D1744883

SIPHON MAGIC

UNRAVELED WORLD - BOOK 1

ALICIA FABEL

Alicia Fabel

Siphon Magic
Unraveled World Series

Copyright © 2018 by Alicia Fabel
All rights reserved
First published in 2018

❀ Created with Vellum

STAY IN TOUCH

Facebook - AliciaFabel.Author

Instagram - @AliciaFabel

Website - AliciaFabel.com

For Aaron, who believed in me before I believed in myself. My biggest cheerleader and best friend.

1

Vera stared wide-eyed up at the mountain lion, the ultimate screw you from Lady Luck. She hadn't seen the beast perched above her as she scrambled up the tree in the darkness. Bloodied fingers latched onto the branch so she didn't end up a nasty splatter of girl-bits on the ground below. Tremors rocked her body while she tried to look like a fierce adversary rather than a juicy flesh-bag of cat chow. The animal could probably see right through to her squishy, terrified core, but this was the only play Vera had. Running away was not an option. A different monster, one that should not exist, hunted in the forest down below. Mountain lions were pee-your-pants-worthy but a deranged centaur? Yeah, nope. Not happening.

Even if there hadn't been a centaur, Vera couldn't have run from the cat. Turn your back on a mountain lion and it attacked. That fun fact was courtesy of Suzie, Vera's old foster-mom. Suzie had taught Vera how to survive a mountain lion encounter after one of the big cats was found napping in a guy's garage down the street. Still, if there hadn't been a mythical monster to worry about, Vera probably would've run. She was not the kind of person who faced down mountain lions, no matter what the experts said. Lady Luck must be rolling on the floor somewhere. The old biddy had plagued Vera with a lifetime of misfortune for kicks and giggles. Someday, Vera was going to punch her in the throat. For now, she drew on the anger twisting in her gut, letting it fuel her bravado. No way would she give up on her alive-and-kicking status the night before her nineteenth birthday. *Lady Luck is screwing with the wrong girl.*

It almost worked too.

Who am I kidding?

Vera had no idea how far away town was or which direction it was for that matter. If she managed to escape dismemberment by teeth and claws, and mutilation by hands and hooves, a wolf would probably eat her. Or she'd starve to death, and a pack of wolves would share her. It's not like they were picky about freshness. A manic giggle bubbled up her throat at the thought. The centaur's croon echoing through the trees obliterated it.

"Come out, sweetness," called the monster. "You can't hide from me. I can smell you."

A bead of sweat rolled down Vera's brow and threatened to flood her eye. She ignored it. She couldn't have pried her fingers from the branch if she'd wanted to. Vera strained to hear a snapped twig or a trampled leaf or anything to tell her how close he was. But everything was drowned out by the pulsing in her ears and the frantic whoosh of her breaths.

"I wonder if you taste as sweet as you smell." His voice surrounded Vera. The hairs on her arms rose. "I hope you're a screamer."

It all fell silent, all the pounding and whooshing. Vera's

vision blurred around the edges. The inky silhouettes of trees shrank farther away. She swayed like a raft anchored to shore by a fraying rope. Only the whisper of fur scraping against bark cut through the hypnotizing stillness. Vera sucked in a quiet breath and locked eyes with the mountain lion.

Stay away from me, cat.

The mountain lion's haunches quivered. It had inched closer while Vera had spaced out. Vera could see the moonlit meadow just beyond their tree reflected in its eyes. A wide-open meadow with all sorts of nowhere to hide from a half-man-half-horse-thing. That's why Vera had climbed the tree in the first place. She wasn't about to run out into the open. The cat whipped its head around to peer down into the darkness, teeth bared. Fur rose on the back of its neck. Vera's stomach clenched. For a wild set of heartbeats, she did not move. Eventually, Vera's gaze inched down toward the shadows.

Vera never got a chance to see if the monster was there. The mountain lion took advantage of her distraction and lunged. The furry mass of hard muscles slammed into her. Crying out, Vera broke her hard-won silence, not that it mattered anymore. Together, they fell from their sanctuary in the trees. Branches tore at Vera's flailing arms. A sharp pain ripped through one leg, and then Vera hit the ground beneath the mountain lion. Air rushed from her lungs with a grunt. Blood pooled beneath Vera's head where it had struck a rock embedded in the soil of the meadow. To be fair, the fall afforded one lucky mercy: It knocked Vera unconscious for her imminent discovery.

KALE'S BARE toes grew cold as he stood eyeing the crumpled body of a girl at the edge of his meadow. It was not improving his current mood at all. Mimi's frantic arrival through the barrier had ripped Kale from sleep. Something he chronically lacked as it was. He hadn't slowed to pull on boots, just charged to his friend's aid. An exceptionally pain-in-the-neck feline friend who now crouched over the broken human. Mimi was protecting the girl from him.

"You have got to be kidding me." Kale was ready to strangle the mountain lion.

Mimi's defiant expression wavered, but she held her ground. Kale looked past her toward the boundary forest where the gates to all the realms of the world circled the meadow, constantly moving and rearranging. He couldn't see them, but he could sense them. Like drafty chinks in his cabin walls. Each realm had a unique combination of scents, which floated on the air when its gate opened. Sienna soil, ash, lotus oil, farmland, salty sea, dung, jasmine, and wood-smoke lingered in the air, but the metallic odor of the human realm, called Earth, overpowered the rest since that was the last world-gate opened. With his mind, Kale felt along the magic that made up the meadow until he found the tendrils which joined the Earth gate to the meadow. Layers of magic threads wrapped securely around the gate, binding it closed. The seals had fallen firmly back into place as soon as Mimi had slammed the gate behind her. Earth's world-gate was the only one sealed shut. Not even a hint of a breeze came from the human realm now. All those humans were safely locked away. Except for this girl.

"Why in the name of the Infernal Ones, did you bring one back with you?" Kale's voice was scary-calm.

Mimi blanched.

Kale sighed and ran a hand through his hair. This was

partly his fault. While Mimi was able to hold the gate open from the other side, just enough to slip back through it when she was ready to return, Kale had to unseal it for her. *Stars blast it.* He knew the risks, but he did it anyway. For Mimi, he would do it again. The magic-less human realm was the only place where Mimi found some relief from the swirling magics that existed in every other corner of the world and which battered her mind endlessly.

"She didn't come willingly, did she?" Kale asked Mimi, knowing it was the only explanation for why his friend would stand against him for a human.

Mimi nudged the girl gently with her nose then looked back at Kale, her slitted eyes pleading for mercy for the human whose presence in the meadow was forbidden. The moment the girl passed through the gate, her life was forfeit. Mimi knew it. And yet, here they were, Mimi silently begging Kale to spare the girl's life, and Kale not doing any killing. The whole situation was preposterous, and Kale was about to make it worse.

"Maybe we can put her back where she belongs before she comes to," he said.

Mimi narrowed her eyes suspiciously. It was understandable. Kale was not known for his mercy. In fact, if it weren't for Mimi worming her way into his affections, along with her over-sized heart, Kale never would have considered anything other than a quick execution. Mimi was probably wondering if it was a trick. In the end, though, Mimi had no choice but to trust Kale or let the girl die. She moved aside to give him access. Kale squatted and brushed blood-matted hair away from the girl's face and neck.

"At least now we know the meadow doesn't discriminate when it comes to healing a human—she's not dying," Kale observed.

Kale wasn't sure that was a good thing, but he was glad to see some of the tension melt from Mimi's face. He considered the girl's awkward position, tilting his head to mimic the unnatural angle of her nearly healed neck.

"You probably should've tipped it back in place before it healed like that." Kale chuckled darkly. "Think the other humans will notice?"

Mimi yowled and head-butted him.

"I can fix it, but you're not going to like it," Kale warned.

Kale wrapped one scarred hand around the girl's throat, placed the other on the crown of her head, and with a quick twist, snapped the girl's neck for the second time that night. Her head flopped to the side. The mountain lion screamed like a woman possessed.

"Enough, Mimi! I told you I was going fix her. See?" Kale indicated the girl's neck. "Still attached, which means she'll live unless someone hears you and comes to see what's going on. If they do, I will toss her out of here and let her live or die at the mercy of her own realm. Like I should have done already."

Want me to do it for you? offered Ferrox, returning home from wherever he'd been all night.

No, you bloodthirsty beast, Kale snapped.

The horse's sudden intrusion into Kale's thoughts had startled the Guardian. Being caught off guard, even by Ferrox whose travel through the gates was as undetectable as his own, was galling. Ferrox threw Kale the horse-equivalent of a one-finger salute through their connection before severing the link. The moody horse sulked off to his barn at the center of the meadow near Kale's cabin. Kale clenched his teeth and pretended not to notice the delighted glint in Mimi's eyes. Mimi couldn't hear the conversations between Kale and Ferrox, but she'd have noticed Kale's jump when the horse arrived. Anytime Kale was not the thoroughly unshakable man the world believed he was, Mimi was annoyingly pleased.

Kale arranged the girl's head so it sat straight on her shoulders and pressed an index finger to her forehead to keep it in place while the meadow repaired the muscles he'd just re-torn. Bone fused beneath the skin while Kale watched. The nerve fractures would take more time to heal, though. If Ferrox was home, the sun would be coming up soon, chasing away the darkness. Shadows were the only thing shielding their treason from anyone who might pop by.

"As soon as this human can survive on the other side, she's out of here. The rest of her injuries will have to heal human-speed."

Kale held up a hand to silence Mimi's protests. Amusement gone, Mimi paced back and forth, throwing him dirty looks. Kale willed the meadow's healing magic to work faster. The first human to land in the meadow was going to give him his first ulcer. He should've just killed her.

"You can stop looking at me like that," Kale finally told Mimi. "I didn't make this mess."

Mimi's glare heated. Stars help him if Mimi learned that —without magic— there was no way human healers could reverse all the damage done to this girl. Even after what the meadow had already accomplished. Mimi would never forgive herself. Or him, since he was knowingly sentencing the girl to her fate. Kale's stomach churned with regret for what the girl would endure in the coming weeks and months.

The girl's eyelids twitched—a good sign. Kale absently wondered what color her eyes were. In the moonlight, the girl's dark hair was such a contradiction to her fair complexion that he couldn't begin to guess. Ever so gently, he ran a thumb across one lid and decided any color would suit her. She seemed so small and fragile. But humans were not helpless. And Kale had nothing to regret. The girl would live, which was more than she was entitled to at this point. Out of time and patience, Kale rose to his feet, gathering the girl into his arms.

"All right, that's good enough. I'll be back. Stay here." Kale silently called for the Earth gate. The meadow provided a narrow trail that would lead him to it.

Mimi, of course, ignored Kale. She spun around and bee-lined out of the meadow. His friend could not see the meadow's trail, but she didn't need it to find the Earth gate. From what Kale knew, Mimi was the only being in all the world able to see the world-gates. It's how Mimi had first ended up in his life. Sighing, Kale cradled his burden as far from his chest as he could manage and carried her into the boundary forest. As expected, Mimi had already found the gate to the human realm before Kale got there. She walked alongside the moving gate until it settled in front of Kale. Her eyes tracing an arched outline was the only visible sign that the gate was actually there. The shifting gates ensured no one could easily skip out on their own realm and hop into another of their choosing. Although some tried. A pixie once hopped realms to escape his debts, only to end up back in the meadow a few days later with a missing wing, begging Kale to send him back home. Other realm jumpers hadn't been as fortunate as the pixie. Most who tried didn't make it past the Guardian to begin with. They never tried a second time.

Kale pulled at the thread bindings until the Earth gate opened. Mimi darted through. Kale didn't bother trying to stop her. Once through the gate, Kale ignored the pull of the meadow calling him back. It was unpleasant, but centuries of practice had made it bearable. Mimi stopped immediately. Lifting her nose to sniff the chilled air, a growl vibrated in her chest. Pressing close to Kale, Mimi's body warmed his leg all the way to his hip where she stood level. Kale frowned, and then smelled it too, lacing faintly through the moldering leaves and spicy butterscotch pine. Even after a millennium, there was no mistaking the scent—an unnatural was in the human realm.

"Is he tracking the girl?" Kale asked on a breath for only Mimi to hear.

Mimi nodded once, keen eyes scanning the forest around them. The abomination was not nearby, but he would be back. He would not stop hunting until he caught his prey. The girl stood no chance. *Stars help me.* Kale had no idea what to do. On the one hand, being Guardian meant keeping the realms safe from outside threats—like a human exposed to magic. If ever someone became a threat to a sibling realm, Kale was their executioner. Obviously, he wasn't doing a very good job with that responsibility at the moment. On the other hand, Kale was also tasked with protecting the world's innocents against perverse magic. An unnatural was the worst sort of perversion.

Damn the Infernals.

Once again, the girl was proving to be a contradiction. She was both human and an innocent. It was a scenario Kale had never considered. Now, he had to decide whether to risk the safety of the entire world to keep her safe or walk away and guarantee her death. The girl flinched in his arms, her dreams plaguing her unconsciousness. Knowing he would regret it, Kale turned back to the meadow, carrying the girl with him. He nudged open the link that tied his mind to Ferrox's and let the scent of the unnatural flow through it.

Old friend, I'm going to need your help to wipe out the infestation before it is unstoppable.

"Keep her quiet and hidden," Kale instructed Mimi, who bounced along beside him like she'd earned a special prize. "I mean it, Mimi. If anyone discovers the girl, I will still kill her." In this, he would be as helpless as the girl.

Mimi sobered while Kale's long strides ate up the distance to the cabin. Ferrox waited for them, eyes smoldering red.

"Maybe we'll get lucky and get the human back to her realm before she even knows she left," Kale said, more to reassure himself than anyone else. Mimi stretched out her neck and licked Kale's elbow. "You really have to get control of yourself. Or go get some help."

Mimi hissed at the suggestion as Kale had known she would. Kale smirked.

VERA WOKE in a small whitewashed room. Blinding sunlight streamed through sheer lace curtains to warm her face. She didn't have a chance to wonder where she was because staring at her, only a swipe away, was the mountain lion. Naturally, Vera intended to scramble away. All she managed was a single violent jolt, like someone whose dream-self just toppled down a staircase. Then her body was still, unable to answer her mind's call to run, unable to move at all. Vera squeezed her eyes closed, breathing in a lung-full of whatever floral scent clung to the white sheets tucked around her and hoping it would be over quickly.

After a minute of nothing happening, she cracked open

one eye. The mountain lion sat watching her, a statue of black fur with silver-gray around its mouth and down its chest. One ring of silver looped the tip of its black tail, which twitched side to side. Vera tipped her head to make sure her arms and legs were still attached. Everything was there, but no amount of power-stare made anything below her neck move. Swallowing hard, Vera wondered how long she could hide her weakness from the predator. Honestly, Vera couldn't understand why she wasn't already a pile of bloody nibbles. She wasn't complaining about her wholeness, though. She just hoped to stay in one piece until someone came to her rescue.

The room was small and clean. A rocking chair swayed near the open window, and a bundle of tiny purple flowers sat in a jar atop a plain wooden dresser. It definitely didn't vibe with the monster from last night. Then again, if centaurs existed, this was probably the lair of a tidy cannibal who was off heating up the stew pot. After everything else, it wouldn't surprise her. Movement drew Vera's attention back to the mountain lion. The animal's fangy mouth stretched wide with a huge yawn, a pink tongue falling forward. Afterward, the lion stood and slowly approached. It lowered its boxy head until its chin rested on the bed near Vera's face. Vera didn't blink or even breathe, but the lion had no such reservations. The cat's breath warmed Vera's face. The residual moisture cooled as the cat inhaled. Warm then cool then warm again. Just as Vera's heart slowed and her breaths evened, the danged thing did the unimaginable. It flicked out its sandy tongue and swiped it over Vera's cheek. Vera sputtered and jerked her head back. The animal followed, intent on giving her a full saliva bath.

"Stop it!" Vera hissed.

The mountain licked her nose.

"Ewww. So gross. Stop."

Looking rather pleased with itself, the cat sat back.

"There is something seriously wrong with you." Vera scowled.

A spark of giddiness lit in Vera's chest when she noticed the fingers on her right hand had closed weakly around the edge of the blanket while the cat had violated her face. Vera tried to move them again, her face scrunched with effort. At first, she thought her efforts had failed. A moment later, though, two fingers twitched. The delayed response was bizarre, but hey, it was something. A glorious smile lit Vera's face while the cat went back to breathing on her.

"Thank you for scaring away that monster," Vera whispered to the strange animal. "I assume that's what happened since, you know, I'm still here and all. So, thank you."

After counting one-hundred-and-two breaths, Vera fell asleep. Both hands were curled into loose fists.

2

The sky was shifting from obsidian to blue when Vera woke again. She wiggled her fingers then her toes. Hallelujah, she had control over her body again. An unexpected shock of pain caught her off guard when she tried to move her legs. Vera whimpered. The mountain lion, curled up on the quilt at the foot of the bed, peeked at Vera through sleepy eyes before tucking its nose under a paw, intent on going back to sleep.

"You suck," said Vera while panting.

Vera feigned annoyance at the cat but having it around was oddly comforting. As a bonus, if it kept shadowing her, Vera wouldn't have to worry about weirdos anymore. That would be excellent since Vera was a weirdo magnet. Centaur-freak was only the most recent in a lineup of wackadoos Luck had thrown at her over the years. Although, with Vera's current track record, a mountain lion might just become an appetizer for whatever came next. On that note, it was time to get up and going before Vera's mysterious host checked on her. While Vera appreciated not being abandoned in the woods—maybe she'd send a thank-you note—she was not waiting around to see what kind of person brought a strange, injured girl into their home instead of to a hospital. She'd learned the hard way to trust her instinct when things seemed sketchy. And this was sketch-tastic.

Easing herself up, Vera pushed the blankets down over her knees. Her right leg was bandaged neatly from calf to thigh. *Fan-freaking-tastic.* Vera scowled at the cat, which gave up on sleep at that point. It slid from the bed, pressing its front paws forward and stretching out its long torso. Then the cat sat and looked expectantly at Vera.

"Show off." Vera rolled her eyes. "How about next time I ride you to the ground, huh?"

After an embarrassing amount of grunting, Vera was upright and clinging like a barnacle to the bedpost. She eyed the window, wobbling on her one good leg. There was no way she'd manage climbing out. Which left the front door. Hopefully, if anyone was at home, they were still sound asleep. The sun was coming up fast, though, so Vera needed to be quick. *Ha.*

"Are you going out the window or coming with me?" Vera asked the cat, but the thing didn't move. "Well, pick one. But if you come with me, you'll probably get eaten."

A chuckle brought Vera spinning around, almost dropping her to the floor. In the doorway, loomed a hulk of a man.

"Mountain lions don't taste so good," the man said, his voice deep but not quite smooth.

Vera was relieved the man had manly legs and only two of them, but they were blocking her escape. He smiled. It didn't reach his eyes. They were the same black as the coffee she served at the diner every morning to the wretched men who'd lost everything because they couldn't walk away from the tables. Vera wondered what unpleasantness this man kept tucked in his back pocket. He might look decent enough. Okay, he looked incredible in those faded jeans and that white thermal with the sleeves pushed up his toned arms, but she still had a niggling feeling that something wasn't quite right. Why hadn't he called the authorities or an ambulance? She'd been there for at least a full day and was obviously injured. If she had to bet, her leg was broken. Why hadn't he let someone know he'd found her? Unless he didn't want anyone to know. It might sound paranoid, but Vera's luck demanded a bit of paranoia. Otherwise, she'd be dead in a gutter many times over by now. The man's forced smile wilted while Vera eyed him.

"My name is Kale." He stepped forward, holding out a calloused hand.

Vera jerked back and nearly fell over the mountain lion.

"Whoa, I won't hurt you," he said.

Lie! It rang in her ears, a familiar chime that settled in the base of her skull.

Sure, you lying sonofa-. Gah, she hated that she was even a little disappointed. Vera had no idea how her built-in lie detector worked, but whenever someone lied, bells went off in her head. It had always been like that for her. As a kid, she'd thought it was like that for everyone. Until she'd called out the boy in first grade for lying about the rock he'd thrown at her friend, Crissy. None of the other kids had gone near her after that. Not even Crissy. Whatever. She'd been transferred to a new home and school soon after anyway. From then on, she kept her bells to herself.

In the end, the bells became an invaluable tool that saved her from falling prey to the wrong sorts of people.

Like the bastard standing in front of her. Vera wondered if she could make it to the window, without tripping end over rear, and throw herself out before the man caught her. Probably not. Instead, she looked for something nearby to chuck at him. Preferably something spikey. All she had was a couple of pillows, though. If she had two functioning legs, she could charge the man and hope to catch him by surprise. Obviously, she did not, thanks to her new furry shadow. And what was her "fearsome bodyguard" doing while Vera stood there helplessly? Absolutely zip.

"Her name's Mimi." Kale tipped his head at the mountain lion. "She, uh, led me to where you fell. And we, uh, brought you here to get you patched up."

Of course the mountain lion was his pet. *You actually believed you forged some sort of bond with a wild animal? Stupid.*

Vera backed away from the man and his overgrown cat. There was no way she could make it past them both. Her chest rose and fell faster than it should have from those few backward steps. The only option left knocking around in Vera's head was to keep playing the fool. She hated the idea, but she'd done a great job of it so far. If she could play along until they weren't paying attention, she might have a chance to get away. First, she had to relax so it didn't look like she was about to bolt. It took everything Vera had to release the quilt, when she noticed Kale frowning down at the abused bedding in her white-knuckled fist. Now, she just had to make conversation.

"Your mountain lion knocked me out of a tree," she blurted. Ugh, not really the conversation starter she'd been going for. Vera wanted to poke out the man's eyeballs when he raised an amused brow at Mimi.

The animal growled and shook its head.

"Did your mountain lion just shake its head at you?"

"She's not mine," he answered. "We're friends."

Uh huh. Sure psycho. "And she understands what we're saying?"

"Yeah, Mimi's not exactly, uh, normal," said the man. "But she's good people."

Yep, he's cuckoo. "Well, Mr. Kale, thanks for helping me and everything—" *Holy Crap! He's the one who took off all my clothes and put me in this nightgown.* The blood drained from Vera's face and she swayed.

"You okay?" Kale swept in but jumped right back when Vera squeaked and cringed away.

Nice job being chill, dipstick. Breathe. "Yeah," she said, plastering on a smile. "Just a little dizzy. It's going away. I'm fine."

The man studied her carefully. In the meantime, Vera tried to figure out how to describe him to the authorities when she got away. He said, "uh" an awful lot, and he spoke with a strange accent that she couldn't place. He also reminded her of the scotcheroos she and Suzie used to make together. Butterscotch melted with creamy peanut butter, all topped with that dark chocolate hair.

"You probably need to eat. I'll go get you something," Mr. Butterscotch—Scotchie—said, seeming to follow the direction of her thoughts.

Vera almost laughed at him. As if she would eat anything he brought her. But if it made him go away. . . "I am a little hungry, thanks," Vera said. To Vera's horror, her stomach corroborated with a whale call.

Scotchie turned to leave.

"Can you take the mountain lion with you?" Vera asked quickly.

The cat looked sadly up at Vera then dropped its head

and followed the man out without having to be told. *Dang it.* Vera felt a little bad. It actually seemed like she'd hurt the mountain lion's feelings.

———

KALE RAN a hand through his hair and stepped outside to do another survey of the tree line for any sign of a wanderer or envoy. It had been a relatively quiet few days while the girl had slept and healed, but the meadow never stayed quiet for long. Every day the unnatural evaded him and the girl stayed in the meadow, it increased the odds of her discovery. Even if he kept her hidden, the magic around them would eventually unleash whatever magical force lay dormant inside her, and he'd have to kill her anyway. He wondered for the thousandth time if he had done the right thing by bringing the girl back here.

It didn't help that the girl was hiding something from him. Black marks had swirled up her hands as she'd clung to the bed to keep from falling over. After Kale's willful ignorance had contributed to the unraveling of the world, he'd been cursed to see deception as markings on the flesh. That way he could never ignore deceit again. Unfortunately, knowing someone intended to deceive him did not mean he knew how they would do it. He had no idea what the girl was planning. *Stars blast him.* He couldn't demand answers without revealing his ability, which would mean explaining that the world is much bigger than she realized. Which was something he planned to avoid if he could. He was already going to have to explain the unnatural. That would be bad enough. At least no one would believe her if she started blabbering once she got back home. Humans didn't believe in magic anymore.

A nudge on Kale's lower back made him flinch. "You are a cruel girl, you know that?" he asked Mimi.

Mimi grinned, displaying an impressive set of fangs. She was one of the few who could sneak up on him. She took pleasure in doing it as often as possible. Kale propped his elbows on the porch railing and hunched over to rest his forehead against the heels of his hands.

"I have to inform the realms of the unnatural," Kale told Mimi. "When I do, people are going to come looking for updates and reassurances. The girl has to be gone before then." Kale pressed his hands against his eyes until he saw stars. "I know you don't want me to kill her, but it would be a greater mercy than sending her back with the unnatural still out there."

Mimi wedged her face between Kale's forearms, tears trickling down her cheeks.

"I've tried, Mimi. I can't find him." Kale's frustration at his own incompetence seeped into his tone.

Mimi lowered her head. A tear splattered on the wooden plank below. Just last spring, Mimi had brought him a newborn fawn, which she'd discovered only after killing the doe. She had cried over the orphaned animal for days while Kale figured out how to get the thing to eat and stay alive. *Blast her bleeding heart and me for being a sucker for it.*

"Two more days," Kale said finally. "If we can't find the unnatural in two more days, the girl has to go, no more arguments. Maybe with the whole world gunning for the unnatural, the girl could run long enough to out-survive it."

And maybe the entire broken world will set aside their differences for a little Kumbaya, added Ferrox who was supposed to be sleeping.

I know the odds, dimwit.

You know them, but you won't accept them. You act as if the life of the human matters to you.

You know it does not, Kale answered. *I'm fulfilling my duty, that's all.*

Yes, yes, your duty to the Axis Mundi. All hail the center of the world. Ferrox snorted in Kale's head. *Has the meadow charged you with the human's protection?*

Kale was silent.

Exactly. And it never will. Humans are curs, Ferrox said.

Do you not care that the girl's death would destroy Mimi?

I would not like that, Ferrox said truthfully.

Then Mimi needs our help a little longer, Kale said. Ferrox reluctantly conceded before withdrawing from his head.

"If you want to help the girl, go get Addamas," Kale said to Mimi. "If anyone can find the unnatural, he can."

Mimi winced. Kale felt for her, but if she was serious about saving the human, Addamas was their best bet. Kale petted Mimi's cheek then turned to go inside. Time to stop avoiding the human. She did need food. When Kale looked back through the screen door, Mimi was gone.

Kale opened the cupboard and looked over the contents. He had no idea what the girl would want to eat, but he couldn't exactly have her use the magic cupboard to summon whatever she wanted. The farther away from magic hot-spots she stayed, the better off they'd all be. He pulled out a loaf of bread and some cheese, sliced both, and arranged it all on a plate with a plum. Taking a deep breath, he walked down the short hallway and pushed open the door to the guest room.

"Knock, knock. I've got some—"

The room was empty, or nearly so. The girl hadn't quite made it all the way out the window yet. Both of her legs dangled over the sill, and she was just ducking out when Kale intruded. Kale recoiled at the sight of the girl's dark hair turned to waves of crimson by the sun rising behind her. She startled, her indigo eyes widening as she teetered, headed for a nosedive. Kale leaped forward, squashing the unwanted memory of a much different woman. He snatched the girl's flailing wrist before it followed her out the window. The inky webbing snaking over the girl's fingertips and around her hands faded away. Well, at least he knew what she'd been hiding from him—plans to climb out the window as soon as he turned his back.

Kale hooked an arm around the girl's waist and hauled her back into the room. He completely forgot to be careful of her leg. She screamed. Swearing, he apologized and set her carefully on the bed where she lay gasping. For a moment, he wondered if he should have just let her fall, and then scraped her up afterward. The drop was only as high as his shoulders. She probably wouldn't have fared too badly. Maybe even better than with his clumsy assistance. Kale pulled out a pouch of crushed polovraga leaves from the nightstand drawer and pinched out a wad of the black, waxy substance.

"Here, this will help." Kale held the mass to the girl's lips, which she clamped closed. "It's just to help with the pain."

She narrowed her eyes. Kale was almost certain she would refuse, then she parted her lips, allowing him to deposit the leaves on her tongue. Her face screwed up with disgust.

"Sorry. It's foul but it works. Chew it up," Kale instructed. She complied, *mother of miracles*. Soon her body relaxed, and Kale relaxed marginally too.

"Thank you," the girl said through clenched teeth, even though her pain should be gone.

Kale nodded and asked, "Why were you climbing out the window?"

"I've got to get home. My dad's gonna be going crazy. He'll have search parties out by now." The girl's left eye twitched.

Kale was going to point out that the window was not the best choice of exits, but obviously, the girl had determined walking out the front door was not an option available to her. She was perceptive. *Fiends take me, that's going to make things even more complicated than they already are.*

"Please let me leave," she said quietly.

"I will. Two more days and I'll take you home."

"Why can't I go now?" Her eyes narrowed. Kale figured he should get used to that look from her.

"The creature that was chasing you is still out there," Kale explained.

The girl froze. Kale half expected her to attempt another flying leap out the window. Her eyes rolled like Ferrox's when he was scared.

I do not get scared, Ferrox piped in, offended.

Of course not. Go Away.

"How do you know about that?" she asked.

"I saw his tracks in the woods," Kale answered. "He's an unnatural."

"Of course it was unnatural," she replied trembling. "It was a frigging centaur."

"No, not a centaur. Centaurs are born what they are. An unnatural, what you saw, is created by merging a man with a horse. They are as vile as the magic used to create them."

"Magic," she said doubtfully.

"You have to know it exists, you saw a magical creature.

You also broke your neck falling out of that tree and went from paralyzed to climbing out a window in three days because of magic. We don't even speak the same language, but in this place, there are no language barriers because of magic."

"You're saying some Sorcerer Frankenstein is out there building monsters? And that's what was chasing me?"

"Something like that," Kale said as the girl began to shake in earnest. He was a little surprised she wasn't calling him a lunatic, but then again, she had seen the unnatural for herself. He'd have to warn her later not to talk about magic with humans unless she wanted to become her town's crazy person. "What's your name?"

The girl didn't answer right away. She was wary and smart. Which made Kale think she might be able to survive hide and seek with the unnatural on Earth for a while, if it came to that.

"Vera," she said finally.

"Vera, I will find the unnatural and I will kill it so you can go home. Just give me two days."

Vera's head snapped up. She flipped from distressed to calculating like a hummingbird flitting between blossoms. "I have to get back to Gu–my dad," Vera claimed. "I'll steer clear of the forest. We won't even leave the apartment for a month, but I can't leave him there alone. He won't be safe by himself."

"You would not be safe there either."

"If I'm not safe there, I am not safe anywhere," Vera argued.

"You are safe here," Kale insisted. "The unnatural cannot come here. That's why you will stay for now."

"Can I at least call my dad and let him know I'm okay? I don't know, warn him or something?"

"Oh, uh, I don't have a telephone." Kale squirmed under Vera's gaze.

"You're kidding."

"I'm not. It would be difficult to get phone service out here." Kale considered his next words carefully. "Maybe I can send him a message."

"You don't get phone service but the mailman comes by?" she asked. "Do you use pony express or carrier pigeons or something?"

"Not exactly."

A new network of deception stains slipped through Vera's fingers. Kale should not have promised Mimi two more days.

VERA SNUCK to the kitchen window and peered through the darkness for any sign of Scotchie or his mountain lion. They'd both disappeared, leaving Vera alone in the cabin all day. Vera's fluttering heart dropped when she realized woods surrounded the cabin on every side. There wasn't a single driveway or path anywhere. *Seriously? I officially hate meadows.* She spotted a creek. She could follow it back to civilization. That decided, Vera turned to ransack the kitchen for food to take for the trek.

Despite Vera's earlier claims, no one was looking for her. Suzie was dead. Suzie's husband, Gus, rarely came out of his room anymore. Vera was just glad Gus hadn't kicked her out when she'd aged out of the system a month after Suzie's accident. She knew Gus only took her in because it's what his wife wanted. He'd have gotten Suzie Jupiter if that woman had asked for it. Vera would've too.

Between serving coffee and cleaning toilets, Vera was

able to slip Gus a little money each month for her part of the living expenses. She hoped it would encourage Gus to keep a roof over her head for a while longer. Every other penny Vera made went to pay for online college courses. Next year, she planned to transfer to a university and really start her life. But that would only happen if she could get away from the man, Kale, who lied about her being safe and about her going home soon.

Wearing her own clothes and a stolen pack full of trail mix—Scotchie had a whole cupboard of the stuff—Vera slunk to the door, leaning on a walking stick she'd pilfered from a closet. She paused with a hand on the screen door to steady her nerves. The man owned a *for reals* sword, which was propped against the wall beside the door. Vera wished she could take it along in case she ran across the unnatural, but it was too heavy to lift, let alone heft through the woods. *Whatever.*

Most of what came out of Scotchie's mouth was lies, but he had been honest about finding no trace of the unnatural. Which meant that monster was long gone, probably hunting some poor person in Canada by now. Vera took a breath and eased the screen door open. It swung as sound-lessly as every other door in the place. She closed it behind herself so it would not slam.

The creek was a hiss of water off to her left. Vera made it down the four porch steps when there was movement off to her left. She whipped her head around as a large shadow detached from the cabin. It was Kale's horse, head hung low to graze. Sucking in a relieved breath, Vera pressed a fist over her racing heart. The horse stopped at what must be a particularly delicious clump of grass, directly between her and the creek. Vera angled to go around the animal, leaving him a wide berth. The horse shifted too, cutting off her path to freedom once again. As Vera transferred her weight, planning to go the other way, the animal mirrored her. Vera hesitated. That was a strange coincidence. The horse pulled up another tuft of grass, never looking at her.

"Hey there, big guy," Vera said with a tremor in her voice. "Don't mind me. I'm just going to be on my way and leave you alone."

Vera shuffled forward slowly so she would not alarm the horse. When she was close enough to feel the warmth radiating from his body, the horse lifted its nose to look at her. Vera staggered back under the gaze of two glowing red eyes. He advanced toward her. Vera hopped back until she tripped over the porch steps and fell on her butt. The walking stick smacked against the steps beside her. The horse's head loomed inches from hers. After a moment, Vera forced herself to lift a shaking hand to pat his nose. It was just a horse, after all. He was probably curious about her and just wanted to say hello.

"Good boy," Vera said soothingly.

The horse's face shot forward, teeth snapping at her fingers. Vera barely pulled them away in time. Then the beast snatched the stick from beside Vera with his teeth and tossed it away. Vera scrambled backward up the stairs. Horse teeth clacked after her. She dragged herself through the screen door and kicked it closed, wondering if the animal would charge it. It didn't. When she stood and peeked out the window, the horse was staring back at her, an impassible obstacle.

Back in her holding-cell-of-a-room, Vera closed the window and jammed the rocking chair under the doorknob before collapsing on the bed. She'd been worried about getting past Scotchie and his mountain lion but had no idea the man owned some kind of possessed horse too. *How in the world do I get past that thing and out of this magical freak show? Yep, magic. Might as well get used to that word, Vera. Not like you can pretend none of this is real, can you?* At least the horse hadn't trampled her. Or gnawed on her. That was reassuring. Now she had to figure out a new way out of this mess.

3

W ithout realizing it, Kale had picked his thumbnail ragged. Vera was haunting him. She was snatches of movement lurking around corners and a whisper of breaths grating on his nerves. If he looked in her direction, Vera scurried away. She'd be back soon enough, though, watching him. She'd refused to let him check her injuries first thing that morning, although it seemed her leg was improved based on how well she was getting around. That was unfortunate. When Vera flat-out ignored his knock and offering of lunch, Kale left the plate outside her door and fled outside.

You ran away. From a teensy human girl. Ferrox cracked up while Kale raked the comb over the horse's mahogany coat, which rippled with delight. There was no way to block out the horse when he was so close.

A girl with knives. There're at least two missing from the kitchen, Kale replied defensively.

You are becoming such a namby-pamby. It's not like she could kill you. I'd love to see her face when you pulled a knife out of your back. Ferrox bumped Kale in the shoulder. *Go back in there, and let's have a little fun since executing her is off the table for now.*

Kale brushed harder, but Ferrox only leaned into it, thoroughly enjoying the attention. *You're so sensitive,* griped Ferrox.

There's an unnatural in the human realm and a human in the meadow. I think I have a right to be a little tense.

An entire flight of wyvern found a forgotten passage to the human realm just last century. They took out half a countryside before you wiped 'em all out. You didn't bat an eye at all those human bodies. Ate whenever you got hungry and slept every night, calm as a swaddled babe. You most certainly didn't hide. The muscles in Kale's jaw jumped while listening to Ferrox's tirade. *Now this girl shows up, and you are as pissy as a protective mama bird. Only you're protecting the cuckoo and not your own chicks.* Ferrox turned to scrutinize his companion, pulling away from the brush that remained suspended in Kale's hand. *Is it a pride thing? I'd understand that. It's not every day you meet a girl who wouldn't give her left tit to spend some one-on-one time with you.*

What? Kale sputtered. *Don't be a fool.*

You're the fool. There isn't a female out there who doesn't lust after you, Ferrox said with a snort. *Even the ones who think you're the bogeyman or who hate you on principle. They still want you. But not this girl. You should conquer the human so you can get your head back on straight and send her home.*

You are not serious. Kale gaped at the animal.

Completely.

I am not interested in the human. At all, Kale added firmly, cutting off Ferrox's retort. *She's only here for Mimi's sake.*

You keep saying that.

Because it's true. Kale felt like his brain might explode. *After tomorrow, she goes back home one way or another.* The twinge of anxiety that accompanied that acknowledgment made him cringe. Ferrox was going to pick up on that and take it the wrong way.

Goddess help us, muttered Ferrox

I don't—

No, not that, you fool man. Heads up.

Kale followed Ferrox's gaze and caught a familiar flash of green from the girl's ratty sweatshirt through the barn slats. He barely had time to drop into a crouch behind a pile of hay before the girl eased inside the barn.

Oh my goddess, said Ferrox. *I just lost the last of my respect for you. Get out here you yellow-bellied elf.*

She runs away from me like I'm a jinn spawned from Jahannam, Kale argued. *Maybe she'll warm up to you, if she doesn't know I'm here.*

Ferrox's displeasure seeped into their connection as the horse faced off with Vera. Understandably, Ferrox was unwilling to turn his back on the girl even long enough to force Kale out. The human was likely armed with blades after all. The musty-sweet smell of dried grasses swirled around Kale as he maneuvered to spy on the two. Vera maintained a wary distance from Ferrox, despite her calm mask.

"Hey there, handsome boy," said Vera. "I brought you a little treat."

Vera held out a trembling palm, displaying a pile of sugar cubes. Kale didn't keep sugar cubes in the kitchen, which meant the girl had used the cupboard. Again. *Stars help us all.*

You hear that? She wants to give me a treat, Ferrox crowed.

Ferrox, Kale warned. *Watch yourself.*

Vera sidled forward. Kale was grudgingly impressed. Not a lot of people would approach the demon horse after an encounter like she'd had last night. Kale had gone out to meet Addamas as soon as his friend pathed into the borderlands. Another day of hunting had not gotten Kale any closer to finding the abomination, so setting the renowned tracker on the trail of the unnatural had been Kale's priority. Ferrox had reveled in his role as terrifying watchdog, going overboard as only Ferrox could. And yet, there Vera was, trying to buy the bully's friendship with a fist of sugar.

She's desperate, Ferrox said. *Didn't you tell her she's going home in a day?*

Yes, but she doesn't seem to believe a word I say. She's the most distrusting creature I've ever met.

Can't be worse than you, Ferrox said.

Vera lifted her offering higher. Ferrox leaned in curiously.

She smells delicious. Ferrox breathed deeply. *I won't take much.*

Before Kale could blink, the horse nipped Vera's fingers, leaving the sugar untouched. Ferrox deliberately licked a trace of blood from his teeth while the girl watched. Vera yelped and raced from the barn. Sugar littered the straw at Ferrox's hooves.

Hades take you. You were supposed to help calm her down. Kale prepared to chase after the girl.

Relax. The girl went back to the cabin. She'll probably steal another knife, though.

Not funny, said Kale.

It totally is. But you were right, she has trust issues.

You bit her.

She offered, Ferrox pointed out.

Sugar. She offered you sugar, Kale said. *Had she known you have a thing for girl-flesh, she would not have, I am sure.*

Girl, boy, undecided. Ferrox shrugged in his mind. *I don't discriminate. She should be careful what she offers to strangers.*

Curse you to Helheim, you blasted beast.

Cool your tool. I won't do it again. She's nasty, Ferrox said with regret, not for his behavior but rather because the girl was not tastier.

I hope her innocence gives you indigestion.

Nah, I just got a few drops. But I do want that taste out of my mouth. It's ten times worse than I remember it being. Ferrox spat. *That's why I stick to the stuff steeped in evil.*

Serves you right, you big brute, Kale said with some amusement.

Careful. You're the only one around right now with my favorite tidbit dangling from your person. Ferrox flooded their connection with memories of savoring his favorite "delicacy." *Would cleanse my palate in no time.*

Disgusting. Kale's stomach turned uncomfortably. *Cut it out.*

Don't knock it till you try it.

That will never happen. Kale attempted to push the thoughts out of his head. Ferrox reined them in slowly to prolong Kale's discomfort. Just then, something occurred to Kale. Grinning, he pointed out, *You do realize you technically accepted her offer of friendship, right? You better hope that bargain doesn't come back to bite you.*

I did not. Ferrox's eyes widened with dawning horror. *The ancient ways are forgotten and gone.*

Forgotten by you, obviously. Kale chuckled. *Be nice, or I might let slip that you owe her a debt of friendship.*

Not if she's dead first. Ferrox oozed satisfaction. *She just took off, by the way.*

Kale felt the ripple a moment later as Vera breached the barrier between the meadow and the boundary forest.

"For fiends' sake."

Kale sprinted from the barn with Ferrox getting the last laugh in his head.

ONE MINUTE, Vera was running for her life, and the next, Kale tackled her to the ground. Vera yelled in surprise, and then with rising fury at the man above her. She stabbed frantically with the knife clutched in her hand. He dodged it easily then captured her wrist in mid-air. Vera flailed with her remaining limbs and bit Kale's arm when she could not buck him off. He pulled back with a howl. Straddling her chest, Kale pinned both Vera's arms above her head with one hand while the other went around her throat to fend off her teeth.

"Enough," said Kale, his face uncomfortably close to hers.

Vera responded by lifting a leg and kneeing Kale in his back. She did it again harder after he flinched. Kale responded by shifting to trap her lower half with his legs. That meant the man was practically lying on top of her. Vera flew into a flurry of growls and curses.

"Stop attacking me, and I'll let you go," Kale hollered.

The truth in Kale's words sank in slowly. Vera's instinct was to keep fighting, but she stilled, chest rising and falling heavily.

"Thank the stars," Kale mumbled. "I'm going to get up. Before you take off running, look behind me, okay?"

He rose and backed quickly out of stabbing range. Vera scrabbled to her feet. Kale stepped farther back, tipping his head to indicate what he wanted her to see.

"No." Vera's heart fell. She was back in the meadow. The cabin and barn were right where they'd always been.

Vera stood exactly at the edge of the forest. She'd sprinted past that spot just a couple minutes before. The burbling creek she'd followed drew her attention. Before, it had been on the other side of her. Somehow, Vera had gotten turned around and run right back without even realizing it. Kale started laughing, a deep rolling laugh with an edge that made Vera bristle.

"I wasn't attacking you." Kale plopped onto the ground, looking up at Vera with a grim smile. "I was coming to make sure you didn't get yourself killed out there, sure, but before I even left the meadow, you came crashing into me. And then you tried to kill me."

What the—Vera looked at the forest behind her again. How had she screwed up that badly? However she'd managed it, she wouldn't make the same mistake twice.

"I know you are not comprehending what's is happening here," Kale said, as Vera prepared to run again. Forget that she wouldn't make it far before he caught her, she had to at least try. "There's no way you could. So, I want to make sure something is very clear—this is not my fault."

That made her bristle. This was all his fault. He was holding her captive, for freak's sake. Kale waved a hand at the forest and said, "Go ahead, go."

Vera froze, dumbfounded, wondering what his game was.

"I won't come after you and neither will he." Kale indicated the horse skulking by the barn.

Truth. Alrighty then. Vera turned and ran. Gimpy as could be and throwing out her hands to the trees for support. Soon, the deepening shadows cooled the sweat on the back of her neck. She stopped looking over her shoulder and focused on not tripping over the roots and debris. A rustle made her jump, but it was only a squirrel or something in the undergrowth. That's what she told herself anyway. After a few minutes, Vera burst from the forest into the meadow again. Kale sat waiting for her, unmoved, tearing blades of grass between his fingers. The whole time Vera had run, the creek had been on her left. Now, all of a sudden, it was on her right, as though she'd spun around. Only she hadn't.

Vera reeled around and tried again. She decided to break away from the creek once she couldn't see Kale behind her. Obviously, it was leading her in a loop back to the meadow. Bark scraped the skin from Vera's palms as she weaved through the trees. She kept an eye out for a hidey hole in case Kale changed his mind about letting her go. With that in mind, Vera dug the second knife from her pocket. A moment later, she emerged into the meadow, right beside the creek she hadn't even been following that time. Kale held up both hands in surrender as Vera brandished the serrated blade at him.

"As I said, this is not my doing," Kale spoke slowly. "It seems we get to spend more time together than either of us would prefer."

"I'm just catching my breath, and then I'm going home," Vera assured him.

"It's a waste of energy. You won't be able to leave."

"Watch me." Vera turned and limped purposefully away.

She moved slower this time to ensure she did not get turned around. In the end, it just took her another minute or two to make it back to the meadow where Kale sat patiently.

"What kind of trick is this? Are you a witch or something?" She now knew there were mythical baddies in the world, but she'd hoped Kale was just an average run-of-the-mill wacko.

"No, I'm not a witch. I'm a man. You can't leave because the meadow has decided to keep you."

"A meadow can't decide anything."

"Like other things around here, the meadow isn't normal. And it must like you."

"What does that mean?"

"Once in a while, the meadow detects a person out in the world who needs rescued or protected from something extraordinarily evil. It scoops them up, drops them on my front steps, and keeps them here until it is safe for them to leave."

"The meadow holds people hostage?"

"That's a bit sinister. More like the meadow acts like a meddling old woman sometimes, but yeah, you won't be leaving just yet."

"I don't need help from you or a meadow."

"The meadow clearly thinks you do." Kale flicked the grass from his fingers. "Since there's an unnatural hunting you, I tend to agree."

"How can this be happening to me?"

"Honestly, I'm as surprised as you are, and I'd rather you went home too. For now, though, we're stuck with each other. And I'll keep you safe."

Everything coming out of the man's mouth was one hundred percent truth, and it was blowing Vera's mind. He'd been lying to her since he'd first opened his mouth, so the sudden one-eighty was jarring. But more importantly, he hadn't denied the existence of witches, which seemed very bad. And the whole meadow twilight-zone stuff? What the actual heck was that about? Vera needed to get back to her reality where things made sense.

"If you don't want me here, help me go home," said Vera.

"I can't."

"Can't or won't?"

"Can't. This," Kale said, gesturing at everything, "means your life is my responsibility. The meadow is the only place I can keep you safe."

"Still sounds like a 'won't' to me," Vera said with venom. "You also sound like a lunatic."

"Wondered when you'd call me that. And you're probably right on both accounts." Kale stood and brushed off his jeans. "I'll keep you safe whether we like it or not."

No bells sounded in Vera's head. She wondered for a second if they were broken. Anytime he'd spouted crap about her being safe before, she'd had a collection of bells ringing in her head. Now, it was all crickets.

"Telling you that the world unraveled, and that this meadow tethers all the broken pieces together, probably won't make me sound like less of a lunatic, but there it is. Somehow, magic got into your realm, where magic should not exist, and now there is an unnatural there hunting you. I have to protect you from it as the meadow commands because, well, the meadow is kind of my boss."

Truth.

"You actually believe that load." Vera infused her words with disdain. "But I don't."

A deafening chorus of church bells went off inside Vera's skull. They weren't broken. Vera winced. No simple chimes for her own lies, nope. Unfortunately, Vera did not have the luxury of willful disbelief even if the truth was too much to believe.

"That's not surprising," Kale replied. "Doesn't change the facts, though."

"The facts are this: I am a captive, and I don't want your protection." *And I still don't trust you*, she added silently.

"And you want to go home, right?" Kale asked sarcastically.

"Any idea when that will happen, Deputy Scotchie?"

"After I eliminate the unnatural," answered Kale, not acknowledging Vera's slip with his nickname. "But you won't truly be safe until I find who created it in the first place and stop them too. So, my guess is the meadow won't send you home until there's no more threat."

"Are you serious? How long will that take?" Dread uncurled in Vera's stomach.

"I am not sure."

"Fabulous," Vera said tiredly. "Any chance you have a computer so I don't flunk my online courses?"

"No. Sorry."

"Sure you are. Just like I'm sure university admissions won't mind that I couldn't even hack online school." Vera's throat tightened. She was never going to get into one of the colleges she wanted. Plus, all those hours saving tips to pay for online classes this semester were for nothing.

"If it helps, I went to your apartment last night and your dad was gone. From what I could tell, he packed up and left before the unnatural found where you lived."

"You went to my apartment? The unnatural was there too?" Vera's voice rose as she spoke.

"Not while I was there, or all of this would be over already. But yes, probably soon after you vanished. That must have been a shock for the abomination." Kale appraised her. "You don't seem surprised that your dad was gone. Was he planning a trip?"

"He travels for work." Gus hadn't traveled for business since Suzie had died. Vera wasn't aware he was going to start accepting travel assignments again, but it was a good thing he had. Otherwise, he'd probably be splattered all over the walls at home by now. "Will the unnatural go after Gus?"

"No," Kale answered thoughtfully. "He won't hunt Gus. He won't stop hunting you, though."

"Why me? How has it not found me here?"

"Why you? For fun. And pride—losing prey won't sit well with him," Kale explained. "An unnatural cannot find you here because this meadow does not exist on Earth where he is. You were transported here through a gate of sorts. Even if the unnatural could find the gate, his kind cannot cross the meadow's boundary unless I allow it."

"That makes it clear as mud. Thanks."

Kale mumbled something under his breath before explaining, "Think of the world as a giant palace. Each realm is a room with a hidden door. The only way to get from one room to another is through this meadow which is like a corridor."

"And that makes you the hall monitor?" Vera snarked.

"I monitor the meadow and guard the doorways, yes," Kale said. "People come here when they pass through their gate."

"How do people get back to their room, if the doors are hidden?"

"When they are ready to leave, their gate comes for them. Only the gate to a person's home realm will answer their call to leave."

"Call? But not on a phone because you don't have those here." Vera was trying hard to stay calm.

"The gates respond to intention. If you leave the meadow with the intention to go home, you'll go home."

"But not me. Because I had every intention of going home and here I am." Vera spread her arms.

"You are an exception. The meadow will reroute you back here until it is safe to go home."

"And there's no way to get around that?" asked Vera.

"No," Kale lied. "The gate to your realm is sealed anyway. I'll have to unlock it for you when it is time to leave, or you won't be able to go through it.

"What stops someone from choosing a different door?" Not that she wanted to go to a different realm than hers, but since her way home was locked up tight, it seemed like a good idea to have options.

"Being invisible makes them rather difficult to find," Kale said. "Then there's me."

"So theoretically, to get into another realm, someone just has to sneak past you and be lucky enough to stumble upon a gate?"

"The odds of stumbling upon a gate are slim."

"I did it," Vera pointed out.

"Not everyone is so lucky. Besides, I am a good deterrent." Kale smirked. "You're very curious for someone who doesn't believe any of this."

"Maybe I'm just trying to gauge how whacked you really are." Vera scowled. "What happens to the people who do get past you?"

"No one has tried in a long time, but the person is hunted down and either returned home, or executed, if they've caused enough trouble and aren't already dead."

"Wow, that's harsh. So what, the realm sends out the Hounds of Hell to take them out or something?"

"Hellhounds do not leave Dubnos," Kale said. Vera gave him a what-the-heck-are-you-talking-about look. "Balor only sends them out of Dubnos if one of his demons gets loose."

"And Dubnos is?"

"You don't know of it." Dawning lit Kale's eyes as he tried to backpedal. "It's not important."

"I'm not going to drop it." Vera folded her arms and stared at the man until he ran a hand through his hair in frustration.

"Dubnos is the underworld, ruled over by Balor."

"Lovely. Glad to know the hounds of hell are real. I'll watch my back if I end up in Tartarus." Vera paused when Kale looked at her oddly, head tipped to the side and brows furrowed.

"You'd have to watch out for Cerberus is in Tartarus, not the Hounds," Kale corrected as if she were a child.

"Hades is real too," Vera said to herself but Kale misunderstood.

"Yes," Kale replied slowly.

"Holy buckets of devils. How many hells, or whatever, are there?"

"Each realm has its own underworld and an Infernal Host to keep order there. Did you think Hell was the only one?"

"To be honest, I'm not sure I believed in the existence of Hell until now. Now you're telling me there's—how many hell-underworlds are there?"

Kale's jaw jumped. "It's not important."

"You know, I've heard you say those names before," Vera pushed. "Places like Tartarus and Helheim. I recognized those. But you've also said things like Diyu, Duat, Avici, and others I can't even pronounce. Always to curse them. Those are underworlds too, aren't they?

Kale didn't reply, but Vera could tell she'd struck a nerve. He was shutting down. *Guess that's a yes.* Time to back off before he clammed up completely. She needed him to keep talking if she was going to figure out a way home. Hopefully she wouldn't be around long enough to get a sense of just how many hells were out there. Her nightmares had enough material to work with already.

"You didn't tell me how the people who sneak into other realms get caught."

"If they don't get caught by the inhabitants first, then the trespasser is brought to my attention. I am the hunter and executioner when someone violates the accords agreed upon by the leaders of each realm," he said. "That includes anyone who invades another realm and anyone who threatens the security of another realm."

Vera tried not to react as the man admitted he was a murderer like it was no big deal. Just a normal day in the twilight-zone neighborhood. She was fairly confident he wouldn't try to kill her, though. Not after his whole protector spiel. It wasn't like she had any intention of invading a foreign realm. Not when there were hellhounds and Cerberus and countless demons out there living, breathing, and drooling. All she needed to do was open a few gates and peek inside until she found the right one. Once she got home to Gus, hopefully before he unknowingly returned home to the new-world-order-of-monsters, the two of them could go somewhere no one could ever find them. On a boat in middle of the ocean, far away from forests and meadows for instance. Kale looked up sharply, into the forest behind Vera. The hair on the back of Vera's neck stood on end.

"Get inside. Now."

Vera hesitated.

"Run!"

Vera took off for the cabin. She glanced back and saw Kale stride into the forest. Where he vanished, Vera noticed a narrow game trail. She was sure it had not been there before and made a mental note to investigate later. For now, she followed the command of her self-proclaimed protector. Scotchie was hands-down the scariest person she'd ever met, and something like fear had flashed through his eyes just then. Vera was stubborn, not stupid. Crashing through the front door, Vera hoped to survive another day.

4

V era was pacing when the screen door slammed. She'd been waiting for that sound. She grabbed the go-bag from under the bed and took off down the hall to follow Kale. He had come back tight-lipped the day before, the trail he'd taken had vanished. Vera was sure she hadn't imagined it, though. The same thing had happened two more times since then. Whenever Kale trekked into the forest, for whatever reason, a narrow trail appeared in his wake, only to disappear upon his return. It wasn't hard to figure out those trails were how Kale left the meadow. Vera figured she could leave the same way.

She crept ninja-style across the front room, ducking under windows and hopping over the creakiest floorboards. After all, Kale could be hanging around right outside for all she knew. She really hoped not. At the front door, Vera tipped her head to peek through the screened opening without being seen. She wasn't disappointed. Kale walked out of the meadow, looking straight ahead the whole way. A trail out of crazy-town materialized behind him.

When the coast was clear, Vera slipped outside after

him. The shadows were beginning to lengthen, but it was still too early for Kale's nocturnal guard-horse to be out and about—creepy thing only came out when the sun went down. Like a Vampire. Man, she hoped he was not part vampire since he'd already sunk his teeth into her. Last thing she needed was to develop an aversion to sunlight and a craving for bloody smoothies.

Vera ran with a hitch in her step across the yard. There was no time to remove the bandaging from her leg. Kale had only been gone a few minutes last time. With the pain gone, she'd manage well enough. Kale, of course, didn't know that her leg was all hunky-dory. While he'd changed the wrappings that morning, Vera had clutched the mattress and grimaced for dramatic effect. No way was she giving away the one advantage she had. She'd been rather pleased with her performance too. Scotchie's brow had furrowed with all kinds of concern while watching her hands twisted into fists. The memory made Vera smile a little.

She slowed at the tree line and took a tentative step onto the trail. Nothing happened. The trail stayed put. No lightning struck. *Oh, happy day.* Vera trotted forward cautiously for a bit. When the meadow didn't yank her back, she knew she'd been right. This was the way out that Kale hadn't wanted her to know about. Now, all she had to do was find the right gate and pick a lock—cake. At the sound of voices, Vera jumped to the side of the trail, ducked behind a girl-sized fern, and froze. The fronds made it nearly impossible to hold still. Thousands of miniature leaves tickled Vera's face and arms. She was desperate to scratch all the places. As soon as Vera blew a frond away from her face, another took its place. Fortunately, the voices weren't getting closer because she was twitching like a criminal.

Vera finally held a handful of the fronds away from her

face to inspect them closer. All the tiny serrated leaves on the fronds in her hand shivered and wiggled. But there was no breeze. The white veins of the mottled leaves flexed and strained toward her all on their own. Stealth abandoned, Vera leaped away from the possessed fern. Frantically, she shook out her clothes and hair to make sure there weren't any leaves on her. The fronds uncurled, reaching after her. *So, the plant-life here is not exactly normal either,* she thought hysterically. At least it didn't sprout legs and come after her. Vera waited to be sure of that fact before she turned her back on the fern.

Head swinging side to side, Vera slunk along the trail toward the voices and away from touchy-feely flora. She was suspicious of anything that moved now, no matter how innocent it seemed. Around the next bend, Vera spotted Kale, his back to her. He leaned casually against a tree a little off the path. Only one shoulder, an elbow, and part of one leg were visible from Vera's angle. She probably would've missed him, if he'd been silent. Vera dropped into an awkward crouch, her wrapped leg stuck slightly out to the front. Like a lopsided crab, Vera inched ahead until she could make out Kale's conversation.

"Mara doesn't know about this?" Kale asked someone Vera could not see.

"Not at all," said a woman with a musical voice. "I thought it best to keep things between the two of us."

A hand with long violet nails slid into view, caressing Kale's arm. *Oh, Lady.* Whatever was happening, or going to be happening, Vera did not want to be there for it. Then again, with Kale distracted, she had a decent shot at sneaking past him. If she'd had semi-normal luck that is. As Vera edged to the right, an angry gray squirrel in the tree above squawked and threw a pinecone at her. In addition to its big bushy tail, the rodent had a single horn curling out from its muzzle, above its nose. Vera tried to duck out of sight, but the creature kept yelling and threw another pinecone. That one ricocheted off the hand she put up to cover her head.

Kale whipped around, shielding the mystery woman behind him, and startling the squirrel. Seeming to realize it was outnumbered, the bizarre squirrel darted away. Vera wished she could do the same. Instead, she pulled on her defiant-girl panties and rose to her feet wearing her best glare. Redness crept up Kale's neck, which Vera could see clearly thanks to a couple of newly-opened buttons. *So yuck.* He noticed her runaway bag when she looped her fingers under the frayed straps. Kale's expression darkened as an otherworldly face peered around his arm. The woman's skin had a silvery glow. Her hair was the same purple as her nails. She was all violet and shimmer like a princess, or a goddess. Grape Goddess was stunning. She was also tiny, coming only up to Kale's sternum. The woman smiled cheerfully at Vera with the palest lavender lips and a mouth full of pointed teeth.

"Oh, my. Hello." Grape Goddess gave a friendly wave.

Vera liked the woman immediately.

"Go back, now," Kale said to Vera through gritted teeth.

"No," Vera replied obstinately. "I'm going home."

"Home is not this way. You are somewhere else," Kale said.

Uni-squirrel and grabby-plant flashed in Vera's mind. *Crap-ola. This is another realm.* Kale had made it sound like stumbling across a gate was hard to do. Vera glanced around curiously. She hadn't even noticed she'd gone anywhere.

"What's going on here Kalesius?" asked Grape Goddess.

47

A bubble of hope inflated in Vera's chest. The woman would help her, Vera knew it.

"He's holding me captive," Vera announced.

Kale groaned.

"Guardian?" asked the woman, backing away from Kale.

Kale did the oddest thing then. He squatted down, placed the fingertips of his right hand on the ground and lifted his left hand toward the canopy, cupped like he held an invisible ball.

"Go back to the meadow. Please," Kale said to Vera.

Vera was prepared to ignore him until the "please." Kale was a shady, controlling muscle-head—he didn't plead. What had Vera missed? Her heart beat faster.

"You cannot protect a siphon. The realms will not allow it." The woman's beautiful features twisted as she struggled and failed to take a step toward Vera. "She is already dead. She just doesn't know it yet."

With some alarm, Vera realized that her usually infallible intuition had been wrong about the woman. She should've realized it too. When had she ever liked someone immediately? The answer was never. Even Suzie had needed to earn Vera's trust over time. And yet, Vera hadn't thought to question her reaction to the purple woman. If Vera couldn't tell the good guys from the bad in this place, she was completely screwed. Worse than that, even knowing Grape Goddess wanted her dead, didn't stop Vera from wanting to get closer to the woman. Only shock kept Vera's feet from moving. Whatever Kale was doing, was somehow holding back the would-be murderess while Vera struggled to regain her senses.

"The girl is my charge. Quit your assault on her," Kale ordered Grape Goddess.

"The realms are tired of being bound to our enemies,"

said Grapey. "If they learn the banished are escaping their prison…" She *tsked* and plumped her bottom lip. "They will raise armies to destroy the axis once and for all. And you with it."

"They would not succeed," replied Kale.

Vera noted the gentle chiming near the base of her skull.

"But that doesn't really matter because you will not reveal her presence here to anyone."

"I am beyond your reach," taunted the woman. "As soon as your fingers leave the earth, I will be at my father's side." The woman rubbed a lock of her hair between her fingers thoughtfully. "If you release me now, I could convince my father to consider an alternative solution for you. The siphon, however, is past saving."

"You mean you'll talk him into blackmailing me in return for your silence," Kale said.

"Give a little, get a little." Grapey smiled sweetly. "The Guardian releasing humans is no little thing, but Father can be reasonable. I'm sure you could come to an arrangement that would be better than destruction and death, no? I've heard it will be a bloodbath when the Infernal Ones battle for the privilege of torturing your soul for eternity."

Holy crap. Vera really wished she could turn tail right about then, but she was incapable of anything so sensible at that moment.

"Or you can let me destroy the siphon now," suggested Grape Goddess. "It'll save you from having to kill your little pet yourself. Perhaps the world need not know about your little indiscretion. I could even keep your secret from father."

"What's your price?" Kale asked.

"No price." Grape Goddess radiated warmth.

Vera knew the sincerity was phony as all getup, but she couldn't even be angry with the woman. *Dammit.*

"Just don't forget about the deal we were discussing before the siphon interrupted."

"If I decide I don't like your deal?" asked Kale

The woman shrugged one shoulder. "Sometimes I am forgetful. Things slip from my tongue. But either way, you cannot save the—" Grapey's voice cut off on a choke before she closed her mouth and stood there looking bored.

Vera's flight response finally kicked in once the woman was silent. Stumbling back, she spun around to leave.

"Wait, Vera," Kale called out.

Vera most certainly did not want to stay there for another second, but the exhaustion in Kale's voice gave her pause. Sweat beaded his forehead and the muscles in his neck strained. *I can't just leave him here. Right?* Whatever he was doing, it had kept the hypnotizing woman away from her. Without Kale, Vera would be a goner and she knew it.

"She can't get out?" Vera eyed the purple woman. "Is she a demon?"

"A jinn. She can't get out until I let her." Kale blinked slowly and dug his fingers deeper into the ground like he was keeping himself from floating away. "I need to know how you got here."

"I followed the little trail you made." Vera pointed at the narrow path.

"You shouldn't be able to see that. You definitely shouldn't be able to follow it through any gates." Kale's eyes narrowed at Vera and she squirmed. "You've started absorbing my magic."

"Excuse me?"

"Even Samhira calls you a siphon, not a human. I've

been trying to keep you away from magic so this wouldn't happen. But you won't stay put like you're supposed to."

"Am I supposed to apologize for not being a docile hostage?" *Maybe I can leave him here.*

"You're not a hostage," Kale declared with more of his usual crankiness, and then sighed. "That's not important right now. If you can siphon magic, you can manipulate it. And that means you can help me stop Samhira, now that you've exposed yourself." The accusation in his words made Vera defensive.

"I can't help you. I am just a human." Vera folded her arms. "This is not my fault."

"You're right. If I'd simply let the unnatural have you, none of this would be happening."

"I can take care of myself," Vera said adamantly.

"Yeah, you were doing a great job of that a few minutes ago when Samhira threw a little of her charm at you."

"If you'd let me go home, I never would've met your psycho girlfriend."

"Right now, I'm the only one standing between that realm you are so anxious to get back to and all the other realms that want it gone. So you can help me stop Samhira, or you can go home and wait for her people to wipe out your realm when she tells them all that humans are roaming the world once more."

"Gah! Like that's even a choice." Vera threw her arms in the air. "I don't know what you expect me to do, though."

"Have you ever seen someone spin wool into yarn?" asked Kale.

"Uh, sure. On cartoons." Vera shrugged. "Afterward, the little yellow sheep knitted it into a scarf to give to his best friend, the blue horse, for his birthday. The chickens ground up their corn to make him a cornbread birthday cake too. How is this helpful?"

"Can you picture how the sheep pulled and twisted the soft bits of wool together?"

"Yeah, sure."

"Good," said Kale wearily. "See what I am doing with my hands? Do what I am doing, right hand down, left hand up." Vera followed the instructions feeling immensely stupid. "Now, this is the tricky part. You need to pull in the magic around you."

"I don't understand. Is this about siphoning or whatever? You want me to siphon magic? Because I can't," Vera said with frustration.

"There's no time to teach you how to siphon. I'm basically going to throw magic at you. You'll just catch it and hold it."

"I should warn you, I'm not good at catching things."

Kale rolled his eyes. "It's not that kind of catch. Just keep your hands like that and you'll be fine. Oh, and it will tingle a bit."

A moment later, Vera shrieked and cradled the hand she'd been holding in the air to her chest. That had not been a little tingly. It had felt like touching a live wire, which she had done once before—when she was eight. Vera's foster sister had convinced her that it would show her what happiness felt like. It had not. Although, after the trip to the hospital in an ambulance, Vera had gotten her a new home placement with Suzie out of it. So in a way, it had brought her happiness. According to Kale, if she sucked it up and grabbed that electricity again, Samhira wouldn't slaughter her. Which would make Vera happy once again. It was going to totally suck though.

Vera threw her fingers into the air. Her arm buzzed with scorching fire.

"Relax," Kale coached Vera.

Sure, no problem, Vera wanted to snap at Kale but the fire zinging through her, which Kale called magic, had locked her jaw shut.

"Magic is like the fibers of wool. You need to tighten them into a cord to make them useful. Like spinning wool into yarn. Picture it in your mind. Pull all that tingling from all your limbs and twist it into a single strand."

This is freaking insane.

"Come on, Vera, concentrate. If a little yellow lamb can do it, so can you."

Bite me, Scotchie. Vera reined in her mind and imagined the overwhelming burn receding from her skin and muscles. She pictured it spinning into a length of electric yarn. Tighter and tighter, until all the tendrils became a single vein of lightning that pulsed from her upraised hand to the center of her chest.

"Now, ground it. Stretch the end of your cord into the earth beneath your hand. Keep your other hand raised, though. The cord can't pull your hand down if you won't allow it."

It didn't take much coaxing to get the lightening strand to anchor itself. Once it made contact with the soil, it happily planted itself, stretching deeper into the ground than Vera would have thought possible. What had begun as a span of magic was now at least twenty times that long. A tug on Vera's upraised hand let her know the cord was finally out of give. Kale was right. It didn't fight for more length than she gave it.

"Good," Kale said to her. "I'm going to tie your thread to mine. Don't pull away."

When Kale's magic prodded Vera's, it was like a finger stroking her flesh. Vera's fought the urge to recoil, reminding herself that Kale was not touching any part of her, despite how it felt. Where Vera's cord was blistering electricity, Kale's was a swirling void that threatened to steal away her breath. Kale's magic slid along hers until both cords were aligned, then it wove itself into Vera's. It only took a moment before their magics were completely intertwined. Gently, Kale guided their shared cord upward through the earth to the feet of Samhira. To Vera, it felt like having another limb. The magics emerged from the soil and looped around Samhira's feet and leg. *We just lassoed a jinn with invisible magic cords. Holy crazy buckets.* The purple woman's mouth opened on a soundless screech while the magic pinned her arms to her sides, rendering her motionless.

"Hold it tight," said Kale. "In just a minute, I'm going to let go. You'll have to hold both our magics on your own. If you remove your hand from the ground, they will snap back and kill you. So don't."

Vera stared at him wide-eyed, wanting to tell him she'd changed her mind. But it was too late. She couldn't speak. Instead, Vera pulled on the magics with all her might.

"If you lower your other hand, even an inch, Samhira will slip free." Kale looked at Vera with regret and said, "It is going to hurt. Count to ten, and pull tighter on the cord with each count. If you don't think you can pull any harder, find a way to do it anyway. When you get to ten, release it. But not before ten, okay?" He waited for Vera's nod. "Get ready. Pull now, Vera."

One, Vera counted in her head. The electricity was a familiar burn. *Two.* Kale dropped his raised hand, releasing the magic, and the burn multiplied exponentially. *Three.* A scream tore from Vera's throat. She squeezed her eyes closed. *Four.* She pulled on the cords until her arms shook, and then she pulled harder. *Five.* Tears slid down her face, obscuring the world. *Six. Lady, help me. Seven. Please. Eight. Pull. Nine... Ten.*

Vera fell over and curled into a ball. The magic, once freed, slithered away, but the lightning had scorched Vera's insides while she'd harnessed its power. It was killing her. The world faded away, the physical agony replaced by a new kind of anguish. Terror ran wild in Vera's mind. The monster had caught her. He pinned her to the ground. Sand coated her tongue while she struggled against his weight on her back. He dipped his face to her shoulder and bit down. Vera opened her mouth to scream but nothing came out.

"Vera, look at me," Kale called her back to consciousness. "Open your eyes."

With one last shake, Vera came to. She choked on a sob and captured Kale's hand before he pulled it away, clinging to the man while the events in her mind retreated to a far corner. She threw a wall up around all of it and fled. Kale knelt in front of her.

"It's over. You are safe," Kale said quietly, staring at her hand in his.

Truth.

Vera saw the body behind Kale then. Beside it was a ball of violet hair splattered with red. Kale tried to block her view, but it was too late. The same red covered Kale's chest and hands. And now her hands too. Vera rolled to her knees, heaved, and threw up. When Kale tried to help, Vera cringed away. She'd held Samhira motionless while Kale murdered her. The woman hadn't even been able to fight back. Some part of Vera had known the woman was going to die, had to die to protect an entire world of humans. However, Vera hadn't let herself think about what that would mean before now. She heaved again.

"She didn't feel any pain," Kale said gently from a few feet away when Vera's stomach stopped rolling.

Vera didn't feel any relief in the hollow ache at her core with that knowledge. The sickness didn't ease. The wailing in her head wouldn't quit.

"Why does the world hate my people?" Vera asked, desperate for an explanation for all of it. "We haven't done anything."

"It isn't what you've done. It's what you could do."

"That's a shitty reason for genocide," replied Vera, directing her revulsion and anger outward.

"Some people would agree, but most have been taught to fear your kind for generations. They cannot help it." Kales eyes scanned the forest around them. "We need to get back to the meadow. Can you walk? I'll explain as best as I can on the way."

Vera stood on shaky legs. She refused to let Kale touch her.

"The realms used to be kingdoms, spread across one world. Now they are fragments, completely isolated and scared," said Kale. "Your kind did that."

"But humans are helpless compared to all of you," argued Vera.

"You are humans because there's no magic to absorb in your realm. Exposed to magic, you would not stay human for long. Look at you."

"We'd all become siphons?"

"No one really knows anymore. When the realms divided, your realm was filled with siphons, half-breeds who absorb the magic of those around them. But there were others too: mothers, fathers, husbands, wives, children, and friends, people from all over the world who chose exile to be with their loved ones. There's no telling how your kind has evolved over a thousand years of intermingling on that scale. No telling what you are."

"Siphons steal magic from other people?"

"Not necessarily. Siphons can learn to absorb excess magic around them, the run-off so to speak. The problems happen when there're not enough magic leftovers to go around or when siphons become addicts."

"Let me guess, that's what happened with my ancestors," said Vera. "Their greed destroyed the world."

"Yes."

"That's no reason to want to kill off all my kind," said Vera. "News flash. Becoming an addict is not genetic."

"The potential threat is enough to scare people. Their memories of that time have not been lost. The only way to protect your people is to keep them locked away."

"And if anyone finds out I'm wandering around outside my prison, that would be enough to doom my entire world," concluded Vera.

It wasn't a question, but Kale answered, "Yes."

So if Vera went home, she could be killed by the unnatural. If she stayed in the meadow, she could be killed by the next person who saw her. Either way, she'd die. However, staying meant gambling with the lives of billions of humans. Vera had never been a gambler. She'd seen what gambling did to people. There was no way she would start now, not when she'd be betting with the survival of her entire race. She had to get home. She'd kill the monster herself if that's what it took.

5

Kale tensed. Vera clung to him in the darkness, hands knotted in the back of his sleep-rumpled shirt. Granted, they were standing in the middle of the kitchen, facing off against an intruder, and Vera was more-or-less using him as a shield, but still. After the bloody mess the day before, she'd threatened to stab him in his sleep if he ever touched her again. At the time, he'd taken it as a good sign. It meant she was okay. The way she trembled against him now, maybe he'd been wrong. Had he damaged her resilient spirit?

"It's okay, Vera. He's just a friend." Kale spoke gently despite clenching his fists. "Grab the lights, Addamas," Kale said to the shadow of a man. "Why are you lurking around my home in the middle of the night?"

"It's basically morning. I was getting some food. I'm starving."

They all squinted against the sudden flare of light.

"You couldn't put on some pants first?" Kale asked with a shake of his head.

"Nope, they crinkle the fur. Besides, it's not like

anything's hanging out." Addamas wagged his eyebrows, and then caught Vera sneaking a peek at him from behind Kale. "Hiya, girly." He winked at her.

"What are you?" Vera asked, following the trail of tattoos up Addamas's arms with her eyes. Tattoos Addamas got to mask his deception marks back when he and Kale were not so friendly.

"I, pretty girl, am the sexiest satyr in all the world."

Kale rolled his eyes, but Vera eased up on his shirt so he kept his mouth shut.

"Do you want to kill me and all humans?" Vera asked bluntly.

"Nah." Addamas didn't flinch at the unfiltered question. "Definitely not you. I mean, some humans, sure. But mostly just the douchey ones." Addamas leaned back against the counter and popped a grape into his mouth.

"I know the type." Vera took a cautious step away from Kale.

"Addamas spends a lot of time in your realm," Kale said. "It's one of his favorite places."

"You can travel to different realms? I didn't think that was allowed. Kale says the gates don't work like that."

Kale didn't miss the pointed look. Or the additional step she put between them. *There's my girl.* Well, not *his* girl, just the fiery girl he'd come to know.

"He's right," said Addamas. "Hopping gates is impossible. Luckily, I'm no ordinary duck. I can create my own pathways and bypass those suckers."

"Ah. So you're not normal either," Vera said with a frown, which Kale did not understand.

"Nope." Addamas beamed. "I'm one-of-a-kind. It used to drive Mr. Guardian here completely mad. But he's gotten over it."

"Speaking of driving people mad, where's Mimi?" Kale asked.

"It's possible she's following a false trail across the human realm, trying to locate the world's most badass tracker," said Addamas innocently, scratching the back of his neck.

"She doesn't know you are here?" *Duat. Mimi is going to be pissed.* "Why do you do that to her?"

"She's sexy as hell when her coat gets all ruffled." The satyr was shameless. "Don't worry, though, she's probably already figured it out and found the pathway I left for her. She should be back here any time now."

"Vera, this idiot is trying to find the unnatural that's hunting you," said Kale. "But don't get used to him. Mimi's going to eviscerate him when she gets here."

"Has found," Addamas corrected. "Already done, my brother."

"You found him? I can go home now?" asked Vera.

It was the first real smile Kale had ever seen from the girl. And she aimed it at Addamas.

"Soon," said Addamas. "Just waiting for the unnatural to lead us to the rest of the horde so we can get his master too, sweetheart."

"Don't call me that," Vera said sharply.

Addamas sobered and Kale bit back a smile. It was going to be nice having someone else on the receiving end of Vera's hostility to commiserate with.

"My apologies," said Addamas sincerely, ditching his devil-may-care charm and trademark teasing.

"Wait, horde?" Vera asked as Addamas's words sank in. "There's more than one of those monsters out there?"

"Unfortunately, there's always more than one," Kale

answered as gently as he could. No need to mention just how many more he suspected.

"But don't worry, girly. We'll get rid of them all." Addamas held out a hand in a gesture he'd learned hanging out on Earth. "By the way, it's nice to officially meet you, Vera."

"You too," Vera replied, stepping forward to take the offered hand. "Sorry I threw a knife at you."

Kale nearly choked.

"No worries. I've got impeccable reflexes." Addamas demonstrated his prowess by throwing his arms about like a fool, pretending to catch invisible blades.

Vera let out a soft giggle.

What the actual helheim?

"Which is a good thing for me," said Addamas. "You're quite the knife-thrower."

"I've been practicing." Vera fidgeted with the hem her shirt. "Between the monsters chasing me, being held captive, and that horse attacking me..."

"You're not a captive," Kale clarified.

"Have you let me leave?" Vera challenged. "Yeah, that's called holding someone captive, Scotchie."

"Understandable," Addamas said with amusement. "I'd be practicing too if I were you. If you'd like, I can show you a couple more tricks. Not even that flesh-eating, demon-spawned horse will bother you anymore."

Vera's mouth popped open.

Damn the satyr to Tartarus.

"Flesh-eating?" Vera squeaked.

"You are completely safe around Ferrox," Kale assured.

"Ferrox probably wouldn't like Vera-flavored snow-cones," Addamas added helpfully.

"What does that mean?" she asked.

"You are too sweet," explained Addamas. "Like undiluted alohra juice. Great stuff, by the way. I love it straight up. But for some, a little whisky makes all the difference. You have alohra juice in the human realm right? I can never... No, that's right. Your realm has..."

"Apple juice?" Vera suggested.

"Exactly. It's like the concentrated stuff in those freezer boxes."

"Gross." Vera scrunched her nose with disgust.

"Ferrox would think so too," Addamas said. "That horse likes his juice diluted with wickedness. The more, the better. You're so sweet, you'd literally make Ferrox sick."

"So Ferrox won't eat me."

"Oh no," Addamas agreed. "He'd have left your carcass for the buzzards for sure."

Kill me, Kale groaned silently.

And end the show? Negative, good buddy. This is hilarious. Of course Ferrox was listening in.

Vera's mouth moved up and down like a grounded fish. Nothing came out.

"Ferrox was never going to kill you," Kale said. "He was only making sure you didn't run away. He was a bit heavy-handed because he was mad at me for making him stand guard in the first place."

"You made him do that?" Vera turned a disconcerting shade of purple.

"I didn't tell him to be a brute about it. I just needed you watched," said Kale.

"You can talk to him like with Mimi?" asked Vera.

Addamas looked over at Kale curiously. If the satyr opened his mouth, he wouldn't have to wait for Mimi to kill him. Kale would do it.

"Not exactly. Uh, Ferrox's mind is linked to mine," explained Kale.

"You're telling me you talk to a demon horse in your head? Were you in his head when he chased me down? How about when he tried to take off my hand for lunch? Did you laugh about it together afterward too?"

Tell her you didn't laugh, that was all me, said Ferrox.

Not helpful.

"Well, you can both go screw yourselves," Vera announced.

Ouch. I'd rather not if it's all the same, said Ferrox.

"Shut up," Kale told Ferrox. Except it was out loud.

Addamas' lips twitched when Vera flipped Kale off and marched to her room before Kale could explain himself. Kale decided he'd rather be back in Hel or Duat or Avici. Any of the underworlds would do.

Diyu is nice this time of year. The man-bit harvest is always at its peak right now.

Kale slammed the door on Ferrox, severing their link.

"Stars above," Kale said slowly.

"You done trying to carry on multiple conversations?" Addamas asked. "Cause you are clearly not that talented."

"That was a train wreck."

"Understatement. But hey, I do like your new redhead. She's feisty." Addamas hooked a thumb toward Vera's room.

"Huh?" said Kale.

"She's spunky. Or hadn't you noticed?"

"Yes, Dam, I noticed." Kale shoved both hands through his hair. "This has been the longest five days of my existence. But her hair's brown, nearly black, not red."

"If you say so."

"I need you to show me where the unnatural's territory is," said Kale.

"Oh good. Avoidance. That's a new tactic for you," Addamas said sarcastically. "I left a path to the place open for you. You can make your own way back once you're done looking around. I'm going to crash for a while."

Kale's stomach fell. "Where's that pathway?" Kale swung around to look for it out the front windows, but he couldn't see it. "Where did you leave the path, Dam?" Kale asked urgently and rushed to the next window, but it wasn't there either.

"Calm down." Addamas was staring at Kale as if he'd lost his mind. "I know how to secure a path. It's one-way only. From here to there. No one can get to the meadow. Your Vera is safe."

"But Vera can get out. The girl can see paths." Kale was already headed for Vera's room, Addamas on his heels. "If she sees that path, she'll assume it's the one for Mimi you were bragging about. A path to the human realm."

Kale barged through the door. Vera was gone.

"The path I left for Mimi leads to Heliopolis, not here. I knew the extra step would piss her off, which is why I did it." Addamas nodded at the pathway visible through Vera's open window while the sun came up through the trees. "That path does go to the human realm, right to the unnatural's territory. It's the path I set for you. I didn't know."

Kale went out the window. It was faster than going back through the cabin.

"I'm truly sorry," Addamas said when he caught up a minute later, carrying Kale's sword. He must've grabbed it before following after Kale. Addamas held out the sword and Kale took it.

"You couldn't have known. Vera's leg's still healing anyway, so we'll catch up to her before she leaves the path. She'll live to run away another day."

Kale and Addamas ran easily beside each other along the path, their breathing unlabored.

"How many times has she run?" asked Addamas.

"I've lost count."

"Seriously, has any girl ever tried so hard to get away from all your hotness?" Addamas laughed a little.

"Yes," Kale replied darkly.

Addamas winced. "You know I didn't mean that. None of that is on you. It's on those siphon bastards and that enchantress wench."

"I didn't want to see it. That's on me. So I'll spend the rest of my eternal life making amends for it."

"Even if that means protecting a pain-in-the-neck siphon girl who could end the world someday?"

"Yes."

"Your only crime was being blinded by a beautiful woman. More people than you are guilty of the same. You deserve a life, man," said Addamas.

"I have a life."

"Not a real one... I do have this cousin who'd be perfect for you. She's no nymph but—"

"Dam?" Kale interrupted.

"Yeah?"

"Shut up for five minutes and I'll think about it."

"Done."

Addamas fell silent. Kale glanced over. The idiot made a motion of locking his lips and throwing a key over his shoulder. Then the satyr batted his eyes at Kale. *Stars, why was this taking so long? The girl couldn't have gotten this far ahead of them... Unless the little faker's leg is healed. Hel.* Kale had ignored her deception marks. He'd thought she was planning another runaway attempt. Since he knew she wouldn't get far, he hadn't worried. After Kale dragged Vera back to the meadow, they were going to sit down and have a nice long chat until all the deception marks she'd been collecting lately cleared up.

Addamas yelped and crashed to the ground under an attacker. Kale spun around. Addamas was flat on his back, Mimi's claws extended at his throat.

"Hey Mimi," Addamas said. "Where've you been?"

The mountain lion growled, and then began to stretch, craning her neck upward. Addamas splayed a steadying hand on her side. There was a crackling blur that lasted only a moment before a fierce woman replaced the animal. The ends of her blunt-tipped black hair swayed by her chin as she knocked Addamas' hand away from her bare ribcage. Mimi balled up a fist and decked the satyr.

"Do you know how many nymph houses I had to go to?" Mimi asked. "And you were here the whole time." She punched him again. "That one's for Sheahna."

"Mimi," Kale called out and was rewarded with all of that fury turned on him. "He deserves it, don't get me wrong, but we need to get Vera before the unnatural does." Kale gestured down the path.

"You let her get away?" shouted Mimi. "I'm going to kill you both."

Mimi leaped off Addamas. She was back on four legs by the time she landed on the path and tore off.

"Hurry up," Kale told Addamas, not bothering to help him up. "If Vera dies, Mimi will never forgive you."

"Damn me to Tartarus," moaned Addamas from the ground.

Kale started to laugh, but just then, Vera's distant scream echoed up the path.

VERA HADN'T EMERGED from the path into a forest as she'd expected. Instead, she was surrounded on every side by sheer rock facings the same color as a prairie sunset. She'd grown up less than a hundred miles from the Badlands, so she recognized the striated formations. Odds were, she'd drop dead from dehydration long before she stumbled across a way out of the dusty clay canyons. Her best bet was tucking tail and heading back to the meadow. She didn't want to be responsible for the annihilation of all mankind, but she wasn't prepared to die without a fighting chance either. There was no way to fight a desert. But it was too late. The path had disappeared. It had spit her out and left her there. Vera's stomach fell. She would've been better off if she'd died falling out of that tree.

Tears of frustration welled in Vera's eyes. Her body's way of wasting precious fluids on stupid emotions. The sun was well overhead, heating the crown of her head and leaving pitiful little shade along the canyon floor. Vera angrily blinked away the tears before they fell. All right, going back wasn't an option. Standing there was a guaranteed death sentence, though, so that wasn't an option either. Time to get over it and move forward. A little ways off to the right, one of the canyon walls had crumbled, leaving a slope of crushed rock. If Vera climbed high enough, maybe she'd get lucky and see a road. Lady Luck had to give her a win eventually.

The unnatural made no sound as it came up behind her.

"You smell sweeter than I remember," he said, tangling a hand in Vera's hair.

Vera screamed. The unnatural wrapped a dirty hand around her throat, silencing her. He lifted Vera by the neck until she was at eye level with him. Her legs flailed while she clawed unsuccessfully at his fingers. When he slammed her against the wall of the canyon, it knocked the fight out of her. Vera's vision swirled and her ears rang. The unnatural pressed up against her, pinning her against the rock wall. Only then did his hand loosen so Vera could drag in shallow sips of air. Barely enough air to keep from passing out. A single disgusting finger ran along Vera's jaw while she sucked in tiny breaths. Vera gagged from the smell of sweat and the feel of the unnatural's touch. The finger traveled down her neck and dipped into the collar of her shirt. The ringing in Vera's ears became a wail.

Suddenly, a shadow landed on the unnatural. He jerked back from Vera, dropping her in a heap. The shadow snarled. Mimi. Latched onto the back of the unnatural's neck with jagged teeth, the mountain lion used her claws to shred the unnatural's skin and hide. With a bellow of outrage, the unnatural balled up a fist and swung it wildly behind him. It grazed Mimi's shoulder. The cat cried out around a mouthful of flesh but did not let go. If the unnatural got its meaty hands on Mimi, he would crush her. Vera wanted to call out to Mimi, to tell the animal not to bother, to just run and save herself, but her throat couldn't form the sounds. She needed to distract the unnatural long enough for Mimi to get away. Using the crevices of the rock face as handholds, Vera hauled herself to her feet. The world spun. All Vera could do was hang on and wait for it to stop.

Vera's vision cleared just in time to see the bloodied unnatural twist around and land a blow on Mimi's head. One solid hit was all it took. The cat's eyes rolled to the back of her head, and she slid to the ground, knocking up a cloud of dust where she landed. Mimi's side twitched once. The cat did not move to get up. An ache punched through Vera's chest. The unnatural didn't stop. With a feral roar of triumph, he kicked Mimi in the ribs. She flew a few feet and slammed against the rock wall with a wet crack. After that, she was still. Vera's arms and legs gave out. Sliding back to the canyon floor, Vera gasped for air. The unnatural bared blood-stained teeth. He ran a hand down his face, spreading gore in stripes down his neck and chest, wearing it like a badge of honor.

Vera braced herself when the unnatural turned on her, but he did not approach. Something on the canyon ledge above had captured his attention. There was a soft clacking. She followed the monster's gaze. Above, perched a white bird with a hooked beak. The bird was bigger than Vera. It hopped from the ledge with a trill, not bothering to extend its wings, and landed gracefully between her and the unnatural. The unnatural stumbled back. Amazingly, the bird seemed unconcerned by the monster's presence. It focused solely on Vera.

The bird placed the tip of its beak against Vera's neck. She tried to pull away but didn't get far with the canyon at her back. The sharp point swept across the delicate skin of Vera's throat without hurting her. A small acorn swung from a leather string around the bird's neck. Exactly like the one Gus wore. Vera had told Gus the cord was too long and made him look like he had a major outie belly button when he wore it under his shirt. Gus had kept wearing the absurdly long necklace anyway.

If it had been any shorter, it would've garroted me when I shed my human form, said Gus's voice in her head. *I'd already be dead, and you'd be headed back to the horde right now. But, since my cry awakens an unnatural's conscience, this one won't get too close while I'm here. That level of remorse is crushing, even though it only lasts a moment.*

Vera stared at the bird, eyes bugging from their sockets. The bird met her gaze with Gus's eyes. *He's a bird?*

Dhalion, corrected the voice. *I'm not some feather-brained creature.*

Gus?

You are being rather slow. The bird ran its beak through Vera's hair like it was grooming her. *Are you sure your head is not damaged?*

It was definitely Gus.

Glad you are catching up. This is my real form. So much better than that human one that itched terribly. Suzie used to chase me off when I became too irritable and wouldn't let me come home until I spent some time away in my own skin. Made me crazy with worry leaving you two alone.

Vera remembered the regular business trips Gus took and how Suzie practically shoved the grumbling man out the door. The truth was so strange.

Figured you'd be getting used to strange by now, Gus said. *What with that Guardian around. Where is that man, anyway? He's supposed to keep you safe now.*

Kale? It's taken me days to finally escape him and that place.

Suzie said you'd be hard-headed about him.

Sorry, what? Suzie knew Kale?

Suzie said she liked him.

I find that hard to believe, Vera said. *You are wigging me out right now.*

Bah. You're fine. Suzie dedicated her life to finding and watching over you. The girl who will rise out of exile and reunite the world. So maybe try not to get yourself killed anymore?

Gus had to be kidding. Then Vera's heart twisted. Had she really only been a duty for Suzie?

Ach, don't pull my words awry in that head of yours. Knowing what you'd become made Suzie search for you, but it didn't make her love you. My Suzie loved you like you were her own daughter. She'd flick your ear right now if she could. Gus thunked Vera on the head for emphasis. *No more running away from the Guardian, got it?*

I can't go back there. If someone catches me, they'll kill me, and then go after the whole human race. And I don't care what you say, I don't trust that man, Gus.

Doesn't matter that you trust him. Trust Suzie. She said the Guardian is the only one who can keep you alive. If you stay alive, the world will too. If you die, the world will crumble. So, if you want to save your kind, you must live. That is your responsibility. You don't get to be a martyr in this story.

You cannot tell me that one life will make that much difference, argued Vera.

That's exactly what I'm telling you. I don't know how or why, but your life does matter that much. Which means so does the Guardian's life.

Something about him scares me, admitted Vera.

Your intuition tells you to fear the Guardian because of the darkness that clings to him. Even those without your sensitivities can feel it. You will see how people steer clear of him. But keep in mind that the darkness which raises the hair on the back of your neck is also what made him who he is. The Guardian and your protector.

I don't think I can be who you want me to be. I just want to go to college, have a life, be me.

Then do it. Do all of that. Being you is how you will succeed. But you cannot be you if you are dead, right? So, don't make it hard for the Guardian to keep you alive, okay?

Vera nodded through her tears. She felt like this was another final goodbye. Gus nuzzled her once more.

Ahhh, he's finally here. I must go. One last thing, though. The Guardian does not know who you are. Not all of it anyway. Be careful, if you should decide to tell him or anyone about your destiny. Not everyone wants the world whole again.

With that, Gus turned and flew from the canyon. Kale loomed on the opposite side of the unnatural from Vera, holding that sword of his. The Guardian scanned Vera quickly then regarded the unnatural, who had turned to confront the new threat. Addamas materialized behind Kale. The satyr shot to Mimi's side, dropped to his knees, and scooped her up. He pressed his face to her bloodied neck.

"Errock," Kale said. "You should be dead and turned to dust by now."

"Ah, Kalesius," the unnatural said. "I knew I'd be seeing you soon."

"Who is your new master?" Kale asked.

The unnatural shifted, revealing caution for the man in front of him. It was scared of Kale. Vera was supposed to put her life in the hands of a man who scared the monsters.

"Tell me and I will send him to Hell after you. That way you can face him without his puppet strings attached," Kale said.

"No one can reattach the strings that were cut centuries ago," Errock said. "I serve the horde at my own will. Someone with your particular skill set would be a welcome addition to the horde. I dare say you'd enjoy the transformation too."

Errock pulled his shoulders back proudly and stomped his hoofed feet. Kale did not react. Eyes flat, arms hung loosely at his sides, and legs set shoulder-width apart. He did not move even a tiny muscle. Vera could not help but remember the severed purple head. Kale could strike in an instant, his prey wouldn't see it coming.

"When you are finished playing whipping boy to the witches that castrated you, come find me," Errock said, anger finally lacing his words at Kale's lack of reaction.

"When you are finished licking the dung from your jailers' feet, finished awaiting their every summons, I will be around. My master would select a magnificent beast to carry you forth to find the dignity they stole from you."

The unnatural reached into the sash at his waist and pulled out a tiny bottle. He dashed it to the ground. Lightening-filled mist joined the sound of shattering glass. It swirled upward, surrounding the unnatural before Kale made it two steps. There was a blinding flash and Errock evaporated. Kale stepped to where the unnatural had been and swooped down to pick up a piece of the shattered bottle left behind. His jaw jumped while he shoved the shard into his pocket

Kale's mask of calm was still in place when he turned to Vera. "Can you stand on your own?"

Vera rose on unsteady legs. "I'm fine," she said.

Surprised that the words had come out, Vera lifted a hand to her unbruised throat—Gus. While Vera marveled, Kale moved to kneel beside Addamas and laid his sword on the ground. The satyr held Mimi's limp body against his chest, rocking gently.

"Are you sure?" Kale asked Addamas.

"Absolutely," Addamas said with conviction.

Kale dug the fingers of one hand into Mimi's matted fur and the others he splayed against the ground. He breathed steadily, but Vera saw an almost imperceivable shudder run down his spine. Mimi seemed to inflate.

"Atinmerit," called Addamas. "Don't you leave us. Or I will go to Aaru myself to find you. And last time I broke into your afterworld, it didn't end well, so get back here."

Mimi's body convulsed and it kept convulsing. Kale kept his hands in place, his eyes pinched. It went on like that for many long, painful minutes. Suddenly, Kale lifted his hands, releasing the magic. Mimi stilled, other than her shallow breaths.

"Atinmerit?" Addamas asked.

The cat opened one eye, closed it, and began to stretch and twist in Addamas' arms. There was so much agony in Mimi's movement, Vera could barely stand to watch. She was sure the cat was in the last throes of death. Kale hadn't been able to save her after all. Vera turned her face away.

"Stop calling me that, idiot," came an irritated girl's voice.

Vera jerked her head up. Where Mimi had been, laid a girl with golden almond-shaped eyes. Mimi's eyes. Vera wondered if anyone was what they seemed.

"Surprise," said the girl to Vera with a pitiful smile. "I would've told you sooner, but sometimes the cat doesn't like to let me go."

"Can you make it home to your healers now?" asked Kale.

Mimi flinched. There was a heavy pause before Mimi inclined her head to say yes without looking at Kale. The Guardian had moved a handful of steps away from them all. His shoulders sagged with exhaustion.

"I will get her there," Addamas assured. "Thank you, Kale."

"Don't," Kale said with a slight shake of his head.

Addamas carried Mimi away, a path opening in front of them.

Vera heard Addamas say, "I like having you naked in my arms."

"Try anything, and I will tear out your innards and feed them to my falcons," Mimi replied.

Vera smiled weakly. Mimi was a shape-shifter girl. She was not sure what to think about that yet, but her chest tightened with relief that Mimi was alive. The rest, Vera would figure out later.

"Are you ready to go back?" Kale asked tiredly.

"Yes."

The truth was, Vera didn't have a choice. Apparently, she had to stay by the man's side and stay alive to save her kind.

6

Vera rested her hand on the doorknob. The metal warmed while she debated leaving her room. She didn't want to, but hunger was beginning to win over pride. When Kale hadn't checked on her that morning, she'd been relieved. Even though it had meant none of the usual breakfast peace offerings. It made sense, though. Kale now knew her leg was good to go. No reason to keep waiting on her. If Vera wanted food, nothing was stopping her from getting it herself. Nothing except overwhelming embarrassment for the trouble she'd caused, which she'd opted to stew in all morning rather than show her face.

Honestly, she knew she was being ridiculous. It was time to get out there, look Kale in the eyes—the super-scary eyes of a man who almost lost a friend because of her—and say sorry. *Ugh. Sorry sounds so inadequate.* She wouldn't blame Kale if he gift-wrapped her for Samhira's family and dropped her off on their doorstep. Only he wouldn't because he was the official bodyguard to her hot mess. The whole situation made her want to crawl out of her skin. *How is this even supposed to work? Like, hey, I think you're uber creepy, but*

I'll let you protect me now because my foster-dad—who's actually a dhalion—said I'd die without you. Then, the world would end. No bueno. Oh, and I know you can't stand me, so it's a good thing you don't have a choice. Just keep me alive. Capiche?

Sounds of Kale moving around in the kitchen floated down the hall. Vera's stomach wrenched, beginning to eat itself since begging for sustenance was getting it nowhere. Vera couldn't put off her appearance any longer. Swallowing, she twisted the knob and forced her legs to carry her down the hall. Kale looked up when she eased around the corner. If he was surprised to see her, he did not show it. He nodded a greeting then went back to piling chips on a plate beside a massive sandwich. The guy did not mess around when it came to feeding time. Vera's stomach called out a pathetic hello to the deliciousness on his plate.

"I was wondering if you've heard if Mimi is okay?" Vera's heart skittered.

"She has some of the best healers in the world to care for her," answered Kale. "She will live."

"And her becoming a mountain lion occasionally won't be a problem for them?"

"They're used to morphs where Mimi is from, so no, it won't be a problem."

"Oh, good. That's good." Vera pressed her lips together to stop babbling.

Kale cut his sandwich in two, placed half on a second plate, dumped some chips beside it, and held it out to her. Vera readied a protest out of good manners. She didn't want to take his lunch, even though she was salivating over it. Rolling his eyes at her hesitation, Kale set the plate of food on the counter in front of her. He grabbed his portion and headed for the table.

"Thank you," Vera said sincerely and got another nod.

Vera popped a chip into her mouth and had to stop herself from wolfing down the rest. Instead, she carried her meal to the table. Like a civilized house guest. The pedestal table had four chairs around it, which meant Vera could sit next to Kale or across from him. Vera chose across from him. Kale went on eating without acknowledging her. Vera followed his lead. She practically inhaled her sandwich before she realized what she was doing. She tucked one hand under her leg, pushed a chip around her plate, then picked it up slowly and put it in her mouth. Vera's toes tapped mindlessly against the center pedestal while she tried not to crunch too loudly. It was dumb, but she was hyper-aware of everything she did all of a sudden.

"Hiya." Addamas strolled through the front door and headed for the cupboard. "Mimi said to tell you both that she's fine and to stop brooding."

Vera startled and choked on a chip. In hindsight, Kale probably should've given her a heads up of that Addamas was coming. He'd sensed the satyr pathing in a few minutes before but hadn't thought to say anything. Kale grabbed a bottle of water and uncapped it for Vera. She took a swig to wash down the food.

"You all right there, girly?" Addamas watched with mild concern.

"Yep," Vera rasped, wiping a bead of water from her top lip.

"You're back sooner than I thought you'd be," observed Kale.

"The food in Heliopolis is abominable." Addamas yanked open the cupboard to reveal a box of breakfast pastries and a bottle of orange soda. "I had to get out of there and get something edible."

"Mm-hmm. Which god did they try to sacrifice you to?" asked Kale.

Kale was not an idiot. The only thing that could've gotten Addamas to leave Mimi's side was Mimi herself. If she'd ordered Addamas away, it was probably to save the satyr from her brothers. They were not fans.

"Pshaw." Addamas dropped into a chair, peeling the silver wrapper from a pair of pastries. "Not god, gods. Plural. They'll never get over it."

"Do you care?" Kale asked.

"Nope." Addamas smacked his lips and shoved half a pastry in his mouth.

Vera couldn't take her eyes off the frosted pastries. Kale wondered if she was still hungry. He went to the cupboard and summoned a couple of the chocolate-covered-peanut butter-crunchy things she was always summoning. Admittedly, he was trying to make amends for the oversight which had led to her chip-choking episode a few minutes ago. When Kale set the treat in front of Vera, though, she wrinkled her nose. So much for that.

"So, girly, been rescued by any more giant birds this morning?"

Vera tensed. Kale threw Addamas his best what-the-hell look. Addamas shrugged, not understanding the problem. All morning, Kale had been careful to give the girl space so she didn't feel pressured into talking and reliving that experience.

"Yeah, no. I'm done running away." Vera glanced sidelong at Kale. "I'm so sorry Mimi got hurt because of me."

By the stars, the girl is apologizing? To me?

"No, no." Addamas shook his head, rubbing the crumbs

from his fingers. "Mimi chose to take on the unnatural. Wasn't your fault. She said she'd do it again, by the way, no matter the cost."

That last bit was aimed at Kale. Addamas was confident, based on his own experience with Kale's healing, that Mimi would bounce back in no time. But Addamas had not been so near death as Mimi had been. He didn't truly understand. Kale had needed to push so much more of the meadow's magic through Mimi. More magic meant more exposure to Kale's darkness. Whatever Mimi had endured as a result would have left unimaginable wounds. Mimi was simply hiding them from Addamas.

"Anyway," drawled Addamas to break the strained silence. "Mimi hates when people try to take responsibility for her choices. Good or bad. And she gets a little bitey when she's angry, so I recommend abandoning whatever misplaced guilt you have and focus on taking down the horde. That's the best thing we can do for Mimi right now."

"How can I help?" asked Vera.

Kale dipped a hand into his pocket and pulled out the shard of the bottle he'd collected after Errock's magically-assisted escape. He set it in the center of the table.

"This gives us some new insight into the source behind the rising horde. It came from a Summartir witch," Kale said.

Addamas swore softly.

"Agreed," said Kale. "I need to inform the Maiden about the unnaturals. Errock said there's a horde, so the infestation has already spread too far to keep it quiet."

"And tell her that one of her witches is responsible for powering up a new Siphon Master," finished Addamas.

"Wait, what's a Siphon Master?" asked Vera.

"A siphon who's creating unnaturals. The master of the horde," explained Kale.

"What kind of person would make them?" Vera shivered.

"They may have been a decent person once, but if a witch got them addicted to magic, that person is gone now." Addamas leaned forward and placed a soothing hand on Vera's shoulder. The girl didn't shrink away from Addamas like she did Kale. "Siphon Masters are worse than the unnaturals they create. Unnaturals are vile, yes, but underneath that, they are just soldiers following their Master's orders."

"At first, I assumed the Siphon Master was an anomaly, someone who'd accidentally discovered they could siphon the traces of magic that cling to some humans." Kale spun the bottle cap between his fingers. "It would've taken someone like that years to collect enough magic to become a Master, even with Errock whispering in their ear. But a witch as strong as the one I suspect now, one powerful enough to break into the human realm without alerting me, could've turned the human into a Master in a matter of days. Like any junkie, an addicted siphon will do anything to get another hit of magic, even creating unnaturals for a witch. What I don't understand is what a witch wants with an army of them."

"Umm, maybe to kill off a bunch of humans?" suggested Vera. "It seems to be a thing around here. How many unnaturals are there?"

"Addamas has found evidence of dozens," answered Kale.

"What happens when people start getting hurt?" Vera asked.

"It's too late for that," said Kale, wishing he could give the girl better news. "Wherever there are unnaturals, there are victims. For now, the Siphon Master and witch are keeping the horde's activities under wraps. As the horde grows, their crimes will not remain secret. Bodies and the remains will begin to surface."

Vera paled. "We need to tell someone. Warn people."

"No one would believe you," said Kale. "When siphons first created unnaturals over a thousand years ago, people didn't believe it. And those people knew magic was real. They had powers themselves. Fae, dragons, and sorcerers, those were real, and yet people scoffed at the rumors of siphons hoarding power to forge half-breed soldiers. To them, siphons were just parasites who leeched the power of those around them. They were nothing to fear. Like those people, humans won't believe until the horde descends upon them. By then, it will be too late. And the rest of the world will gladly rush to amputate your infected realm as soon as they find out."

"How do we stop that from happening?" asked Vera.

"Now that we know the siphon is not working alone, we go after the witch first." Addamas was in his element laying out a plan of attack. "Cut off her power, and the siphon will misstep. We'll be waiting for it. Eliminate the Master, and the unnaturals have no way to evade us or organize themselves. We can wipe them out."

"How can I help?" Vera asked again.

"Stay hidden while I'm gone." Kale released the bottle cap and sat back, folding his arms over his chest. "I'll only be gone a couple of days. You'll be safe here as long as you stay inside. All parts of you. Not one foot on the porch or a single finger out a window. No one can enter the cabin uninvited, and if they don't know you are here, no one will try."

Vera inhaled and opened her mouth as if to argue then said simply, "Okay."

Vera's hands remained as clean as the day she'd fallen into his life. The girl would do as asked for once. *Thank the stars.*

"Addamas will come check on you when he can, but the more time he spends hunting the horde's nest, the sooner he'll find it," said Kale. "Hopefully, we'll be ready to strike the horde as soon as I deal with the witch. This will all be over quickly."

"When are you leaving?" Vera asked.

"In about an hour."

"Maybe you shouldn't tell the Maiden right away," said Addamas thoughtfully. "She's the leader of the coven right now."

"No, I know what you're thinking, but you're wrong. The Maiden is the only one I am sure is not capable of this."

"Looks can be deceiving." Addamas said it gently, but Kale tensed.

"I am aware of that, Dam. It's not the Maiden we are looking for."

"I'm sorry, this is all just a lot to process." Vera stood abruptly. "I think I need some fresh air before I'm stuck inside. Is it safe? I won't leave the meadow."

"It's safe," assured Kale. "I'll know if anyone is coming before they get here."

"Want any company, girly?"

"No, I'm okay." Vera just about tripped over herself to get out of the cabin.

"Oh man," said Addams once Vera was out of range. "She's in bad shape. It will not be happy times if we don't get some pep back in your girl's step before Mimi returns. You know, it would help if you worked a little on your resting-dick-face."

"My what?"

"Your default facial setting. Me and Mimi are used to it, but I think it's bumming your girl out."

"Would you stop calling her my girl? And what do you want me to do, go around smiling like an infernal clown?"

Addamas burst out laughing. "Now that you've put it like that, never mind. No infernal clowns. I'd be terrified, and your girl might start throwing knives again." Addamas's laughter quieted. "I don't understand much about women, but from what I do know, she's probably blaming herself for not being able to prevent her whole realm from going to pot. Especially after yesterday blew up in her face in a bad way. To top it off, she probably thinks you hate her."

"That's absurd. A chance to get home appeared and she took it. I would've done the same thing if I'd been ripped from my world. Plus, what's happening in her realm has nothing to do with her. She's been through more in a week than any innocent I've ever known, but she keeps fighting with a warrior's heart. It's exhausting and infuriating but also admirable. I don't hate her."

"Don't tell me that." Addamas raised both brows with a spark in his eyes that Kale disliked. "I already know all that. Maybe you should tell *her*, though. I mean, skip the part where you call her feelings absurd. It turns out, females don't like that kind of thing. But the rest was good."

"I am sure my opinions of Vera do not matter to her." A spot behind Kale's left eye began to ache.

"You might be surprised," said Addamas. "Even the strongest girls in the world need reassurance sometimes. Mimi taught me that. Then swore to do unholy things to me if I ever told anyone." Addamas winked. "Oh, and you won't lose her—Mimi. No matter what she saw when you linked to her. She loves you too much. And you did just give her a tenth life."

"She might wish I'd let her die instead."

"It's a good thing she has both of us to remind her what she has to live for then," replied Addamas optimistically.

Kale winced. The ache behind his eye was beginning to throb in earnest. He hadn't had a headache like that in hundreds of years. There were no drafts on the air to signal anyone's approach. None of the gates had opened. Nothing to worry about. Kale rose to his feet anyway.

"Kale?" asked Addamas.

"I'm going to check on Vera." Unease had spread through Kale's gut.

The girl squatted precariously near the edge of the meadow. One small hand hung in the air, half-extended toward some shaking brambles in the overgrowth. Probably because whatever animal she planned to extricate from the thorny shrubs had started hissing and snarling at her. The sound carried to him, barely breaking past the uproar taking hold of his mind. Vera had no idea Errock was stalking her in the boundary forest, waiting for her to reach through the barrier since he could not cross it. She couldn't see him. She had no idea she was in danger.

Kale swallowed his warning cry. As jumpy as Vera had been lately, she might overbalance and fall right into the trap if he startled her. Kale surged forward soundlessly. If Errock got his hands on Vera, the unnatural wouldn't waste time before magicking the girl to the horde this time. Kale would lose Vera to them. The messy knot of hair on top of Vera's tilted head was coming loose. She pulled her hand back to push the strands away, considering the struggling animal.

"Shhhh. I'm trying to help you, ya dumb thing," Vera scolded, duck-stepping to the side before tentatively reaching forward again.

Kale barely got an arm around her in time. He swung Vera around, setting her on her feet while positioning her so her back was to the boundary, and Errock. Seeing the unnatural would terrify her, no matter that she was safe on this side of the barrier. Kale had to give it to her, Vera didn't cower at the sudden man-handling but rather went full-on-hell-cat, clawing, kicking, and screeching. When she realized it was Kale, she didn't stop either.

"Why did you do that?" Vera shrieked, punching him in the sternum. "What is wrong with you? Why would you do that? You are so messed up." She punctuated each phrase with another hit. Kale didn't stop her. When he noticed tears pooling in her eyes, he had no idea what to do. Addamas had said she might need comforting, but Kale didn't know how to do that.

"You were about to leave the meadow," Kale pointed out lamely.

"No, I wasn't."

"You almost reached through the barrier with your hand," he told her.

"With my hand? You have got to be kidding me. So you decided to scare the crap out of me to teach me a lesson?"

"Of course not. I was protecting you."

"Protecting my hand?"

"I was protecting all of you," Kale said losing his temper. "If you'd reached through the veil, you would've been gone before I even knew anyone was there."

Vera's eyes widened.

I'm an absolute idiot.

Vera twisted to look over her shoulder, but Kale stepped around her, putting himself between Vera and Errock. She was too short to see anything other than the center of his chest.

"I thought you knew when someone was coming," she said.

"I do," Kale replied.

Vera flinched and narrowed her eyes at him. "I don't believe you."

"It was the truth until now." Kale pushed a hand through his hair wanting to rip it out. "He didn't use a gate, so I missed it."

"He? The unnatural was here, wasn't he?" Vera asked, taking a step back.

"He cannot enter here. You were only in danger if you crossed the barrier into the boundary forest."

A sob burst from Vera's throat. Kale instinctively wrapped his arms around her. She stiffened at first but wilted into the embrace with another sob that tore at his stone of a heart.

"You are safe," he told her.

Kale looked over his shoulder. Errock removed a tiny fox kit from the thorns. It was too young to have left its mother's side on its own. The unnatural met Kale's gaze with a gleam in his eyes and snapped the tiny animal's neck. He tossed the carcass through the barrier before pulling another disappearing act. Errock couldn't pass through the boundary veil, but the dead kit landed near Vera's feet without obstruction. Once again, Kale failed to protect her from another horror. Vera cried out and covered her face to block out the scene. Desperate, Kale swept her up into his arms and carried her to the cabin.

Inside, he laid her on the couch where she curled up into a tiny ball. Addamas draped a blanket over her, and both men moved a few steps away.

"I'm going to see how far I can track him," Addamas said, voice pitched low.

"Vera's coming with me to Summartir," Kale told the satyr.

"Is that a good idea?"

"She isn't safe here anymore. There's someone there who may be able to disguise what she is. We'll go to her first. If that goes wrong, I have the authority to execute any who threaten my charge. The entire coven if needed."

"And the witches know that, right?" asked Addamas

"They wrote the law. Right before they made me immortal and unraveled the world."

"It could get tricky protecting her while fighting that many, though," Addamas pointed out.

"I'll avoid it if I can."

7

Vera spun in a slow circle, taking in the boundary forest and pretending not to notice Kale's outstretched hand. Trees, trees, and more trees. She was beyond sick of trees. However, she hadn't realized hand-holding would be on the agenda, and she needed a moment to prepare mentally for it. Kale might have carried her like a blubbering baby a few hours ago—anyone would've fallen apart after the day she'd had—but Vera was still entirely uncomfortable around him. Her cheeks warmed just thinking about his arms holding her. To make things worse, her little break-down had convinced Kale to drag her along to Witchville with him. *So much yay for being a pathetic ball-and-chain. How mortifying.*

"What if the gate doesn't come?" asked Vera

"It will."

"What if the wrong one comes?" she persisted.

"It won't."

"How do you know if you can't see it?"

"I can sense it." Kale stuck his hand out again. "Done stalling yet?"

Vera wanted to deny it, but she was totally stalling.

"I don't have cooties," Kale said. Now he was just taunting her.

"Shut up." Vera snatched his hand.

Despite spending the last twenty minutes grumbling about not needing to be babysat, Vera was secretly relieved to be going along. If left in the cabin all alone, she knew she'd end up huddled in a corner, clutching knives, and jumping at every benign sound by nightfall. Not that she would admit that truth to Kale for all the chocolate in the world. She just wished she wasn't such an inconvenience for him.

"I better not get killed by this mystical gate for trespassing," Vera said.

"You've been through a gate before."

"Yeah, by accident."

"You'll be fine. There's a country road on the other side, so it will be a little more disorientating than transitioning to another forest. Otherwise, it'll be the same. It'll be painless."

"'Kay. Let's do this." Vera started forward and almost jerked her shoulder out of its socket when Kale didn't move with her.

"How about I go first and make sure you don't get run over by a cart?" he suggested.

"Oh. Yep, good plan." Vera gave a sharp nod, but Kale still didn't budge. "Are we going?"

Kale threw her an exasperated look before proceeding straight ahead, supposedly toward a gate. After a few steps, Kale dissolved, except for the seemingly-dismembered hand still clasping Vera's. He towed Vera along before she could balk, right into a blazing white tunnel. Heavy air encased Vera, holding her immobile. She was alone. The air compressed until Vera's lungs could no longer expand to draw air. Her head swam. A woman flickered in front of her, red hair burning darkly against the whiteness. Vera blinked slowly, painfully. The woman pressed against her. Warm lips kissed Vera's throat. There was a seductive smile, and then the woman plunged an icy blade into Vera's chest. Cold speared though Vera, burning hotter than fire.

Vera blacked out and came to in Summartir. She was flat on her back in the middle of a dirt road with Kale hovering over her. Shivers racked Vera's frame. Kale rubbed his hands over her arms and propped her up, facing the sun. The warm rays spread across Vera's face.

"You lied to me. I mean, you lie all the time, but I believed you this time," Vera said angrily.

Kale's brow furrowed.

"It'll be painless," Vera quoted, using a generic dumb-guy voice impression.

"That shouldn't have happened," Kale said in his defense. "I had no idea the gate was cursed until I passed through the spell. By then, you were already coming through it too."

"So, a redheaded bombshell stabbed you in the heart too?"

Kale winced. "The curse was keyed specifically for you. It didn't affect me."

"I feel so special," Vera said sarcastically. "Who exactly knew I was coming again? I'd like to avoid them while we're here if possible."

"No one knew. All I can think is the witch we're hunting orchestrated that stunt with the fox kit so I'd bring you here. And I fell for it." Kale paced circles around Vera with a constant string of curses. Vera only recognized a fraction of them.

"Calm down there, Scotchie. Let's go back, then."

"We can't. The spell hasn't turned off. I only got you through alive because it wasn't already powered up. There's no way for you to get back until it's disabled. It would destroy you."

"Fabulous. I love being a fish on a hook."

"I don't follow," Kale said.

"Hurts like crap getting caught, and there's no way to get free unless I wanna lose a chunk of my face. Or, you know, die," explained Vera.

"You have a strange way of looking at things."

"Are you saying I'm wrong?"

"No, I'm saying you are strange," he replied.

"Back at ya, buddy."

"Someone's coming. We need to get off the road." Kale pointed out a cloud of dust rising in the distance.

Vera pushed to her feet with Kale supporting her under one arm. As soon as she could do so without being obvious, Vera inched away from him. The dirt road was narrow. Two cars might fit if they were compact. To one side of the road, rolling hills of farmland stretched into the distance where a mountain range sliced across the horizon. On the other side, was a narrow field edged by a forest of gnarled trees. Vera understood that, logically, the forest was the best place to hide, but she was not thrilled about it. Kale helped her down the shallow embankment beside of the road.

"Run or ride?" Kale asked.

Vera gaped. He meant piggyback ride. And he was completely serious.

"Run," she answered quickly.

Kale locked a hand around Vera's wrist and hauled tail. Vera struggled to keep up. The dash across the empty field took a couple of minutes at most but it seemed much longer. After a week of being cooped up in the cabin, Vera hadn't expected to be so out of shape. Her legs ached and her lungs were wrung out. She was glad to stop and catch her breath when Kale tugged her behind a tree trunk that was as wide as a dumpster—Vera had hidden behind a lot of things in her life. Vera panted while Kale was completely unaffected. Several nerve-wracking minutes passed before a cart pulled by a dozen billy goats rattled past. A boy with a wide-brimmed hat held the reins of the noisy team. The cart was a simple wooden box on wheels, without even a bench for the kid to sit on. Instead, he perched atop a mound of cargo, tied down by a green tarp.

"What is that?" asked Vera.

"Corn. Each week, one of the fourteen families takes a turn delivering a cart to the palace stables. The green canvass marks it as the Sanford family's crop."

"That's a lot of corn. Is this one of those places where the people starve to feed the monarch?" Vera asked.

"Magic ensures healthy crops and abundant harvests. Laws ensure everyone contributes, and no one starves. Famine and poverty do not exist here."

"Wow, sounds like a real utopia," Vera said.

Kale squinted an eye and bobbled his head a little side-to-side. "It's not as idyllic as they'd like to believe." Kale stood. "Let's go. We need to visit someone before the Coven sends witches out to look for us. The Maiden will have felt the ripple of our arrival and be expecting us to appear soon. With a good explanation as to why we're in Summartir."

Kale headed deeper into the woods. Vera didn't follow immediately.

"This mysterious person we've got to go see seriously lives in there?" Vera asked unhappily.

"No, but that's where she'll be waiting for us."

Vera grudgingly trailed after the man and was rewarded

with a spider web to the face. She let out the tiniest squeak, batting away the webbing, and shook out her hair. Kale spun around looking for the threat and scowled when he realized what was happening. *Screw you, buddy. There's no telling what kind of spiders they have in this place.*

"Do you see any spiders in my hair?" Vera asked.

"No."

"You didn't even look."

"We need to hurry. The weaver doesn't like to stay in one place for very long." Kale walked away without making sure Vera was behind him.

Vera gestured rudely at the man's retreating back and patted her hair one last time before chasing after him.

"Anything else I should know about this woman?" Vera asked after a few minutes.

"She's a witch, and she's not as patient as I am. So be careful what you say around her."

If that was true, it might be best to skip meeting the lady altogether. The farther they went into the forest, the higher the tree roots arched out of the ground, like pulled stitches. Vera made sure she didn't hook a foot in one and fall on her face.

"I'm kind of surprised these people don't guard their gate better."

"Some realms do guard them. Other realms positioned their gates in such dangerous places that no one would will- ingly go through their gate. A few, like Summartir, magicked their gates so the most powerful people know when someone shows up, and there's no hiding from them at that point."

"And Earth?"

"Sealed closed and placed somewhere humans would not likely wander."

Vera snorted. "Yeah, that worked well." She didn't realize Kale had stopped until she bounced off him.

"We're here." Kale grabbed her before she fell. "Don't freak out, okay? You are safe."

Well, that sounded positively terrifying. Kale reached toward Vera's face, and she dodged to the side.

"What are you doing?" she demanded.

Kale was faster than Vera. He plucked something from her hair. It looked like a wingless, eight-legged bumblebee. A hint of a smile tipped one side of his mouth when Vera gasped and started shaking out her hair again. He deposited the spider on a branch above his head.

"Kalesius! And you brought a friend," called a smoky woman's voice. "You've never brought a friend before. She must be someone special."

The old woman who spoke was tall and lean with a multitude of white braids trailing down her back. Leaves and twigs stuck out between the plaits of hair, and bits of dirt clung to her bare feet. That's where the witch's naturalist vibe ended, though. She had on rainbow zebra-print leggings and a pink tee-shirt with a sun-glasses-wearing porcupine printed on it. Around the witch's neck hung a thick, yellow rope necklace. She stood on the steps of a purple Victorian house with yellow gingerbread molding. Vera hadn't even noticed the house before, which was impossible since it towered over them. In fact, Vera was sure that spot had been covered in trees a minute ago. The witch assessed Vera and gave a big toothy smile.

"Well, look at you. I think I was right about you after all," said the witch.

Vera frowned. Kale bumped her before she could ask what that was supposed to mean.

"My name is Marianna. Welcome to my home. Come in,

come in." Mariana waved them in before disappearing through the front door, which she left open for them.

"This is a pretty impressive house for someone who doesn't like to stay in one place for long," Vera mumbled, reminding Kale of his earlier assessment of Marianna. She hadn't even picked up on his boloney that time. If Vera lost her lie-detecting in this place, she was going to be pissed.

Kale shushed her with a sharp look. Just then, the entire house shuttered and groaned. Vera grabbed the railing to keep from falling over.

Inside, Mariana yelled, "Knock it off! We'll leave when I say we leave!"

The answering reply was a chorus of hisses which emanated from the foundation of the house itself.

"The house moves," said Vera.

"Nice deduction." Kale smirked.

Okay, so Kale hadn't lied after all. The truth just happened to be completely outrageous. A whole big house of nope. Vera did an about-face, planning to skip right back down the steps and away from the possessed structure but skidded to a stop. Cats surrounded them. Hundreds of cats. Orange, black, gray, white, spotted, striped, mottled, fuzzy, fat, skinny, and even naked cats. Vera had never seen so many different kinds of cats in one place. They ringed the house, standing shoulder to shoulder, ruffs spiked and teeth bared. Vera did another one-eighty and hurried inside, urging Kale to close the door quickly behind her.

The inside of the house was like a library. It even smelled beautifully musty like one. But rather than books, the wall-to-wall shelving held neat piles of fabric. Marianna had not organized the fabric by color, or in any way that Vera could discern. Vera trailed her fingers across the various textures of cloth in awe as Kale led her through the maze of shelves to another room. The walls of this room were lined floor-to-ceiling too, but the center of the room was open and filled with living room furniture. Additional bolts of fabric littered the floral sofa, but otherwise, everything was clean and impressively dust-free. An arched doorway to Vera's right framed yet another room. This one filled by a massive loom. A partially-finished piece of cloth stretched between the supports. There were cats in there too. They batted around bits of yarn and lounged in the windowsills.

Kale scooped the fabric off the sofa and stacked it with some other bolts already leaning against a rolling ladder, which stretched all the way up to the abnormally-high ceiling. He settled in the cleared space and patted the cushion beside him. Vera sat stiffly and fidgeted with her sleeve.

"You look hungry, dear." Mariana entered the room, carrying a tray of teacups and cookies—suspiciously-brown cookies.

"Are those gingerbread cookies?" The question tumbled out before Vera could reconsider.

Mariana's smile dimmed. Kale cringed and pinched the bridge of his nose. It's not like Vera had intended to be rude, she'd just been surprised was all. In her world, accepting gingerbread from a witch was generally a bad idea. Vera held her breath while Mariana studied her closely. Suddenly, the witch started laughing, a full-bellied laugh. Soon, there were tears on her weathered cheeks too. The witch plopped into the blue-and-white-striped armchair opposite the sofa and set the tray on the table between them.

"Ahhh. You are delightful," said Marianna. "Isn't she, Kalesius?"

"Always," Kale lied.

Vera's lie-detecting superpower was definitely still working.

"I see you are familiar with some Coven lore which has survived the generations in your realm," said Marianna. "You need not be distressed, though. These are brown-sugar cookies. I do love a nice gingerbread cookie sometimes, but I would not eat you. I'm not that kind of witch."

"I didn't mean any offense." *Wait, did that mean there was a kind of witch that did eat people?*

"Oh, I know, dear. And you have caused none." Mariana giggled a bit more. "You have caused me a lot of curiosity, though. What exactly are you? Kalesius has not shared this with me yet."

"Oh, uh." Vera looked to Kale for direction.

"Vera is a siphon," said Kale, surprising Vera by revealing her secret so easily.

"Is that so?" The witch cocked her head to the side. "I haven't met a siphon in a very long time. Now that you mention it, I do see the resemblance. Forgive me if I'm wrong, but I believe it is illegal for a human to cross the barrier from their realm. If you are siphon, you were human once. The guardian would have been duty-bound to execute you immediately after you left your realm. You would not be sitting in my living room right now having tea. Do have some tea, dear," Mariana picked up a teacup with green vines painted on it and handed it to Vera.

Vera took it reflexively, but all her attention zeroed in on Kale. She already knew he'd been lying his butt off when they first met, when he'd told her she was safe. Her heart stuttered now with the understanding of how much danger she'd been in. All the while, Kale opened his mouth to protest, closed it, and then tried again.

"It's not...I don't . . ." he tried.

Mariana waved off his efforts.

"Don't worry about him, dear," Marianna said to Vera. "If the Guardian was going to kill you, he would have done so already. I'm afraid that chance has come and passed. No going back now that he's your protector. What great luck you have. Drink your tea. It's getting cold."

Vera stared blankly at the yellow-tinged liquid until Mariana cleared her throat. She took a polite sip to appease the witch. It was bitter and sweet. Not awful, but not great either. One more sip out of good manners and Vera returned the cup to the tray. That was all Vera's pitching stomach could handle. Mariana gathered a clay bowl from the side table into the crook of her arm, cradling it like a bowl of popcorn, and watched Vera like she was the entertainment. The witch popped something from the bowl into her mouth and chewed it up. Vera squirmed under Marianna's scrutiny.

"Want one?" Mariana offered, extending the bowl filled with acorns toward Vera.

Vera shook her head with a side-long glance at Kale. His face revealed nothing of what he thought.

"No thank you. I'm not hungry," Vera said.

"Too bad. You'd like them, I think," Marianna replied.

Mariana popped a third or fourth nut into her mouth, shell and all, and then set the bowl aside. She stood abruptly, brushing acorn fibers from her chest. At the same time, Kale went to pick up a teacup. The witch smacked his hand away.

"You wouldn't like that," Marianna told him. "It's cold now anyway."

Kale narrowed his eyes at their host but didn't argue. He also didn't relax back into the seat after that. Vera was getting twitchy from the undercurrents in the room. Mariana padded over to the ladder and rolled it along its track to a set of shelves. The pile of fabric which had been leaning against it toppled over onto the floor. Mariana didn't seem concerned about it. She began climbing, pausing at every shelf to ruffle through the fabric until she found what she was looking for on the tenth one up, three down from the ceiling.

"Ah ha. I knew it was here," Marianna proclaimed.

A moment later, Marianna presented Vera with a wooden box, inlaid with a sun made from various stones. Even with one of the sun's rays missing, it was stunning. Vera wasn't sure what to do with it.

"Well open it," instructed Marianna.

Inside was a silver chain with a black tear-shaped stone dangling from it. The stone shone like polished glass. Freed from the box, it sparkled like a starry sky.

"It's incredible," said Vera.

"It is yours," said Marianna

"Oh, you don't have to—"

"Shh. Do not argue with me, dear. It is yours. It always has been. The box is yours too, but I will keep it safe until you need it." Mariana snagged the wooden box and tucked it away on a different shelf. "That charm is a cloak. As long as you wear it, no one will know what you are."

"What will they think I am?"

"I'm not sure. Isn't that exciting?"

"Weaver," said Kale.

"Watch yourself, Guardian. You are in my home."

Mariana's eyes flashed, her fingertips crackled with angry lightening babies. *Well, that escalated quickly.* Kale's warning had not been an exaggeration after all.

"Apologies." Kale dipped his head, contrite.

"I know you are worried about your charge, so I will not remember it. But do not push your luck, young man."

"It will keep her safe?" asked Kale.

"Oh, yes. Perfectly. Vera won't siphon a drop of magic while she wears it either." Mariana had switched right back to the friendly quirky witch. "Oops, it is time to say goodbye. Your escort is nearly here." Mariana pulled Vera to her feet, clasped the charm around her neck, and tucked it into her shirt. "Keep that hidden, okay dear?"

"Oh, okay. Thank you again," Vera stammered.

Mariana patted Vera's cheek. "Such a good girl. Come back and see me again when you have time to listen to some of my stories." To Kale, Marianna said, "I'll have that curse on the gate taken care of in a sennight. Until then, be careful. The witch you seek is more dangerous than you realize. If you do not stop her, you will lose your charge. I am rather taken with this one, so I would be very put out if you let that happen."

"I will not fail," Kale promised.

"Good."

The house began to tremble and hiss like before. A skittish gray kitten dropped its scrap of yarn on Vera's foot on its way to Mariana's shoulder, where it burrowed beneath the witch's hair. Vera picked up the yarn and was surprised that it was not soft, but more plastic-like. Mariana tucked a few cookies into Vera's empty hand.

"For the road." Marianna ushered Kale and Vera out the front door. The army of cats parted to let them pass.

"Move out!" shouted the witch.

The ground beneath the house began to heave and roil at Mariana's command. Then the entire house lurched into motion. Kale tapped Vera's arm and pointed at a cat who had broken away from the pack. The tabby picked a snake up carefully with its mouth, trotted back to the house with it, and tossed it under the porch with the others. Mariana's house was slithering across the ground on a nest of snakes, which were being herded by a pack of tabby cats. Vera danced in a circle, checking for any stray snakes, her arms up in the air. Mariana's laughter rang out while she watched Vera hop around like a dodo. The witch stroked her necklace which writhed beneath her touch. That was no necklace. Vera lifted the yarn in her hand to get a closer look at it. Nope, not yarn. She dropped the rolled piece of snake skin.

"Oh, Kalesius," Mariana shouted. "I forgot to remind you, the celebration of fear is tomorrow. You have terrible timing." The woman cackled until the house disappeared into the trees.

"Care to explain what that means?" asked Vera

"Not right now, we don't have time," answered Kale. "Our escort is close. We need to get back to the road."

"Anything I should know about these witches and any pets they have, first?" Vera questioned.

"Don't walk behind the chickens," he said cryptically. "Hurry, we'll have to run again."

Vera didn't have enough air to ask any more questions after that.

8

"Your talent for withholding important information is astounding," Vera said icily.

Kale had been expecting something like that. The girl did not like surprises. To be fair, he'd have wanted a heads up that Summartir witches rode horse-sized chickens with beady red eyes and serrated beaks too. But there hadn't been time to warn her. He'd barely had time to remove all the leaves—evidence of their forest excursion—from Vera's hair before the four witches had arrived, saddled high on the birds' necks. As Kale and Vera walked a safe distance behind their escort to the palace, one of the hens relieved itself. The steaming white goo fell into the dirt ahead of them. Fortunately, not near enough to splatter either of them. Vera leaped to the other side of the road, gagging.

"I don't know. It seemed important that you not walk too close to the chickens. Or that would've landed on your head."

Vera opened her mouth, probably to call him a nasty name or two. The girl caught sight of the excrement behind him and gagged again. Facing the other direction, she flipped him off over her head instead. Kale hadn't laughed much in over a millennium, but with Vera around, he might pick up the habit again. Not even Dam or Mimi was brave enough to insult him as she did. Oh, she was definitely scared of him like the rest, but she was too hot-headed for her own good. She was like a tiny kitten, claws out, ready to take on a beast, and peeing herself the whole time.

Vera stumbled over her feet while attempting to walk forward with her head craned to the side. Kale steadied her reflexively. One of the witches, a middle-aged witch in maroon-colored festival robes, noticed and sneered. As soon as the woman realized Kale watched her, she whipped around to hide her expression. Summartir witches were usually more careful with their expressions around Kale, not wanting to give him power over them in any form. They also wore full arm-length gloves when he was around, for the same reason. Showing up unannounced had thrown them off their game. It also hadn't helped that Kale and his outsider guest were crashing the kick-off of one of their transition festivals. Or that Kale had refused to reveal the purpose for his visit when the entourage questioned him. Nothing stung a witch's pride quite like a reminder that, even in their home realm, they had no authority over him. Cassie, one of the witches Kale knew by name, had attempted to soothe her own ego by going after Vera. The witch did not dare assault the Guardian head-on.

"I'm surprised someone with so little magic was deemed worthy of the Guardian's efforts. Honestly, I cannot even tell what you are." Cassie sniffed the air like she smelled something rotten. "You poor child. That must make you feel quite wretched about yourself."

Vera met the insult with a blank stare until the young witch, who was only a year or two older than Vera, turned away uncomfortably. Kale's mood improved considerably watching that play out. Plus, Vera walked closer to him afterward, in a clear show of solidarity against the unpleasant witches. The girl was still pissed at him for "withholding" certain facts about Summartir but progress was progress.

"It's the Guardian," a child called out.

They'd entered the herb district, located on the outskirts of Summartir Proper. An extensive network of cottages with large gardens spread out before them. Most of the gardens looked half-wild, but each plant was carefully tended and harvested for a variety of uses by the coven. The little girl's mother gathered her up and rushed her inside. More doors slammed throughout the neighborhood. At first, Vera frowned in confusion at the men and witches dropping their garden tools and scurrying into their homes. After a few minutes, Vera seemed to follow the eyes of all those people right to him. Dawning, that Kale was the bogeyman they all ran from, lit her eyes. She peeked at him and winced. Usually, Kale couldn't be bothered by how people reacted to him, but Vera's pity irritated him.

"How do you feel about lizards?" Kale asked to distract her.

"Huh?" Vera's eyes narrowed. "I feel like they are snakes on legs. Why?"

"Oh, no reason. Just curious."

"Kalesius." It was the first time she'd said his full given name and she'd growled it. "If you tell me there are lizards here the size of horses, I swear I will march back to that gate and throw myself through it."

"You would die."

"A risk I'm willing to take."

"It's not a risk. It's a certainty," Kale told her.

"I'd be okay with that," she said.

"You would really—"

"Oh my gosh, Kale." Vera came to an abrupt halt, hands fisted. "There really are horse-sized lizards, aren't there?"

"No. There aren't. I promise... They are house-sized lizards, not horse-sized. And they have wings—we call them dragons." Kale waited until Vera's eyes were the size of dinner plates."I'm kidding. Dragons live in a different realm." Kale smirked. "You don't have to worry about them while we're here."

"Not funny."

"It was a little funny." Kale offered a rare genuine smile.

"No, it wasn't." Vera pretended to be angry, but the corner of her lips twitched. "Whatever."

They caught up to their escort with the mood between them notably lighter. The conversation hadn't gone the direction Kale had intended, but at least the pity in the girl's eyes was gone.

"I'm never going to that other realm, by the way," Vera informed him.

"Probably a good idea. Dragons like to take pretty girls hostage and keep them locked away in their caves."

"Oh, they're relatives of yours then?" Vera asked.

"Ha. Ha," Kale said dryly. "Look, you can see the palace now."

They'd taken the final bend in the road, and the palace peeked from behind an outcropping of trees. Only a short walk through the temporary market— set up for the coming festivities— separated them from the courtyard. The palace was relatively isolated, exactly how witches preferred their homes. In a week, the stalls would be teeming with witches selling their wares. Hopefully, the Weaver would have the curse stripped from the world-gate, and they'd be gone from Summartir before then.

"It's incredible," Vera said. "Like a castle and a log cabin had a baby."

"And it's alive," said Kale ominously.

"I assume that does not mean what it sounds like."

"The trees, they are alive. They were woven together by magic, without being cut down."

"Incredible," she repeated with greater awe. "I have no idea how I'm going to describe all this when I get home."

Kale frowned. "You can't."

"I know, right? No description would do all this any justice."

"No, I mean you cannot tell anyone about this place. Or the meadow. Or any of it. If humans knew what was out here beyond their world, they'd tear down the walls to catch a glimpse."

"Maybe there shouldn't be walls," Vera said with feeling.

Her intensity worried him. Those deep-blue eyes flashed with the magic she'd been siphoning recently. He hoped no one else noticed. The charm around Vera's neck must have awoken, though, because the magic faded. Kale breathed a sigh of relief. He wasn't sure how he'd hide the girl in Summartir for an entire week if someone discovered her origins. Not even the witches' fear of the Guardian would be enough to protect Vera if mob mentality kicked in.

"Do you know how many humans spend their entire lives looking for magic? Knowing that something's missing from their lives?" Vera continued. "But they never find it. They don't know it's been locked away from them because they were born with the wrong genetics, according to the rest of the world."

"You don't understand," Kale replied. "If there were ever any hint that humans might rise up to reclaim magic, even just a taste of it, Earth would be wiped out before anyone knew what was coming. That's why you cannot ever tell anyone."

"That's so messed up."

"I agree," Kale said earnestly.

"It's stupid." Vera's face was turning red.

"It is," he agreed, hoping to diffuse her.

"I hope you aren't talking about me," said the Maiden, walking out to meet them as they entered the courtyard.

"Maiden," Kale dipped his head in a respectful acknowledgment of her presence. "We were just discussing world politics."

"Oh, then I'm sure I would agree. It is stupid." The Maiden placed a bare hand—she was the only one to leave her hands bare in his presence—to the center of her chest in greeting to Vera. "Happy meet and welcome to Summartir. My witches say you are the Guardian's charge."

"Maiden, this is Vera," introduced Kale. "Vera, this is the Maiden of Summartir."

"You can call me Maiden," the young witch said. "Very creative, no?"

The four escorts urged their mounts on toward the barns without a backward glance. The remaining elite witches, who'd already arrived for the festival, gathered on the palace steps behind their leader.

"We require a private audience." Kale pitched his voice low, but the women lining the steps heard anyway. They stirred unhappily, despite the vacant expressions they maintained for his benefit.

"I had suspected as much. Come, let's get inside," Maiden said.

The Maiden looped Vera's arm through her own as if they were longtime friends. Vera looked at Kale, unsure of what to do. He gave the slightest nod to let her know it was okay. Maiden didn't acknowledge their audience as she lead Vera past them and through the carved stone doors. A bright blue newt darted from the Maiden's platinum hair and down to their linked arms to investigate the new arrival. To her credit, Vera didn't flinch or whimper or fling the familiar away. Tendons in her neck stood out sharply, though. The maiden whistled a soft trill of notes. The tiny lizard flicked his tongue once more before retreating to his hiding spot in Maiden's hair.

"Sorry, that one likes to greet people," Maiden explained to Vera. "He's always popping out to say hello."

"No worries."

The blasted girl smiled calmly at the Maiden as if she hadn't been upset one bit. She was good at wearing those pleasant masks when she wanted to. As soon as she could get away with it, though, Vera threw Kale the evil eye over her shoulder.

"I tried to tell you about him, but you distracted me with dragons," Kale informed her.

MAIDEN LOOKED like a golden-haired prom queen. It boggled Vera's mind that someone so young could be the leader of an entire realm, a realm of witches no less. Maiden could probably obliterate Vera with a few words and some wiggled fingers. *Better not forget that. Then again, Kale hasn't gone protector-mode yet, so Maiden must be harmless enough. Or the witch is so powerful that Kale doesn't dare challenge her. Oh happy thought.* Vera checked to be sure Kale was still behind them. The man was freaky-quiet thanks to the thick rugs underfoot. That's when Vera noticed the symbol woven into the carpets, just like the one carved into all the doors. It was the same sun that was on the cover of the wooden box Marianna had given her.

"What does that sun symbol mean?" Vera asked, pointing at the image.

"It's a reminder of who we are and the consequences should we forget," Maiden answered.

"Oh." Vera fell quiet, wondering how to politely ask for more information.

"Kalesius said you were speaking of dragons. You have dragons in your realm, Vera?" Maiden turned the conversation before Vera got her own questions out.

"No, thank the Lady," Vera answered.

"I'd love to meet a dragon someday," said Maiden.

"Really? Not me. The stories I've heard? Not good."

"My grandmother was engaged to be married to a dragon before the Unraveling," Maiden revealed.

Maiden turned them down a third hallway, or maybe it was the fourth. Smooth tree trunks, like giant wooden serpents stacked on top of each other, curved and draped over pairs of arched stone doors and floor length windows. The windows were open to let in fresh air that smelled of the forest around them. Thick white candles lined the hallways, none of them lit. It seemed like a terrible fire hazard. There were no pictures or curtains, nothing to tell one hallway from another. If Vera needed to escape later, she'd be royally screwed.

"Grandmother's family didn't approve, of course," continued Maiden. "Grandmother eventually broke it off with the dragon and married a man from the Luca family, my grandfather. They were very happy together for all of their lives, and yet Grandmother never stopped loving her dragon. She tells me stories about him and his kind."

"Maybe she can tell me some nice dragon stories," Vera said.

"I'm sure she would, but she's been dead for a thousand years," Maiden replied.

"I'm so sorry." Vera's brows pinched in confusion.

"Goodness me, I forget not all the realms remember our history. You must be completely baffled by us." Maiden paused for a second to consider their route, and then tugged Vera up a winding staircase. "Summartir is home to tens of thousands of witches and their families. However, unlike what some may think, witch magic is not limitless. What magic there is must be harvested like precious stones. Also like stones, it can also be gifted to other witches."

"How do you harvest magic?" asked Vera.

"We absorb the energy of nature while tending the land. Although, Summartir's harvests have depleted over the years. There's very little new magic anymore. What we have is essentially the last of it. We are careful not to use magic when there is another way."

At the top of the stairs was a hallway filled with portraits of every shape and size. The pictures were not hung with any sense of organization. There were so many of them that very little of the stone wall, unlike all the other wooden walls in the place, was visible. Paintings of women even packed the ceiling space. Some were portraits of women smiling or scowling back, while others were candid images of women gardening, dancing, or cradling small children. Maiden pointed at a large rectangular portrait with an aged gold frame near the center of one wall. It was of a group of women huddled together.

"Summartir's founding circle of witches. Our governing families are each descended from one of these fourteen women."

"Respectfully, is there time for this, Maiden?" asked Kale.

"Are you worried the world will tear itself apart while I share a little about my people with your charge?" Maiden asked.

"No. Not so soon as that," Kale said delicately.

"That's reassuring. And I will not be wanted for anything for a few minutes at least. However, we should walk and talk just in case."

Kale dipped his head in acceptance.

To Vera, Maiden said, "The palace is fairly small, but the corridors do not take the most direct paths to anywhere."

"I've noticed," Vera said ruefully.

"The row of portraits over here are of our current triads, the head witches from each of the fourteen families. Triads are made up of the three most powerful women of their family, and they govern their family's region." Each portrait showed three women of various ages, and each triad wore a unique color scheme. "A maiden still in her youth, a witch in the prime of her life, and a crone in her wisest years. When all of these witches come together, as they will tomorrow for the start of the Transition Festival, they form the Maiden Circle, the Witch Circle, and the Crone Circle. Linked together, we are the most powerful magical force in all the world."

The matching frames all had a small placard with a name. Vera recognized the name Sanford from the cart of corn they'd seen on the road earlier. The Sanford triad wore shades of grass-green, just like the tarp stretched over the corn. So the triads were wearing their family colors. The Luca family, Maiden's family, wore pale blues and gold.

"Wow," said Vera.

"Indeed. Finally, these," said Maiden, pausing to let Vera

take in the three life-size portraits in spun silver frames. They were all three of Maiden in various outfits. "Only one is me." Maiden indicated the one of her in Luca-blue with an electric-blue lizard clinging to her throat. "The next is the High Mother and the third is the High Crone. Together, we are the head of the Summartir Coven."

The three women in the portraits looked identical. However, the High Mother wore shades of black with crystals sewn onto the fabric, a fox curled around the hem of her gown. The High Crone wore a color that Vera could not describe. She was sure she'd never seen anything like it. It was yellow and blue but neither color at the same time. It was not green either. On the Crone's shoulder perched a large black crow.

"You're triplets?" asked Vera

"Not at all. We simply share this same body. Oh, but not at once," Maiden added quickly when Vera looked startled. "I am alone in here. Only one of our spirits possesses this form at a time, and it is my season to do so. For one more week anyway. At the end of this week's festival, Mother will transition here, and I will transition out and take my rest on Kyopili Mountain. That is where the spirits of the Mother and Crone are now. When we aren't here, we attend to the spirits of murdered witches who haunt Kyopili until their deaths are avenged. My grandmother is one of those spirits. That's how she's able to tell me stories about her dragons."

"Are there a lot of spirits there?" asked Vera as they left the hall of portraits behind.

"In the past, no. Summartir witches are a rather vengeful lot," Maiden said with a fond smile which unnerved Vera a bit. "After the Unraveling, the numbers grew, though. Most of the witches killed at that time are still there and always will be. Their deaths cannot be avenged because there is no one to hold accountable anymore."

"That must be awful," Vera said.

"For some. My grandmother has forgiven those who caused her death. She is at peace with her existence, so I cannot be angry. The High Mother's mother remains bitter, though. She wanted Mother to avenge her death. However, after the Unraveling, the chance for vengeance was gone. Time is more painful for them."

"That's—" Vera had no words.

"Too much?" asked Maiden

"Maybe a little, but I... I think Summartir is pretty amazing too." Vera had almost said, like an idiot, "...but I only learned about magic a few days ago." That would have been spectacularly bad.

"Maybe if your guardian will permit it while you are here, you can come visit me and share a little about your realm. I'm sure it is equally amazing."

"Umm, yeah. That would be great." Vera's skull felt like it would crack from the lie.

Kale sidled closer when Vera faltered.

"Is everything all right, Vera?" asked Maiden, cocking her head to the side slightly.

"It's just my head. I'll be okay."

"Well, we are here—my rooms. We can be assured privacy to speak. There should be tea. Perhaps some refreshment will help your head."

Maiden threw open a set of stone doors. There was nothing Vera could see to set them apart from the dozens they'd passed on their way. For a second, Vera thought Maiden had picked the wrong ones because these led outside to a woodland garden. Except they didn't. On the other side of the doors was an immense room, more like a loft really, where nature had seeped inside. Stone floors gave way to a carpet of moss and ferns. Flower-studded vines grew along the walls, and a waterfall murmured in one corner. The waterfall fed a small pool sunken into the floor. Lilly pads with flowers that glowed pink and green dotted the surface. Clusters of white candles burned all over the room, giving the space a warm glow. A young girl was setting a silver tea set out in the sitting area just inside the doors.

"Maiden," the girl bobbed a curtsy.

"Thank you, Margory," said Maiden with a nod.

The girl slipped out the room, taking a wide circle around Kale. Maiden knelt beside the pool, trailing a finger over the surface. Her lips moved, but Vera could not hear what she said over the sound of the water on stone and wood. Whatever the witch said, called forth an entire troop of little lizards from her hair and clothes. Vera schooled her expression, but inside, she felt a little ill. The creatures were all brightly colored, like the poisonous frogs at a zoo. A blue one, probably the same one from earlier, draped itself over Maiden's ear and flicked its tongue out to lick the witch's temple. Maiden rubbed its tiny head then turned her attention back to her guests.

"All right, Guardian. Why have you come to Summartir and brought an outsider with you?" asked Maiden.

Whoa. Mild-mannered Maiden had just shifted seamlessly into her head-witch persona. No one would doubt this woman's ability to rule. Or to lay down a ruthless magical beating.

"There are unnaturals on Earth," answered Kale.

"For how long?"

"Weeks at least. I've only just discovered them," Kale said.

Lie.

"Tracking them is proving more complicated than I'd anticipated. They are using portals." Kale offered up the shard of evidence on an open palm. Maiden took the glass into her hand and closed her fingers around it. Both Maiden and Kale wore dark expressions.

"You are suggesting a Summartir witch is responsible for creating a Siphon Master?" Maiden's voice was even but had a sharpness to it.

"An unnatural portaled into the boundary forest."

At those words, Maiden deflated. "Then it is definitely someone from the Coven, a threadbearer."

"How do you know?" asked Vera.

"The symbol you asked about earlier is not a sun. It represents the meadow and the fourteen strands of magic that now hold the world together. When the world unraveled, the founding witches came forward to save the fourteen kingdoms. Each witch used their magic to tie one of the kingdoms to the meadow. There are only two ways to find the meadow. First, is to cross through one of the world-gates Kalesius guards. No creature from Earth can do this because the Earth gate is sealed."

Vera stilled, hoping her guilt was not obvious.

Maiden continued, seemingly oblivious to Vera's sudden discomfort. "The other way is to follow a thread from one of the threadbearers to the place where their magic binds realm and meadow together—the boundary forest. Only a threadbearer can do that. Which means one of the threadbearers had to have directed the unnatural to the meadow."

"So, one of fourteen possible witches?" asked Vera.

"To protect the threads, the identities of the threadbearers are known only to them. It is possible that a threadbearer doesn't even know what they are, although all witches teach their daughters about the world threads. In theory, the betrayer could be any witch. However, they will be among the most powerful in Summartir and most likely a member of one of the triads."

"High Mother and High Crone are not living at the moment and your hands are clean. That leaves thirty-nine triad Witches," Kale said.

"How could a witch not know they are a threadbearer?" Vera asked.

"Witch magic is tied to a witch's spirit. When a witch dies, what magic they have stays with their spirit and is reborn with them in their next life. But a witch has no memories of past lives. So, no way to know that they are a threadbearer unless they discover the thread inside them and follow it."

"If a witch is dead, how does their thread not come loose?" questioned Vera.

"Oh, it does. That is why we put in a second layer of stitches. The Mother, the Crone, and I hold the sure-stitches. The first layer of stitches, held by the threadbear-ers, ties the fabric of the world together. But as you guessed, it falters when a threadbearer is not living. That is why members of the High Triad cannot die and move on to another life. We have to ensure the threads never come undone. When a threadbearer is between lives, we strengthen our own threads in that part of the world."

"What if someone tried to kill you?" asked Vera.

"They could try, but they would fail. All I would need to do is call on the magic of the Mother and Crone. Combined, we are stronger than any being in the world. Even on my own, few could beat me."

"Well, that's good," Vera concluded. "Whoever's making unnaturals can't just drop a realm off the face of the world. Would a realm float away or something if that happened?"

"It would crash. Like a kite with its string cut," explained Maiden.

Then it was very good that couldn't happen. Vera had a suspicion that Earth would be the most likely target. Although, at this rate, the unnaturals were probably going to decimate Earth anyway.

"Anyone who helps create unnaturals could attempt anything, though," admitted Maiden, turning to Kale. "They must be found and stopped. However, I ask you to proceed delicately. Our traditions are important, and I'd like to see this festival proceed without a bloodbath. You both have my invitation to attend the Passage and the banquet following it tomorrow evening. With any luck, the betrayer will give themselves away when they see you there."

"Thank you. We accept your offer," replied Kale.

Vera wondered what the man had just gotten them into. Maiden's fingers moved at her side as though she were typing on an invisible typewriter. Blue mist, the same pale color as Maiden's gown drifted from her fingertips. The girl from before came into the room.

"Are our guests' accommodations ready, Margory?" asked Maiden.

"Yes, Maiden. I'll show them the way."

"I apologize you did not get refreshments, after all, Vera," said Maiden, "I got caught up with the news and was not a very good host. I will have something sent to your rooms."

Just like that, they were dismissed. Kale ushered Vera out the door to follow Margory. Something caught Vera's attention. The little blue lizard scurried across the floor and disappeared into the pool. From this angle, Vera noticed rivulets of blood seeping through Maidens fingers as she clenched the glass in her fist, marking the side of her gown with crimson streaks. One drop fell to the floor before Maiden caught the direction of Vera's stare and shifted her hand out of sight.

"Rest well, Vera. Merry meet." Maiden's smile did not reach her eyes.

9

Kale bit back a groan when he saw Cassie waiting inside the room.

"I'll make sure our guests are settled in, Margory," said Cassie, dismissing the young witch.

Margory opened her mouth to argue, reconsidered, and closed it. She abandoned Vera and Kale without a peep. *Smart girl.* Kale envied her escape.

"There are gowns for you in the closet through those doors," Cassie told Vera. "And a washroom through the second set of doors. The cook will send your evening meal to your room. I do not suggest you go wandering around. You wouldn't want to get lost."

"No worries, wasn't planning on it," Vera replied absently, surveying the room.

It was a spacious room, but nothing like the High Maiden's apartment. Simple wood floors and walls, a bed with silver and white linens, and silver curtains. There was also a small table with two chairs and a vase of fresh daisies in one corner. The tea that Maiden had promised was already waiting. Cassie must have brought it. Vera eyed the wide bed, fidgeting. She had to be exhausted.

"Is Kale's room next door?" asked Vera.

"No," Cassie said as though the idea was absurd.

"Where will he sleep then?" Vera asked, her voice laced with worry.

Kale coughed to hide his laugh, suddenly realizing what was bothering Vera. *Does she think we'll be expected to share a bed?*

"There are no other available rooms in this hall, I'm afraid. Tomorrow is the start of the festival. All the triads are staying here," Cassie said. "There is a spare cot for the Guardian in the loft over the coop. He'll sleep with the liverymen."

Generally, that's where Kale would have preferred to stay —away from the maze-like castle full of witches. If only he were on his own. With Vera here, that was unacceptable.

"I will sleep on the closet floor," Kale said.

"That would be completely indecent," spluttered Cassie. "Do you believe your charge is in danger in the palace?"

Kale bit his tongue. The witch was fishing.

"If it would help, I could just sleep in the loft too," Vera offered.

"It would not," Cassie said firmly. "The Maiden said to ensure your absolute comfort."

"Well, the only way I'll be comfortable is to be close to my guardian." Vera folded her arms. "So, unless you have another room to spare nearby in this massive castle?"

Vera had given Kale that look plenty in the past week. His charge was losing her temper. Based on Cassie's pinched lips, the witch recognized it too.

"We're good with the closet arrangement then?" Kale

asked Cassie unnecessarily, to ruffle the witch some more. She'd earned it.

"I'm a lot smaller than you," began Vera. "I'd fit better if you want—"

"Absolutely not!" said Cassie shrilly.

"It's okay," Kale assured Vera, touched by her offer. "I like sleeping on the floor. It reminds me of when I was a boy."

"Naturally." Cassie snorted under her breath.

"You may leave," Kale said, making sure the warning was clear.

Cassie wisely stepped back, ducking her head. Surprisingly, the witch stayed, though, her hands fisted by her sides. Kale grew wary.

Finally, Cassie said to Vera, "As long as you're sure you're all right with him staying in your room."

Kale's jaw would've hit the floor, if that were possible. He hadn't imagined Cassie capable of being so bold. The witch had just earned a smidgen of his respect. The world might really be going off-tilt.

"Thank you," said Vera, softening. "I'm sure. Kale's not so bad."

Cassie didn't look convinced, but she turned to leave, having fulfilled her perceived duty. Kale stepped aside, giving a slight nod when the witch glanced at him from the corner of her eye. The witch's steps sped up, but her head did raise a few degrees too. After Cassie's exit, things became awkward. To have something to do, Kale moved to the table, poured two cups of tea, and offered one to Vera. Vera took a sip of hers, shifting uncomfortably.

"Your head still hurting?" asked Kale.

"What? Oh, no. I have got to pee, though."

"Have you forgotten how or something?" Kale smirked.

"Oh, shut up."

Vera practically threw her cup back at him before heading for the second set of doors. Kale swallowed a mouthful of the liquid from his cup and grimaced. How Vera drank the stuff with a straight face was a mystery. It was disgusting. He set the cups aside and moved on to inspect his sleeping quarters. It was worse than he'd hoped for but not as bad as it could be. If Kale angled himself just right, he might be able to stretch out all the way. As Kale reached above his head to grab some extra linens from the shelf, the walls flexed, and the floor heaved. Kale grabbed the doorframe to steady himself. Something was wrong.

Vera.

The water in the bathroom had stopped. Kale couldn't hear her moving around anymore. He raced from the closet and stopped dead in his tracks. The cursed enchantress was waiting for him. Her seductive smile and red hair awoke memories he'd worked hard to forget. She was supposed to be rotting in Dubnos with the Fomori demons. Kale had made sure of it.

"What have you done with her?" Kale demanded, scanning the room for Vera's body.

"With who?" asked Talia with fake innocence.

Kale charged the woman and threw her against the wall, shoving his forearm against her throat. Talia struggled unsuccessfully. She was weaker than Kale remembered.

"If you hurt her, I will rip your arms from your body before you die."

"Kale," Talia gasped. "Stop. Please. I didn't hurt anyone."

"Tell me where she is. Tell me where Vera is."

"Are you kidding me right now?" rasped Talia.

Except it didn't sound like Talia. While Kale was trying to puzzle this out, Talia stabbed him in the arm. He hadn't seen her reach for the blade. As fire sliced across Kale's skin, Talia flickered and became Vera.

"Vera?"

"Obviously, you freaking maniac." Vera shoved against him until Kale released her and backed away.

"I don't know how... Did I hurt you?" Kale lurched forward, searching for injuries on her, but Vera swiped out with the blade. "You brought my kitchen knife?"

"I swear if you take another step, I will stab you again."

"I'm sorry. I didn't know it was you. I thought you were... someone else."

Vera didn't lower the knife. Her hair flickered red. Kale put his hands on either side of his head. *What is happening to me? It's like I've been drugged.*

"I think I've been poisoned," Kale said with a hollow laugh.

"How?"

"Something had to have been in the tea. It's the only thing it could've been."

"I drank the tea too. I'm fine," Vera said.

"I know. I can't figure that out right now. My head is not... It must be something about you. You're special," Kale slurred.

"Dude, you're freaking me out right now."

"Lock yourself in the bathroom. Don't come out until it is safe."

"Done." Red-headed Vera was already on the move.

Kale staggered across the room to the door. Using the last of his mental acuity, he engaged the door's magical lock. It wouldn't let anyone in or out until he unlocked it. He would only be capable of that after his body got rid of the poison. Kale collapsed once the lock was in place.

In the dreams that followed, Vera fought Talia. Kale

tried to stop the human girl, tried to pull her away. He had to keep her safe. But Vera wouldn't listen to him. She stabbed him. Over and over. He kept trying, but she punched like a demon until she slipped free. Vera wouldn't let him save her. There was so much blood. Vera and blood. Kale's stomach heaved. Vera stopped fighting long enough to place a hand on his brow. She wiped away the sweat there. Then she was gone again. Kale couldn't catch her. He tried so hard, but he couldn't. Finally, he called out to Vera, begged her to come back to him. This time, she listened.

"I'm here," Vera said.

Kale rested.

He woke choking. Twisting, trying to force air down his throat, he fell, landing hard on hands and knees beside the bed. Sheets wrapped around his legs and torso. He'd pulled them with him when he'd fallen. Vera stood in the center of the room, feet planted shoulder-width apart.

"Why aren't you in the bathroom?" Kale wheezed. "Did you just punch me in the throat?"

"Yep. Punching you in the arm wasn't working."

Kale pushed himself into sitting position, propped up against the side of the bed.

"Are you hurt?" he asked.

"Just my hand from hitting you. It'll be fine."

"I told you to stay in the bathroom. I could have killed you."

"You were really sick."

"Which is why I said to stay in the bathroom," Kale said.

"You said to stay in there until it was safe to come out." Vera shrugged one shoulder. "I decided it was safe."

"How long did it take for you to make that decision?" he asked with a hard look.

Vera didn't respond. She pressed her bottom jaw forward stubbornly.

"Do you have a death wish? Or are you really that stupid?" he asked.

"You're right. I should've let you drown in your own puke."

"I can't die, Vera!" Kale ran a hand through his sweaty hair. "But you can."

"I didn't know that. Well, I knew I could die. The whole you-not-being-killable thing is news to me, though." She hesitated. "I did figure out you heal fast, though."

"And how'd you figure that out?"

"I had to stab you a couple times." She scrunched her face up. "Maybe more than that. But it was getting everything bloody, so I stopped."

Kale let his head fall back against the bed in exasperation. "So all the blood was real."

"Huh?"

"Nothing. I guess I'm glad you snuck a knife into Summartir since it kept me from killing you, but don't go waving it around and upsetting our hosts. A knife won't do much good in a witch fight." He tipped his head to look at her. "I should've told you the poison couldn't hurt me."

Vera frowned at him, and then pulled her shoulders back. "I still would've helped you. You needed help."

"You're impossible." Kale rubbed his temples, trying to massage the lingering throb away. "How did I get into the bed?"

"I've manhandled plenty of drunks into cabs. It wasn't so different. Although I did have to give you that." Vera pointed at Kale's face then indicated her eyebrow.

Kale lifted a hand and felt the cut on his brow. "Is your hand really okay?" he asked.

"Yeah. I didn't do that with my hand. The vase from the table didn't survive, though. How angry will Maiden be that I broke it?"

Kale couldn't help it, he laughed. A laugh that would have taken him to his knees if he hadn't already been sitting. The girl was unbelievable. Standing there after fighting him off for half the night and she was worried about upsetting a witch over a vase. Vera started then smiled too. Her shoulders relaxed.

"I'm sure she'll forgive you when she finds out why you had to sacrifice her vase." Kale sobered. "How long was I out of it?"

"I'm not sure. Someone brought our dinner. You tried to get out the door to go after them but it's locked. Pretty sure they ran away as fast as they could. That was a few hours ago. Right about the time when the candles lit by themselves."

"Well that's good. I'd have guessed it would take all night for my system to kick that stuff."

"The candles are magical, right? They can't burn down this castle made almost entirely of wood while I sleep? Because I don't want to asphyxiate in my sleep in a couple of hours."

"You're worried about dying by candle accident after what you risked tonight?"

"You were trying to protect me from your hallucinations, not hurt me. Whenever you forgot who I was, I just had to remind you."

"By stabbing me."

"Once I realized how fast you healed, I didn't even feel bad about it." Vera's stomach rumbled.

"You're hungry," Kale observed.

"Starving. I'll live, though. Don't we need to, I don't

know, alert Maiden that someone poisoned you? Do you think it was Cassie? I don't want it to be her. I don't think she's so bad. But she was here when we got here, and—"

"Breathe." Kale wondered if the girl had smuggled caffeine into Summartir along with the knife. "Cassie is the most likely suspect. If it was her, she could be the one working with the Siphon Master. I'll talk to the Maiden, and we'll watch Cassie closer. For now, would you like to go raid the kitchen for food that no one's touched and won't be poisoned?"

"You know where the kitchen is?"

Kale nodded. Vera did a happy dance. It was as though fighting him off all night had used up all her anxious energy, leaving her the most relaxed he'd seen her. Or she was giddy from sleep deprivation and adrenaline. She was also looking at him expectantly just then.

"I should probably clean off all the dried blood, so if someone sees us, we don't cause a midnight panic in a palace of witches," Kale said.

"Good plan. Be quick, though." Vera's stomach growled again, in anticipation this time.

Kale paused on his way past her. "Thank you for what you did for me tonight, Vera."

"It's not a big deal."

"Yes, it is. You were braver than anyone I know, to do what you did."

"I'm not brave."

"You're wrong about that," Kale said firmly then his lips twitched. "But I still think you're an idiot too."

"Back at ya, Scotchie." Her strange nickname for him didn't sound like an insult that time.

"You'll be fine," Kale told Vera for the twentieth time.

Vera stuck her tongue out at the back of his head, and then stepped on the hem of her skirts—also for the twentieth time. That's what she got for not paying attention. Her arms chafed against the crystals sewn into the bodice as she untangled herself from the layers of fabric. She hiked the front of her skirts higher, showing off her tennis shoes beneath. The pointy boots with heels she'd found waiting beside the dress had been a no-go.

"This thing is ridiculous," she grumbled. "This whole fear thing is ridiculous. Who has a banquet to celebrate fear? It's dumb."

"You have nothing to worry about," said Kale, tugging at the neck of his high-collared shirt.

"Sure, sure. Just a quick walk through a magic passageway that's going to make me face my greatest fear. I won't be able to turn back or the stupidness will get worse. It will seem like I'm totally alone, but you promise you'll be right there. Oh, and everything I see will be tailor-made to make me crap my pants, but it won't be real. You're right, nothing to worry about at all." Vera tipped her head back and spoke to the ceiling. "Lady, please don't let me end up catatonic tonight."

"You're being dramatic."

"I swear I'm gonna kick you," Vera threatened. "Again."

"You kicked me too?" he asked.

"Repeatedly."

"Where did you kick me?" Kale's eyes narrowed.

"I'm betting you've already guessed." Vera scrunched her nose with an evil half-smile. "Be grateful you have that super-healing mojo of yours."

"You are an insane woman."

"Better crazy than dead, right?"

"With you, I'm not always sure." Kale dragged her around one more corner where the "festivities" were kicking off.

All fourteen triads were gathered and waiting for Maiden to open the passage. It was just another hallway, but this one looked like it had been formed around a ginormous balloon, which they'd popped afterward. The distended walls left plenty of room for all the mingling witches. They were all smiling and chatting, obviously excited for the banquet. *Yep, they're all completely mental.* At the sight of Kale and Vera, those smiles evaporated. A few witches stared, others tried to sneak inconspicuous peeks but mostly failed.

"Well, this is fun," said Vera through her teeth.

"It won't be long," Kale assured. "I timed it so we'd get here at the last possible moment."

"Ah. That's why you were walking like a speed demon. I approve."

Another hush fell across the room. This time, for Maiden's arrival. The women parted, leaving a path for their leader. Vera searched for lizards in Maiden's hair as she passed but saw nothing. Knowing the things could hide so well was equal parts impressive and disturbing. Kale, on the other hand, did not look Maiden's way. He was scanning the room and the other witches. Vera was supposed to be doing the same. She had no idea what she was supposed to be looking for, though. Kale had said anyone acting strangely. Yeah, they were witches. Everything about them was strange.

"Welcome sisters," said Maiden cheerfully once she reached the passageway doors. "Merry meet."

The room erupted in greetings and hugging. From their enthusiasm, Vera would've thought they were all seeing each other for the first time in forever. Except, they'd been standing around gabbing a few seconds before. Vera moved closer to Kale to avoid getting caught up in the touchy-feely-ness. It was a riot of colorful gowns, gems, and flowers on all sides, with each triad decked in their family's colors. Vera and Kale stood out in their silver and white ensembles. Those were the only colors not claimed by an elite Summartir family. Apparently, wearing any family's colors to a formal event was frowned upon if you were an outsider.

"Is this strange enough for you?" Vera asked Kale.

Kale rolled his eyes, but the corner of his mouth twitched.

"Cassie's not here," Kale observed.

"Does that mean we are off the hook for this schtick?"

"No," Kale said, frustratingly.

"Tonight, we celebrate fear," said Maiden when the outpouring of affection subsided. "Fear protects us from that which would harm us. We embrace our fears and we face them. Only by facing them, can we understand what they are trying to show us. Then we can move forward, stronger and wiser."

Maiden ran her fingertips over the doors. A gray mist stood out against the pale material of her gloved hands. She whispered reverently to the stone. With a click, the doors swung outward. Beyond them was a short hall. The hall was so short, Vera could see the tables of a banquet hall on the other end. Tables filled with tureens of soup, platters of fruit and roasted vegetables, and tiered plates piled with desserts. *Maybe this won't be so bad after all.* Vera had expected a long haunted-house-style passageway, not something that was maybe twenty-feet long. More importantly, there was cake.

"As you have noticed, the Guardian and his charge are joining us this year," announced Maiden. "They have agreed to be the last in our progression. The feast is ready. Please follow me."

Maiden stepped into the passageway and vanished. Literally vanished.

"Where'd she go?" Vera whispered to Kale.

"Keep watching," he answered.

A moment later, Maiden emerged on the other end of the passage. She turned and beckoned to them. One by one, the witches followed their Maiden's lead, each disappearing for a minute or two before popping out on the other side. There went Vera's momentary calm. She mentally urged the women to slow down but in no time, the conga-line of terror had moved into the banquet hall. And it was Vera's turn.

You got this girl. Come on, now. Vera closed her eyes and stepped forward.

An alarm wailed. Vera slapped her hands over her ears to block out the sound. Her inner ears throbbed. Sure the hall had detected her human-ness, Vera started to turn back before it was too late. Behind her stretched an abyss. In front of her was an endless expanse of nothingness. It was already too late. The alarm intensified. Vera's ears popped, and her fingertips came away wet with blood.

It's not real. It's part of the allusion. The banquet is right there. Vera hoped the reminders would slow her heart. Suddenly, Cassie was there. The witch spun in a circle like she was looking for the exit. When she saw Vera, she stopped.

"You," Cassie accused. "What have you done?"

"Me? This is your ritual, not mine. If something's going wrong, you should probably talk to your people."

"I have to get out of here," Cassie said, panicking and walking quickly through the passage.

Vera was about to point out that Cassie was going the

wrong way, but realized the witch was coming straight for her. Cassie yanked a curved blade from her skirt and jabbed it toward Vera's chest. Vera barely got out of the way in time. Holy deja vu. It was like the passageway had pulled the memory of Vera's Summartir-gate nightmare right from her mind. Then added a dash of Cassie-the-betrayer into the mix for an extra kick of awful. It was a total jerk move. Vera's cheeks flushed with heat as she turned to face the Cassie illusion. She was done with all the magical bullcrap.

"I will kill you," yelled Cassie.

"Try it, witch," Vera shot back.

The psychotic allusion leaped at her, blade swinging. Vera dodged, twisting around to shove the witch from behind. Cassie fell hard at the edge of the abyss. Vera raced for the banquet hall before Cassie got up.

"Vera?" said Cassie with confusion.

Vera looked back, heart pounding in her blood-crusted ears. The witch had flipped onto her back and was staring down at the knife protruding from her chest. She'd fallen on her own weapon. Vera tensed, wondering if fake-Cassie would get up and attack again but she didn't. Blood pooled around Cassie's body. Vera sprinted the rest of the way. She didn't want to think about how the blood was so much darker than she would've imagined.

Kale was waiting for her, his hair disheveled from running his hands through it. Vera was going to kill him for making her go through that.

"How are you already here?" Vera asked.

Kale didn't answer. He tipped her head, looking at her neck and face. His jaw jumped, and he was breathing faster than Vera had ever seen. *Why is he upset? I'm the one who begged not to have to go through that to begin with.* Vera batted Kale's hands away angrily, blinking back the tears sting her eyes. She didn't want to cry—she was mad. She wanted Kale to know she was furious at him.

"How are you here already?" Vera demanded. "Did you go a different way?"

"No, Vera. I went through just like you. An hour ago."

Vera finally looked around. The witches were not feasting, they were clustered near the passage, watching for something.

"Did you see Cassie?" called out a young witch.

A buzzing started in Vera's ears. Kale used a cloth to wipe away the blood. It was real.

"It wasn't real." Vera's voice hitched. She shivered. Kale pulled her to him, wrapping his arms around her to warm her up.

"Shh," he whispered into her ear just as the screaming began.

The passageway had cleared, revealing Cassie's body just inside the doors. Vera struggled to breathe. An elderly woman, dressed in the same burnt-red as Cassie, elbowed through the witches. She knelt beside Cassie, resting an age-spotted hand on the dead witch's head. A sob tore from the woman's chest. A young witch, with a halo of dark curls and porcelain skin just like Cassie's, also rushed forward and fell to her knees beside the woman. As the old woman and young girl clung to each other, the other witches gravitated toward those dressed in the same colors. They were seeking out their families for comfort as they grieved.

"What happened?" Kale whispered into Vera's hair.

"She tried to stab me. I pushed her away. She fell on her knife."

Kale stepped away, lifting Vera's hands between them with a long exhale.

"You didn't kill her," he said with relief.

"Yes, I did," Vera argued.

"Shh. It wasn't you," Kale said. "Someone set it up to make it look like you, though."

The witches began to hum. Cassie's family bent to kiss her closed eyes. The old woman and young girl placed both hands on Cassie. One on her head, the other over her chest. Rust-colored mist gathered around them, shrouding Cassie's body. When the mist melted away, Cassie was gone. The blood was gone. All that remained was a black stone the size of Vera's thumb where Cassie's body had been. The old witch picked up the stone, and the young witch helped her to her feet.

"It's a bloodstone," explained Kale quietly. "The last drops of blood turn to stone when a witch is murdered. They'll use it to find Cassie's killer."

Vera couldn't breathe.

"It's not you," Kale said, reading her distress.

Kale maneuvered Vera into the circle forming around Cassie's family. Kale was wrong. Soon, they were all going to know it too. They probably already did. Vera looked around the circle. A few witches looked back, suspicion written on their faces. Maiden caught Vera's attention. The leader of the witches drained her cup and set it on the table behind her. The old witch in orange began to chant. At the same time, Maiden's fingers twitched, that dark mist dripping from her hands. Vera's palm stung. Scalding heat flowed up her arm. Vera flinched. Kale looked over, frowning, but before Vera could say anything, the heat cooled and was gone just as suddenly as it had begun. Around Vera's neck, the medallion was warm and heavy. The old woman kept chanting. Maiden stumbled, confusion flashing in her eyes just before they rolled back and she collapsed. With a burst of light, the bloodstone winked out of sight.

No one moved toward Maiden until Kale did. He didn't release Vera, so she stumbled along behind him. The witches backed away, whispering and covering their mouths. Kale dropped by Maiden's side and felt for a pulse.

"She's okay," Kale said to himself more than anyone.

The relief in Kale's tone made Vera look at Maiden a little differently. Were Kale and Maiden a thing? Maiden's eyes popped open. She looked at something that wasn't there. Blue mist shot from her fingers and made a hole in the plaster where she'd been staring. *Well, this feels familiar. Good thing Kale couldn't shoot magic from his hands or last night would've gone a lot differently.*

"You will not help your Maiden?" Kale asked the room of witches. "You'll turn your back on her when she needs you?"

"She has been found guilty by the bloodstone," called a witch.

"Your kind always was quick to decide guilt," Kale said with disgust as he restrained the thrashing Maiden.

"We have the evidence. The pain of the bloodstone was too much for her," said another witch.

Kale took Maiden's hands and slid the gloves down her arms. One hand, and then the other. The witches watched closely. Kale lifted her hands to show the room.

"How about now?" Kale asked. "There's no mark. The bloodstone didn't brand her. She's been poisoned."

The witches surged forward to aid their leader after that, their mouths stretched into huge O's of horror. Vera wondered if it was because their leader had fallen, or because they'd been willing to leave her there. Kale planted himself between the mob of witches and Maiden.

"You've seen that her hands are clean," Kale said. "If you want to touch her, you will show me yours first."

"You cannot demand that," they cried in outrage.

"I already have," Kale said flatly. "Now, it's up to you how long your High Maiden stays on the floor without assistance."

Vera was shocked when the witches did not move. What were they waiting for? None of them had killed Cassie—she had. Still, the witches glared and stood unwaveringly.

"For all we know, Cassie's killer is here and is responsible for poisoning your Maiden. Are you willing to let that witch go free for your damned pride?" Kale asked the witches.

Finally, a crone in candy-apple red stepped forward and peeled off her elbow-length gloves. She presented her hands to Kale for inspection, flipping them back and forth. Kale let her pass. The crone knelt beside Maiden. As one, the rest of the witches followed suit. Gloves were stripped off and dropped to the floor, clean hands presented to Kale for inspection.

"Show them your hands, Vera," Kale said after he'd cleared the final witch.

Vera held out her hands, flipping them in the same way she had seen the witches do. She'd already looked and known there wasn't a mark that she could see. The witches seemed satisfied, which made absolutely no sense. If the trick with the bloodstone was to be believed, no one there had killed Cassie.

"Tonight, we will mourn and watch over the Maiden. Tomorrow, we will begin a witch hunt," said the crone who had cried over Cassie. "We will find the witch who killed our sister and poisoned our Maiden."

"Could Cassie have poisoned Maiden's cup before she died?" Vera asked Kale when they were far enough from the witches that none could overhear.

"I saw Maiden dip that cup of wine from the bowl after you came out of the passageway," said Kale. "No one else was poisoned so it was added to Maiden's cup later. After Cassie was gone."

"Will Maiden be okay?"

"Yeah, she's powerful enough, she'll be fine. No one else here would survive that particular poison, though."

"Except you," reminded Vera. "So, you know what the poison is?"

"Yes and tomorrow we're going to visit the only possible source and see who's got something to hide."

"Why did the witches not want to show you their hands?" Vera asked.

"That's hard to explain." At Vera's look of impatience, he added with a sigh, "You're not going to like it."

Vera tapped her foot, impatiently waiting for Kale to get on with it.

"When someone tries to deceive me, I see it manifested as black marks on their hands and arms. Just like Addamas's tattoos. That's why he got them, so I couldn't see his deception. I always know when someone is trying to deceive me."

"Always?"

"Always. Every time you planned to run away."

Vera's mind emptied. It was like being speechless but more complete. Her well of emotions was dry. She wasn't sure how to react.

"I expected yelling," Kale said

"Don't worry, that'll probably still happen. I think I'm too tired to process what you're saying," Vera informed him. "None of the witches had deception marks, I take it?"

"Nope. Surprisingly, none of them were hiding anything," Kale answered.

"Does that mean none of them are responsible for the Siphon Master and the unnaturals?"

"That's what it means," Kale said tiredly. "Hopefully, we'll have better luck at the farm. Come on. Let's get out of here and get some sleep."

"Best thing you've ever said to me," Vera replied.

Kale picked up a plate of fruit and cheese as they walked through the room. Vera lifted one brow.

"Once the adrenaline wears off, you'll be hungry," he explained.

"Careful. I might stop hating you." Vera snagged a plate of pastries too.

10

K ale braced himself.

"I hate you," seethed Vera while shaking strings of saliva from her shoe.

"I didn't mention the velvet worms because you would've freaked out. They typically steer clear of the chickens, anyway, so I didn't think it would matter. That's the whole reason why we're riding, not walking. Plus, they're generally nocturnal. It was unlucky that an aggressive one was still above ground this time of day."

"First off, I'm still ticked you didn't warn me that I'd have to crawl onto a chicken's back this morning. Second, how about if you assume from now on that if there's a chance something unlucky will happen, like a watermelon-sized worm with a mouth full of razors losing its mind and leaping from a hole to try and eat my foot, it will."

"Your luck's not all bad," Kale argued. "You were lucky the chicken moved so fast. Your hen probably feels pretty lucky after that unexpected snack too."

"I'm serious," Vera said. "Full disclosure from now on."

"Then you should know the beetles are big around here too."

"Oh, Lady." Vera spun around in her saddle, looking for any sign of a giant beetle, her eyes bugging from her skull.

That's why he hadn't told her in the first place.

"The beetles are scavengers, not predators like the velvet worms," Kale said patiently.

Sweat from the humid Velvet Wood air coated their skin even though they'd skirted the outside of the woods, avoiding the most humid areas where the worms lived. Vera swiped a hand across her forehead, trying to appear calm. The third time she jumped at a noise, Kale sighed.

"What is your deal with Lady Luck?" Kale asked as a distraction.

"Suzie believed in her." Vera shifted in the saddle and shrugged. "After Suzie died last year, I needed someone to talk to. I figured if Lady Luck was real, maybe she'd listen. The way my luck's been going ever since, I should've kept my mouth shut."

"You didn't have anyone to talk to? What about Gus, the bird shifter?"

"He's Suzie's husband. I didn't know he was a shifter until the Badlands." Vera fiddled with the pommel on her saddle. "Gus was always around, but we never talked. Even before Suzie died. Wait, how did you know that was Gus?"

"Smelled him at your apartment. I was surprised because magic doesn't last long on Earth. Somehow, your foster parents had a supply of it, though. I'd like to meet Gus sometime and ask him about that."

"And then execute him?"

"No. There was only a trace of magic, not enough to be dangerous or to expose humans." Kale ducked under a branch. "So, no other friends?"

"I've never been good with people. They're pretty much all liars. Except for Suzie, she never lied... Never-mind, I take that back. Even she was a liar. She was hiding magic from me that whole time. That leaves one homeless guy who hung out near our apartment as the only person I know who never lied to me. Suzie and I used to take him food, but he stopped coming around after Suzie died." Vera inhaled deeply. "That's my sob story. How about you? You slept on the floor when you were a boy? And when was that, exactly, Mr. I-Can't-Die?"

"A long time ago," said Kale wryly. "When I was a boy, I slept in the loft with my big brother. Sometimes he'd let me use him for a pillow when I couldn't sleep."

"Did something happen to your family?" Vera asked perceptively.

"Pirates. They came in the night and killed everyone except me. Decided I had a pretty enough face, so they sold me alongside my family's sheep."

Kale hadn't thought of that night in a long time. After so many centuries, the rage and pain had dulled. It was just a story of facts now. Vera's eyes shone with heartache, though. *Stars blast. I only meant to divert her curiosity from how long ago I'd been a boy. The last thing I wanted is for her to forget who and what I am. She's already proven to underestimate how dangerous I am to her.*

"Don't worry. I got my revenge. Killed my owner and his closest friends when I was ten. Then I hunted down and slaughtered the pirates and the Tempestarii—a sect of magicians—who'd hired them. Along with anyone who ever hurt my family or me. Everyone who stood in my way too. By the time I was fifteen, I stopped keeping count of the bodies. When I found the last tempestarii, he was having dinner with his wife and children at his mansion in the country, as far from his past and me as he could get. It wasn't far enough, though." Kale smiled viciously. "The screams of his wife and children as they watched him die were beautiful. Afterward, I kept killing. I enjoyed it too much to stop. People started paying me for my services. Eventually, the Infernal Hosts took notice. Once I worked for them, I had a warm bed in every village and town I went. Never had to sleep on the cold floor again."

Vera's sorrow twisted into a familiar mixture of disgust and horror. It was a look Kale was more comfortable with.

"If I'd known that story would shut you up, I'd have told it to you days ago," Kale said with a smirk.

"You're such an ass."

With that, Vera turned away and sealed her lips shut. She seemed to have forgotten about the worms and beetles, though, as she stared straight ahead without flinching. When they emerged from the Velvet Woods, the Monroe farm lay ahead, nestled in the crook of a bluff. At the center of the compound was a massive white barn. It wasn't like a human's barn. It was only shaped like one. The upper levels were apartments that housed five generations of the Monroe family. The lower levels were the family commons areas.

Large igloo-shaped structures—chicken huts—sat in rows to one side of the barnyard. Hens, cocks, chicks, and goats wandered around the barnyard. A creek flowed around one side of the compound, creating a natural barrier to contain the animals. It fed through the pass and into a small lake on the other side of the bluffs. Opposite the chicken huts were rows of silos, filled with leftover corn and grain from last year's harvest. The rest was miles of fresh-turned farmland.

Vera took in the whole scene with awe but otherwise

remained quiet. Normally, she'd have asked a million questions by now. It had to be killing her.

"The Monroes are the most well-known, non-elite family in Summartir," Kale explained unprompted. "They have always been loyal servants to the triads. Monroe daughters become handmaidens, Monroe sons farm the land. Together, they raise the flocks. Monroe land rivals most of the elites'. Perhaps there's a Monroe who's tired of playing second-fiddle and powerful enough to do something about it."

"By poisoning the Maiden and you? But why create an unnatural army on Earth?" Vera wondered aloud, obviously forgetting that she was not talking to Kale.

"A long memory and someone to avenge?" suggested Kale.

Two men rode out toward Kale and Vera. Kale recognized the burly older man carrying a pitchfork as one of the family patriarchs. His olive-toned skin, darkened by many hours in the sun, contrasted with his thinning white hair. Interestingly, the white hair was a family trait, not due to age. Even the children in the family had snowy heads of hair. While taking in the range of bluffs, Vera hadn't noticed the approaching welcoming party. Kale wondered what she was thinking.

"Incoming," Kale said as the stamp of chicken feet reached his ears.

"Guardian," greeted the older man as he neared. "Why have you come to our farm today?"

"Someone's been making milktooth poison. I'm here to see if anyone in your family is that stupid, Mitch," answered Kale.

"What makes you think it's milktooth?" asked the young man, who looked like a younger version of Mitch.

"Who are you?" asked Kale.

"My son, Gage," answered Mitch. "He's our Hatchery Master."

"The triads confirmed it," Kale answered Gage.

"You're sure it's not an old batch someone's had tucked away in their family vault?" Mitch licked his lower lip nervously.

"Someone tested it out on me," said Kale. "It's fresh."

"I assure you, everyone here values their life too much to do something like that, Guardian." Mitch laid the pitchfork across his lap and tugged off his work gloves, baring his hands. "I see the rumors of your invincibility are not exaggerated, though."

"Not much about me is," Kale replied, honestly.

"A nest was raided four days ago," revealed Mitch. "Lost all but one chick. Been trying to keep the little guy alive, but he won't last long. His egg tooth is missing."

"Why didn't you report it?" asked Kale.

"We thought it was an animal attack. All that was left of the other chick was feathers and gore. Found this little one floating downstream the next day, half his beak chewed off. Their mama looked to be chewed open too. We hadn't believed there was anything to report," explained Mitch.

"Why has the Maiden sent you instead of coming herself?" asked Gage.

"Your Maiden was poisoned too," Kale revealed and Mitch pulled back startled by the news. "She'll live, but it will take some time for her to recover fully. I also have reason to believe the person responsible for the milktooth poison is also responsible for a threat on my charge's realm."

"Ah," said Mitch slowly. "Then you have the authority to seek whatever answers here you want. You do not require our permission."

"No, but your family's cooperation would make things a lot easier."

"I will do my best to ensure it. We have nothing to hide regarding these matters," assured Mitch. "We'll take you to see the surviving chick if you'd like? Let you see why we thought it was an animal attack."

"It's as good a place as any to start," said Kale agreeably.

The two men turned their hens toward the farmyard, leading Kale and Vera to their home. Gage was clearly not pleased. The young man kept throwing meaningful looks at his father. Mitch didn't acknowledge his son's attempt at silent communication.

"I don't trust them," said Kale under his breath.

"His hands are marked?" Vera asked.

"No."

"Then what's the matter? He said they have nothing to hide. I think he was telling the truth."

"You're wrong," said Kale

"Want to make a bet about that?" Vera asked, bristling.

"You don't want to do that," Kale warned.

"Oh, I think I do."

"Fine. When you figure out that you're wrong, you'll owe me one act of obedience. No questions, no defiance. Whatever I say, goes."

"Done," Vera said smugly. "And when you figure out I'm *not* wrong, you'll owe me one favor. I get to decide what that favor is whenever I'm ready."

"Done."

Vera urged her hen after the men, looking like she'd already won. She was going to be angry when she realized her error. Kale just had to keep her in one piece until then.

THERE WERE KIDS EVERYWHERE. One little girl was trying to ride a goat. The goat wasn't having it and flipped her off. The girl jumped up to the cheers of a small group of boys and girls. Farther out, teens tossed handfuls of corn at the feet of the chickens. Chicks as big as ponies followed after the feeders, cheeping until someone reached up to pet their fluffy heads. Whenever a chicken wandered too far from the yard, a goat chased it down and rammed it with its head, herding it back to the flock. A couple of little boys laughed at the squawks of the herded chickens, and then ran to collect any dislodged feathers. Vera couldn't imagine what a childhood like this would've been like.

Mitch led them to a platform, like the one at the palace they had used to mount the chickens. A young boy ran forward and grabbed Vera's reins, unworried when the hen tussled his mop of hair with her jagged beak. Vera pulled her legs to one side of her saddle and slowly slid down the chicken's side on her belly, holding onto the saddle so she didn't fall on her butt. The platform was lower than Vera had thought. She reached with her tippy toes, feeling blindly for it. A pair of big hands grabbed Vera around the waist, plucking her from the chicken and standing her on her own two feet. Vera whipped around to inform Kale she didn't need his help. It wasn't Kale. It was Gage. Kale was on his way toward them, though. With a death glare.

"Thanks," Vera said, putting herself between Kale and the man.

"Sure thing," Gage said, eyeing the Guardian before ducking his head and walking away.

"You good?" Kale looked Vera up and down like she'd just come from battle.

"What's your problem?"

"Just stick close to me," said Kale grumpily.

"Sure, I'll be the sprinkles to your doughnut. That work for you?"

Vera was distracted as a young woman walked from the barn, to small kitchen garden, and out a side door. She wore linen pants and a white shirt. The same as everyone else at the farm. Her dark skin, against the silvery braid down her back, was striking. But that's not what caught Vera's attention. Out the corner of her eye, the woman seemed to glow. Looking at her straight on, there was nothing unusual about her. The woman saw Vera staring and froze. Her eyes scanned the yard like a startled rabbit sniffing out danger. When the woman's eyes landed on Kale, she nearly fell over her own feet to get back inside. Soon, adults were showing up to usher the kids inside too.

"Come on, Sprinkles," called Kale.

Vera's nose flared at the new nickname. She really had to learn to keep her mouth shut.

THE HATCHERY TOOK up a small corner in the lower level of the barn. It allowed easy access for monitoring the at-risk eggs and chicks brought for specialized care. Heat lamps hung over half a dozen stalls. Only two were on. Someone in the Monroe family had enough magic to keep the devices powered. One lamp heated an egg the size of a beach ball. The other warmed what looked like a dead bird. The mutilated chick was flopped in the corner of its stall, not moving beyond the shallow rise and fall of his chest. Blood matted the delicate down-covered flesh that outlined his ribs. One wing was scored by what looked like claw marks. A jagged hole in his beak had been patched, but the bandaging was coming loose as though he'd tried ripping it off. There were teeth marks all over his beak. It looked like something had used him as a chew toy.

Kale turned to tell Vera to brace herself but she'd already seen. Before he could catch her, Vera squeezed past him and into the stall. The chick jerked, frightened, but not able to get away. Vera clicked her tongue and shushed gently. The chick stilled, tipping his head to peer at her through his only remaining red eye. *Stars, the girl's a chicken whisperer too?*

"Don't!" hissed Gage.

Vera didn't hear, or more likely didn't care to listen. She dropped to her knees beside the bird, placing a hand on the chick's beak. The chick looked at her pitifully then nuzzled her hand.

"Well, that's unexpected," said Mitch, shoulders relaxing. "No one else has gotten that close to him without having to go to the healer to be patched up."

"He's violent?" asked Kale quietly so not to frighten Vera.

"Honestly, we thought he'd gone feral," Mitch answered equally as quiet.

Kale's blood heated. Neither man noticed because they were too busy gawking at Vera and the mad bird.

"You didn't think to mention that fact sooner? Before my charge was beside him?"

That got their attention. The men moved a couple steps away.

"I'm sorry, Guardian," spluttered Mitch. "We had no idea your charge would run in there like that. Most people take one look at him and stay back, all proper. Without needing to be told."

Kale's hands clenched by his sides. Admittedly, it wasn't their fault that Vera's sense of self-preservation was faulty.

Telling her wouldn't have made a difference either. He could have tied her up, though, if he'd known.

"He doesn't seem to mind her for some reason," said Gage. "I think she's plenty safe in there with him. She can probably walk out any time she wants."

"But I wouldn't go in after her, he might get spooked," added Mitch.

"Vera," Kale said calmly. "These guys think it's best to let the chick rest now. Why don't you come out here?"

Vera scowled at him and asked Gage, "When was the last time this chick ate?"

"He hasn't. Not in the three days we've had him here."

"You poor thing," Vera cooed to the chick.

"We won't let him keep suffering," assured Mitch. "After today, with him not getting any better, he'll be put to rest."

Vera looked at Mitch with wide eyes. Then at Kale as though any of this was his fault.

"You're gonna let them kill him?" Her voice rose, upsetting the chick who began to squirm.

"Stay calm," said Kale. "It's not my decision to make."

"He won't feel a thing." Mitch thought to assure Vera.

Again, Vera looked to Kale. *Damn the moron to the depths of Diyu.* Kale was prepared to toss the man into the stall and let Vera and the chick have at him if he said another word.

"Bring me some water for him. And some food," Vera ordered with frightening calm.

Mitch began to argue, but Kale grabbed the man's arm, squeezing tightly.

"I'll get it," Gage said and ran away.

"Can I have a cloth or something to clean him up too?" Vera requested.

Kale released Mitch's arm once the man said, "Yes, of course."

Mitch fled too. Hopefully to do as Vera asked, or Kale would hunt him down.

"I'm being stupid, aren't I?" Vera asked Kale.

"Caring for a helpless creature is not stupid."

"Yeah but we're here to save a lot of people, and I'm worried about a chicken."

The hatchery was empty except for them, but Kale was relieved Vera had chosen her words carefully. Witches knew too many ways to listen in on a conversation when they were motivated to do so.

"I think we can manage to save countless people and one chick too. As long as you're prepared to let him go if you can't help him."

"You can heal him," Vera said. "Like Mimi."

"I can't."

"Lie," Vera accused.

"I don't have magic, Vera. I can only call on the meadow's power when there's no other choice. But there's a cost. That cost would drive this chick insane. They'd have to put him down for sure."

"What's the cost?"

He did not want to tell her, but she had a right to know. "When I draw the magic through me, a memory attaches to it. It's sent into the person I'm healing. For them, it's like living that experience through my eyes."

"What memory did Mimi see?"

"I'm not sure. But Mimi didn't see it, she lived it. As though she was me."

"And you think the memory was something really bad," Vera concluded.

"There's little good to be found in my memories."

"So, she could've become a murderer?"

"Or worse. Now she has to live with the memory of what

she did, even though she didn't do anything wrong." Kale let out a slow breath. "I did do those things, though. Mimi has to decide whether or not she can forgive me for that too."

"It's all because of me," said Vera. "Because she tried to rescue me."

"Don't be dumb," Kale scoffed.

Vera's back straightened at his rebuff as he'd intended.

"Then help me some other way," said Vera. "Please. This chick doesn't want to die."

Kale frowned. *Is she making a general assumption based on the fact that no animal wants to die? Or is it something more than that?* He couldn't ask because Mitch and Gage were back with the requested supplies. Vera busied herself cleaning the bird and trying to coax him to open his beak for some water.

"Answer a question for me, Mitch," said Kale when the man drew near. "Do you want to find out who butchered your chicks and poisoned your Maiden?"

"Right now, it's all I can think of," said Mitch.

"If that person turns out to be a member of your family?" Kale asked.

"Anyone who's capable of butchering chicks, and performing the unspeakable magic necessary to make that poison, is no family I'd claim," Mitch answered.

"You'd disown them? Just like that?" Kale snapped his fingers.

"Even if it was my own child."

"I have a proposition for you then," Kale said.

"I'm listening."

"Don't put the chick down tonight. Give Vera twenty-four hours to try to save him. I'll give you that twenty-four hours to talk to your family, see if you can learn anything before I step in."

"Why would you do that?" Mitch followed Kale's pointed look at Vera. "Ah, I see how it would be challenging to keep an eye on that one and search for a would-be murderer."

"Not would-be. We're hunting for someone who's responsible for deaths in this realm and another." What Kale didn't admit aloud was that Mitch would be able to get the answers Kale needed faster that Kale could himself. No one wanted to talk to the Guardian.

"There's no one here with that kind of magic," Mitch said, shaking his head.

"I know you don't want to believe it could be one of your family, but everything's led us here," Kale said.

"You can rest assured that whoever brought your attention here and endangered the Monroe family will receive no mercy. To be truthful, though, I hope what I find will take your search away from here."

"Then you should work quickly," Kale suggested. "Twenty-four hours starts now."

Mitch had only been gone minutes when Gage slunk back inside the hatchery. He'd brought along a coat and mittens for Vera. Sure, the nights got chilly this time of year, but didn't the fool realize that Vera was practically toasting beneath the heat lamp? Gage cleared his throat to get Vera's attention then passed her the items. *Stars, it's painful to watch the man fumble.* Vera smiled, and Gage blushed to the roots of his hair. When Vera's attention returned to the chick, Kale angled his body to face Gage, who remained hovering. In Kale's peripheral, Vera dribbled water on the chick's beak and tried to get him to swallow some.

"You're awfully young to be the Hatchery Master." Kale pitched his voice low. "Perks of being the son of the Monroe matriarch and patriarch, I guess."

"I'm the Hatchery Master because I work hard and do a good job, not because of my parents," Gage declared.

"Isn't it your job to watch over the spring nests and chicks? It doesn't seem like you've done such a great job to me." Kale indicated the chick.

Gage's face turned red, his gloved hands gripped the stall door tighter. When his work gloves shifted, Kale noticed the black spirals underneath. The man didn't turn to meet Kale's gaze, but at least he wasn't making googly eyes at Vera anymore either.

"There was no way to know someone was going to raid that nest," Gage insisted.

"Unless you planned the raid," countered Kale.

"I had nothing to do with the raid," Gage said, his voice rising in anger.

Kale raised a dubious brow at the man's gloved hands.

"I believe him," piped Vera.

"Of course you do," replied Kale. "But he's either been neglecting his responsibilities, giving the raiders an opportunity to plan and carry out their task, or he was involved in the raid himself." Kale turned back to Gage. "So, which was it?"

"I have not been neglecting my responsibilities," Gage said, but his shoulders slumped slightly. "That night I missed my rounds. I'd been up with a sick brooding hen the night before and most of the day. When I woke late, I hurried to inspect the nests and found the raided coop."

"Why were you awake with a sick hen? Where was the flock healer?" asked Kale.

"I am Flock Healer. In addition to being Hatchery Master."

"I thought the healer was a witch's position," said Kale.

"It is. Our last healer died a few years ago. There was no

one to replace her. I learned how to treat the flock without magic. It takes a lot more time that way, though. Sometimes I don't get much sleep."

"Based on the number of healthy birds I've seen, you must be skilled. I'm surprised you are willing to do both."

"I'm the best option the flock has," Gage said.

"You care so much for some chickens?" Kale asked curiously.

"Yes. I would never be able to harm one of my chicks. I knew exactly when each was laid and when they would hatch. I've not missed a hatching since I was twelve. This chick was due to hatch the day someone ripped him from his egg. Milk teeth become potent several hours before a chick hatches. Whoever did this knew that. To take a chick from their egg before their time, it's abhorrent." Gage took a steadying breath and said quietly, "Even if this chick survives, he'll never be strong. Most likely, he'll be bullied and ostracised by the flock. I'm not so sure we're doing him a favor by keeping him alive."

"Say any of that to Vera, and I'll rip out your tongue. Got it?"

Gage nodded quickly, looking at the oblivious Vera.

"Is there someone who might have had access to your intimate knowledge of the eggs?" asked Kale a little louder. "A wife? Girlfriend? A friend who's been keeping your bed warm lately?"

Vera pretended to be busy tending her chick, but Kale could practically see her ears standing at attention.

"There's no one. I've been too busy for relationships." The man blushed again. "Maybe soon I'll find someone who will make me want to look up from my work."

Oh, for fiends' sake.

"I wasn't asking for your hopes and dreams," said Kale. "Just seeing who might have gotten you talking."

"Even if someone had been watching me, there's no way they could've known the hen would get sick, or that I'd sleep through my rounds that night."

"What was wrong with the hen?"

"She managed to find some bracken. It grows wild in the hills. Sometimes a seed blows down and takes root. Unfortunately, no one saw it before the hen found it. She has three eggs that will hatch soon, I had to make sure she didn't destroy them while she was ill."

"Do you keep records of whose turn it is to feed the hens?" asked Kale.

"Sure. Mitch keeps stuff like that."

"Maybe you should consider the possibility that the hen getting sick wasn't an accident," said Kale. "I know you don't like it, but if you want to make sure they won't do something like this again, you need to check it out. Have Mitch track down who was on the feeding crew. If nothing else, maybe someone saw something."

"He's swallowing," cheered Vera. "Look!"

By the stars. The bird tipped his head back to swallow a ladle of water. Vera tried to offer some corn gruel next, but the chick turned his head away and closed his eyes to rest.

"You are incredible," said Gage with wonder.

Vera smiled but it wobbled when she looked at the chick. The bird hadn't eaten.

11

Vera couldn't sleep. The moon was too bright. Okay, maybe she'd been obsessing over how cute Gage was when he'd blushed earlier. And how she'd blushed back. *Gah.* Her face heated thinking about it. The look he'd flashed her when she'd gotten the chick to swallow some water. . .Vera's stomach flipped. She kicked a foot out from beneath the blankets. It was too warm. A minute later, she pulled it back under. It was cold enough out there to freeze a boob off. Spring acted as drunk in this part of Summartir as it did back home. Or more likely, the Palace had been heated magically, so she just hadn't noticed how chilly the nights still were. At the farm, cold seeped through the plank floors and walls unhindered. She hoped Eggbert was okay. That's what she'd been calling the chick when no one could hear. It was a silly name, but she liked it. What if his heat lamp went out? She hadn't thought to ask how that thing worked.

Vera sat up and peeked over the foot of the bed where Kale slept in a patch of moonlight. He was on his back, one arm curved under his head. The thin wool blanket draped over his chest wasn't long enough to cover his bare toes. For some reason, seeing him barefoot made him seem deceptively harmless.

"Kale?" Vera whispered.

He didn't flinch. She felt bad for all the sleep he was not getting lately. Kale shivered, making Vera feel even worse. She'd offered him one of the comforters, but he'd said he'd be fine with the blanket he had. So full of his tough-guy self. Vera slid from the bed, dragging along the thickest comforter, still warm from her body heat. Stepping lightly, she edged around the bed and lowered the comforter over Kale, making sure to cover his feet too. Soon, he stopped shivering. Vera's lips curved into a tender smile. She'd let him sleep while she ran down for a quick check on Eggbert.

Vera tugged pants on under her nightshirt and pulled the coat from Gage over her shoulders with a stupid smile. Getting the feels for a man who lived in a witch realm was such a bad idea. Then again, if he turned out to be a douche, Vera would definitely never see him again. Shoes on, Vera tiptoed to the door. She used one mittened hand to muffle the slight click of the lock. One perk of this place, the locks were magically low-tech. Vera hadn't been able to unlock the palace guestroom door no matter how hard she'd tried. Twisting the doorknob slowly, Vera cringed, anticipating a creak, but it was silent. Because the door didn't open when she pulled. She pulled harder. Still nothing.

"Going out?" asked Kale, his breath warm on Vera's neck.

Vera jumped and spun around to face him. She pressed her back against the door and looked up at his face right above hers. Kale's arm was extended up to the top of the door where he'd held it closed to keep her from leaving. At least she wasn't just an incompetent door-opener. Kale swiped his other hand across his face, rubbing away the remnants of sleep. Vera couldn't see his face from the shadows, but the moonlight at his back high-lighted the curves of his shoulders and arms. His sides narrowed above the waist of his pants, the only things he'd worn to sleep in. Vera realized with horror that it probably looked like she was checking him out. She wasn't, though. She'd just been fascinated by how the moonlight framed him. How it highlighted the crisscrossing scars all over his skin. *Crap, I'm doing it again. He's really going to get the wrong idea now.*

"You have a lot of scars," Vera said pathetically.

"I know," Kale replied. "What I don't know is why you're sneaking out in the middle of the night."

"I was just going to make sure Eggbert's okay. It's really cold."

Vera wasn't feeling the cold anymore. Kale radiated heat. No wonder he hadn't thought he'd need a thicker blanket.

"Eggbert?"

Double crap. I didn't mean to say that either. "The chick." Vera prepared for Kale to laugh.

He tipped his head and studied her. He didn't laugh. Pushing off the door, he turned to retrieve his shirt and boots. The cold flowed back around Vera. The moonlight outlined Kale's tense jaw.

"Next time wake me, okay?"

No scolding or berating. Half-asleep Kale was unusually mellow and non-jerkish. Like this, he'd be incredibly easy to get along with. Vera's throat was too dry to speak, but she nodded her head. Kale must have seen it in the darkness because he didn't ask if she'd heard him.

"Let's go," Kale said once he was fully clothed.

Vera wanted to tell him he didn't have to go if he didn't want to. But there was no way he would let her go alone.

Arguing would probably bring out his normal crank. Vera pressed her lips closed. Better to not screw up a good thing.

KALE LOOKED OVER THE CHICK. Vera's Eggbert was fine. The lamp over his stall was going strong. Kale hadn't expected otherwise, but after whatever had been happening upstairs, with the girl's eyes all over him, he'd needed out of that room.

"He looks better, right?" Vera whispered.

Eggbert woke. Vera's voice was a siren call to him. The chick strained to get closer to Vera but was too weak to stand.

"Hold on, buddy. Don't hurt yourself." Vera unlatched the gate and hurried inside.

The chick was no threat to Vera, but Kale suspected he'd lose something if he got too close. The cord that tied Kale to the Meadow threaded up his spine, so his back and head were indestructible but his fingers not so much. A few dismembered digits wouldn't kill Kale, but once something was cut off, it didn't grow back. He had to reattach it. Vera would not appreciate how he went about getting a finger back from the chick's gut should the thing swallow one. Eggbert pressed against Vera, jostling her with his uncoordinated movements. Vera overbalanced and fell on her butt, giggling. Eggbert did look better, but he still looked like he could be dead in a day or two. *Stars help me, I want the thing to stay alive so Vera keeps smiling like that. First Mimi, now Vera. These women are killing me.*

"It seems he missed you," said Kale. "I'll refill his water and see if I can find something he'll eat."

Kale carried the empty water bowl back through the

doors separating the hatchery from the family's common areas. There was a sink in the hatchery, but they stored unfertilized eggs for eating in the kitchen pantry. He weaved through the rows of dining tables and stepped over some forgotten playing cards near the kitchen entrance. The Monroes would not approve of feeding the chick an egg, but it was precisely what Eggbert needed. It'd give the chick a super-dose of nutrition. And Eggbert would love it. Hopefully. Kale would deal with the repercussions later if they came up.

After pumping a bowl of fresh water, Kale found six eggs in the pantry. Half that many would be more than enough to feed everyone at breakfast. Kale collected a ladle and a large mixing bowl. He smacked the top of one egg with the ladle. The shell splintered. Kale hit it a couple more times until he'd made a hole big enough for the ladle to fit. Egg-white dripped over the side of the shell and onto the floor. Some crone was going to throw a fit in the morning when they discovered Kale's messy handiwork. He would have to look for duck nests tomorrow. He wouldn't dare try something like this again.

Balancing both bowls, Kale headed back into the hatchery. He'd only been gone a few minutes. Vera crouched near Eggbert and startled when he walked in.

"Kale," Vera said, letting out a relieved breath.

"What happened?" Kale turned in a circle, searching the shadows for what had her scared.

"It's nothing." Vera blushed. "Someone walked by the window outside, it surprised me is all. Probably just someone making rounds. I'm a little jumpy now, but it's fine." Vera started to stand.

"Stay down where no one can see you. Just in case." Kale

lowered himself, so he was hidden as well, and set the bowls inside the stall. "Keep your voice low too."

"I really don't think there's anything to worry about." Vera pointed at the orange-streaked liquid that she could see now. "What's that?"

"A little egg for Eggbert," Kale said, listening for any sounds of movement beyond their stall.

"That's disgusting."

"He won't think so."

"Isn't that cannibalism?" Vera asked.

"There's no baby chick in there. It's just egg—what baby chicks eat before they hatch." Kale glanced over his shoulder.

"Oh, I hadn't thought of it like that." Satisfied, Vera reached over, snagged the bowl, and pulled it toward Eggbert. "How do I feed it to him?"

Eggbert submerged his beak in the slimy liquid without any encouragement, and then tipped his head up to let the egg slide down his gullet.

"I think he's got it handled," said Kale. "Stay with him. I'm going to take a quick look outside."

Kale slunk to the window. Moonlight lit the yard, but even without it, he wouldn't have missed the huddle of chickens off to the side, near the loading platforms. Chickens loaded with travel bags. Men and boys climbed onto the saddled hens. A couple of sleepy toddlers were handed up into the arms of their fathers. From their angle, there was no way to see through the hatchery window. The runaways had no idea the Guardian watched them. Mitch and Gage oversaw over the whole procession, arguing back and forth. Eventually, Mitch threw his marked hands in the air and stalked away from his son. Something must have happened since they'd made their arrangement for Mitch to choose this course of deception. Kale was about to go find out what.

"Kale?" Vera called out, anxiously.

She stood in the middle of the stall, a crease between her brows, and her hand held out to display magic-stained fingertips. The same stain trailed down her cheek. *Stars help us, she's crying tears of healing.* Vera had gotten hold of magic from somewhere.

"We need to get back to our room," Kale said urgently. "Now."

Eggbert was too busy cleaning his bowl to pay any attention to Kale, who was suddenly in his stall. The chick's head was dotted with Vera's tears, the magic already absorbed. Vera's breath caught when Kale brushed away the magic tears from her cheeks with his thumbs. He worked quickly, knowing his nearness made Vera uncomfortable. Grabbing Vera's hand, he towed her out of the stall and latched the gate behind them. Vera slowed to look back at Eggbert. Belly full, the chick was dozing off.

The Monroe men would get away. Right now, Kale had to figure out how Vera was still siphoning magic. More importantly, he had to figure out how to stop it before she siphoned from someone powerful enough to catch her at it.

VERA RUBBED HER EYES AGAIN, but the glowy stuff was gone. Kale locked the door of their room and closed the curtains.

"I can't see in the dark, Kale." Vera stuck out her hands feeling for anything she might run into and ended up groping Kale's pecs when he stepped close.

"And neither can anyone else who might look this way."

Kale captured her hands and lowered them to her sides. "That's what I'm going for right now."

"Oh." Vera's chest rose fast when Kale began unbuttoning her coat. "What are you doing?"

"An experiment."

Mother of butterflies, what just happened in my stomach?

"I can do that," Vera insisted, trying to brush aside his hands.

"It's fine, I've got it. Can you even feel your fingers right now?" Kale popped the next button. "I think you gave me frostbite through my shirt with those things."

"I left my mittens downstairs."

"Was tonight the first night you cried near Eggbert?" asked Kale, unaware of her distress.

The heat of Kale's hands soaked through Vera's nightshirt. Actually, it was Kale's shirt. Vera had stolen it after she'd gotten so tangled up in the lacy gown the witches lent her that she'd fallen out of bed trying to free herself.

"No, it wasn't the first time." Vera screwed up her face, trying to regain control of her senses. "I've been a little weepy around him. A mutilated baby animal seems to do that to me. Sue me."

"Then we know why Eggbert's improved so quickly. You were healing him with magic you didn't know you had." Kale tugged at her coat sleeves. "Take this off. I want to try something."

"I have magic?"

Vera pinched her thigh, desperately trying to keep her mind anywhere other than where it suddenly seemed interested in going. *This is Kale, for freak's sake. Kale!*

"A siphon only has magic by siphoning it. Your charm should block you from doing that, so I want to see if it is failing."

"Which would be bad," Vera said slowly, like she knew what she was talking about.

"If you siphon from a witch powerful enough to notice, yes. Very bad. Run-for-your-life bad."

"Wouldn't I feel something if I was leeching someone's magic?" Vera summoned an image of Gage to her mind to replace her awareness of Kale.

"Maybe. Have you taken the charm off at all since you got it?"

"No." Vera pictured Gage's dark eyes.

"Not even when you bathed?"

"No. *Dammit. Kale has dark eyes. I have no idea what color Gage's eyes are.*

"You're sure?"

"Yes, Kale. I'm sure." She was going to figure out what Gage's eyes looked like ASAP. "I was completely naked, except for my necklace."

"I want to try something," Kale told her.

"It better not involve me getting naked," Vera retorted.

Why did I say that? Obviously, it wouldn't. Right? Gage, Gage, Gage.

Kale released a slow, patient breath that stirred Vera's hair. "Can I see your charm?" he asked calmly.

"You want me to take it off? But you just—"

"Please, Vera." He sounded weary. "You're killing me right now. Can you please just let me see your charm?"

Vera pulled the charm over her head and held it out. Kale was closer than her addled mind realized, and she punched it into his chest.

"Sorry," she mumbled as Kale's fingers brushed hers to take the charm. She yanked her hand back as quickly as she could.

"Hold still, okay?"

Vera was going to ask for more information, but Kale stepped into her and placed his hands on either side of her neck. His thumbs curled over her jaw. The words died on her tongue. Her brain shorted out completely. Vera swallowed hard. A gentle hum began in Vera's toes. It crept up her legs to her thighs. *Holy lucky pennies. No! No lucky anything, Vera.* The hum moved up and up. Her lower stomach tightened. Vera's breath was ragged by the time the hum reached her chest and finally her neck.

Then Kale stepped back, releasing her abruptly. The loss of his touch was painful. Kale swept the hair from Vera's face and looped the charm back over her head, settling it carefully beneath her throat. Vera swayed. When the stone touched her skin, the hum echoing through her blood converged to the spot between her breasts, where the charm rested. The stone heated as the hum left her, flowing into it instead. When the last of the hum was gone, Vera's legs felt boneless. Kale swept her into his arms when she sagged and carried her to the bed. Gently, he laid her against the pillows and tucked the blankets around her. Vera's eyelids were heavy.

"What was that?" Vera asked, her voice breathy.

"That was me feeding you a little magic." Kale placed a hand on her cheek and asked, "Do you feel anything now?"

"That was your magic?" Vera asked.

"I borrowed a little from the Meadow."

"What magic did we use that time with Samhira then? This felt different than that."

"Samhira required a bit more abrasive magic to restrain her. This time, I only used a gentle current. I didn't want to knock you out."

"I appreciate it," she said wryly.

"What do you feel now?" Kale rubbed her cheek.

Kale's hand was warm and soft. Softer than she'd have thought. Gentle for a killer's hands. She wanted to press into his palm. *What is wrong with me?*

"Nothing," Vera answered in a carefully measured voice.

Vera was glad her hands were hidden safely under a thick comforter, and for the darkness to hide her wince. *How in the heck would I explain to him what I'm feeling right now? I can't even explain it to myself. Except as temporary insanity from being high on meadow-magic. Kale's hot, yeah, but he's Kale, come on. He'd laugh his butt off if he knew what was going through my head right now. Heck, I'd laugh too if I weren't so freaked out. Do I have Stockholm syndrome? Even though, technically, he didn't kidnap me? I mean, crushing on my mass murderer-turned-bodyguard, that's got to be a syndrome too, right? Oh man. If Gage is a bad idea, Kale is the mother of bad ideas.*

"Well, the charm does stop you from siphoning magic," Kale said. "Without it, you suck up magic just fine. With it, you can't."

"Then how come I was crying lightning-bug juice?"

"My guess? You aren't just a siphon. You're something else too, but I don't know what that is yet."

"Yay, I'm a mutt," Vera said with a yawn.

"I've been assuming that every magical act you've performed was from siphoning magic, but I think you're creating your own magic too. I don't know what's what anymore with you. Except your healing tears, those must be one of your natural abilities."

"Creating magic?"

"Some magical beings, like witches, enchanters, and sorcerers are magic manipulators, harvest and control magic threads in an endless number of ways. Other beings, like trolls, sirens, and dwarves, are made of magic and create their own magic to use for a few specialized tricks."

"You said siphons don't have their own magic," reminded Vera.

"They don't. Or they didn't used to anyway." Kale gave a rueful laugh. "You're a walking contradiction."

"Explain."

"At first, you were human and innocent. Two things that don't naturally belong together. You've got an attitude that cuts like ice, but you have a heart that warms like a flame. Now, it turns out you're both siphon and magical. Whenever I think I have you figured out, you go and throw something else at me."

"If I didn't know better, I might think you like me a little," Vera said.

"Like is a strong word," teased Kale. "You are growing on me, though. I guess I'm glad I decided to stay your execution."

"I can't believe you would've killed me just because I'm human."

"You're not human anymore."

"Nope, I'm a freak like you now."

"No one's a freak quite like me," said Kale. "Now get some sleep. Eggbert's going to want breakfast in a few hours."

"We can stay here for a little longer then?" asked Vera.

"If there's anyone here sensitive enough to notice you have magic, they won't be surprised because most outsiders do. Even if they don't recognize your brand of magic. The problem only comes up if you siphon magic and get caught. Since you can't siphon, you're fine. Maybe keep the healing waterworks in check, though. Preventing people from killing you is hard enough, I don't need to worry about people wanting to keep you." Kale stood to leave her.

"Take one of the comforters," Vera said, closing her eyes.

"I'm fine."

"Don't be dumb. You were shivering like crazy earlier."

"You were watching me sleep?" Kale asked with exaggerated shock. "You know that's creepy, right?"

"Says the man who plotted to kill me."

"I plot to kill everyone. I just don't actually do it most of the time. So you're not that special," Kale informed her.

"What's scary is you aren't lying."

"How would you know?" asked Kale.

Vera pretended to be asleep until she didn't need to pretend anymore.

12

Vera felt like she'd just closed her eyes.

"Vera," Kale called gently from nearby. "Wake up, Vera. Come on. I'm hungry." Vera groaned and cracked open one eye. "The sun isn't even up yet."

"They've got donuts. We're going to miss out if we don't hurry," Kale said.

He was such a liar. If there were donuts, she'd have headed for the door in a heartbeat. Instead, Vera pulled the pillow over her head and curled into a tighter ball.

"Gage is here to see you," said Kale, the lying jerkwad.

"Go away. Leave me alone."

Kale was quiet for a minute. Vera dozed off.

"I'm going to lick you," Kale said beside her pillow.

Not a lie. Vera ducked her head and scrambled to the other side of the bed.

"What is wrong with you? Are you ten or something?"

"Well, then." Kale perched on the edge of the bed, looking rather irritated by the silly insult. "I don't suppose you have anything interesting to share about yourself with the class?"

"Um, I really don't like being dragged out of bed by a jerk." Vera blinked hard, trying to see straight.

"Tell me, Vera. Do you have the hots for Gage?"

"What? No." *Ow.* It was too early to have those gongs going off in her head.

"I can't believe I didn't figure it out sooner." Kale pinched the bridge of his nose.

"I just met Gage yesterday," Vera protested.

"I'm not talking about your love-sick chicken boy. You know that game, two truths and a lie? We just played two lies and a truth. You performed remarkably well. Licking you was the most preposterous thing I could come up with. But I couldn't fool you, could I?"

Vera's stomach dropped.

"Ah, you've finally caught up," Kale observed. "So how does it work exactly? It must be tough not even being able to lie to yourself."

Vera's first instinct was to deny any understanding of what he was talking about. Kale looked down at her hands resting on the bed. *Crap.*

"Fine." Vera threw her hands in the air. "It sounds like bells going off in my head. Big bells. When I lie, it's like I've shoved my whole head inside a freaking church bell."

"How long have you been able to hear lies?"

"All my life."

"Interesting. Another natural magic ability you have, which means you've been producing a tiny amount of magic all your life. No wonder you've had a tough time with the wrong kind of people. You've been attracting would-be magic addicts without knowing it."

"Good to know being a sleazeball magnet wasn't just in my head." Vera held up her hands, twisting them back and forth for Kale's inspection. "Happy?"

"Actually, yes. Now get dressed. We're going to breakfast."

"Why are you happy?" Vera asked warily.

"What's wrong with being happy?"

"Nothing. Unless you happen to be you. Then it's suspicious."

"You don't want me to be happy?" Kale asked with mock offence.

"I want to know *why* you're happy."

"Because I have my own lie detector and no one knows it."

"You can already tell truth from lies."

"No, I know when someone intends to deceive me. It's different. A person can lie without deceiving. Like you not telling me about your little superpower. Obviously, you weren't being deceptive or trying to use your ability to deceive me, you just didn't want to tell me. On the other hand, people can also deceive without lying. It's all about intention. But since people know what I can do, they hide their hands."

"Make them take off their gloves, oh-scary Guardian."

"I can't, not without breaking an agreement I made yesterday. Well technically, they've already broken our agreement, based on the midnight event I saw last night. But no one knows I'm aware of that, and I don't want to show my hand yet. Not since I have you and don't need to."

"What agreement? What happened last night?"

"An agreement that doesn't affect you."

"Are you for-real right now with the lying?" Vera scowled.

"I was just checking."

"Lie."

"I think I preferred your silent scowls when I lied to you

before. When you couldn't argue without revealing your little secret."

"I think I prefer getting to call you on all your BS." Vera bared her teeth in a mockery of a smile.

"It's obnoxious."

"So are you when you're evading my questions. What agreement did you make?"

Kale sighed. "The Monroes gave you one day to work your magic on Eggbert, which turned out quite literally to be magic. In return, I gave Mitch a day's head start to find me a lead before I step in and do things my way."

"Oh." Now Vera felt like the jerk.

"Do you smell that?" Kale asked.

"Smell what?" Vera raised her nose to sniff the air. "I think someone's burned breakfast."

A scream echoed through the walls. Up and down the hall, doors began to open and slam. People were running.

"There's a fire," said Kale. "Hurry."

Vera had fallen asleep with her pants on so Kale grabbed her shoes and coat and ushered her out the door, into the stream of families hurrying down the stairs. At the bottom, Kale pulled Vera into the kitchen, which seemed the likeliest place for a fire to be raging. And the worst direction to go.

"Shouldn't we follow those guys?" Vera hooked her thumb toward the back door where parents led their children outside.

"The fire is already out," replied Kale.

"Oh, good. How do you know that?"

"No smoke. But someone was burned. That's what that smell is."

"And we're gonna go check it out," she concluded. "Obviously."

Kale didn't respond but pressed on. Vera lifted her shirt over her nose, feeling ill. As a precaution, Vera made sure Kale's back would block her view once they got to the end of the hallway. She was not prepared to see a charred body in this lifetime. Someone hurried around the corner and ran into them. A woman mumbled sorry then realized who she'd bumped into and stumbled back. It was the woman from the garden. This time, she was definitely glowing. She glowed all the way out the back door as she ran away, throwing one last terrified glance in Kale's direction. He didn't seem to notice. It turned out, the woman wasn't the only glow-worm around. A middle-aged woman, with tear tracks through the soot on her face, sat on a stool while a witch wrapped her arms in white bandages. The hands of the young witch glowed faintly. It wasn't quite as dense as the magic mist Vera had seen at the palace, but Vera knew that's what it was—magic. Kale stopped after a few more steps.

"Mitch," Kale said.

Vera's heart stuttered. She braced herself and peeked around Kale. Mitch laid on his back on a dining table. One side of his face was red like a sunburn and half his hair was missing. Down Mitch's neck, the red became blistered. His shirt had been removed, showing the same blistered red down most of his chest. Two women, whose hands and fore-arms glowed, had wrapped Mitch's arms to the elbows in the same cloths as the other burned woman.

"Did you do this to yourself?" asked Kale flatly.

Vera gaped at Kale. What kind of people was Kale used to dealing with to think something like that?

"How dare you," growled one of the glow-women.

"It's okay," rasped Mitch to the woman. To Kale, he said, "No."

Kale twisted to look at Vera. He wanted to know if Mitch was telling the truth. Vera nodded.

"You're sure?" Kale asked her.

"Uh, yeah. You really thought he'd do that to himself?"

"It crossed my mind."

The offended woman said, "Listen here, Guardian. Mitch is the reason my sister is not lying here in his place. Or dead. You can—"

"Your sister? Is she the woman over there with the burned arm?" Kale asked.

"Yes. The pan caught fire with no warning. If Mitch hadn't acted so quickly..." The woman sniffled.

"Was anyone else nearby?" asked Kale.

"Liah," said Mitch.

"Liah wasn't anywhere around, Mitch," said the woman. "I was there."

"Liah fed chickens. Wasn't her turn." Mitch labored to speak clearly.

"Okay, that's enough," said the other woman, speaking up for the first time. "Mitch needs to heal. He's not thinking straight through the pain. Please, Guardian."

Mitch mumbled something, shaking his head.

"Dad?" Gage's cheeks were red from cold when he rushed into the room.

"You're right," Kale told the women. "We'll go."

Kale turned Vera by the shoulders, nudging her to leave. Vera hesitated, eyeing Gage. The poor man. Vera wanted to help him.

"Careful," Kale whispered mockingly into Vera's hair. "Don't want to make it too obvious."

"Shut up," Vera mumbled, blushing.

She could feel Kale laughing at her as she marched from the room without looking back a second time.

KALE STOOD on the bedside table, one foot braced against the far wall, trying to catch a butterfly with a basket from the wardrobe. The butterfly had been resting on the center of the bed when they'd returned to the room. Vera had oohed and aahed, seeming to forget that she was angry with Kale for steering her away from Gage. Kale had been less enthusiastic at the sight of the winged bug. They hadn't left a window open, so it hadn't gotten in by mistake.

"Don't hurt it," Vera said, tugging on Kale's pant leg.

"I'm not going to hurt it."

Kale swiped with the basket and missed. The butterfly flitted across the room. Kale stepped down from the bed, waiting for it to land again.

"What color is that?" Vera asked.

"Aejoh," he answered.

"A-Joe," Vera repeated. "It looks strange. Red and green but neither of those. Not brown either, but red and green make brown."

"It's not a color that exists in your realm. It's a shade of magic."

The insect landed on a wall. Kale inched toward it, just as the butterfly started to pump its wings. He swooped in, trapping it beneath the basket.

"Now what?" Vera asked.

"Now, you need to get dressed." Kale wiggled the basket's lid under the rim, careful to not lift the edge high enough for the thing to escape.

Vera lifted an uncooperative brow.

"If you get dressed, we can let the butterfly go by the stream and look for eggs to feed your overgrown chick," Kale amended.

That made her compliant. Vera grabbed the pile of borrowed clothes and hurried into the bathroom. Kale sat on the edge of the bed with the basket on his lap. He cracked the lid. The butterfly fluttered its wings. Slowly, Kale lowered his hand into the basket and waited. Sure enough, after a couple more wing flaps, the butterfly walked onto his hand and spread its wings flat. Kale pushed the lid away and lifted the messenger out.

Kale inhaled through his nose and gently blew across the butterfly's wings. As his breath brushed across, they sparked, igniting a flare of violet script that swept and curved across the wings. The butterfly had a message for him. *Threadbearers dying. Danger Monroes. Corydalis. Moonset.* The words flared only once then burned away. Kale placed the butterfly back in the basket. Now that the message was received, the butterfly would fly home once it was released.

Corydalis flowers bloomed at the edge of the Velvet Woods this time of year. It didn't narrow down exactly where this mysterious informant wanted to meet, but Kale assumed they'd be watching for him. They'd show up wherever along the forest edge he chose. Without knowing who this person was, Kale couldn't risk taking Vera with him. Nor could he leave her safely behind. What he wouldn't give for one of the magicked doors from the palace to lock everyone out, but more importantly, lock her safely in. Hopefully, he'd figure out what the message meant before he had to decide what to do about it.

"Hey Kale," Vera began as she exited the bathroom. "Why does magic here look different than the Elite's magic?"

"You can see magic?" Kale asked with surprise.

"Yeah, I figured everyone could."

"Nope. Add that to our list of your magical oddities."

"Any closer to figuring out what I am?"

"Not yet," he said. "What does magic look like to you?"

"Back at the palace, it looked like colored mist."

"And the witches here?"

"A whitish glow. Some glow bright, others not so much. The women healing Mitch glowed up to their elbows. Only that one girl gets all glowy, like a glow-worm."

"Which girl?" asked Kale.

"The one who ran into us downstairs before."

"Of course. The one running away from a magical crime scene."

"Crime scene sounds pretty serious," Vera said.

"A fire has to feed on something, but this one barely charred anything. If it fed on magic, it would explain why there was no smoke and no damage."

"You think someone set Mitch on fire?"

"Maybe Mitch has a secret." Kale handed the basket to Vera. "Do me a favor and point out that glow-worm next time you see her. And be careful around Gage. He's hiding something too."

"That's two favors," Vera pointed out. "I don't think Gage is dangerous."

"I do."

"I'll take your opinion into consideration," Vera said flippantly.

"How'd that make your head feel?" asked Kale.

"Peachy, because I wasn't lying. I considered your opinion and decided to ignore it unless you have a real reason for not liking Gage."

Kale was quiet, letting Vera think she'd won. He hadn't had a chance to tell her about the exodus of Monroe men last night. And he wasn't going to so long as the people involved were being targeted. Kale wished he knew what

Mitch and Gage had been arguing about out there under the moonlight.

"Ready to find Eggbert some breakfast?" Kale asked.

"Yes." Vera bounced excitedly on her toes. If Gage's secret hurt her, Kale would kill the man slowly.

13

Vera peered through the duck egg Kale held up to the sun.

"See, no baby duckies," he confirmed.

"I still feel kind of bad about stealing them." Vera chewed her bottom lip.

"Mama duck will lay a new clutch. This nest smells like me now anyway, so they'll be abandoned."

"Something you knew would happen before you touched them in the first place." Vera rolled her eyes.

"Guilty. Are you going to release that butterfly so we have a way to carry these?" Kale picked up a second egg.

Vera pulled the lid off the basket. The butterfly was still until Vera shook the basket gently. Then it pumped its wings and lifted into the air. Wobbling on the breeze, it hovered for a minute before following the stream back toward the farm. Had the butterfly flown the other way, it would've headed for the lake instead. A wedge of glistening water peeked between the bluff walls at the opposite end of the pass.

"Don't get yourself eaten by a giant chicken going that way," Vera murmured.

"Are you talking to a butterfly?" Kale raised a brow.

"It's no weirder than talking to you." Vera stuck out her tongue and handed Kale the empty basket.

"Touché. Make yourself useful and find another nest. We'll need twice this many to have enough until you wean Eggbert off eggs."

Vera wandered down the rocky streambed, checking under shrubs and behind outcroppings as Kale had done. The smell of juniper and musty soil rose into the air as Vera used her foot to part the thick shrubs. When Vera bent to peak under a tall scraggly shrub near the sheer cliff walls, a pointy red face bared its teeth at her, growling low. Vera jumped back with a yelp and raced back down the bank. Kale had crossed to the other side of the stream. He looked up sharply.

"What happened?" Kale stepped up to the water's edge.

"There's a fox in that bush." Vera scanned the bank for the ferocious animal.

"You do have terrible luck, don't you?" Kale chuckled. "Foxes aren't usually this far from the mountains so early in the year."

"It's not going to come after me, is it?"

"You probably scared it away. But maybe you should come to this side of the stream, just in case."

"How do you suggest I do that?" Vera eyed the water, which was at least waist-deep and twice as wide as she was tall.

"It's pretty narrow here. Jump."

"Yeah, that's not happening. Have you seen how short my legs are?" Vera planted her hands on her hips.

"Every time I want you to move faster," Kale answered.

"There's a rocky ledge farther down you can use to get across."

Vera scowled but followed the stream to the rocks Kale pointed out. There was a section of rough water with four stones peeking out of the water at uneven intervals. The one in the center was only as big as her foot.

"This is snowmelt, isn't it?" asked Vera, the chill from the water wafting over her face.

"And we do not have an extra set of clothes," Kale said. "So no swimming or getting naked will be involved this time." He was laughing at her.

"Maybe I should stay over here and make friends with the fox. See how fast you get your protector-butt wet getting over here to save me when I get mauled," Vera suggested irritably.

"You're being absurd."

"You're being a dick."

Kale turned stony, waiting impatiently for Vera to get her big-girl panties on. Trying not to think too much about how many shades of wrong things could go, Vera stepped onto the first stone. The second was a stretch, but Vera made it just fine. On the third stone—the itty-bitty one—Vera's heart spiked while she balanced on one foot in the middle of the stream. Icy mist puffed up her pant leg. One more step and it was an easy hop to the other side, but that last rock turned out to be a problem. While the stone appeared big and solid, it was unstable. As soon as Vera put all her weight on the rock, it wobbled. Unfortunately, she'd already committed, and there was no way to get back to the tiny rock without a swim. Vera windmilled her arms, trying to regain her balance, the rock shifting beneath her feet.

Kale grabbed a fistful of Vera's tunic and yanked her forward just as she lost the fight for balance and fell backward. He didn't worry about being gentle either. Vera slammed into him. The hand he'd tangled into Vera's shirt ended up pressed between them. Right up against Vera's pounding heart. Kale's other hand pressed into Vera's hip where he steadied her. Neither of them moved. Vera's face was plastered against Kale's chest. Kale seemed to be breathing hard too. Feeling Kale's body against hers only sped up Vera's frigging traitor-of-a-heart. Vera's stomach flipped. *Aww, crap on a sexy cracker.* Vera lurched back, and submerged her foot into ice water.

She gasped, jerking away from both Kale and the stream. Cursing the Lady up and down, Vera shook the water from her shoe. Silently, she was cursing herself. At least the wet foot gave her an excuse to not look at Kale for the moment. *Holy nightmare, Vera!* Admittedly, she didn't have much experience with men, but this was a definite sign that she needed to spend some time with a man other than Kale. Before she lost her mind. Or her dignity.

"Come on." Kale headed into a shallow alcove. "I found another nest just before you started shrieking like a banshee."

Vera followed, gritting her teeth with each squelchy step.

"You checked them, right?" Vera asked as Kale added an egg to the basket.

Kale lifted an egg to the sun. "They're good."

Vera held her tongue while Kale transferred the rest of the eggs to the basket. His shoulders were tense when he stood. Without warning, Kale grabbed Vera and pressed her into a crouch, setting the basket off to the side.

"Shh." Kale pointed down the pass.

Vera followed his finger and saw a woman picking her way along the streambed. The woman looked over her shoulder a few times and cast long glances toward the bluffs above.

"That's the glow-worm woman," Vera whispered. "She's not glowing now but that's her."

Kale placed a hand on Vera's lips as the woman drew closer. His leg, pressed against Vera's, tensed.

"Stay," Kale ordered as he rose to his feet and stepped into the woman's path.

Glow-woman startled. She looked at Kale, and then past him toward the end of the pass. If Vera had to guess, the lady was wondering if she could outrun Kale. Vera would tell her the answer was no. The woman didn't run so she must have realized that for herself.

"Out for a walk?" Kale asked pleasantly.

The woman did not respond.

"All right then. Care to show me your hands?" asked Kale.

"My hands are bare. I'm sure you see them well enough," the woman replied flatly.

"Yes, I can see deception written across your fingers and curling up the backs of your hands to disappear beneath your sleeves. But what I'd like to see are the palms of your hands."

"Why?"

The hands Kale and the woman were discussing began to glow. The glow deepened, spreading past the woman's wrists and all the way to her neck.

"Because I'm looking for a bloodstone brand."

The woman slowly lifted her hands, palms down. The glow intensified.

"She's going to use her magic on you," Vera called out, rising from her crouch.

The woman's eyes widened with surprise at Vera's

sudden appearance. Kale quickly grabbed Vera and tucked her behind him.

"Yes, I figured she would," Kale said tightly. "That's why I told you to stay put."

"Oh. Whoops."

The woman didn't blast them. Instead, she rotated her hands to show off unbranded palms.

"She didn't kill Cassie," Vera said, earning an annoyed look from Kale.

"Cassie's dead?" the woman asked with alarm.

Kale nodded once.

The woman moaned, threaded both hands into her hair, and pulled the strands while pressing in on her head at the same time. The woman turned her back to Vera and Kale. Her glow flared as she screamed. Part of the bluff wall popped, and then crumbled with a roar to the streambed. *She caused a freaking landslide by screaming.* Vera stared with wide eyes while Kale tried to nudge her safely behind him once more. Startled by the noise and dust, the fox from earlier darted out of his hidey hole.

"No!" cried the woman, spinning back toward the two of them with a wildness in her eyes. "Stop her. Don't let her get away."

Vera gave Kale a what-the-hell look when he swooped to pick up a stone the size of his palm. Without looking, Kale pulled back his arm and winged the stone over the landslide debris. Vera wondered what he hoped to achieve since the fox had disappeared already. A pained yelp followed, answering Vera's unasked question. She covered her mouth with both hands. Kale had killed the fox. Blindly. With only a pebble.

"What's your name?" Kale asked the woman, unruffled by what had just transpired.

"Liah," The woman rubbed away her tears, leaving streaks of grime.

"Liah, I need you to answer a few questions." Kale hadn't flinched at the name, but Vera was sure he recognized it from Mitch's babbling that morning.

"I did it," Liah said simply and without prompting.

That was unexpected. And way too easy. Then again, this Liah woman was obviously nuts. Nuts enough to create an unnatural army on Earth and poison her own people.

"What did you do?" Kale asked Liah.

"I set the fire. I tried to kill Mitch."

Also not what Vera had expected.

"Why?" Kale asked, unaffected.

"To stop him from talking to you."

"About what?" pressed Kale.

"I cannot say. Too many lives are at risk." Liah scratched her arm anxiously.

"Are you afraid of what I'd do if I knew?" Kale asked.

"No, you're not the one I'm afraid of."

Well, that can't be good. What's scarier than Kalesius, Terror of the World?

"Who are you afraid of?" asked Kale.

"The fox in the hen-house," Liah replied.

"Did a fox raid the nest a few days ago?" Vera asked, finding her tongue. "Is that what happened to the chick in the hatchery?"

"No fox did that," said Liah.

"You know who raided the nest?" asked Kale.

"Not a who. A what," said Liah. "A what did that. A what that is not from Summartir. Not from anywhere. Not supposed to exist."

"How did the what get to Summartir, Liah?" asked Kale

"I cannot say. The fox might hear me."

"The fox is dead," reminded Vera.

Liah pressed her lips together, refusing to speak about it.

"Did you help feed the chickens the day before *the what* raided the nest?" asked Kale.

"Yes. She asked me to."

"Who asked you to?" Kale asked

"I don't know." Liah shrugged.

"You don't know who asked you to feed the chickens?" Kale frowned.

"She didn't tell me her name. I did not see her face."

"She's not a member of the Monroe family?" asked Kale.

"No," Liah said irritably. "I know all the Monroes. I'm not stupid. She has no home."

"Do you know how we can find her?" Kale kept his voice smooth and soothing. He was good at this interrogating thing.

"No, she is hiding. She hides among the witches, but she is the most powerful."

"Why did she ask you to feed the chickens?" asked Kale.

"To save the hen house."

"But that did not save them," Vera pointed out.

"It will," said Liah confidently.

"Did she ask you to feed them something special?" asked Kale

"Yes, I had to go all the way to the edge of the fields to find it. But I did. Now we will be safe."

"Did she make milktooth poison?" asked Kale

"She had to," Liah said as though this should be obvious.

"Why did she have to? Who was it for?" asked Kale

Liah smiled a sly smile that sent chills up Vera's spine. "You already know that, Guardian."

"Was it for the Maiden?" Kale guessed.

"No," Liah frowned, becoming agitated. "That's not the plan. That's not the plan!"

"Shh," said Kale gently. "The Maiden is okay."

"She is not okay," yelled Liah.

"She will be, though," assured Kale. "The Maiden will be okay."

"Yes," said Liah. "She will be. We will all be okay."

Holy smokes, the woman was certifiable. Yet everything Liah said was the truth. Or at least the truth as Liah saw it. The woman hadn't lied once, even though everything that came out of her mouth was nonsense. Suddenly, Vera's heart ached for the woman.

"Who did she tell you the poison was for?" Kale rephrased his question.

"Her." Liah pointed at Vera. "I need to go. My son is hungry."

"Why poison Vera?" asked Kale

"To save the hen-house," Liah said, scratching her arm harder. "I already told you all this."

"One more question, and we'll take you back to the farm, okay?" said Kale.

"Okay."

"Do you know what Vera is?"

"Vera is not a what. Vera is a who. She does not want Vera here. It makes her scared."

Liah's words knocked the air from Vera's lungs. A buzzing sound started between her ears. Somehow, the witch they were hunting knew Vera was in Summartir and wanted her dead.

"We'll walk with you back to the farm," Kale said to Liah. "We do have to tell the family what you've done."

"I know." Liah smiled a bitter-sweet smile. "They won't understand, but it's all right. I had to save us all."

KALE EYED MITCH'S BANDAGES. With magic stores as they were, the witches could not afford to heal the man any faster. They'd done enough to prevent infection and mini-mize scarring. The rest was up to Mitch's body. Until then, proof of Mitch's deception remained hidden from Kale. In the meantime, Kale noticed that the motivation behind Liah's attack had gone unquestioned. Kale still had to figure out if it had anything to do with the unnaturals on Earth. Everyone in the family who might have given Kale some of the answers he needed was either hiding or gone. All of them smuggled away by Mitch, a man who'd not intended to deceive Kale a day ago.

Kale kept himself calm by sheer will. Sinking his hand into Mitch's burned flesh and squeezing until the man answered for himself was tempting. It would accomplish nothing, though, except to ensure hostility from the rest of the family. And he needed their cooperation since he couldn't very well torture them all. Well, he could, but he'd given up those methods centuries ago. At this point, whoever had sent that butterfly was Kale's best lead.

"I'm probably not as surprised as I ought to be," Mitch said, after a few family heads escorted Liah to her apart-ment until they decided what to do with their errant member.

"What happened to her?" Vera asked Mitch curiously. "Has she always been like that?"

"You mean has she always been paranoid and delusional?"

"I didn't mean—"

"It's fine," Mitch assured. "No, Liah wasn't always like that. She's my niece, my brother's daughter. Liah grew up an ornery little girl, for sure, always looking for the next adventure. She preferred sneaking out with the boys to watch the worms hunt over playing with the girls. Too smart for her own good. Figured out a way to get her cousins to do most of her chores by the time she was ten. When the High Crone visited to find a new handmaiden, Liah jumped out of her seat to volunteer. Literally. Her mama about had a heart attack. Most of the family was scared to death that Liah would drive the Crone mad and earn us a curse for generations. But the Crone's eyes lit on Liah, and she barely looked at anyone else the family put forward."

"That girl was over the moon to get away from the farm. Instead of wearing the Crone out, she brought the High Witch's youth back. The two were partners in crime. When the Crone rested for her seasons, Liah came home, but she was never content here. She packed her bags weeks before the Crone's return each year. Then one winter, Liah returned changed. That season, the Crone had been ill and Liah caught it. No one realized how sick she was until she'd been missing for a couple of days. The Crone was so ill herself that she didn't notice Liah's absence. By then, Liah was out of her mind, babbling about the monsters. When she came home, it was like something had broken her soul."

"Soon, we learned Liah was expecting a baby. And that baby turned out to be two—twin boys. She told us the father was not someone in a position to be a father. She planned to raise the boys alone. Waiting for those boys to come gave Liah back some of her old self. Shortly after they were born, Liah started having nightmares. Dreams about animals following her. She was exhausted but insisted she didn't want help. One afternoon, she fell asleep while the boys played together on a blanket in the sun. She woke to one of the boys crying and alone. His brother had scooted away and ingested some berries that an animal must have scattered there. That baby was gone. Liah never talked about her nightmares again after that, but I know they still haunt her."

By the end of the story, Mitch was pale and deflated. Vera and Kale left him to rest.

"So, we need to find the most powerful witch hiding among other witches," said Vera as they walked down the hall toward the hatchery. "A witch who summoned unnaturals—the things not of this realm, which should not exist—to Summartir. Had them raid a nest for poison ingredients in order to kill me because she's scared of me. Oh, and she's a witch-bitch who takes advantage of broken women. She manipulated Liah into becoming her accomplice by convincing her that she was saving her people. Which Liah needs to believe because she couldn't save her own son. Am I missing anything?"

"Sounds about right," said Kale.

"Now what? We go back to the palace and see who's the most powerful witch among witches?"

"I already cleared the most powerful witches at the palace. She's not there."

"Or you missed something." Vera's voice cracked.

"Hey, it's okay. We're getting closer," assured Kale.

"It doesn't feel like it."

"Not right now, but we know more than we did a few days ago. Tomorrow we'll know more." Because he was going to make sure Vera was sound asleep that night, and then go meet his mystery informant. He'd be back before Vera was awake, and he'd make sure to have a clear view of her window the whole time. If he left the window cracked, he'd even be able to listen in on her while she slept. A bit of meadow magic woven into her so he could track her, and hopefully, that would be enough. Although, with Vera, nothing would probably ever be enough.

"By the way, I can't believe you killed that fox," Vera said, pulling herself together.

"I didn't."

"What?" Vera shot him an incredulous look.

"I just knocked it out for a bit. She's fine."

"I really didn't think you'd have an issue with killing it."

"Don't get the wrong idea about my morals, Vera. I am fine with killing a fox. Or doing just about anything to fulfill my responsibilities."

"Then why didn't you kill it?"

"I'm trying to think of a good lie," he said when Vera grew impatient with his silence and waved a hand to get his attention.

"I'll just call you out."

"Which is why I'm having a hard time." Kale sighed. "I didn't kill it because I knew you wouldn't want me to."

Vera tried to look away, but Kale caught the shimmer in her eyes.

"Apparently, that makes you sad," Kale teased gently.

"Shut up." Vera rolled her eyes then reached out and squeezed his hand. "Thank you."

Kale's heart lifted. "You're welcome."

14

Kale stood motionless just inside the Velvet Woods, arms folded over his chest. The moon had slid behind the bluffs nearly an hour before. He'd been tapping a finger against his leg until a pack of worms peeked from the undergrowth, assessing whether they could eat him. Embedding one of Vera's blades into the pack leader's head had dissuaded them. Vera would be unhappy if she found her knife missing in a few hours. He was going to have to retrieve the slimed blade from the worm's corpse, clean it, and take it back to her. The prospect made him irritable. Worm slime burned like acid.

Kale clenched his jaw impatiently, listening through the hum of beetles and rustling of leaves for the approach of his informant. He nudged a strand of meadow-magic through Vera's window and listened to her breathing deeply and evenly. Just when he decided the informant must have changed their mind, there was a scuffle through the trees. And it was getting closer. Whoever was coming, they were moving fast, unconcerned with concealing their presence. Kale plucked the blade from the worm's head.

He swiped it through the grass to get off the worst of the mess. His hand burned. If the person headed his way turned out to be a threat, they'd be too dead to mind the dirty blade.

A woman emerged from the trees, dressed in black with a black scarf over most of her face. She staggered in a circle, looking for something. Or possibly for him. Kale didn't immediately move forward.

"Guardian," called the woman, dragging a hand over the scarf to reveal her face.

Kale dropped the knife and hurried from his lookout to catch the High Maiden under her arm before she fell.

"Are you being pursued?" Kale positioned himself between the witch and the woods. "Why are you on foot?"

"A pack of worms took my hen. There is no one else."

"Your magic couldn't chase them away?"

"The poison." The Maiden swayed. "I don't remember..."

"You're still healing. Why did you come alone?"

"The Monroes are in danger. I need to find the last threadbearers before it is too late. I don't know who I can trust," the Maiden explained.

"In danger? Not the source of the danger?" *Diyu, I had it wrong.* "Is one of them a threadbearer?"

The Maiden's eyes rolled back into her head as she collapsed. Kale scooped her up easily and headed toward the farm. If the Monroes hid one of the last threadbearers, then Kale didn't have to figure out where the betrayer was hiding. That witch was coming for them.

VERA WOKE to a knock at the door. *What is wrong with people? Doesn't anyone sleep until the sun is up?*

"Kale? You get that?" Vera groaned when the person knocked again. "Kale?"

No response. A quick survey of the room and Vera knew why—Kale was not there.

"Vera?" called Gage softly through the door.

Welp, that got her awake. Vera kicked off her blankets and rolled out of bed. She didn't exactly dash to the door—her legs weren't that coordinated yet—but she stumbled as fast as she could. Hand on the door, Vera acknowledged that Kale would not approve. *He'll be furious when he gets back. From wherever he's gone without letting me know. Yep, forget him.* Vera opened the door.

"Sorry, it's Eggbert..." Gage's eyes widened, dipping to take in Vera's nightshirt before flicking back to her eyes.

"What's wrong?" asked Vera. "Is he okay?"

"Where's the Guardian?" Gage looked past Vera for the man in question.

"I don't know. Who cares?" Vera waved her hands dismissively. "What's wrong with Eggbert?"

"He's digging at the straw and ready to go outside, but I didn't want to throw him in with the flock until we know how they'll react to him. I thought you might want to come with us to the Woods so he can scratch for worms before they go underground for the day."

Gage did not take a breath in that entire spiel. *Poor flustered man.* Vera bit her lip to keep from grinning. Her shirt came down halfway to her knees. Girls wore shorter dresses than that every day. Just not in Summartir. Gage cleared his throat, suddenly interested in the doorframe above their heads. Then the words, "woods" and "worms" sank in.

"You are not taking Eggbert to those woods," Vera said, sharper than she'd meant. "Those things would eat him. And me."

"They won't attack when a chicken is nearby. Even a little one," Gage said.

"Yeah, that's what Kale said. I still have dried slime on my shoe that proves you both wrong."

"I didn't know you'd had a run-in." Gage was slowly relaxing. "I'm sure it was a fluke."

"Or really bad luck," Vera said. "Can we take him somewhere else? The lake?"

"Sure. That'd be a good place to find some frogs and mice."

"He eats mice?"

"Yep. He'll like those as much as the eggs you've been sneaking him." Gage winked.

"You know about that." Vera winced.

"I figured it out."

"Kale said you guys wouldn't like him eating eggs."

"It's not a good idea. But it was the first thing that worked for Eggbert, so I let it go."

"If it works so well, why don't you allow it?" asked Vera

"When a chicken eats eggs, they can get a taste for them and go after nests."

"What if that happens to Eggbert?"

"He'll have to be adopted out immediately or be put down," Gage said seriously.

"Someone would adopt him, though, right?"

"Hopefully, it won't be an issue. But maybe cut him off from here on?"

"Absolutely." Vera nodded. "Give me two minutes to get dressed and we can go."

Vera's words reminded Gage of her attire. He blushed. Vera shut the door, ripped off the shirt, and threw it across the bed. On went another set of white-on-whites. Pulling on shoes, Vera realized her knife was gone. It was not under the bed or in the wardrobe. Kale must have it. Vera had not been without a knife since Errock. When Vera saw Kale next, he was not going to be the only one with a bone to pick.

"I'M FINE," the Maiden insisted from the bed in her commandeered room.

"Is she fine?" Kale asked the Monroe witch assessing the Maiden as they spoke.

"From everything I can tell, yes. The Maiden simply ran her body past exhaustion."

"Is there anything you can do to help her?" asked Kale.

"Magic cannot fix fatigue. She needs rest," said the witch.

"Then you can leave." Kale opened the door for the witch. "Go use your talents where they are needed—get Mitch back on his feet. There's no time to let him heal naturally anymore."

The witch spluttered, looking back and forth between Kale and the Maiden. Kale considered the few people loitering in the hall. They'd been making breakfast preparations for the day when he'd carried the Maiden through the front doors.

"If any of you reveals the Maiden's presence here before the Maiden is ready to announce it herself, you will get a visit from me. The family heads are the only ones to know for now. Do you understand?" Kale looked at each person in turn until they nodded. "Now, out before I toss you out," Kale told the reluctant witch healer firmly.

"That was cruel of you," Maiden said after everyone scurried away. "To scare them like that."

"This place is the worst gossip-mill I've ever seen,"

Kale informed the Maiden. "If I hadn't scared them, you'd have a steady stream of well-wishers until sunset. And no rest."

"Well, I don't want that." Maiden covered a yawn.

"No sane person would."

"I appreciate your vote of confidence in my sanity after what you've seen today."

"How many threadbearers are gone?" Kale asked.

"Cassie was the first. I didn't know she was a threadbearer until I felt her threads fall away while I was in and out of my mind from the poison. Eleven others were murdered the day you left. All were members of the triads. They met in secret to honor Cassie's service to the realms in this life. A tradition of the threadbearers none knew about except them."

"Which means only two realms remain double-bound," said Kale.

"Summartir and Earth," the Maiden confirmed.

"Do you know who holds the threads?"

"No. But they are rumored to be Monroes, Summartir's most beloved subjects."

"I'll talk to the Monroe family heads and see if they can identify the threadbearers," said Kale. "I may already know who one is. Once I know for sure, I'll lock the threadbearers up with Vera to keep them safe if I need to."

"Where is your charge, by the way?" the Maiden asked, eyes slipping closed.

"Sleeping." Kale frowned, noticing the pink sunrise through the window. "I should check on her. You rest."

EGGBERT SNAPPED UP ANOTHER MAYFLY. Vera cringed. A

tentacle hung from his beak before floating to the ground. He'd eaten more bugs and frogs than Vera could count.

"You're disgusting, Berty." Vera patted the chick's head affectionately when he rubbed against her leg.

Something caught Eggbert's attention near the water. He raced across the rocky bank to chase it down. Vera shivered. The sun had come up, but the bluffs still shadowed the lake. She shuffled closer into the narrow wedge of sunlight shining through the pass.

"I can't believe how healthy he seems," Vera marveled.

"Do a lot of people where you're from have healing magic?" asked Gage.

Vera chest constricted. "What do you mean?"

Gage pointed at Eggbert with a gentle smile. "He didn't get better that fast without some help."

"Oh. I, um..." *Lady, have mercy.*

"I'm sorry, I shouldn't have asked about your realm," said Gage. "I know it's improper, but I'm finding myself very curious about you, Vera."

"Oh." *Wow, you're impressively articulate this morning, Vera.* "It's okay, don't worry about it. I didn't even know it was improper or anything."

"Honestly, if the Guardian had been around, I wouldn't have brought it up. He'd have ripped out my spine already."

"Kale can be a little intense," Vera agreed.

"I'm surprised how relaxed you are around him."

"Kale's not as scary as people think."

"Oh, I think he's every bit as scary as people think he is," Gage said. "But around you, he's tempered. Perhaps you have won the Guardian's affections?"

"Noo." Vera blushed, which was infuriating. "I'm just a job for Kale. He's counting the seconds until he can send me home. Trust me, we do not get along at all."

"You must be fearless, then."

"Not at all." Vera laughed lightly.

"You dashed to Eggbert's side without a second thought for your safety."

"Stupidity and fearlessness are not the same things."

"I know. I didn't mix the two up." Gage bumped Vera softly. "While I'm being honest, I'm relieved I'm not competing against the Guardian for your attention."

Vera blushed again. *Dang it.* "Nope."

Gage didn't move away. His arm brushed against Vera's when she shifted. Vera turned her face away to check on Eggbert, using the chick as an excuse to hide her silly grin. Eggbert trotted across the beach toward them with a stick in his beak.

"He's like a puppy," Vera observed.

"What's a puppy?"

Way to go, genius. Puppy doesn't translate. Now that Vera thought about it, she hadn't seen a single dog in Summartir. That's why Kale told her not to talk to anyone more than necessary. A little flirting and Vera's mouth was misfiring.

"It's what we call baby goats," Vera said lamely.

Gage eyed Eggbert. "Huh. You must have strange goats."

"Uh huh."

Eggbert shoved the stick at Vera. She grabbed it, wondering if the chick would play fetch. Her fingers closed around something slimy and squishy, something that moved. With a squeak, Vera flung the stick into the water. One of the squishy bits stuck to her hand. It was a slug. Vera flicked it to the ground and wiped her hand on her pant leg, scowling at Eggbert.

"He's trying to make sure you get fed too." Gage chuckled.

"So sweet of you," Vera said when Eggbert cocked his

head at her, looking at her through his one eye. "But ya know, I'm not hungry right now." Vera's stomach rumbled. "Okay, I'm hungry, but I'm not that hungry."

Eggbert's excited bouncing slowed. Had she hurt his feelings? Gritting her teeth, Vera bent down and pinched the slug between her fingers. *The things I'm willing to do for this chick.* Vera wiggled the slug in front of Eggbert. His tail feathers waggled. When Vera tossed the slug into the air, Eggbert snatched it, his beak clacking. Then he looked at her for more.

"That's all I've got," Vera told him.

Eggbert waited another minute before wandering back down to the water's edge, looking for more treats since Vera had thrown his slug-stick into the lake. Three slugs sat on top of the bobbing stick to stay dry. Eggbert nosed around the weedy patches, moving farther and farther away. After a few minutes, he stopped to peck at something in a shrub. Vera sighed and went to see what he'd found while Gage sat on the bank to watch them, arms draped over his knees.

"Hey, Berty," Vera cooed when she got close. "Whatcha got there, buddy?"

Crap. Vera tried to nudge Eggbert away from the nest of duck eggs. These had not been empty. Eggbert was slurping up the tiny forms along with the egg matter. Gage couldn't find out.

"Stop," Vera hissed, trying to push Eggbert without alerting Gage.

The stick of slugs. It had floated away but not too far. Maybe Vera could distract Eggbert away from the nest with those slugs. Vera kicked off her shoes and pulled up her pant legs. *Gah, this is gonna suck. Stupid chick.* The water was freezing. *Just a few steps out, that's all I need.* Holding both pant legs with one hand, Vera reached for the stick. One pant-leg fell loose, dipping into the water before she could catch it. She snagged the wet fabric, hiking it up before it got wetter.

A shadow beneath the surface of the water caught Vera's attention. She opened her mouth to scream when something powerful clamped down and yanked her off her feet. Pain sliced through Vera's leg. The water hurling past swallowed Vera's scream as something towed her into deeper water. Silt and pebbles from the lake-bottom scraped Vera's cheek. Instinctively, Vera kicked out, trying to free herself. The creature held tight. Vera's arms pulled helplessly at the water. Something coiled around Vera's ribs, squeezing. Inside Vera's chest, her lungs heaved, demanding air. Then the water began to glow. Only it wasn't the water, it was something hurling through the water. The glowing thing slammed into the creature, which released her. She floated limply. Faster than the creature had traveled, something else flung Vera toward the surface.

Gage sucked in air, tugged Vera closer, and kicked for the bank. She coughed up water. Eggbert paced at the edge of the lake, cheeping for Vera, who did not respond. Dragging her onto the beach, Gage pressed a palm to the center of her chest. A pulse of white light flashed between Gage's hand and Vera's chest. She expelled water from her lungs. Gage tipped Vera to her side and sent another pulse through her, forcing the last of the water out. Eggbert's cheeping turned frantic.

"Eggbert?" Vera pushed herself up, looking for the bird.

"He's fine. He's just mad I won't let him crawl on top of you." Gage moved aside, letting the chick see Vera.

"What was that?" Vera pulled her feet from the water then gaped at Gage. "Are you glowing?"

Gage's eyes widened. "You can see that?"

"Yeah," Vera said slowly. "Another thing my kind can do, apparently."

Vera put a hand to her forehead. Her head swam. Eggbert splashed into the water to get to Vera, tired of waiting for Gage to get out of the way.

"Eggbert, get out of there!" Vera yelled.

A tentacle shot from the water and wrapped around the chick's leg. A broad, flat mouth full of teeth rose from the water. Vera screamed, grabbing the chick and trying to dislodge the tentacle. Gage sent a pulse into the tentacle and it released. The creature hissed. A different tentacle flew from the water, wrapping around Gage's neck. It shook Gage then slammed his head to the ground. Vera snatched Eggbert's stick, floating near the bank, and swung it down, pointy end first. The creature let out a raspy cry as the stick pierced through its tentacle and out the other side. The lake monster recoiled, sinking back into the water. Vera pulled Gage past the beach, onto the grassy edge. Eggbert hopped around anxiously, favoring one leg.

"Hey, buddy. It's okay. We're okay." Vera's voice cracked.

She shivered. Gage groaned, holding his head. He rolled to his side, trying to sit up. Vera noticed a growing, red puddle around her. Strange. The world spun.

"Vera," bellowed Kale, as he scrambled over the bank.

"Kale?"

"Are you okay?" Kale pushed the hair back from Vera's face.

"I feel dizzy." Vera blinked slowly. "Don't hurt Gage. He saved me."

"I'm going to kill him for getting you hurt."

Vera put a weak hand on Kale's face, leaving a smudge of blood when she turned his face toward her.

"Promise me. Not hurt him." Vera was having trouble catching her breath. "Promise."

"I promise," Kale conceded.

"Sorry," Vera slurred.

"For being stupid and sneaking out when you know you're not supposed to?"

"For blood on your face."

Vera passed out.

15

Smoke filled Vera's lungs. All around her, huts burned. An entire village was on fire. A woman screamed. Vera twisted to look over her shoulder. An unnatural held the woman in the air by the throat. Blood and dirt were smeared over the unnatural's arms and legs, like war paint. Vera looked away when the unnatural shoved the woman against a hut wall and pressed against her. Vera couldn't help the woman so she walked away. Slipping between two huts, Vera hoped none of the unnaturals would see her. The last thing she wanted was for anyone to notice her. A young boy raced around the corner and stopped short when he saw her. The child's frightened face contorted in fury then. He charged Vera, holding a shovel above his head. Vera batted the shovel away and threw the boy to the side. The boy grunted then pulled back into a pile of straw and dung. If he stayed there, the unnaturals might not notice him. She didn't stay to see if the boy was that smart.

Vera kept moving. She ducked into a hut when two unnaturals galloped by with their most recent trophies. One held a young girl's head by the hair, adding more blood to his already stained coat. The other dragged an old man behind him. The man's clothes were gone, his skin ripped away by either hands or dirt. Unfortunately for the man, he was not quite dead yet. He would be soon enough. A noise behind Vera made her turn around and eye the room. She didn't see anyone, but she wasn't alone. Vera moved farther into the hut, knocking chairs out of the way. There was a single bed, which Vera flipped over, tossing it to the other side of the room. Two young girls huddled together. One was a toddler and the other a girl barely past the edge of childhood. She'd be a prize for the horde.

"Please don't hurt the baby," said the older girl, pulling a chain from around her neck and extending it toward Vera. "You can have me but please take this instead of her."

The door crashed open behind Vera. Vera's nose flared. If it hadn't been for these girls, she'd have been away from here already. They'd slowed her down, gotten her caught.

"What have we here?" asked an unnatural, shifting to get a better look at the hut's occupants.

Vera kept her back to the unnatural. Her shoulders tensed as she reined in her anger at the girls for the trouble they'd brought her. Part of Vera wanted to bash both girls' heads in and be done with it.

"Please," repeated the oldest girl as she rose to her feet.

"Well, well," said the unnatural. "Look at that."

"You can have her," Vera said simply.

"You're not going to fight me? Try to stop me from taking her from you?" There was disappointment in the unnatural's tone.

"No." Vera picked up the girl by the front of her dirty shirt and tossed her to the unnatural.

"If you insist." The unnatural carried the girl from the hut.

He wouldn't go far or take long. Then he'd be back for Vera and the toddler who'd remained hidden by Vera's stance. The tiny girl began to moan.

"Cry, and I snap your neck," Vera warned.

The tiny girl hiccupped. Vera reached for her neck.

"Vera," called Kale.

What does he want? Vera picked the child up by the neck. The smelly thing choked and wriggled.

KALE SHOOK VERA FIRMLY. "VERA!"

Vera jolted. Her eyes snapped open. Kale pulled back cautiously, shuttering his expression. He hadn't had a choice. An artery in Vera's leg had been nicked, she'd been bleeding out, and one of her broken ribs had pierced a lung. A few more minutes and Kale would have found Vera dead.

"Are you okay?" Kale asked Vera.

"You healed me..." Vera sobbed, lifting a hand to cover her mouth.

Kale's gut heaved. He'd promised Vera that he wouldn't harm Gage, otherwise Kale would have eviscerated the man at that moment. Instead, Kale looked away.

"If you could walk, or if Gage could carry you, I promise I would not touch you," Kale told Vera before lifting her into his arms. "As soon as I can set you down, I will."

Kale did not speak as he carried Vera through the pass toward the farm. Eggbert ran alongside them, picking at Vera's hair with concern. Gage stumbled behind, doing a decent job of keeping up despite his injuries. Vera's chin quivered.

"I'm going to be sick," Vera said suddenly.

Kale stopped, knelt to the side of the pass, and tipped

Vera so she could retch. Gage hurried forward and held Vera's hair away from her face. Afterward, Gage wiped Vera's mouth with his hand. Snaking up Gage's wrists were the deception marks Kale had glimpsed before. And yet, Kale would've handed Vera over to the man if he could. After whatever she'd just experienced in his memories, she shouldn't have to endure his arms around her. Vera shook. Kale was not sure if she was cold or in shock. Probably both.

"We're almost there," Kale assured her.

Up ahead, two figures moved into the pass. Apparently, Mitch had received his dose of witch healing as Kale had prescribed. Someone also must have told Mitch that the Guardian was going after his son. Kale didn't mind that, except Mitch had dragged the Maiden along too. She was supposed to be resting.

"What the hell are they thinking?" Kale asked, not speaking to anyone in particular.

"Who?" Gage swore and ducked into a crevice in the rocks.

"What are you doing?" Kale asked the moron.

"She cannot find me like this," Gage explained.

"Like what?" Kale eyed Gage with disdain. "I'm sure the Maiden has seen a wet man before. She's as old as me."

"No, it's not that. I can't..." Gage shut his mouth and ran a hand over the back of his neck.

"The lines on your hands are growing," observed Kale. "Either explain how your deception involves your Maiden, or I'll toss you at her feet and let you explain it to her yourself."

"You can't do that." Gage backed farther into the crevice.

"I can if you don't start talking. Quickly." Kale angled his body so Mitch and the Maiden would not see him talking to Gage, just in case.

"The Maiden can sense magic," said Gage.

"Try telling me something I don't know," Kale replied impatiently.

"I am a witch," Gage announced.

Kale laughed. The man had hit his head too hard.

"He's telling the truth," Vera said, but Kale already knew that because the marks on Gage's hands faded.

"Keep talking," Kale said.

"Monroes have been passing magic to their sons ever since the world unraveled. Stitching the world together required more magic than the triads possessed, so other witches lent their magic to the cause. But the triads took more than they needed. My many-times-great-grandmother knew they'd never give any of the magic back—and they didn't. So, she gave the last of her magic to her infant son to keep it safe. My family has continued to keep our magic safe that way ever since."

"Men cannot harness witch magic," Kale argued.

"When we have sorcerer's blood in our veins, we can."

"How has your family kept that a secret for so long?"

"We make sure we don't get noticed. As long as we don't use the magic, it lies dormant, undetectable."

"You used magic to rescue Vera," Kale concluded.

"A lot of it."

"What will happen if you're discovered?" asked Kale.

"The triads will come to collect all the magic from our family. Like they did during the unraveling. We would fight."

"The other men, the ones who left in the middle of the night, they're witches too?" asked Kale.

"Yes." Gage lifted his brows with surprise.

"Unless you can heal yourself, you won't make it to your

hiding brethren before you fall and kill yourself with that head injury," said Kale.

"I have to try." Gage was determined.

The sounds of approaching steps reached them.

"Put me down," Vera demanded.

"That's not a good idea," Kale replied carefully.

"I said put me down." Vera put every shred of her pain in those words. "I want to say good-bye."

Kale set Vera on her feet. She wobbled but put up a hand when Kale reached for her.

"I want Gage," she informed Kale.

Gage tucked an arm around Vera's waist. Vera shifted her weight to the other man and wound her arms around Gage's neck. Rising to her tippy toes, Vera pressed her lips to Gage's before pulling back to look the man in the eyes. Kale flexed his fists and turned away.

"We have to head the Maiden off so Gage has a chance to sneak away," Kale said.

"Here," screamed Vera without warning. "We're over here."

"What are you doing?" Gage backed away as if Vera had slapped him.

"I gave you my cloaking charm." Vera grabbed the rock wall to stay upright. "You're safe. I won't let you go out there and die." Vera tapped her charm, now resting against Gage's chest. "Tuck that under your shirt."

"Vera," started Kale.

"This is my decision. I didn't get to decide what I did when you..." Vera closed her eyes, trying to block out her new memory. "But I do now."

Kale clenched his jaw and didn't say a word. She'd made sure he couldn't object, in the most effective way she could.

Stars help me, she's right. He'd have to figure out a way to keep her alive without the charm.

"You wore a cloak?" Gage looked at Vera wide-eyed. "What are you?"

"No idea. If you figure it out, let me know," Vera said lightly.

She wobbled. Kale scooped her up before she hit the ground. Mitch and the Maiden were upon them. If Kale had to run, he would, but for Vera's sake, he hoped he wouldn't have to. Although Kale had healed her, Vera's body needed as much rest as if she'd healed naturally. Running from a siphon-hunting mob would not be ideal.

"How am I supposed to keep you safe now?" Kale asked Vera quietly.

"Maybe you can't." Vera blinked long. "I'm not human anymore. So as long as I don't slurp from someone else's slushy I'll be fine, right?"

"As long as nothing unlucky happens," Kale said.

"I'm always unlucky."

"That's why I'm very worried right now," Kale said seriously.

Vera didn't respond. She was asleep.

VERA KNOCKED on Liah's door. Kale had tried getting Vera to go back to sleep but she'd refused. There was no way she could sleep, knowing that Liah could be Earth's threadbearer. The woman could be all that stood between a maniacal witch and the destruction of Vera's people. And Liah was in danger so sleep would wait. Seeing Vera's determination, Kale had stepped aside without further discussion. So far, the topic of

Kale's memories had not come up, for which Vera was glad. While Kale had always been brutally honest about his past, seeing it had been an entirely different thing. Not even being thrown out of her own realm had made Vera feel so completely unbalanced. The world had just tipped beneath her feet.

On top of that, guilt for how Vera had unfairly judged the world gnawed at her. She'd been willing to condemn the world for banishing her people and throwing away the key. Her self-righteous anger was dampened now, though. All it had taken was the smallest glimpse of the atrocities her people had committed. Vera was ashamed of the monster she carried within her. Siphons had not wanted respect and rights, they'd wanted to torture the world, to make it bleed. They'd enjoyed doing it too. Siphons happily became monsters, relishing the bloodshed and violation of the people who'd repressed them. For the first time, Vera understood why the world felt the only option was to lock siphons away for good. It wasn't hard to understand why, even after all these centuries, a witch might decide to unleash a horde on the people who'd caused so much destruction. Or possibly want to drop their realm from the world altogether.

Vera knocked again, louder, wondering if Liah was asleep. The woman was not supposed to leave her apartment so she should be there. When the betrayer came for Liah, Kale and Vera would be waiting for her. While Vera no longer wanted her people unleashed upon the world, she also didn't think they deserved extermination. Once they stopped the witch and wiped out the horde, Vera would go back home, enroll in school, and live her life as she'd planned. She'd forget about Summartir, the meadow, and all things magic. She'd leave the world in peace from her and her kind.

"Let me try," Kale said.

Vera stepped aside. Kale knocked loudly, then jiggled the doorknob. It was locked.

"Liah," Kale called, but there was no response. "Something is wrong. She should've answered by now."

Kale threw his shoulder and hip into the door. The frame cracked. One more time and the door fell open. Vera followed Kale inside. They passed the sitting area, taking the hallway to the right. The first open door led to a small room with two empty cradles. Kale crashed through the door at the end of the hall. Liah lay on the bed, choking on vomit and foam. One of Liah's arms hung off the bed, fingers stained purple from the berries that lay scattered across the floor. Kale rolled Liah onto her side and used a blanket to wipe her face, before removing the soiled material.

"She's tried to kill herself," Kale said. "Those are belladonna berries."

"Should I get a healer?" asked Vera.

"They can't save her now. It's too late," Kale said.

"Can you save her?" Vera asked.

"No." Kale sat on the bed beside the dying witch.

"Yes, you can," Vera argued.

"She already doesn't want to live." Kale ran a hand through his hair. "How can I save her only to bring her mind more torment?"

"But what about the thread. And her son."

"I'll protect the Maiden. The sure-threads will hold, your realm will be safe." Kale's voice broke. "Whatever you saw today, I promise there's worse. If you'd seen the worst, you would not be standing beside me now. I cannot do that to Liah. It would destroy her."

Vera's heart fell. "Kale, you once found sisters hiding under a bed during an unnatural attack on their village. Do you remember that? A baby girl and an older girl."

"The older girl asked for the baby to be spared in exchange for her own life."

"I saw what happened to the older girl. How I... You threw her to one of those monsters without a second thought." Tears fell down Vera's cheeks. "What happened to the baby?"

Kale stared silently at Liah, who convulsed.

"What happened to her?" Vera's voice rose. She fell to her knees to look up into Kale's eyes.

"I squeezed her neck until she blacked out. Until her bulging eyes fell closed. Then I shoved her into a flour sack and gave her to the first creature I found—a dragon."

"Save my son too," Liah gurgled.

"Your son will be safe," Kale promised.

"No—" Liah gagged and gasped for breath.

"We'll make sure he's safe." Vera placed her hand on Liah's forehead. "She's so warm."

Kale frowned and placed his hand on Liah's cheek. "She's cold to the touch."

"No, she's burning up." Vera touched Liah with her other hand to be sure.

Heat spread up Vera's arm. Sweat beaded Vera's brow. As soon as Vera pulled back, the warmth was gone, and Vera shivered from the loss of heat. Kale reached out and touched Vera's hair. Surprised, Vera jerked away, and Kale lowered his hand.

"Did you fall asleep beside me after I was poisoned?" Kale asked suddenly.

"What does that have to do with anything?" Vera blushed.

"I'll take that as a yes," Kale said. "Try resting your forehead against Liah's. Trust me, okay?"

Vera hesitated before raising to her knees and leaning forward to press her forehead to Liah's. She felt silly. As soon as their skin met, it felt like the room was a sauna. Sweat beaded across Vera's skin. She started to pull away from Liah, but Kale urged her to wait. Using a clean blanket, Kale wiped away the sweat as it formed. Vera felt drowsy. Her eyes dipped closed.

"Whoa, that's enough," Kale said, catching Vera as she slid away.

Slipping an arm under Vera's knees and one behind her head, Kale swept Vera into his lap, cradling her to his chest. Vera yawned and blinked sleepily, too tired to protest. Liah placed a hand on her forehead and pushed herself into a semi-seated position.

"Well, I think that answers some questions we've had," mused Kale. "Look at that, Liah's hands are clear now too. I'm going to take a wild guess and say your secret has something to do with the unusual Monroe men."

Liah's eyes widened. "I was going to tell you. You already know?"

"Yeah, Gage saved me from an octopus-alligator. Octogator." Vera giggled. "But then I saved him too. He used magic, but I used a stick. A slug-stick." Vera looked up at Kale and giggled again. "I feel funny."

"You'll feel better after you've slept it off," Kale said with a sad smile.

"I have to find my son." Liah struggled to get untangled from the bedding then swayed and held the sides of her head.

"The poison is gone, but the damage it caused is still there," Kale said. "You need to rest and heal. I'll bring you your son later."

"You don't understand," Liah wailed. "The fox will get

him. If you know about the Monroe witches, so does the fox."

"Liah, is your son a witch?" asked Kale.

"He has my magic now. I knew the fox would come for me."

"We'll make sure the fox doesn't come," Kale said.

"The fox is already here," Liah insisted. "She shoved the berries down my throat. I didn't care because I don't have what she wants."

"She? The fox is a woman?" asked Kale

Liah placed both hands over her mouth, and then whispered between her fingers, "I was not supposed to tell you that. The fox will be angry."

"Are you a threadbearer, Liah?" asked Kale

"Not anymore."

"Who has your son, Liah? I'll go get him." Kale rose with Vera in his arms.

"He's with Calla. They were going to feed the chickens. My little boy loves feeding the chickens."

"Go. Leave me here with Liah," said Vera.

"I can't leave you," argued Kale.

"Well, I can't go. Those green swirls are making me dizzy." Vera tracked the green swirls floating in front of her with her eyes.

"She can rest here," said Liah. "I'll watch over her. I do not wish her harm."

"Truth," Vera slurred.

Kale lowered Vera to the bed. She curled up contentedly.

"Lock the bedroom door. I broke your front door." Kale strode from the room, and Liah did as instructed.

"You aren't crazy, are you?" asked Vera.

"It depends on who you ask," answered Liah.

"I thought you were crazy. You talk nonsense."

"When you have to be careful not to speak the wrong words because things are listening for those words, what you say does sound like nonsense."

"I told Gage about puppies," Vera said. "But I didn't tell him about kitties."

"Now you sound crazy like me."

"Kale would be angry. He's always angry. But I'm angry at him too."

"You should not be angry with him."

"I *am* angry with him." Vera lifted a hand to trace a line of violet light that came to play with the green.

"That story about the little girl he gave to a dragon, I know that story," said Liah. "Do you want me to tell it to you my way?"

"I already know it. I don't like that story." Vera turned her back on the witch.

"I'm going to tell you anyway." Liah was as stubborn as Vera. "A very long time ago, there was a little girl who lived in a sorcerer's village. The little girl's father was very sick. She had to feed him and buy him medicine, so she worked the only way a little girl could. Soon her father was dead anyway, and the little girl had a tiny girl of her own. The world was becoming a scary place then. The little mother used to climb into the hills and pray that someone would take her tiny girl away and give her a better life. A dragon lived in those hills, you see. He'd listen to the little mother. Finally, the evil came to the little girl's village. The little mother begged mercy from an unlikely place—the most feared man in all the world. When he could've turned his back, the man let the little mother sacrifice herself to save her baby. The man took the baby into the hills and gave her to the dragon. The dragon saw the man's goodness. It was buried deep inside, never snuffed out. If a fire could survive in that man through all that he'd seen and done, the dragon knew there might be hope for the world after all."

"The dragon flew the baby girl to the home of a past lover, a witch in Summartir Kingdom. When it was time to unravel the world, the witch found the man who'd saved the baby. He became the Guardian. The only man whose fire was strong enough to be tied to the meadow. The world was almost completely destroyed by then, but what little remained after all those evil years, survived because of him. The tiny girl was not tiny anymore. She stayed in Summartir and had a tiny boy. She learned to care for the chickens and serve the triads well. That family is my family. The Monroes."

"Kale saved the baby." Vera like that story better. "But everyone is scared of him."

"He's a scary man," said Liah.

"I don't think he's scary. I think he's a jerk."

"Yes," laughed Liah. "I noticed. Just remember that under the Guardian's hard demeanor burns the fire of a man who helped save the world. The same fire the dragon saw. It's buried, but not as deep as it once was. I think you're good for him."

The apartment door crashed open. Liah turned to place herself between the bedroom door and Vera. The doorknob twisted. The lock did not stop it. When the door opened, Maiden stood on the other side.

"Kalesius said I'd find you together," said Maiden.

"They will stop you," Liah spat.

Black mist gathered around Maiden's fingers, dripping to the floor. The tendrils stretched up and snapped around Liah's mouth and nose. It wrapped around each of Liah's limbs and yanked her to her hands and knees. Liah didn't struggle. The crazy witch looked defiantly up at the High Maiden.

"What are you doing?" Vera tried to stand, but the room lurched, throwing her off her feet. "You shouldn't do that to her."

Maiden tipped her head. "My, my, Vera. You have changed since I first met you. I wish I'd realized sooner that you were cloaked. It made things very complicated for me." Maiden reached up and pulled off one glove, finger by finger, to reveal a palm covered in brands shaped like Cassie's bloodstone. Maiden pointed to one of the marks. "That one was supposed to go to you. Not to fear, though, I'll give you the next one, now that your siphon is uncaged."

"How do you know what I am?" Vera swayed.

"The Crone cursed the gate so siphons could not get through," Maiden explained. "To stop me from getting my hands on another one. I was very grateful for the Guardian pulling you through, except you didn't feel like a siphon. I thought he must be wrong about the gate attacking you, but he wasn't, was he?"

Liah convulsed as the Maiden's mist cut off her air. Vera crawled across the floor and tried to pull Liah from the mist but she couldn't.

"Stop. Please," Vera begged.

Maiden did not listen. Vera wrapped her hands around a tendril of magic. A piece pulled away and sank into Vera's hands. It slunk up her arms like roaches skittering beneath her skin. Panicking, Vera snatched the mist and flung it away. It smacked against the Maiden, and the High Witch absorbed it. Maiden's eyes widened at Vera. Liah stopped struggling. Her body stilled, her eyes stared blankly ahead as the mist retreated. Maiden's smile grew sharper then turned brittle.

"I'd really thought she was one of the final threadbearers." Maiden sighed coldly. "But it's not all a waste, I have you now. You're even more useful than I realized. Not even the Guardian can save you from our laws now that you've murdered a witch."

"But I didn't," Vera protested.

"That's not what it will seem like. A word of warning, if you mention that you're a siphon, the Monroes will kill you outright. So I'd keep that to yourself. And don't say a word against me, or I'll show them what you are myself. They won't believe a siphon over me."

The Maiden's mist spiraled up Vera's arms and legs and sank into her skin. The last of the effects of Liah's poison dissipated. Vera's head cleared. Maiden snatched the bloodstone from the floor near Liah's open mouth.

"No," cried the Maiden dramatically. "The outsider killed Liah!" Maiden winked at Vera. Tugging her glove back on, Maiden yelled until a mob of Monroe men and women rushed into the apartment. Witches gathered at the front. Maiden made a show of holding Vera off with her magic, but the witch wasn't actually using a drop of magic against her. It wasn't necessary. She had Vera trapped.

Mitch shoved his way through the crowd.

"I came to visit Liah, and that girl was strangling her." Maiden held the bloodstone up to show the Monroes as proof.

"Did you kill Liah?" Mitch asked Vera.

Vera pinched her lips together, staring at Liah's lifeless hand.

"The bloodstone will find her," said one of the witches who had healed Mitch.

Immediately, the women in the room hummed as one. The Maiden began to murmur the words that would supposedly send the stone to the murderer. Vera knew that would not happen this time. The burning of the brand on Vera's hand confirmed it. There was no way to ignore the searing pain. Vera clutched her hand to her chest and screamed. Mitch's shoulders slumped as he looked between the Maiden and Vera. He turned to leave the room, not needing to see the rest to know the stone had found its mark in Vera. When the chanting subsided, hate-filled faces surrounded Vera. Only Kale bursting into the room held them off.

"What is happening here?" Kale demanded. "Vera?"

The Monroes parted, leaving the Guardian a path to Vera. Kale walked forward, and they filled back in behind him. Standing in front of Vera, Kale looked over Liah's body. His eyes dipped to Vera's scarred hand.

"You are convicted of murdering a witch," Kale said darkly.

Vera glanced at Maiden, and then nodded.

"Stand," Kale commanded Vera.

"She deserves to face the triads for her crimes," said Maiden to Kale. "Not a quick execution."

Vera's heart dropped. She hadn't even thought of that. She'd become a threat to an outside realm. Kale had the responsibility of killing her for that. Vera quaked as Kale stared her down, deliberating her fate. Then his face softened, and he rolled his eyes in exasperation.

"Your luck couldn't hold out for a whole day?" Kale asked Vera.

He charged her. Scooping Vera up, he pressed her face into his chest and curved an arm over her head. Then he leaped backward through the window with her. Vera clung to Kale as they fell together. When Kale hit the ground, he tucked his legs up, curving around Vera until they rolled to a stop. Vera was shaken but completely unharmed. People screamed out the window.

"Hurry." Kale shoved Vera to her feet.

At the corner of the barn, Mitch yelled, "Here." The man held the reins of a saddled chicken.

"What are you doing?" asked Kale.

"Setting up a getaway. Figured you'd need it," answered Mitch.

"I didn't kill Liah." Vera brushed at the burn on her hand. "The Maiden killed her, not me."

"I believe you," Mitch said, echoing Vera's proclamation from their first meeting. "I don't know what's happening, but my son said you gave up your cloak to protect him. The Monroe family owes you a debt and our trust. But you need to move now."

"There's no way we can outrun Maiden," Vera pointed out. "Your family thinks I killed Liah too."

"I have some tricks of my own," said Mitch.

"Holy cow, you're a witch," Vera gaped at the glowing man. "The Maiden will see you."

"Gage left me your gift." Mitch patted his pocket.

A moment later, Mitch slapped the chicken, and it raced toward the passage carrying Vera and Kale.

16

Kale shifted so Vera could stretch out her legs. They'd been squeezed behind the crates in the hatchery storage closet for over an hour, ever since Mitch sent that chicken from the barnyard carrying a magical phantasm of the two of them on its back.

"This seems like a bad idea the longer we sit here," Vera whispered.

"It's better than trying to outrun witches," said Kale. "And I assume you'd prefer I not have to kill a bunch of Gage's family."

"You assume correctly."

"Then we'll stay until Mitch says it's safe to go."

"What happens if they realize that's not us on the chicken? How long can Mitch hold that illusion?"

"He only had to hold it long enough for the chicken to get a head start. They'll be following its footprints."

Something clattered to the floor beyond the storage door. Kale pressed Vera into the shadows, pulling an empty sackcloth over them. The door cracked open.

"What are you doing in here?" demanded Mitch of whoever was on the other side of the door.

"That chick dumped his water bowl again," said a young girl's voice. "I can't find Gage."

"I'll worry about the chick. You go help your father get dinner to the children while the witches track the Guardian."

The door clicked closed. Vera released the breath. Only the door swung right back open, and Vera jumped.

"It's just me," said Mitch. "I packed a couple bags with food and supplies for you. I tucked the knife I found in your room in there too. Had to clean the velvet slime off it, though."

Kale had forgotten about that. Vera pinned him with an accusing look. That was going to come up again later.

"Thought you'd need this." Mitch tossed Kale a clean tunic. "Stay close to the barn until you put the silos between you and us. Then you can get to the woods without being spotted."

"Thank you, Mitch." Kale tugged the clean shirt on, and Mitch collected the bloodied one.

"I think we're about even after this," Vera said.

"We will never be even. You and the Guardian are going to save all my people. In that endeavor, you have our support, whatever it may be."

"I'm not sure your family would agree," Kale said.

"It's not safe for them to know the truth right now. Not with our High guest watching over all. When it is time for us to stand beside you and take back our land, they will know."

"You suspected it was her all along," guessed Kale.

"Not something to speculate out loud, but Liah's ramblings always made me wonder."

"The fox in the henhouse," said Vera.

Kale wanted them to be wrong. He wanted to believe there was no way he'd misjudged the Maiden. Addamas's words of caution floated through his mind. He'd underestimated another beautiful woman. But how was he supposed to have known when she never intended to deceive him? It was like Mitch's double-crossing all over.

"When did you decide to send the men away in the night?" asked Kale. He needed to know how he'd missed Mitch's deception. Maybe then he could understand how the Maiden had accomplished hers.

"I didn't," answered Mitch simply. "I planned to tell you the truth if it came up and beg your silence. It was Gage who sent them away. I found them already loading up."

Tension melted from his shoulders. He hadn't screwed up as badly as he'd thought. But badly enough. How had he missed the Maiden's deception?

"There are only a few days until the High Mother's transition here for her season," Mitch said. "The last threadbearers are out of the Maiden's reach for now. We'll keep them that way until she's gone. You worry about keeping Vera safe. For some reason, the Maiden wants Vera bad."

"That I can promise," said Kale. "We're headed to Kyopili next to warn the High Mother. She'll need to be prepared to fight the Maiden if needed during the transition. Vera will be safe until the Maiden is gone."

"Good. I'm going to make sure everyone stays inside so you two can escape. Don't dawdle."

Mitch held out his hand to Kale. Kale was surprised by the gesture. Humans shook hands without thought, but outside their realm, the gesture meant more than a simple greeting. It was a contract of friendship, an offer of assistance should they need it. Kale wondered if it was right to accept, but Mitch waited until Kale grasped the offered hand.

"May you find luck on your travels," Mitch said.

Vera snorted lightly behind them.

To Vera, Mitch held out a chain. "Gage carved this for you. It is a piece of Eggbert's shell to keep for good luck. It comes with a promise that Eggbert will be waiting for you when you return."

Vera flew into the man's arms and hugged him tightly. "Tell him thank you for me." She clasped the token around her neck and swiped away the tears before turning to Kale.

"Go," Mitch urged, tears shining in his own eyes.

Kale crept to the door and peeked outside. His breath caught when Vera slipped a hand into his. He squeezed it, then pulled her behind him out the door, motioning for her to stay low. The bag slung over Kale's back slid back and forth as they ducked under windows, and then sprinted for the cover of the silos. There they waited, making sure no one was watching, before sprinting to the wood's edge. They didn't slow until they were well inside the shade of the trees. Vera breathed heavily, hitching her pack into place. She already had a sheen on her skin from the humidity of the Velvet Woods.

"So, how do I make sure I don't become worm food in this place?" asked Vera.

"Stab anything that looks at you." Kale pulled the knife from his bag and held the handle out for her to take. "They travel in packs. Kill one, the others will decide you're not worth it."

"Will do." Vera flexed her hand around the knife. "Don't take my knife again or I'll stab you too. 'Kay?"

"Understood," Kale answered. "Once the sun goes down, they'll start surfacing, so we need to get through as much of the woods as we can in the next few hours. If you need to pee, do it now, we don't want your scent anywhere near us when they wake up."

"I'm good," Vera looked skeptically at the undergrowth. "Even if I did have to pee, the idea of one of those things sliming me while my bare rear hangs in the air would scare the urge right out of me."

Kale's lips twitched. "Walk ahead of me so nothing can sneak up on you. This time, I'm the sprinkles to your donut."

Vera walked ahead, holding the knife in her right hand.

"If you don't move a little quicker, we won't get out of here before midnight," Kale informed her.

Vera threw him a look over her shoulder but picked up the pace. Kale stayed close behind her. Only one beetle tried to drop onto her head. Kale batted it away without her even knowing it. The undergrowth became more humid as they got closer to the center of the woods. Wet tendrils of hair fell loose from Vera's braid and clung to her neck. Every once in a while, she lifted the hair and waved a hand to fan her neck. Even though the sun was well on its way down, the heat trapped between these trees never let up. Vera rolled her sleeves up over her shoulders. The damp material clung to her. Kale focused on the trees until Vera lifted the front of her shirt up to wipe away the sweat from her face, baring her waist and lower back. *Internals take me, why am I paying attention to her waist?*

Kale had enough when Vera pulled her hair up and piled it on top of her head. Her shirt rode up as she stretched to hold the hair in place. Kale used his teeth to tear a strip from his tunic sleeve. He reached forward, twisted Vera's braid and loose tendrils into a knot, and wound the strip of fabric to hold the hair in place so she would stop playing with it. When Kale finished, Vera gave him a funny look over her shoulder. And tripped over a branch. Even Kale was too distracted and didn't catch her that time. He leaned over to help her up and noticed the smell of rot. Then he saw the white feather.

"The Maiden lost her chicken on her way through here. I think it must have been nearby, which means we're on a pack's hunting ground."

Vera moved forward slowly. This time Kale didn't correct her pace. When they came to a fallen tree, Kale guided Vera around it, not wanting her too close to an easy hiding place. As Vera circled the mass of uprooted roots, she whirled away, gagging. *Aww Hell.* The Maiden hadn't just lost a chicken, she'd lost a couple of witches and their mounts too. The mass of slime-coated body parts and feathers turned even his stomach. At least the slime contained most of the stench. The worms had laid eggs too. With the abundance of food, it was the perfect time to grow the pack.

"She wasn't overcome by worms," Kale concluded. "Her hen probably went down while she fought her own witches, and then she left them all for the worms. I knew her story was strange, but I didn't question it." Kale punched a tree.

Vera eyed his bleeding hand. "Is blood a good idea right now?"

"The worms aren't hunting. They've gorged themselves already and left this here to snack on when they get hungry again."

"I still think we should go now." Vera avoided glancing again at the desecrated bodies.

Vera was right. As they turned to leave, she jumped back, bumping into Kale.

"I saw something," she said.

"A worm?" asked Kale.

"I don't think so. It was too tall."

"Probably a beetle," Kale said.

"And those won't attack, right?"

"No, it was probably here for the bodies and is waiting for us to leave so it can go back to them." Kale squinted through the gathering darkness. "We're only halfway through the woods and sunset is very close. We have to get moving."

Vera moved cautiously, head swinging side to side. They walked until it was nearly pitch black. Vera occasionally tripped. She moved slowly out of necessity. Kale kept his eyes mostly on the brush but occasionally checked the limbs above. Something had been leaping from tree to tree earlier, keeping pace with them. He hadn't heard it in a little while, though, which may or may not be a good thing. There was no telling what lived above.

"Maybe it's time for me to lead," Kale said when Vera stumbled again. "Hold onto my shirt."

"Can you see in the dark?"

"Better than you, apparently," Kale said, catching her before she walked into a tree.

"How much farther?"

"Not long. The humidity is letting up."

"Maiden shoved magic in me," Vera said suddenly. "I can still feel it inside me. Like when you eat so much you think you'll be sick. And it won't go away."

"She gave you too much." Kale imagined how things would be different if Vera had told him that before he'd thrown them out a window. He would have ripped the Maiden's head from her shoulders, High Maiden or not. "To stay with your analogy, your stomach is too small for what she gave you. You can stretch your stomach with time. That's what happened to your ancestors. They kept taking a little too much each time until their stomachs were too big. They were afraid every bit of magic they pulled might be their last, so they binged whenever they could. Until their appetites were unquenchable."

"I don't want to become like that," Vera said with worry.

"You won't. Because you don't want to."

"How do I get it out of me?"

"Use it."

"I don't know how to use magic."

"You've handled it before. It's all about spinning a thread, and then casting it out of you like a fishing line while telling it what to do."

Vera became quiet for several minutes. Then there was a flash of light that blinded Kale. He grabbed Vera, wrapping himself around her until he saw spots and could see the outlines of the trees again.

"Crap. Sorry."

"That was you?"

"I was trying to make a light."

"Were you thinking about lightning by chance?"

Vera stilled. "Oops."

"Next time try something gentler." He shook away the last of the spots. "Not fire. The last thing we need is to be burned alive."

"Oh," Vera squeaked. "Nope, we're good."

"You were thinking about fire, weren't you?" Kale closed his eyes, seeking patience. "For now, I can see. Maybe we should leave good enough alone."

Vera didn't respond, which he took to mean she disagreed. *Stars help me.* Kale started moving again, Vera's hand on his back. Once or twice, her hand slipped, and Kale had to remind her to pay attention. Finally, dots of amber light began to pop in and out of sight above them.

The lights twinkled, casting a glow over the space they took up.

"Fireflies?" Kale looked with wonder at the incredible insects only found on Earth.

"I love them," Vera said with an upturned face, smiling at her casting.

"They're a good choice."

Vera tipped her head down to share her smile with Kale but it fell flat. Her eyes widened, looking past Kale's arm. Kale twisted in time to see the fox launch itself at him. It latched its teeth on his shoulder and shook. Kale reached back to grab it, but the fox released him almost immediately, falling to the ground. It lay in a heap, twitching, with Vera's knife in its back. Kale jerked the blade to the side, ending the vixen's life quickly.

"Are you okay?" he asked Vera, who trembled.

Vera nodded rapidly. "You?"

"I'm fine. I think that's the fox I hit with a rock." Kale looked around, regaining his bearings. "I'm pretty sure we're out of the Velvet Woods, but I want to go a little farther to be sure. Can you keep going?"

"I said I'm fine, Kale," Vera snapped. "Will there be more foxes?"

"There shouldn't be."

Kale cleaned the knife in the dirt and handed it back to Vera. She took it without batting an eye. As the moon began to filter through the trees and the chill returned to the air, Vera jabbed her finger against a spot on Kale's shoulder. His skin was bare from where the fox had shredded the fabric. Kale hissed at the bite of pain.

"What is that?" Vera asked.

"Glass."

"Why is there glass under the skin of your shoulder?"

"There's glass under a good portion of the skin on my back at the moment. I went through a window earlier today. Didn't have a chance to clean it out before the skin healed. I was too busy hiding and running."

Vera was quiet. "I'm sorry."

"I think we've determined none of what happened this afternoon was your fault."

"Not that. I'm sorry for how I reacted to your memory."

"Don't," Kale bit out.

"Shut up and let me talk," she said irritably, and then took a steadying breath before charging forward. "You never lied about your past or who you used to be. I know you're not that person anymore. I had no right to judge you for a past I only saw because you were saving my life. All I was thinking about was me. You've only cared about my well-being since, well since you decided not to off me. So, I'm sorry. And thank you. For not doubting me when that High Witch-Bitch framed me for murder."

"It wasn't hard to trust you. I know there's no way you could kill anyone. Unless you were defending someone. Or my back." Kale winked at Vera. "We can rest here. It's too dry for the worms to come this far."

Vera nodded, dropping to the forest floor and pulling off her shoes. Kale set about making a small fire to deter anything else that might come sniffing around.

"Will the Maiden be able to find us here?" Vera poked at the fire with her knife.

"I don't think she'll be anxious to lead a hunting party past her killing grounds. They'll have to take the long way around the Velvet Woods. Plus, Mitch said he'd make sure we had at least a day's head start. That means we have until tomorrow afternoon before we have to start looking over our shoulders."

"Good. Take your shirt off," said Vera without missing a beat.

Kale swung around to stare at her. The girl had surprised him before, but his heart just about choked him that time. He was not thrilled that part of him was excited by her odd demand.

"I'm going to get the glass out of your back," she explained.

Well, that made a lot more sense. But now there was no denying the woman had more power over him than he was comfortable with.

"You don't need to do that," Kale said.

"Obviously. But I'm going to. Sit."

"You should eat," he argued.

"Yeah, that's a really bad idea with what I'm about to do." She waved him over and patted the ground, pulling her blade from the fire. She hadn't been playing in the fire. She'd been sterilizing her knife. Kale ran a hand through his hair then sighed. She wasn't going to give up. He pulled the shirt over his head and sat in front of her as directed. Vera did not touch him, though.

"It's okay," Kale assured, assuming she'd lost her nerve. "I'll be fine until Addamas can get it all out."

The blade slid across his skin without warning. Kale stilled and took a shallow breath. Vera's fingers pressed into his skin. *Stars above.* His stomach dropped. This was a really bad idea. Kale clenched his teeth while Vera's fingers and the knife flitted interchangeably over his skin. Kale began to think he preferred the bite of the glass under his skin to the new sensations he felt when he thought of Vera or felt her touch. He had to get himself together. All she was trying to do was make amends for something he did not hold against her to begin with. If she had any idea what he was thinking now, she'd run away screaming.

"That's it. There's enough glass to make a new window here," Vera announced finally. "Stay there, let me clean off some of the blood first."

She hopped up and retrieved his torn and bloodied shirt. He only had one more in the bag after that one. Vera's face was pale. Her hands trembled when she touched the cloth to his back.

"I think most of them have already healed over," she said absently.

Kale began to wonder how much blood there had been as the fabric moved up and down his back. Finally, he spun around to catch her hand.

"That's enough," he said. "It's good enough. Thank you."

Vera looked down and nodded, tucking a lock of hair behind her ear. The lock escaped as soon as she released it. Kale moved before he realized what he was doing and tucked the errant hair back again. Vera's chin trembled.

"Healing you was not as selfless as you want to believe," Kale said and swallowed hard. "I think if I lost you now, I wouldn't know what to do with myself."

"You'd probably go save the world a lot faster without having to save my butt every two minutes."

"You do realize that you've cleared poison out of my system, saved a chick's life, stabbed a lake monster with a twig, and rescued me from the jaws of a fox? You're hardly a helpless burden hanging around my neck."

"Huh. I guess I am pretty awesome, aren't I?" Vera teased.

"You're going to make me regret those words, aren't you? You know you do owe me an act of obedience since I won your little bet."

"You did not. I said Mitch and Gage could be trusted, and you said I was wrong. So, I won. Ha."

"Actually, you said Mitch and Gage had nothing to hide, and I said you were wrong. Which means I won. Because what he said was that his family had nothing to hide regarding the nest raid. You're the one who translated it into him having nothing at all to hide."

Vera gaped. "That's..." Vera stuttered. "But that means you let me make that bet, knowing I'd worded it wrong."

"I did try to tell you."

"You're a butt." Vera yawned through a scowl.

"Why don't you eat something and rest?"

"I'm not hungry. I'm just going to close my eyes for a little while." Vera pulled her pack over and laid her head down. "I bet Ferrox is missing you by now."

"Nah, he doesn't like people. He only tolerates me because he has to."

"At least I'm not the only one." Vera's eyes slid closed and did not open again.

"Funny enough, he did accept your offer of friendship that day."

"Huh?" she asked, half-asleep.

"The sugar. When Ferrox took it, he made a contract. If you ever need anything from him, he's obligated to return an act of friendship."

"That's crazy."

Above them, the magical fireflies slowly winked out as Vera fell asleep, and the last threads of magic frayed and dissipated.

17

Vera stirred. Her nose and fingers were freezing. She snuggled closer to the yummy warmth radiating beside her. Warmth which turned out to be a sleeping Kale. Vera's icy touch jarred him awake. All of a sudden, Kale was crouched protectively over Vera, a knife in his hand. Blinking to bring the lunatic-man into focus, Vera felt her waistband for where that knife should've been.

"How do you have my knife?" she asked sleepily.

Behind Vera, someone hooted with laughter. Vera startled, huddling closer to Kale while craning her neck to see who'd found them. In the process, she bashed her head against Kale's chin. Ducking, Vera wrapped both arms over her head, squinting from the pain. Kale clenched his jaw and winced. The laughing turned hysterical.

"Weaver," Kale gritted out.

"Wondered when you two cuddle bunnies would wake up." Marianna sat on a fallen log a few feet away, elbows resting on her knees and eyes crinkled with laughter. "Breakfast is about ready."

Behind Marianna loomed her traveling house. The trees

had spread out to make room for it. The witch looked between Vera and Kale with undisguised interest. Vera's face flamed. She desperately wanted to explain that getting handsy with Kale had been unintentional. *Girl, you know protesting will just make things worse. Ugh. We'll just pretend it didn't happen at all.*

"I made gingerbread cake for you, dear," Marianna said to Vera with amusement.

Kale ran a hand over his jaw and rose stiffly to his feet.

"Don't feel bad, Guardian." Marianna rose to her feet as well, brushing debris from the seat of her green pinstriped jumpsuit. "I'm confident you'd have woken sooner had I been anyone else. I'm old. I've had more practice sneaking around than most." Marianna tilted her head, listening to something. "Oh, I picked up some stragglers yesterday. They were looking for you two."

Kale tensed when the girl-version of Mimi burst from Marianna's home. Mimi leaped from the porch, easily clearing the steps, and plowed into Vera. Vera threw out a hand to keep them both from falling over. Mimi clung to Vera's neck while Vera sat there awkwardly. She knew Mimi, but she didn't really know Mimi. Addamas strolled through the door eating what looked like a piece of bacon. *Holy manna, could it be?* Marianna plucked the strip of meat from Addamas's fingers and walloped him upside the head.

"Satyr hooligan," Marianna scolded.

"What?" Addamas asked innocently, ducking Marianna's next blow.

Mimi snorted. Vera hid her smile.

"Let's go see if there's any breakfast left for the rest of us." Marianna glowered at Addamas and tossed the confiscated bacon to the nearest cats. The cats pounced.

Marianna disappeared into the house, and Addamas pouted while the kitties devoured his treat.

"Satyr," Marianna bellowed in outrage inside.

"Be right back," Addamas said and vanished.

"Where'd he go?" Marianna was at the front door, holding an empty grease-streaked platter.

Mimi pointed at the spot where Addamas had disappeared. Marianna squinted, then gave a satisfied nod. "He better bring back extra this time." Marianna headed back inside. "Get a move on, you all."

The three were quick to follow Marianna's bidding, Mimi pulling Vera to her feet. On the way to the house, Vera caught Kale throwing furtive glances at Mimi. He'd not spoken once since Mimi appeared. In return, Mimi had not acknowledged Kale at all. Well, breakfast was going to be loads of fun. Mimi was not willing to let things get that far, apparently. The girl hit the top step and swung around, hands on her hips.

"Are you even glad to see me?" Mimi demanded of Kale.

"I thought you might prefer if I didn't speak to you."

Mimi rolled her eyes and launched herself at Kale. Kale caught her, holding her above the ground. The strain on his face drained some. Mimi pulled back to press her forehead to Kale's. Vera pinned her gaze on the new hole in her tennis shoe, wondering if it was best to leave or hold still.

"I love you, dummy." Mimi licked Kale's cheek and grinned when Kale looked a bit uncomfortable.

Kale set Mimi back down on the top step and waved her inside fondly along with Vera. Inside, Marianna had transformed her loom room into a dining room. A large pedestal table held bowls of fruit, oatmeal, nuts, honey, cheese, and, yes, sliced gingerbread with butter. Vera's stomach gurgled. Addamas returned with a fresh plate of bacon. He'd added a pile of sausage links as well. With his most charming smile, Addamas offered the platter to their host. The weaver sighed with annoyance but her lips twitched. Marianna pinched Addamas's cheek affectionately, and then patted it before taking the plate. Not a gentle pat either. Addamas didn't flinch. The satyr winked at Vera when he noticed her staring.

"Eat. Then talk," Marianna instructed.

Vera didn't have to be told twice. Her eyes rolled into her head with her first bite of bacon in months. Back home, bacon had been an expensive luxury they didn't indulge in often.

"Did I shut the cupboard?" Addamas asked himself aloud, a sausage halfway to his mouth.

"You're cleaning it up if you didn't," said Kale.

"Nope, we're good. I'm sure I did." Addamas shoved the whole sausage into his mouth.

"What cupboard?" Vera asked curiously.

"The food cupboard," explained Mimi. Vera shrugged her shoulders in ignorance. "Kale didn't tell you about his magic cupboard? The one in his kitchen that conjures whatever food you want at any moment?"

"It didn't come up," Kale said defensively at Vera's pointed look.

"That's why it was full of trail mix when..." Vera pressed her lips closed.

"When you were trying to run away for the hundredth time," finished Kale. "You spilled that stuff all over my kitchen, you know."

"I was in a hurry."

"If you leave the cupboard open, it keeps spilling food onto the counter." Mimi wrinkled her nose. "If no one's home for a day or two, it can get disgusting."

"And after a week..." Addamas whistled. "I kept away until the place aired out."

"Because you knew Kale was going to kill you, idiot," said Mimi.

"How do you get a magic cupboard?" Vera asked.

"It was a gift from a leprechaun," Mimi answered.

"It was payment for my help," Kale clarified.

"Kale saved the guy's pet bunny from a hawk." Addamas leaned his chair back onto two legs.

"Really?" Vera couldn't hide her surprise.

"Our Kale's got a squishy middle." Addamas pressed out his lips, making goo-goo noises.

"And a secret following of worshipers," Mimi added.

"You're both ridiculous." Kale pushed the food around his plate with a scowl.

"Um, no. We're not," said Mimi. "That leprechaun tried to give you his pot of gold for saving his precious friend, but you wouldn't take it. Which won his complete and total adoration." Mimi turned to Vera conspiratorially. "The leprechaun offered Kale his fealty."

"Kale promised to cut off the leprechaun's legs beneath the kneecaps if the little man ever bowed to him again." Addamas laughed. "Leprechaun was so enamored by Kale's threats, he had that cupboard fashioned as a gift."

"Does he still pop up once in a while to ask if you require his service?" Mimi asked, but Kale had turned stoney.

"Kale threw a shovel at the leprechaun once. He brought it back to Kale gilded in gold." Addamas guffawed.

Kale flicked out a foot, and Addamas's chair fell over.

"Keep my chairs on all four legs, satyr," Marianna berated Addamas over the lip of her teacup, but her eyes sparkled with amusement.

While Addamas righted his chair, Marianna poured a cup of tea for Vera. Vera took it politely, wanting nothing to do with it.

"You'll like this one," Marianna assured. "It has ginger to keep your stomach settled while we're moving."

"We're moving?" Vera spun around in her chair. Trees passed by the window—*yep, we're moving*.

"My cats noticed a search party headed our way. I decided it was best for us to get going."

"Was the Maiden with the search?" Kale asked, seeming surprised by the news too.

"Could be. They sensed some strong magic." Marianna turned to Vera. "Speaking of magic. That charm doesn't look like the one I gave you."

"It's not." Vera rubbed the piece of eggshell between her fingers. "I gave the other one to someone who needed it more than me. I hope that's okay."

"It was your charm, dear. You're free to do with it what you will. Are you sure that was wise, though? You seem to have sucked up some magic recently, and I haven't got another cloak."

"More like I was force-fed. By the Maiden." Vera had everyone's attention with that.

"The Maiden is the betrayer?" asked Mimi with alarm.

"For the record, I'm really trying not to say I told you so." Addamas kicked back in his seat, folding his arms over his chest. He kept all four chair legs safely on the floor.

"It is interesting that you missed her deception, Guardian," noted Marianna.

"I haven't figured out how she did it yet," Kale admitted.

"How did she force-feed you magic, Vera?" asked Mimi.

"She shoved tendrils of her mist through my skin."

"Fun fact: Vera can see magic," Kale explained for the group. "She's only part siphon it seems."

"What else can you do?" Mimi sat forward excitedly.

"Her tears can heal," Kale answered for Vera. "She cannot be poisoned, she can purify someone who is poisoned, and she can swear like a sailor when she's really angry."

Vera flipped him off.

Marianna cackled and said, "I knew I liked you, Vera dear."

"You're part kargagon," Addamas said confidently.

"That's what I was thinking too," agreed Kale.

"What's that?" Vera tilted her head curiously.

"Unicorn," said Mimi.

"You cannot be serious." Vera looked between her friends. "A unicorn? Then where's my horn?"

"A unicorn's horn is made of magic, not bone," Addamas informed Vera. "You could still sprout one at will."

"Um, guys, I don't want a horn." Vera rubbed her forehead anxiously.

"Ignore him," Mimi said. "He's just messing with you."

Lie. Vera cringed. Kale covered his mouth with a hand, pinning Vera with an intense stare. *Interesting that he left out that little ability of mine.* Vera got the feeling she wasn't supposed to mention it either. The man was going to have some explaining to do.

"But human myths describe unicorns as horses or goats," Vera said, breaking the staring contest with Kale.

"They're not wrong," said Addamas. "Kale, how much time did you spend tracking down horny unicorns who'd snuck into the human realm looking for a frolic? Especially once that rumor got started about maidens sitting around in forests, waiting for a unicorn to come lay their heads in a warm lap."

"Not my favorite century," said Kale.

"Their realm is right beside yours, that's why there are so many images of unicorns in human records," explained Addamas. "When the witches stitched your realms together, there were some residual cracks. Those naughty boys found them."

"Unicorns sneak to Earth?" asked Vera.

"Not anymore. The unicorn's king finally hunted down every last crack and sealed them after a few herdsmen got killed. Human men-folk were never happy to find their maidens were not maidens anymore, if you know what I mean." Addamas wagged his eyebrows.

"She knows what you mean," Kale said dryly.

"But girls and unicorns? How?" Vera closed her eyes, hearing what she was asking. "Never mind. I seriously don't want to know."

"Hey, once you go furry, you never go—"

"Enough, Dam. They can use glamour, Vera," said Kale. "Sometimes they look like animals, but other times they look like us. Or like a troll or demon or giant or whatever they want. That's why it's very difficult to find a unicorn who doesn't want to be found."

"I could turn into a horse? Or a troll?" Vera's voice rose with panic.

"No," Mimi and Addamas lied at the same time.

Kale did not hide his smile fast enough at Vera's wide-eyed horror.

"It's not funny, Kalesius," Vera said with warning.

"You're right." Kale sobered. "How about we stop the Maiden and get you home so you don't have to worry about any of that?"

"Please." Something inside Vera's chest twisted at the reminder that she was going home soon. "How do we stop the Maiden?"

"I found where the horde is hiding in Montana if that helps," said Addamas. "Managed to keep up with Errock that last time."

"Why doesn't that sound like good news?" Vera asked Addamas.

"Because there are a thousand unnaturals with him," Addamas answered.

"I didn't expect there to be so many already," said Kale. "What about their master?"

"He's not there much, but he checks in every day, brings in a load of food and booze," Addams said thoughtfully. "He didn't use magic once."

"You think the Maiden has him on a diet?" asked Kale.

"I'd almost guarantee it. He was twitchy like an addict too long between hits."

"That has to have the siphon pretty upset with the Maiden," Kale said.

"Too bad you couldn't toss him, the unnaturals, and the Maiden into a pit together and let them kill each other off," said Vera.

"That's surprisingly blood-thirsty coming from you," said Addamas. "It'd be a great plan, though. If only we had a pit."

"We don't need a pit," said Kale. "I'll kill the siphon so the horde cannot be released, then we'll face the Maiden with the Mother's and Crone's help. Once the Maiden is dealt with, and the Mother has transitioned, we'll ask the Mother to assist in destroying the horde."

"We're headed for the base of the Kyopili now," Marianna informed them. "You'll have a chance to get the High Witches up to speed soon."

"The only way to get close enough to the Siphon Master to kill him is by joining the horde," said Addamas, who'd grown quiet.

"I know," replied Kale.

"No," said Vera. "First off, without the siphon to command the horde, what happens if the unnaturals go on a rampage? Can you fight off a thousand of them? What's to stop them from tearing across the Earth at that point? Secondly, based on everything I've seen, joining the horde is the worst possible idea there is." The thought of Kale joining them was a vice around Vera's chest.

"If Kale kills the siphon, he'll become their leader," Addamas revealed. "They won't do anything without Kale's okay after that.

"Which means everyone would be safe," Kale said. "It's a good plan with little threat of casualties."

"Except you," Vera pointed out.

"I can handle it." Kale turned to Addamas. "Would it work, though?"

"There's a lot of variables, but yeah. It's a solid plan."

"Are we agreed then?" Kale asked the group.

Everyone nodded except Vera, who sat dumbly.

"Come on," Mimi stood and grabbed Vera's hand. "Let them talk out the details. We'll go watch the trees go by."

Vera followed Mimi to the front porch. "What if something goes wrong? Kale will be alone in the middle of the horde. What if they turn on him? He says he can't be killed, but I don't know."

"Don't worry, we won't let him go in without backup," said Mimi.

"What backup?"

"Like we were talking about earlier, some people will stand beside Kale. That number is growing all the time. We'll make sure people are in place should things go sideways."

The tight coiling in Vera's chest loosened some, but Mimi seemed lost in thought now.

"So," drawled Vera. "You're a cat."

"Ha. I'm a morph. Not a very good one, though. Once I'm in my cat form, I have a hard time getting back to this one."

"Does it hurt?"

"It's not too bad. I have a hard time quieting my mind so I can change over, though. It takes a lot of focus."

"I can't imagine."

"So, who gave you this?" Mimi picked up Vera's charm for closer inspection.

"His name's Gage."

"Ohh," Mimi sang. "Is Gage hot?"

"He gave it to me because I had to leave my chick, Eggbert, behind. It's a piece of his shell. Apparently the acorn he carved is a symbol of luck."

"That's a yes on the hotness thing then." Mimi nudged Vera's arm. "He must like you quite a bit to be that thoughtful."

"What? No." Vera protested. "He was just being nice. He's like twenty-three or something. He's too old for me."

Mimi choked a bit, looking past Vera. "Hey Kale. What's up?"

"I wanted to make sure you two hadn't fallen off and been run over by the house."

"Now that's something I never thought I'd hear." Vera smiled ruefully up at Kale.

"Wanna come sit with us?" Mimi asked, fluttering her eyelashes.

"I don't think so. Be careful." Kale left them.

"What do you have against older men?" Mimi jumped right back to their previous conversation.

"Huh?" Vera peeled her mind away from the look on Kale's face just then. "Nothing, I... Nothing."

Mimi studied Vera's red cheeks suspiciously. "Gage totally likes you and you know it. You're being bashful right now. Aww, you're adorable. I'm glad I found you." Mimi leaned against Vera.

"Pretty sure I found you," Vera said.

"Then I shoved your butt out of a tree," Mimi replied. "How could we not be friends after that?"

"Mimi, dear," Marianna said from the doorway. "I just wanted to let you know we're almost to the world-gate."

"I thought we were on our way to Kyopili," Mimi said, puzzled.

"We are. The satyr said you'd be headed back to the meadow rather than joining the rest of the group."

"By Duat, I am." Mimi jumped up fuming. "I'll be back. You can keep this house moving."

"How are you holding up, Vera dear?" Marianna plopped into the spot Mimi had just vacated, cradling her bowl of acorns.

"I'm doing okay, I think."

"Well, your head hasn't exploded yet, so that's a good sign." Marianna patted Vera's knee.

"Don't speak too soon. I'm trying to figure out a plan B, and my head may still explode."

"What's wrong with the plan they have now?" asked the weaver.

"Oh, ya know. Either Kale could die or turn into a monster."

"And you care," said Marianna.

"Of course I care. He's an infuriating jerk most of the time, but he's my friend."

"Don't fret yet," Marianna said. "With a little luck, everything will work out."

"I don't have good luck, Marianna."

"Maybe that good luck charm around your neck will help with that."

Vera lifted the egg chip, eyeing it. "Mitch did say it was for luck.'"

"I think it will bring you just the luck you need," Marianna said optimistically. "In the meantime, you know what helps me when I'm stressed?"

"What?"

"Food." Marrianna popped an acorn into her mouth and thrust the bowl under Vera's nose. "Want one?"

"No thanks," Vera said with a polite smile.

18

Rock crushed beneath Kale's feet. Addamas tapped Kale's elbow and angled his head toward the empty branches where the Crone's crows should be roosting. This time of year, the trees should be teeming with newly hatched chicks and their mamas to yell at trespassers. The pools near the base of Kyopili were empty because the newts wintered at the palace with their Maiden. Kale wondered if any of the Mother's kits would be playing on the rocks outside their dens. Based on the unusual fox activity in Summartir, Kale was thinking not.

"I'm getting a bad feeling about this," Addamas said quietly.

The smell of new grass and spring were at odds with the ominous hush over the mountain. Addamas slowed, falling back to bring up the rear behind Mimi and Vera. The group clambered up the narrow ledge to the gaping mouth of the soul cavern. From there, they had a clear view of the deserted valley below.

"I don't like the idea of being in there with no lookout," Addamas said, eyeing the dark cavern. "Why don't Mimi and I keep watch while you and Vera have a chat with the High Witches?"

"Don't worry, Addamas," Mimi patronized the satyr. "I'll protect you if any dead witches come to say hi."

"I'm not scared of a few old ghosts, woman." Addamas's nose flared at Mimi's insult.

"You might not be, but this girl is." Vera pointed at herself using both thumbs. "In fact, I might pee myself really soon."

"You'll be fine. It's just like an old folks home for women," Mimi said.

"Only the women are crankier, can become invisible, and float through walls," Addamas said.

"Don't listen to this moron." Mimi punched Addamas in the arm for emphasis. "His sister dropped him on his head when he was a baby."

Vera's eyes widened.

"It wasn't her fault," Mimi said. "Addamas bit her, like a little demon."

"I regret nothing." Addamas raised a brow at Mimi. "My sister was obnoxious when we were kids. Like someone else I know."

"Suddenly, I'm ready to face a cave of ghosts," Vera mumbled.

"You and me both." Kale tugged Vera's arm, pulling her into the cave.

They'd gone barely more than a dozen feet when Vera whispered, "Now what?"

"Why are you whispering?" demanded an old woman, hunched with age. She hadn't been there a moment before. "I'm old. Speak up so I can hear you."

Vera jumped about twenty feet in the air and spun to face the High Crone, who sat casually on a stone altar. She appeared to be alone. Of course, other spirits could be surrounding them. They stood in what amounted to Kyolipi's reception area. If spirits didn't want to be seen, they weren't. He was just relieved the Crone had come to greet them. There was always a chance that she'd ignore them. In that case, they would've probably wandered the caves all afternoon without seeing anyone. Vera's attention latched onto the solid rock wall behind them, where the cave entrance had been moments before. He'd forgotten to mention the cave would seal them in until the witches were ready to let them go. The girl pinched the back of his arm to let him know she was not pleased. Kale resisted rubbing the spot. *Infernals be damned, that stings.*

"Crone," Kale dipped his head respectfully at the Crone.

"Took you long enough to come see me," chided the Crone. "If I'd had a crow left, I'd have sent it to peck out your eyes."

"Apologies for our delay," Kale said humbly. "We came as soon as we knew the truth."

"Bah." The Crone slashed a hand in front of herself. "You know nothing yet."

"We know the Maiden is responsible for trying to tear apart the world and destroy my realm," Vera said with a tiny edge of offense.

Kale pressed his lips together to contain his groan. One second the Crone was standing across the room, the next, she was inches from Vera's face.

"Child, I am tired. My crows are all dead. I am trapped here seeing all that wretched excuse for a witch is doing to my home, and I can do nothing. When I tell you that you know nothing, do not think me a fool. You. Know. Nothing."

"I've seen what the Maiden has done too," Vera said, quieter, but still not backing down.

"You saw, but you did not see," replied the Crown harshly.

"What did I not see?" asked Vera.

"What color magic does the witch use?" questioned the Crone.

"Black," answered Vera.

Kale's eyes fell closed. Of course. It made sense now.

"Did the witch ever use blue magic?" Kale asked Vera.

"Twice. The first day I met her, and when she blasted a hole in the banquet-hall ceiling after she'd been poisoned."

"The only times her clean hands were on display for the Guardian," said the Crone.

"It made sense for her to be confused after she was poisoned." Kale talked it through as the pieces fell into place. "No one questioned it—I didn't question it. That was by design, I suspect. Where is the Mother?" he asked the Crone.

"Now you know the truth," said the Crone, retreating to her spot, perched on the altar.

"Kale?" Vera frowned.

"The Maiden never deceived me," explained Kale. "A witch uses a single color of magic. You saw two different witches. The Mother is there too. The Maiden has no idea she's not alone."

"I'm not sure if I should be glad that she's double-stuffed instead of two-faced." Vera shivered. "How did no one notice?"

"The fox hiding in the henhouse," said Kale. "Like Liah told us."

"Can you stop Mother?" Vera asked the Crone.

"If that were possible, I'd have done it. Our magic is so intertwined, I cannot move mine against the Mother without her knowing what I do before I do it."

"If we weaken the Mother, force her to use her magic?" asked Kale.

"If you could force her to use all she has down to the final drops, I could rip her from the threads without unraveling the whole of the world. But Mother is sly, like her familiars. Getting her to use up her magic stores like that, I'm not sure it's possible."

"If the Maiden found out, could she help?" asked Vera.

"If Maiden could fight from that side and me from this side, we might be able to bind the Mother," said the Crone. "But once the Maiden transitions, she will be as helpless as I am now."

"So, we have less than three days to cut the Mother off from her unnatural army so she has no leverage, and let Maiden know what's going on without alerting Mother. Cake," Vera said sarcastically. "When we fail, the world will celebrate as my realm crashes and burns."

"You doubt your ability to succeed, girl?" asked the Crone curiously.

"Against these odds, absolutely. But that's never stopped me from trying. Ask him," Vera tipped her head at Kale.

"Vera will not be a part of the fight to come," said Kale emphatically.

"Never mind, don't ask him," Vera said. "It turns out he doesn't know me at all."

"I think you just gave me the hope I have lacked." The Crone's face softened. "Take luck with you."

With that final wish, the Crone disappeared. Behind them, the cave opening reappeared.

"Your part in this plan is to stay back and stay alive," Kale said firmly.

"I'm not discussing this with you," Vera turned and walked away.

Kale was working on his breathing when Vera stepped into the sunlight and slowly put her hands into the air. It was a particularly human movement that meant surrender. In a few strides, he inserted himself between Vera and the Mother waiting for them outside.

"I was not happy to learn you'd come here," Mother said. "But once I got here and secured a couple bargaining chips, I felt much better."

Mimi was bound to the mountainside by magical ties that Kale could not see and was circled by foxes. One fox had its mouth around Mimi's throat. Addamas stood back, unable to move without risking Mimi, which the satyr would never do, no matter how much the two bickered.

"I'll let you take your friends here with you," Mother offered Kale. "All you have to do is give me the siphon."

"No," yelled Mimi.

The Mother clicked her tongue, and a fox ripped a chunk of flesh from Mimi's calf. Mimi screamed. Addamas shot forward but Mother *tsked*. With the wave of a hand, she knocked him into a pine tree.

"Stay down. Or she'll lose more of that flesh you like so much," warned the Mother.

"I'll come with you," Vera cried, easing around Kale.

"No." Kale stepped in front of her again.

"I won't let her kill Mimi."

"But you'll let her kill you?"

"She doesn't want to kill me," Vera said loud enough for the Mother to hear. "She wants to use me."

"For someone so dense, that's rather insightful of you, Vera," said the Mother.

"Which means my life is safe for now. Mimi's is not." Vera squared her shoulders.

Vera was scared of spiders and jumpy around strangers,

but put someone in danger or piss her off, and she'd go up against a demon. She'd go up against Kale.

"You're right," said Kale, running a hand through his hair. "But I'm not sure I'm capable of letting you go. I need to figure out a way to save you both."

"Save Mimi," Vera said gently. "Let me save myself. And you."

"What do you mean by that?" Kale's stomach rolled.

"I'm a siphon and Mother has too much magic," Vera whispered. "This is my role in this battle."

"No, we stick to the plan we agreed to," said Kale.

"I never agreed to that plan. In fact, I hate it."

"Vera, you're killing me here."

"I have to try," said Vera. "At least this way we have another option if your plan fails. If something happens to my realm, and I did nothing when I could have, I wouldn't be able live with myself. Let me try to save my people."

"You have a trade," Kale informed the Mother heavily.

"First, I want the Pathmaker to open a path and walk away," instructed Mother.

"That wasn't part of the deal," argued Addamas.

"I'm not an idiot," said Mother. "You're waiting for me to be distracted by this exchange, but that won't happen."

"Go," said Kale to Addamas.

Addamas shook his head.

"I will bring Mimi home alive," Kale promised.

"Go, you fool satyr," said Mimi.

"If you die, I'm going to be pissed at you," Addamas said.

"Fine, if I die, you can chew me out later," Mimi said.

"Count on it." Addamas turned and vanished.

"Stay there, Guardian. Only Vera now. As soon as Vera and I have portaled away, my friends over there will leave, and you may gather your friend. Harm any of my foxes, and I'll repay it on your Vera."

Vera took a breath to steel herself.

"Oh, I almost forgot something." Mother pulled Gus's acorn medallion from her pocket. "I borrowed this from a birdy friend of yours. You'll want to do what you're told, Vera, and not do anything regrettable. Unless you're not worried about how many feathers he keeps."

Vera's breath hitched. Kale twirled her into his arms before she could walk away. He pressed his face to the top of Vera's head and held her tight.

"I won't be able to help you after all," Vera said. "Not when she has Gus. But I don't want to lose you either. If you go face the siphon, what will happen to you?"

Kale felt like he'd been punched in the gut. This girl would be his undoing.

"Look at me," Kale said. "I promise you, you will not lose me. Whatever happens, I will be the same man when I come for you as I am today. Trust that, okay? I'm calling in our bet now. Trust me. No arguments, no questions."

"Got it, Scotchie," Vera said with a pathetic attempt at a smile.

The Mother yanked Vera from him. A portal swirled up to take them away. Kale let them go.

"WHAT ARE WE DOING HERE?" Vera asked, standing over Margory as the young girl slept.

"I want you to siphon Margory's magic and give it to me." Mother brushed Margory's hair back from her face. "I slipped a sleeping potion in her tea. She won't wake."

"I don't know how to do that," Vera protested.

"You threw my magic back at me, don't pretend you didn't."

"But I didn't mean to. I was just trying to get it out of me. I've never even siphoned magic on purpose before."

"I think with the right motivation, you'll figure it out." Mother wrapped her fingers around Margory's throat and squeezed.

"Don't," Vera cried.

"Shh." Mother released Margory's throat and placed a finger to her lips. "You don't want to wake a neighbor. Their blood would be on your hands too." Mother tapped Margory's throat. "Look right here for the magic inside Margory. Feel it, see it, taste its essence on the back of your tongue. Then take it. Stealing magic is in your nature. If you don't, I'll kill her. Your choice."

Vera searched Margory's skin, looking for the glow. "I don't see any magic in her."

"There's not much there. You'll have to look deeper."

Vera squinted, peering into the girl's flesh. There it was, tucked in the back of Margory's throat, like a dying blue ember.

"It's the same color as Maiden's."

"Yes, Margory's a Silvet too. The child only has a touch of magic, though. She won't even miss it."

While Mother spoke, Vera looked for the psycho-witch's store of magic. It was not a tiny ball. It filled Mother's whole being.

"If you're thinking about siphoning my magic, I'll warn you that you'll only get a sip before you can take no more. Then I'll kill the girl."

Vera turned away, hating that she couldn't drain the Mother dry. But the witch was right, Vera had nearly gagged on the bit Mother had thrown at her before. That had been nothing compared to what she still possessed. Defeated, Vera focused on the flickering blue ember within Margory, urging it to come to her. It took little encouragement for the magic to flow to Vera. Like Mother's mist, Margory's magic soaked through Vera's skin, but it did not feel overwhelming like Mother's. Margory's magic settled inside Vera like a tiny nibble of deliciousness. Vera wanted more. She definitely did not want to give it away. Most certainly not to Mother.

"Margory is depending on you," Mother reminded Vera.

Vera gritted her teeth and plucked the magic from its place inside her and threw it at Mother. The tiny blip slid inside Mother, melting into the other magic there. In a heartbeat, it was indistinguishable from the blackness.

"I think with a little more practice, you'll be able to keep a steady stream of magic between any witch and me," said Mother.

"You want me to be your extension cord to endless power," Vera concluded.

"I'm not sure what an extension cord is, but if it becomes necessary, then yes, endless power sounds right."

"You already have so much magic. Why do you want more?"

"You think this is about power?" Mother gave Vera a pitying smile.

"It sure seems like it."

"I don't care about power. I care about avenging the witches who have suffered unrest for a thousand years. Power is only a necessary tool to right that wrong."

"Maiden said your mother is trapped there," Vera said.

"Along with hundreds of other witches who will never be reborn, never move on from their past life and the barbarity they experienced. All this time, their murderer has walked free, unburdened by what he's done to them."

"Their killer is still alive?"

"Oh, Maiden forgot to tell you that, did she? Yes, the man responsible for killing thousands, including my mother, has been by your side this whole time. Touching you. Making you smile."

"Kale." The hole in Vera's heart widened. "But he can't be killed."

"Everyone can be killed if you know how to do it. That butcher-masquerading-as-a-hero is tied to the meadow. Destroy the meadow and you destroy him."

"That's why you're killing the threadbearers," Vera said, finally understanding the endgame.

"I'll remake the world without the meadow, Kalesius, or humans."

"But you're killing your own people."

"I never intended to kill any witches. I only planned to pull their world-threads from them. I couldn't face another season trapped with the unavenged souls of my sister witches so I stayed here and I worked. But I wasn't careful. The Crone figured out what I was doing. She found the siphons I'd smuggled from Earth, the ones I was training to siphon the threads from the threadbearers. She killed them all and put a spell on the gate so I could not bring any more humans into Summartir."

"That's what Liah stumbled across that's haunted her ever since," said Vera.

"To Liah, it seemed like the Crone had lost her mind. Raving mad and murdering what appeared to be men and witches. When I got control, I convinced Liah that the Crone...that *I* had been ill and delusional. That excuse worked until the Crone broke through and told Liah the truth. I thought if I threatened Liah's unborn children, she would keep silent."

"You killed Liah's baby," accused Vera.

"So quick to jump to assumptions for someone who's one of the world's most despicable beings. I did not kill Liah's son. However, his untimely death did make things easier for me since Liah shut up for a time. I hadn't realized how far her mind was gone, though. So far gone that she'd talk to the Guardian himself. Looking back, I should've just killed her in the beginning."

"How did you know Liah talked to Kale?"

"The Guardian should have killed that fox, as Liah asked."

"Instead, your little spy reported back to you, and you came to the farm to tie up loose ends," said Vera. "Using the same berries that killed Liah's son."

"It seemed poetic. It would've made for a convincing suicide too. It was unfortunate that you messed that up. Even more unfortunate that Liah wasn't a threadbearer."

"I don't understand. If you're planning to untie Earth and let it collapse, why do you need the unnaturals?"

"You think those are mine?" Mother pulled the covers up higher over Margory. "Which means the Guardian believes it too. If he's planning to take out the Siphon Master and destroy the horde, I hope he succeeds. They are the only thing that could stop me at this point."

"Someone else made them. To stop you." Vera's lungs constricted. *What have we done?*

"I'm sure of it. When you and the guardian brought news of the horde to the Maiden, I realized the Crone must have confided in someone other than Liah. Someone willing to bring those abominations back to life to save a realm crawling with vermin. Then your ever-trusting Guardian said he suspected Cassie of poisoning him. I thought Cassie might be trying to complete the job that the gate failed at—

keeping you from me. Which would mean she was responsible for the unnaturals too. Only after I killed her, the horde continued to grow. So, she was not to blame after all."

"It must kill you, knowing that whoever is fighting against you got close enough to slip poison into your drink at the banquet. That they're still out there." Vera felt a sense of pleasure throwing that in Mother's face.

Mother laughed. "Yes, I suppose I would be bothered if I hadn't been the one to put that poison in my own glass. I needed Maiden to wake up confused and not question her missing memories of the night. Since someone was already poisoning people, it was convenient."

"That's messed up."

"I admit, I was angry when I couldn't send Cassie's bloodstone to you. But when Cassie's death unraveled some of the world threads, I knew then that killing the threadbearers was the only course left to me. It's the only way to get rid of your abhorrent realm, as I'd planned, before the horde is sent against me."

"What happens if the horde gets here before you find the last threadbearers?"

"That's why I was very excited to learn that you are not like other siphons. Other siphons can take magic, but you can give magic also. I'd never seen that before. If the horde comes before I restitch a better world, you'll keep me powered until I destroy them all. Allowing me to get rid of the meadow and Earth without worrying about any more threats."

"The horde isn't the only threat, though, is it? Maiden can stop you. That's why you don't want her to find out you are here."

"If you attempt to tell Maiden about me, that man-bird will be the least of your concerns. I'll go after your cat friend, the satyr, and that mutilated chick you're so fond of. Everyone and everything you care about. And I'm always there, watching and listening. So don't think you can get a message to Maiden without my getting it too."

"You're a real sick piece of shit, aren't you?"

"Think what you want about me. But know that whoever raised an unnatural horde is ten times worse than me, because they are fools. They have no idea what that horde can do if it's freed. But I still remember. I was there. So yes, I will kill my own people to stop those aberrations from escaping your cesspit of a realm. Even though it is not how I wanted this to play out."

"How are you okay with killing an entire race of people?"

"Killing them protects the other hundred or so races in this world. Unlike the rest of the world's species, yours is multiplying like an infestation of termites. It needs to be eliminated."

Margory stirred. Mother rose and dragged Vera from the room of the magic-less witch girl. Vera had just made a witch into a human. The very thing that Mother planned to eradicate.

KALE ROLLED his shoulders back and walked out of the pathway Addamas had set. A thousand unnaturals turned to eye their prey.

"I want to join the horde," Kale announced clearly, holding his arms away from his body so they knew he was no threat.

With grunts and growls of disappointment, the sea of unnaturals parted to let Kale pass. It was the only declaration that gave a man a chance to live. If the Master decided a man was not worthy of joining the horde, he became the horde's toy until he died. Errock stepped into the path the unnaturals had made.

"Kalesius. I told the Master you'd come."

"He's waiting for me?" asked Kale.

"Waiting for you to realize you're fighting for the wrong side," confirmed Errock. "And here you are."

"You said I'd have a chance to destroy the witches who sentenced me to an eternity worse than Hell in that meadow."

"Oh, you will." Errock grinned. "You're going to lead us through the gates to their doorsteps, brother."

"Perfect. When do I meet the siphon?"

"You just missed him, actually," replied Errock.

"He left you in charge?" asked Kale with surprise.

"He trusts me. I told him he could trust you too, but you understand how it is."

Kale did. "How can I earn the Master's trust?" he asked, knowing he'd have to prove himself.

"See, I knew you'd be ready to go." Errock slapped Kale on the back. "There's only one little thing you have to do first."

"Name it."

"That sweet little human girl of yours—"

"No," Kale said flatly.

"Now hold up." Errock lifted a hand to calm the shifting horde, which wanted the defiant man for their fun now. "I'm not asking you to do anything with Vera. She lived with a peculiar shifter bird, though. Kill him and you're in."

"I won't be able to find him," Kale said, knowing Gus was already a prisoner in Summartir.

"No worries. We've already found him for you and brought him here," said Errock.

It was all Kale could do to keep his expression unreadable. If the horde had Gus, then Vera had gone willingly with the Mother for nothing. Kale was sure he could've found a way to save Mimi without Vera martyring herself. In the end, he'd only let her go because Mother supposedly had Gus. He couldn't force her to sacrifice her adopted father when there was a chance to save him. But Mother never had the man.

"Where is he?" Kale didn't have to force the edge to his words.

Errock turned and pointed at a leaning shack that must have been abandoned years before. "All tied up and waiting for you. I told you, I knew you'd come."

Kale moved unhesitatingly toward the shack. Vera would never forgive him, but Kale could accept that so long as she lived.

Hand on the latch, Kale paused. "Errock, were you responsible for killing a nest of baby chicks and hacking up their beaks recently?"

"Now that was some fun times." Errock winked.

Kale tucked that information away for when he killed Errock then pushed through the door. Gus sat against the wall in his human form. The man's mouth and wrists were bound with strips of stained fabric. The door fell closed. Kale tugged the gag from Gus's mouth.

"Ah, my executioner has arrived," greeted Gus. "It's nice to officially meet you, Guardian."

"You don't seem distressed by your impending death." Kale folded his arms.

"Nah. My Suzie's been gone a year. My kind mates for life, and when one dies, the other follows. I've stayed alive long enough. I'm ready to join my Suzie now."

"You don't care that you're leaving Vera alone in the world?"

"I'm not. I made sure Vera found you first."

Kale frowned at that. "After Vera learns I've killed you, she'll never forgive me."

"Yes, she will. See, I've always known this is how I would die—in this way and in this place. My Suzie saw it the same as she saw her own death. Suzie made me promise I wouldn't die of a broken heart before this moment. She begged me to let my death make a difference for Vera, for the world. I could never say no to that woman."

"How does dying here make a difference?" asked Kale.

"For starters, it's the only way you'll be accepted into the horde and that needs to happen."

"Suzie saw all this?"

"She was miraculous, my Suzie." Gus smiled, a smile full of love at the memory his lost wife.

"Did she say if we would stop the Mother in time?"

"It's one possible outcome," said Gus. "Although for that to happen, I have to die here."

"What else do we need to happen?"

"I cannot share anything of what will come, or you will fail. But all that *has* happened was necessary. Even the Mother capturing Vera. Which is why I made sure it was the path Vera took."

"You gave the Mother your medallion." Kale's hands balled into fists and fell to his sides. "You let that witch use it to manipulate Vera."

"Yes. Want to kill me now?"

"With every inch of my being," Kale growled.

"Good. Take care of Vera for me."

"For as long as I can," Kale said, still not sure he could

kill the man Vera cared so much about. *Kill him, sure, but face Vera after? How can I do that?*

"I know you're still trying to figure out how to get out of killing me. You do have an alternative option."

"Care to share it?"

"I'm going to die in this shack. There's no way around that. However, if I die by my own hands, I will never see my Suzie again. If you kill me, I will. You get to decide my fate."

With that, Gus began to expand, feathers sprouting from his flesh. As he grew, the cloth tied around his neck began to cut off his air. Gus gagged. There was no way for Kale to undo the band. It was sunken into the man's neck too deep. Kale could either stand and watch the bird slowly suffocate or end it quickly. It wasn't a choice. Kale wrapped his hands around Gus' head and twisted sharply. The shifter fell limp. Kale brushed Gus's eyes closed, untied the cloth that had choked him, and walked out of the shack.

Errock checked Kale's handiwork before dragging the body from the shack. The field of monsters roared with delight. Hands grabbed Gus and tossed him into the horde. There'd be nothing left to find of the man once they had finished with him. *Well, Gus, I'm in the horde.*

19

Vera marked the bottom of the door with the edge of a candle. One more palace room checked. Still no sign of Gus. At the next set of doors, Vera looked up and down the hall before wiggling the doorknob. Locked. Taking a breath, she rapped quickly with her knuckles and waited, hiding the candle behind her back. A bleary-eyed witch with tightly-curled orange hair and midnight skin opened the door.

"Oops, I'm so sorry," Vera gushed. "Wrong room."

The witch glared and slammed the door in Vera's face. Vera quickly marked the bottom of the door and moved on to the next. She had no idea where Maiden's room was, but she had to be getting closer. If Vera could figure out where Gus was, she could figure out a way to free him. Hopefully, he wasn't in a dungeon under the palace. Just in case, Vera was looking for creepy passageways and stairs too.

The morning sun hung low in the sky. Light shone through a wall of windows at the end of the hall. Colorful tents and carts belonging to Summartir families filled the rolling hills beyond the palace grounds. People had been showing up in a steady stream by road and through portals to join in the transition festivities. They were blissfully unaware that Mother was already here and murdering their people. The market stalls were full of witches selling bottled magic, charms, herbs, fabrics, toys, furniture, and even cages filled with ferrets, salamanders, and aejoh-colored butterflies like the one from the farm. Now that Vera had siphoned witch magic, it was easy to see the glow of it among the people below. Even dim blips of magic like Margory's. Vera was horrified that her body craved a taste of that glow now.

Vera turned away from the growing crowds, returning to her search. She had to find Gus and get out of there. Kale would be coming to face Mother soon, and Vera would not be a bargaining chip for the witch to use against him. Not to mention, once Gus was safe, Vera planned to latch on to Mother's magic and slurp it up, until she popped from over-siphoning or the evil witch was drained. Whichever came first. As Vera neared the next doors, they burst open. A rumpled young man stumbled out, followed by the giggles of at least a couple women. The man winked at Vera and sauntered down the hall. Vera marked those doors without knocking and hurried on. At the next intersection, Vera recognized where she was—the stairs to the picture hall. Hiking up the ridiculous dress she'd been given to wear, Vera climbed upwards. *Freaking Lady Unlucky*. She'd managed to stumble upon the Mother, who was there admiring a portrait. Vera wondered if it was too late to retreat. Mother looked over and smiled. *Yup, definitely too late.*

"Vera, I'm glad you could return for the end of the transition festival," said the witch while a blue lizard poked its head out of her hair near the witch's ear.

"Maiden," Vera said tensely, checking the witch's eyes for any sign of the Mother who was hiding in there somewhere.

"Where's your protector this morning?" asked Maiden, looking for Kale behind Vera.

"He had something to take care of," Vera answered honestly.

"He's so overbearing, he probably decided you'd be safer in here than out there where everyone is gathering, and where all the fun is happening," guessed Maiden.

"He is very overbearing," Vera agreed carefully.

"When he gets back, can you tell him I want to see him? I want to make sure he gets the Mother up to speed on everything that's been happening as soon as possible tomorrow."

"Sure. But I'm not sure when that will be," Vera said.

"It's okay. Whenever. I'm not going to be busy today. I usually spend my last day enjoying the festival, but my heart isn't in it this year with so many good witches dead and missing this week. I'll have to go out there soon and see how the news is spreading," continued Maiden. "Mother will have a tough season, keeping everyone calm and unmasking our betrayer. I feel rather bad leaving her with this situation."

"It's not like it's your fault," managed Vera. "I'm sure she won't blame you."

"I know you're right, but it's still difficult." Maiden rubbed Blue's head. "Mother is incredible. You're going to like her. And she'll fix everything."

"What were you looking at?" Vera indicated the painting Maiden had been appreciating since there was no way she was touching that conversation.

"Come look." Maiden waved Vera closer. "This is my

grandmother's dragon. I was trying to memorize the details so I could share it with her when I get there."

"Are you glad to be going back?" asked Vera

"Yes and no," Maiden said. "I miss my grandmother when I'm here. But I miss my friends when I am there."

"Does it hurt when you leave your body?"

"No, it feels like letting go of the shore and allowing a stream to carry me away."

"Hopefully not a stream that's as cold as the one I was in this week." Vera forced her mind to flit over the Kale-related details of that experience. "It fed into a lake with a monster which tried to eat me."

"You've had an exciting week."

"You could say that." Vera frowned. "Could you let go anytime? Like, if you wanted to leave early?"

"I can only leave during the solstice. Summartir has three each year. The ties that bind us here loosen for a short time during that period. Only the High Triad witches can come and go from our body, since it is not truly ours. I'll wait for the Mother to get here first, and then slip out. Once solstice passes, the power rebinds to the land and Mother will be safely locked in until the next solstice."

"How will she find her way here?"

"Our people sing for us. She'll follow their voices."

"She won't accidentally end up in the wrong body?"

"Oh no. Every other body is already filled to the brim. I'll push myself aside to let her in."

"What if you don't leave?"

"Vera, enough," warned Mother through Maiden's mouth, and then she was gone.

Maiden shook her head dizzily, "I think I ate too many tarts for breakfast. The sugar is catching up to me. Mother is not going to be pleased with a sugar hangover when she gets here," Maiden bit her bottom lip sheepishly. "Anyway, of course I'll leave. It would be too cramped with more than one of us here. But other than my newts leaving the palace to come be near me at Kyopili, you won't know anything has changed."

"I can't believe those lizards can hide so well." Vera studied Maiden's hair.

"Actually, only Blue is with me today. The rest are getting one last soak in the lily pool. They tend to mope my last days because they know we're leaving it behind for the rest of the year. I should probably go see them so their feelings aren't too hurt. Do you want to see them too?"

"Sure," Vera said with more enthusiasm than she'd intended. She hoped Mother hadn't noticed.

It was a short walk to Maiden's room. Vera glanced around as inconspicuously as possible when she walked through the doors. There was nowhere to hide a giant bird.

"Your rooms are beautiful," said Vera to explain away her interest in the space. "I bet Mother is looking forward to being back here."

"Mother's taste is a little different than mine. Her foxes don't enjoy the humidity in my room either."

"Ah. I hadn't thought of that."

Mother had her own room. Probably near Maiden's. Maiden lifted the edges of the lily pads before brushing aside the flowers at the edge of the pool. The witch's lips pinched tighter with each failed attempt to find her familiars.

"I think those little stinks have already left. They've been extra temperamental this year." Maiden sighed. "I should've spent more time with them. Next winter, I'll have to add more flowers to earn their forgiveness."

Vera's heart ached. She knew the newts likely hadn't left

at all. Just like Crone's crows, Mother had gotten rid of them to keep her presence a secret. Maiden stood up from the edge of the pond and brushed off her knees.

"Sorry, Vera. I know you were excited to see them. You'll have to come back next winter and visit me again. We can share dragon stories too."

"That sounds like fun." Inexplicably, Vera's eyes began to sting, but she yawned to cover it up. "Wow. I didn't sleep much last night. I think I may go get a nap if that's okay."

"I'll walk with you," Maiden volunteered. "I'm headed that way anyway to go see the market. Sure you don't want to come?"

"Maybe later. I need to crash for a bit right now."

"I completely understand."

Vera memorized each turn on the way back to her room and watched Maiden leave before slipping down the hall to do some more snooping. She hadn't made it far before she rounded a corner and nearly mowed over Margory. Vera grabbed the girl by the shoulders so she didn't end up on the floor and apologized. Margory waved one hand to show she was fine and shuffled down the hall.

"Are you okay, Margory?" Vera called after the girl.

"Just tired. I'll be fine."

Vera's shoulders fell. She suspected rest wouldn't help the girl. Humans wished for magic, but since they'd never felt it, they didn't know what it was to miss it. Margory only had a dab of magic, but she obviously felt the loss intensely. Did the girl even understand why she felt the way she did? Vera wondered how long it would take Margory to feel okay again, or if the girl would always feel off. If taking away a drop of magic hurt like that, what would happen to a threadbearer if someone took all their magic? Liah had seemed okay. But then again, Liah had willingly gifted her magic to her son. No one had stripped it from her. Vera would never drain someone of their magic ever again. Except Mother. But to do that, she had to get out from under Mother's thumb.

More determined than ever to find Gus, Vera pushed forward. Mother's rooms were easy enough to find now that Vera knew the way. They were next door to Maiden's rooms. The room was freshly aired out for Mother's return. Unlike Maiden's jungle room, Mother's room was arid. The walls were rock with narrow crevices and burrows. There was nowhere to hide Gus. Ready to shriek in frustration, Vera hit up the hallways again. By sunset, there wasn't a single door without a candle wax smudge. She'd searched the kitchens, ballrooms, meeting halls, and every single room in the palace, but she hadn't found him. Nor had she found evidence of anything like a dungeon. Vera had failed. *How can I help my friends take down Mother and keep Suzie's Gus safe at the same time?*

KALE STARED up at the stars. He'd walked across the prairie until he couldn't hear the whoops of the unnaturals or the screams of their entertainment. A truckload of college kids had the unfortunate idea to drive out to the middle of nowhere to shoot cans and get drunk. They'd tried to run once they realized their bullets didn't pierce the skin of the unnaturals. For a bit of sport, the unnaturals had let a kid or two run for a while. It amped up the fear wafting off of them before the unnaturals hunted them down. Tonight, Kale added five more tallies to the body count he claimed responsibility for. One girl had seen Kale standing on two legs and pleaded for his help. He'd turned and walked away, abandoned her to the horde. Just like he'd done in the memory Vera had lived.

Kale didn't have another choice. He couldn't fight the horde and win while the siphon still lived. If he tried, he'd only blow his cover, and the kids would still die. Possibly worse deaths than they were already guaranteed. With them, millions of other people would die when this realm ceased to exist. If Kale was honest, he didn't care about a billion humans. He cared about one, and she was not even human anymore. Vera was waiting for Kale to rescue her from a witch and get her back home. He couldn't do that if her home was gone.

"Afraid you'll forget what it feels like to stand on two legs?" Grass crushed beneath Errock's hoofed feet as he approached Kale.

"Have you forgotten?"

"Fortunately, yes. I don't miss it. You won't either."

"How did you survive all this time?" Kale asked.

"Magic," Errock answered cryptically.

"I'm surprised you chose to follow a new Master when he didn't create you and yours is long dead. You didn't have to follow anyone. Why not make a different way?"

"Because I enjoy it. I like being part of a horde. And taking what I want. I seem to remember when you enjoyed a little bloodletting yourself. Don't worry, that will all come back to you once you give up those pathetic legs you're wearing now. All those moral dilemmas you're fighting in your head will go away too."

"How soon can this happen?"

"The Master is here. He's ready for you."

Kale followed Errock toward a choice that was going to rip Vera's trust in him to shreds.

Vera woke with a start. The hair on the back of her neck rose. She peered into the darkness surrounding her.

"Who's there?" she called.

No one answered. Not that an intruder was likely to step forward and greet her properly. There were no shadowy forms or anything out of place in her room. Her heart pounded like there were two in her chest competing against each other. Vera pressed a fist to her chest. Something caressed Vera's shoulder, and she bolted off the bed. No one was there. Just the pile of blankets. One must have slipped and brushed against her. Vera's whole body felt constricted like it was stretched too tightly over her bones. In fact, her ribs were crushing her. Vera struggled to draw a breath. She stumbled to the bathroom. At the sink, she pumped water from the faucet. Her hands trembled as she raised a handful of water to her lips. And choked. There wasn't enough room for the water to go down.

Whoa there. Calm down, Vera.

Vera froze. That wasn't her thought.

Suzie always said she wasn't raising no fool, said the voice.

Vera's eyes flew open wide. *Gus?*

Obviously.

How are you in my head? Where are you? I've been trying to find you.

I'm not just in your head. I'm in you, said Gus.

Care to repeat that?

Basically, I'm possessing you. Instead of crawling into your sleeping bag and shoving you to the bottom, I shimmied in beside you so we could share.

Vera was too stunned to move. *How?*

Not really the most important thing to worry about right

now. *Suffice it to say, the solstice has begun so a soul like mine, released from its body at just the right time, has a little extra freedom before afterlife calls. Finding you was easy. You're not like anyone else around these parts.*

You're dead, Vera concluded.

Possession works best that way.

Mother promised she wouldn't kill you if I cooperated.

She didn't kill me, said Gus.

Who killed you then?

Ahh. While we're getting off subject, would you mind scooching over a bit? I'm feeling squished over here.

Vera unconsciously took a small step to the side. Literally. She side-stepped in the bathroom. She immediately felt Gus laughing at her.

"Leave me alone. I have no idea how to shove myself over inside my own body." She was so flustered she'd forgotten that she didn't need to speak out loud.

Here, just relax. I'll help, said Gus, dousing his amusement at Vera's expense. Just like that, Gus smooshed Vera to the side. Like he'd wiggled his butt between her body and her spirit, forcing her aside so he could have the space he wanted. *There, that's better.*

"I'm getting a little freaked out here," Vera admitted.

You're doing very well. If I wasn't here, do you think you'd be able to make room on your own if you needed to?

"Uh. Yeah, I guess. Now that I know what it feels like."

Good. Don't forget it.

"Why would I ever need to do this?"

You never know when a soul may need a little landing spot. It's always good to be prepared.

"In case a dead friend wants to visit?"

Exactly. Suzie would want you to be a gracious host.

"Could Suzie visit me?" Vera's heart spiked with excitement.

Sorry, girl. She's already moved on. But if she were still here, you can bet she'd visit and talk your ear off.

"Oh. That makes sense." Vera was disappointed. "I'm sorry I didn't get to you soon enough to save you."

You couldn't have. I was never here to begin with. Kalesius killed me back on Earth a little while ago.

Vera couldn't breathe. Her lungs wouldn't pull in air.

Breathe, girl! He didn't want to. I didn't give him much choice.

Gus played his memory of Kale and the shack in the middle of a field of unnaturals.

"How could you do that to him?" Vera was appalled. "Plus, you helped Mother trick me into coming here?" Vera was seeing red and wondering how to deck the man possessing her without giving herself a black eye.

As long as you'll forgive him, Kale will be fine.

"There's nothing to forgive him for. You, however, are unspeakable. Get out of me."

I always did appreciate your stubborn temper. Just like Suzie's when she was your age.

Vera gave Gus her metaphorical back.

The important thing is that the Mother has no hold on you now that I'm gone. But she doesn't know I'm gone. Or that you know. Which gives you an advantage."

Vera maintained her silent treatment.

I'm sorry I never tried harder to get to know you. I should have. But I knew what I'd have to do to you when this time came. I thought it'd be easier if you didn't love me like you loved Suzie. I am sorry. Know I have the best intentions and know we are both proud of you, girl. You can have everything you want in this life, so go make it happen.

Wait. Tears dripped down Vera's cheeks. Gus was gone. Her body felt too big now. And lonely. "I'll miss you, Gus. Tell Suzie I love her," Vera whispered to the empty bathroom.

This time Vera knew she didn't imagine the caress across her cheek or the kiss on the top of her head.

20

K ale's bare torso was slick with sweat when he reached Earth's world-gate. A few steps and he'd be back in the meadow. The rumble of thousands of hooves behind Kale echoed the ones beneath him. He'd led the horde over hundreds of miles that night and into the morning. Now, they'd follow him to Summartir.

"Find the Mother witch!" Kale bellowed to all those who could hear him. The rest would follow their lead. "Take her, and no one else will be strong enough to stop you. You'll never have to hide on the prairies waiting for scraps again. Summartir will be yours!"

The horde raised their voices in a cry for blood and power. By withholding magic, the witch had effectively starved the horde, kept them weak and destructible. And very angry. They would slaughter everyone in their path all the way to the witch who'd held them down. They would claim her magic, and then all the magic in Summartir. Nothing would be able to stop them after that.

"But remember, the siphon girl is mine!" Kale said as a warning.

Kale twisted to meet the eyes of his closest soldiers. They nodded, understanding of his orders. None would touch Vera except him. *And once she learns the truth, she'll never want my touch again.*

VERA STOOD JUST inside the palace doors with Margory, hidden in the shadows. They had a clear view of the palace steps, where the transition would take place. Mother surfaced to give Vera a few last-minute warnings and threats before Maiden walked outside. The witch naively waved farewell to the gathered crowd. Vera hadn't worried about anything Mother said except the reminder that the Monroe family was hunting Vera as a murderer. If Vera knew what was good for her, she'd not let anyone see her in case they recognized her.

Maiden stood on the palace landing. Below, a sea of faces looked up toward her. The remaining triad witches solemnly lined the palace steps on either side of their High Witch. After the transition, those most powerful of witches of Summartir would scour the crowd for death brands. They'd kept news of the recent deaths quiet so the crowds would gather as usual without fear. Those happy people who'd come to wish Maiden farewell and welcome Mother back had no idea what was coming for them. Celebrations and merriment would not continue into the night as they'd imagined. Instead, there would be an all-out witch hunt. Among the hunters, Mother would secretly search for witches powerful enough to be threadbearers. Those would all die. As many as necessary until Mother found the right ones. Given enough time, Vera had no doubt that Mother would find Liah's son too. The boy who would grow up without a mother because the High Mother murdered his. Vera's anger rose.

By now, Kale had either dismantled the horde or failed. Either way, he hadn't made it back to Summartir in time to face off with Mother and keep Maiden from leaving. So, Vera would do all she could to take down the witch-bitch herself. Vera took Margory's hand. The girl's face was pale and drawn. Vera located Mother's magic. Mother had squished into a churning mass in the corner of the High Witch's chest, where she could stay hidden from Maiden. Vera braced herself and pulled. The magic barely touched Vera before she directed it into Margory. Unlike when Mother had forced magic into Vera before, this didn't fill her up. Margory was taking all Vera gave her. The girl was a bottomless well. A single voice rose from the crowd as a young girl began singing to show Mother the way to them. The crowd joined in. Vera pulled harder, and then went flying as Mother surfaced. The High Witch yanked Vera off her feet and dashed her onto the steps in front of the palace with a sweep of her hand through the air.

Holy mother of bruises, that hurts. The chorus of songs turned to gasps. Lifting her head, Vera saw Mother stalking toward her enraged. Behind Mother, Margory held a hand to her chest where the magic had pooled. The girl stared at Vera in awe.

"You will get that back for me," said Mother, picking Vera up by the front of her dress. "Now."

"Not a chance, you old bat." Vera grinned.

Mother swung back and smacked Vera across the face. Vera's lip split. Blood dribbled down her chin.

"Do you not care about your bird friend?" threatened Mother.

"You mean my foster dad? He told you not to lie to me,

didn't he? That's why you never actually said that you'd kill him, because you never had him in the first place. I swear it's a good thing he's already dead."

Mother's eyes flinched then hardened. The witch swung back to give Vera another blow, but her hand froze in midair, tangled in white threads.

"Release her," commanded Gage, surrounded by the grown male witches from the Monroe family.

"How are you doing this?" asked Mother.

"The same way we will stop you from destroying Vera's home," replied Gage. "With the magic our mothers gave us." Mother's eyes widened as Gage made a motion with his arm, sending Mother sprawling.

Gage caught Vera before she fell. "Hey there, trouble," said Gage with a wink.

"What are you doing?" Vera looked between the men and the crowd that was backing up like they sensed an outbreak of plague. Even the triads shuffled back. "They'll know your secret now."

"Pretty sure that one's officially out of the bag," Gage said. "It's time Summartir accepts that men can be witches too."

"It's you," said Mother, crawling to her feet. "That's why I couldn't find the last threadbearers. I wasn't looking for males."

It can't be. Vera scanned the men around her. Could the Monroe men be responsible for not one but two world threads? They'd had the perfect hiding place, and now they'd stepped right out and waved their arms to get Mother's attention.

"Run." Vera shoved away from Gage. "Why did you come here?"

Gage pulled a white feather, Gus's feather, from his pocket. "He said you'd need help."

The man to Gage's left lifted into the air. Ribbons of black mist wound around his limbs.

"Which of you is the threadbearer?" demanded Mother.

Strands of white flew from Gage's fingertips and crashed into Mother's. Mother closed her hand and yanked. Her ribbons around the man constricted. He deflated before falling to the ground in a heap. Mother had killed him.

"It's not him," Mother announced. "Which of you is it? Do you even know yourselves? I will figure it out, even if I have to kill every Monroe."

Just then, Addamas appeared behind the Monroe men whose arms and necks glowed with magic they were not practiced at using. Vera's heart lifted. She waited for Kale to step out behind the satyr, or Mimi, but no one else came. Addamas spun in a circle like he was lost.

"Right. Look at the state of you," *tsked* a cockney voice behind Vera.

Vera swung around. A small man, the size of Vera's forearm, lounged on the steps. He had a fancy red suit with several rows of gold buttons and a matching triangular-shaped hat.

"The boss may be glad to see you this way," the little man informed Vera.

No one else seemed to notice the man. The Monroe men stood shoulder to shoulder, shooting strands of white at Mother, attempting to contain her or kill her. The High Witch rolled her eyes. An easy flex and the magic wrapping around Mother snapped and fell away from her. Mother lifted a hand, and another Monroe man lifted into the air.

"Acting like maggots, the lot of them," said the little man. "Watch this."

He flicked his finger against his thumb just as Mother stepped forward. Mother's toes caught on the hem of her gown, and she fell on her face. The Monroe man who'd hung in the air dropped. He was alive. His family caught him. The little man laughed, saluting Vera before poofing away. There was a cry and the triads shifted. One of the witches vanished in plain sight. Then another. The little man was taking them. Mother pushed to her knees and sat blinking at the faces of terrified people around her. Only it wasn't Mother.

"Vera?" Maiden asked. "What's going on?"

"Maiden." Vera made it to Maiden's side in a few steps while the Monroe men yelled for her to stop. "It's Mother she—"

Maiden's hand lashed out and closed around Vera's throat. Vera choked.

"Time for the Maiden to go," said Mother.

Maiden's confused eyes flickered back into view. "I can't hold on. What's happening?"

"Don't leave." Vera shoved herself over, making room. "Stay with me. Don't leave."

"It's too late, siphon," answered Mother. "She's gone."

Oh no she's not.

Vera? Maiden asked. *How are you doing this?*

Look through my memories. I'm a little busy right now.

Mother stood, pulling Vera to her feet as well. Vera reached down, freed the knife from her skirts, and swung it at the witch. A cloud of black smoke stopped Vera's arm mid-swing.

"Uh uh. Bad siphon," said Mother.

The magic ripped the blade out of Vera's hand and flung it behind her. The blade thunked into flesh, and the grunt that accompanied the wet sound was Gage's. Screaming started. At first, Vera thought it was all in her head, but then she saw the people finally begin to run. Not from the maniac Mother, but from the army of unnaturals cresting the road. Kale led them, sword in hand. As the army reached the market, Mimi melted from the shadows. The mountain lion stepped right in front of the advancing army and roared. At her cry, a band of warriors in black-plated metal interspersed with black cats and birds of every type and size joined her. Mimi was standing against Kale.

The witch dropped Vera beside Gage. He must have been coming for Vera when the witch embedded the blade in his gut. Vera screamed in rage. She gathered all the threads of mist and tossed them across the platform, along with Mother who was attached to them. Mother landed on her stomach, sliding a little before she stopped and looked at Vera with hate. The little man in red poofed onto the back of Mother's head and jumped. Mother's head cracked on the steps, and she went still. The Monroe men circled Vera and Gage protectively.

"Gage." Vera's voice cracked.

"I'm okay," he lied. "Okay, I'm not. Looks like I won't get a chance to try to make you mine after all. By the time I get back, you'll have given your heart away."

"I'll be an old lady when you get back," Vera said, teasing through her tears.

"I've always been mature for my age." Gage's breaths rasped through his teeth.

"But you won't remember me."

"I want you to hold on to something for me, okay?" Gage slipped Vera's cloaking charm, the one she had given him, into her hand.

"In twenty years, I'll come find the most overachieving boy in Summartir and give it back," Vera promised.

"Not that. That's yours." Gage laughed, and then wheezed. His eyes closed.

"Gage, wake up. Wake up!"

"Tired," he whispered, shaking.

"All right," Vera said, her heart shattering. "You go to sleep. I'll see you again, okay?"

"Maiden," Gage gurgled, and then he stopped shaking.

Hold tight, Vera, warned Maiden.

Suddenly it wasn't just Vera and one witch – there were two.

"Gage?" Vera asked slowly, trying to breathe through the crush.

I won't stay long, promised Gage. *I have to give this to you.* Gage's magic hummed as he passed a thread to Vera.

I can't take your magic, Gage.

Sure you can. You're who should have it.

No, I mean I literally cannot take it. It's too much magic for me.

You'll get used to it, Gage assured. *You'll stretch like a new shoe.*

I can help you, offered Maiden, and the magic constricted before settling into Vera's lower back.

Why don't you keep it for your next life? asked Vera.

Because of this. Suddenly Vera was following the thread of magic as it flowed outward. Together, she and Gage traced the line with their minds to where it anchored at the meadow. The thread twined around a doorway that Vera had never seen, but the place beyond the door was as familiar as breath for Vera.

You're the Earth threadbearer, Vera gasped.

Was. Now, you're the Earth threadbearer. You see why I cannot take it with me.

It would leave Earth vulnerable. You're saving my realm.

If I'm honest, which I see now I must be with you, I'm mostly doing this for the girl who makes me blush and fumble for thoughts like a schoolboy. At least now I know the odds of you choosing me were not in my favor. I think that makes leaving you a little easier. I would be miserable watching you fall for someone else.

What are you talking about? asked Vera.

I'm sorry, I tried not to look, Gage apologized. *But your thoughts were open for the Maiden. I saw what I'm sure you do not see for yourself yet.*

The memory of Kale's arms around Vera at the stream floated forward.

That was nothing, Vera argued. *Kale's just a friend.* Vera blushed. It was made worse by having Maiden there watching all that play out. Vera never did figure out what those two meant to each other. And apparently, Maiden heard that thought because she startled and began laughing.

I would call us unlikely friends. Never anything more, assured Maiden.

Before you write the Guardian off as lost, look up, Gage said to Vera.

While the warriors in black had held back the unnaturals, they'd let Kale through. Vera's heart wrenched with relief to see the man whole. Kale eyed the witches surrounding Vera as she knelt over Gage's body.

Don't let him kill my cousins, okay? Gage kissed Vera's lips softly, sweetly, and then he was gone.

Kale leaped from the horse he rode and cautiously

walked to Vera. The witches parted. Kale dropped to his knees beside her.

"I'm sorry I was late," Kale said to Vera. "I'm sorry I couldn't save Gage for you."

"I know. Maiden is still here with me, though," Vera revealed.

"You're incredible, you know that?" said Kale.

I cannot transition back into my body unless you weaken the Mother so I can shove her aside.

Vera relayed Maiden's message to Kale.

"Then it's a good thing that's what we're planning to do," said Kale.

"Time to end this together." Vera squeezed Kale's hand.

"You're not scared of me, even though I led the horde here." Kale's brows pinched in confusion.

"A bet's a bet. I trusted you would be you." Vera shrugged a tired shoulder. "That's not Mother's army anyway. They were meant to stop her."

"I found that out too, just before the siphon knocked me out and ran away," Kale rubbed the back of his head. "I decided to let the horde do what they were made for."

"If any unnaturals get loose, a lot of innocents could get hurt." Vera looked at the witches, men, and children hiding and running.

"That's why those guys came." Kale winced and pointed up at a pair of dragons headed their way. "Actually, I was getting worried they wouldn't make it. Mimi's warriors can't hold off the horde forever."

The dragons opened their mouths, spewing streams of fire. They circled behind the horde, laying down walls of flame to corral the unnaturals toward the palace where Mother was beginning to stir. Mimi and the warriors moved, getting themselves on the other side of the flames, a few carried fallen brethren. The dragons continued their path until they'd encircled Mother with the horde. Everyone else was safely outside the arena they'd created. Mother rose to her feet, surrounded by her familiars who had come to guard her while she was unconscious. Kale placed a hand on the ground to steady himself. His brow glistened with new sweat.

"It's not a pit like you suggested," Kale said, breathing hard.

"But it will work," Vera finished. "Are you okay?"

"Monroes, you know your job," Kale reminded.

The Monroe men raced into action, circling the wall of flames and adding nets of magic across the top.

"Kale?" Vera asked with concern.

"I have to lead the horde," said Kale. "Or they won't wear down the High Mother enough." Kale placed shaking hands on the sides of Vera's face and pressed his forehead to hers. "I'm so sorry."

"You're scaring me."

"You never have to be scared of me. Never." Kale groaned, and a horse screamed—Ferrox. "My ride is here. Please forgive me."

Kale pressed his lips to Vera's forehead. Vera's stomach dropped. Kale took off across the grounds without looking back. Ferrox was tearing across the field toward him. Vera covered her mouth. They were going to collide, but neither horse nor man slowed. Maiden flowed forward inside Vera, wrapping around her, holding her together. Kale and Ferrox hit with a crack, folding in on each other. The space between the two blurred, and then they were one. Kale was an unnatural.

"You knew," said Vera to Maiden.

Of course, I'm one of the witches who selected him to become the Guardian. And I'm the one who separated him from his demon steed. As much as I could anyway. They will always be linked.

Kale lifted his head to look at Vera for a heartbeat, his eyes glowing red before he leaped through the fire to join the horde. Mother had worked her way through a good portion of the horde by using a magic shield to fry any who touched her. Vera thought she saw the red man riding a bucking fox inside the arena before both disappeared. As the unnaturals surrounded her, Mother ripped at the net above.

Vera, you need to help the Monroes, Maiden said urgently. *They need another witch to complete their circle.*

I'm not a witch.

But you have the magic of one now. I'll show you how to use it.

Vera was already running while Maiden threw a white thread into the net. The fraying edges of the net healed. Mother howled with fury.

I've got the net. You see how much magic you can siphon from the Mother, said Maiden, directing Vera's attention to the girl on the palace steps. Margory had not run.

Vera tugged at Mother's mist. It was thinner than before, but there was still a lot of it. As Vera pulled, Mother turned to face her with a snarl. The High witch threw her magic against the flames in front of Vera, even while Vera tugged it from her and threw it into Margory.

"Bloody hell," said the man in a red coat. "That was a lot of hopping. I'm right tired." He sat down, leaned against Vera's leg, and closed his eyes like he was taking a nap.

Vera, do not take the final drops, said Maiden. *You have to stop when I say.*

Vera wasn't sure how to turn off the current going

through her and flooding into Margory. It was like asking her to stop a bolt of electricity.

Now, Maiden screamed.

Vera pictured the magic stopping, saw the flow reverse in her mind, but couldn't stop the siphon inside her. Then the magic changed. It wasn't black anymore. It was blue. Vera whipped her head around to look at the woman inside the arena with the horde. It was not Mother anymore. It was Maiden. Vera felt the hollow spot inside her ribcage where the witch had been. Vera was draining Maiden. With a cry, Vera pulled her hands down, closing them into fists. It didn't stop to flow.

"Plant them in the soil," suggested the little man.

Vera dropped to her knees and dug her fingers into the dirt. It worked. The little man poofed away. Maiden was still trapped inside a wall of dragon fire with at least a hundred unnaturals, though. They all looked at Maiden like they smelled honey. Kale yelled, turning on the unnatural at his side and sliced him in two with his sword. Kale pushed his way through the mob of unnaturals, destroying them and ducking their blows until he reached Maiden, who stood in a ring of downed unnaturals of her own. Kale picked Maiden up and threw her. Like a freaking shotput. Right through the hole that Maiden had left open in the net when she'd left Vera. Then Kale turned, facing down the unnaturals that surrounded him. The Guardian's vicious smile matched the remaining horde's as the monsters converged as one, swallowing Kale in their midst. Vera covered her mouth with one hand. The dragons swooped in from above, gliding through the fire to land on surviving unnaturals. The dragons tore them in half with claws and teeth.

The net above dropped as the Monroe witches joined in the fight, using fiery ropes to sever unnaturals. Mimi fought side by side with Addamas, who wore black armor. Together, they destroyed the last of them. Except for Errock. In the last minutes, when Kale had turned on the horde, so had Errock. Now Kale and Errock stood face to face, sides heaving. Errock nodded with a grin and slipped through a gap in the flames. Kale roared and charged after the unnatural. Before Errock made it a dozen steps, he cried out and stumbled. When the unnatural fell, his eyes remained open and vacant. A small yellow snake slithered into the undergrowth. Probably on its way back to Marianne.

"Well, that was lucky," said Maiden.

The dragons turned their attention to the last of the unnatural bodies, charring them to ash.

"Mother?" Kale asked Maiden while Vera averted her eyes, unnerved to see him in that form.

"Mother is defeated," announced Maiden. "Her spirit will remain locked away with me until the next solstice when I can send her on from this life."

"What of the world-threads?" asked Mimi. She had returned to her two-legged form and wore an over-large shirt draped over her shoulders. Beside her, Addamas stood bare-chested.

"For now, the sure-threads are all intact. Only two threadbearers survived, however." Maiden pulled Margory beside her. "This witch will take the place of Maiden. I am to become Mother. Over time, the threads will be reborn. Changes will need to be made so nothing like this can ever happen again. Although, I'm not sure what that will be. I do know if the Monroes had not kept their secret, the world would be very different right now. Witches would be the monsters."

"I have to take my people home," Mimi said and

wrapped Vera in a hug to say goodbye. "If I could stay right now, I would," she said quietly to Vera.

"It's okay. I'm so grateful your people came forward to help save mine," said Vera.

"They've had practice recently with accepting differences. There's still work to be done, but we're getting there." Two warriors, who had shadowed Mimi, shifted when Addamas tried to get closer. "Guys, let him through," Mimi said.

"Yes, your Highness," one said and let Addamas pass. Although, if looks could kill.

Holy hell. "Highness?" Vera squeaked.

"It's no big deal." Mimi rolled her eyes. "My brothers here are just uptight."

"You're a princess?" Vera persisted

One of the warriors snorted. "She's our Queen."

Vera gaped. "Very big deal, Mimi. You have as many secrets as Kale."

Mimi's head drooped a little. "Will you still be friends with me?"

"As long as you don't push me out of any more trees."

"I want a girl's night when I get back," said Mimi.

"'Kay." Vera refused to cry any more. She was sure she'd used up her saltwater quota.

Mimi hugged her one last time. "He's still the same guy," she whispered.

"I'm not so sure." *Dang it, there are more tears in me after all.* "He's one of them."

"I know," Mimi said sadly. "If you need time to figure things out, I get it. We won't talk about any guys at girl's night."

"That sounds perfect."

Mimi released Vera and stepped back. Mimi's brothers tried to block Addamas.

"You guys want to walk the whole way, or let the satyr make us a path straight home?" Mimi asked the brutes.

Vera could tell they were undecided, but one more look at Mimi's limp, and they let the Addamas pass. Mimi's band of warriors and morphs slipped out as quietly as they'd come.

"I have to go take care of my people too," said Maiden. "There are a lot of answers and reassurances that they need from me right now."

"What about the dragons?" Vera looked dubiously at the golden lizard the size of a house and the red one that was only slightly smaller.

"I think they're planning to stay for a while," Maiden said nonchalantly.

"I can see that tears you up," Vera teased.

Maiden winked at Vera, took one more look at the dragons, and left to check in with her people.

"How hangs the onions, boss?" asked the little red man, poofing in to stand beside Vera.

"You did well, Seamus." Kale replied.

"Now that I've saved ye all, I must go check on my Felicity girl." The man bent at the waist in Kale's direction.

"I'll knock your head off if you do that again, Seamus," said Kale.

Vera frowned at the threat, but Seamus beamed before poofing away. Kale and Vera were the only ones left inside the charred line of grass. Vera couldn't bring herself to look at the man shaped like an unnatural, with glowing demon eyes.

"Are you ready to go home?" Kale asked quietly.

Home. I can go home. Her heart lifted, and then she

remembered that there was nothing at home. Suzie was not there. Now Gus was not there either. Home was an empty apartment, alone. But at least there were no more unnaturals there.

"You'll have to ride, though. Ferrox and I cannot be separated when we are in the same realm."

"That's why you don't travel together," Vera said feeling betrayed. Kale had purposely not explained that part to her. He'd lied again, without saying a word.

21

Kale considered suggesting that Vera spend the night at the meadow and go home the next day, but he knew she wanted to be far away from him. Ferrox sank into a corner of their mind to rest, not caring to be part of Kale's turbulent thoughts. Vera held around his waist as loosely as possible. If she hadn't been too tired to stand, he suspected she'd have refused to ride.

"Are you sure Ferrox doesn't mind my riding him," Vera asked.

"He's not paying attention right now," Kale replied.

"Oh, well tell him thanks for me?"

"I will."

Fiends take me. Vera ran a hand over the hide on his equine side. Her fingers made the skin quiver. Kale stumbled.

"Vera," he said as calmly as possible. "Ferrox is sleeping. That's me right now."

Vera's hand froze against his hide, then she jerked it away.

"How many times have you healed me?" Vera asked suddenly.

"Three. At the lake, at the gate to Summartir, and in the forest after Samhira."

"You weren't just passing through that village when the horde came," she concluded accurately.

"I led the horde there. I was their commander. The very first unnatural."

"But you didn't want to join in their destruction."

"I retained more of my mind than I should have. As corrupt and bloodthirsty as my mind was to begin with. That's why they chose me. I was a siphon the world feared and respected. A golden ticket to world destruction."

"You're a siphon?"

"All unnaturals begin as siphons. Being tied to the meadow's magic makes me something different now."

"Why didn't you lose your mind?"

"Ferrox. They didn't realize he was demon-spawned when they captured him. He was drunk off his tail at the time. Being merged with him instead of a normal horse changed the dynamics. I wasn't alone in that fog of anger and thirst. I had a demon in my head with me."

"Who's the redheaded woman I saw when you healed me at the Summartir gate?"

"The honey-trap. They sent Talia to gain my trust and affection. When I was fully under her spell, she shoved a blade into my heart. The only way to live was to go willingly into the army of creatures they'd decided to create."

"Do you remember the little girl you—" Vera stopped when her voice cracked, remembering how she'd been the little girl that Kale had held down. In the memory she'd experienced while on the forest floor beside Sahira's body. A memory Vera had locked away, believing it was a simple nightmare.

"I wish there were things in my past that I could take back. But I cannot. I am sorry you had to experience them."

"I just want to be home," Vera said, pain lacing her words.

Kale's hearts wrenched for bringing her that pain. In this form, he had more than one heart to break. It nearly brought him to his knees. "Hold tighter, and I will run."

Kale ran as fast as he could toward the moment he would walk away from Vera for good. Which was the plan all along. Somewhere along the way, though, he'd gotten used to her by his side. He didn't want her out of his life. But it didn't matter, because he'd already lost her. Best to get her home quickly and get it over with. Like a Band-Aid, the humans said.

VERA WAS HOME. It had been three months since Kale had dropped her off and run as quickly as possible out of her life. She'd wanted nothing more than for him to be gone. But everywhere she turned, he was still there. The glowing eyes of Ferrox out her window at night, watching over her. Baskets of food, including her once-favorite scotcheroos. Not to mention, the full-ride scholarship to the local college that had come in the mail the month after she'd gotten home. Issued by the Meadow Institute. Vera hadn't planned on going to the small college in town. She'd planned to get as far away as possible. She even debated tearing the scholarship up, but who was she kidding? She was working at a fast food restaurant. That scholarship would give her a way out of South Dakota, to some career far away from the world-gate. Someday, she'd pay Kale back. With interest.

There was a knock at the front door. Vera hesitated. She didn't get visitors. Especially not after dark. Careful not to make a sound, Vera moved to the door and peeked through the peephole. Mimi waved. Vera pulled the locks back and opened the door. Mimi charged her as Mimi always did. Vera hugged the morph girl back this time.

"What are you doing here?" Vera closed and relocked the doors.

"Girls' night." Mimi held up a bag. "I brought snacks."

The girls spread out their goodies, laughing as Mimi described what it had taken to sneak away from her body-guard brothers. Battling an army of unnaturals had made her people more concerned about their queen's comings and goings than usual. Mimi popped a lid off a sour cream container before snatching a nacho-cheese chip from an open bag. The chip left a trail of orange as she slid it through the cream. Mimi popped it into her mouth.

"Nasty," Vera made a face.

"Don't knock it till you try it." Mimi ate another. "What's your favorite snack?"

"I don't have a favorite," Vera said.

"Everyone has a favorite."

"It used to be scotcheroos, but I think I lost my taste for them."

"What's a scotch-uh-roo?" Mimi tripped over the word.

"It's a peanut butter cereal bar with chocolate on top."

"Sounds like those things you used to summon at Kale's."

"I did not," Vera argued.

"Uh, you so did. None of us had any idea what those things even were. They kept popping up in the cupboard. It was way weird, cause the cupboard only summons what you're thinking about or wanting. But then, you'd never eat them."

Vera blushed. Mimi zeroed on it. "Spill."

"No." Vera leaned back on the couch and put her hands over her face. "It's so embarrassing."

"Now I'm thinking all sorts of naughty things."

"It's nothing like that." Vera threw a pillow at Mimi, but the girl caught it mid-flight.

"Then tell me."

"Fine. When I met Kale, I thought he looked like a scotcheroo."

"Huh. I can kinda see it. So, they were popping up because you were thinking about Kale?" Mimi's voice rose as she talked.

"Only about how much I hated him. The cupboard apparently couldn't tell the difference."

"Do you still hate him?"

"The things he did. . ." Vera shook her head.

"I get that. It's hard to forget the man he was when you've lived through his eyes. He told me you'd had a rough time. He doesn't hold it against you. Can I ask what you're having a hard time getting past?"

"I was a girl in one of them. His victim."

"Whoa. Stop. When you're in his memories, you're always Kale."

"No, I was a little girl."

"Did you see yourself in a mirror or something?"

"No. I just felt—"

"Like you were a girl," Mimi finished. "That's because, although you were in Kale's memories, you were you. Obviously, you think of yourself as a girl. But the part you played, that was Kale's part in real life."

"When he was a boy." Vera sucked in her lips and squeezed her eyes closed while her understanding rewrote itself. "He was sold after his parents died."

"He was sold to a brothel. Oh goddess," Mimi dropped her chips and encased Vera into her arms. "I'm so sorry."

"I didn't know it was a memory after it happened. I thought it was a nightmare from being chased by the unnatural. Then when I found out, I just assumed..." Vera's stomach churned.

"Let me assure you that even when Kale was out of his mind, that was the one crime his entire being rebelled against. After spending his whole life getting revenge and escaping the fear that comes from being a victim, he could never act on that particular urge of an unnatural. Although there are plenty of other crimes he had no objection to."

Vera brushed away the tears with her fingers and gave a self-loathing smile. "What a great friend I turned out to be, huh?"

"Eh, we all have our demons that we're trying to run from. That means we don't share some of the darker regrets and fears we have. Kale has more than most. Believing in someone who only reveals themselves by pieces is no easy thing." Mimi studied Vera. "Why don't you come for dinner this Sunday? This week Dam gets to pick what we eat, so we'll be having something fried or covered in barbeque. Or both."

"Thanks, but I don't think that's a good idea. Pretty sure I'm supposed to keep my siphon butt away from magical meadows. Also, I'm sure Kale would prefer I don't rain my crazy on his parade again."

"I think Kale misses your crazy."

"Sure, like a drunk girl misses her panties."

Mimi choked and took a sip of soda. "Goddess, don't do

that to me." Mimi laughed. "Don't you have the cloaking charm? Wear that. Siphon problem solved."

"It's not just that. After what I thought about Kale and how I treated him, I think it's best if I stay out of his life."

"He'd understand."

"I thought there was a rule about no boy talk allowed at girls' night."

"You started it," Mimi replied.

"Well, I'm ending it. Unless you wanna talk about how fast Addamas ripped his shirt off to throw over you after the horde was dead."

"That boy just likes to take his shirt off. He doesn't need a reason." Mimi bit her fingernail. "But you've made your point. No more boy talk."

KALE SIGHED when Mimi winged a chicken leg at Addamas's head. A few days ago, Addamas had suggested they start a new tradition of weekly family dinners. Kale seriously doubted his sanity for agreeing.

I cannot believe you told her, Ferrox barged in Kale's head all of a sudden.

Why are you back? You're supposed to be keeping an eye on Vera. Is everything okay?

Everything is not okay, Ferrox stated emphatically.

Damn the Infernals. I shouldn't have let her go home with that siphon still out there. He stood up from the table and headed for the door, just as Ferrox marched across the boundary. Kale felt her then. Moments before he saw her riding Ferrox. Ferrox glared at Kale across the yard while Vera slid from his back. The girl rubbed Ferrox's forehead head shyly. The demon horse's eyes cooled to black.

"You came," Mimi squealed and raced to greet Vera.

Addamas stepped onto the porch beside Kale and propped his shoulder against a beam.

"Mimi made you talk me into family dinners, didn't she?" Kale asked the satyr.

"Yup." Addamas held out his tattooed arms "Now that you know, all that's left is ink."

"Why didn't you both just tell me you'd invited Vera? You didn't need to create a whole event."

"Honestly? Mimi didn't think Vera would actually come. She didn't want you to be upset. And she's been talking about doing family dinner forever, anyway."

"That's ridiculous." Kale rolled his eyes. "Why would I care if Vera came or not?"

"Why indeed." Addamas winked then skipped down the steps to join the girls.

Fiends. Kale had no idea what to do right them. He felt like a stars-blasted fool. If Vera had come to see Mimi and Addamas, he didn't want to make her uncomfortable. So he'd keep his distance. However, he didn't want her to feel unwelcome either.

Goddess, if your junk is finally going to fall off, I get first dibs on it, Ferrox interceded.

Don't be an ass, Kale replied, knowing how much Ferrox loved being compared to one those creatures.

How about you get over here and say hi to the girl who just threatened to stab my face while I sleep if I ever bite her again.

What? Kale choked on a laugh and swiped a hand over his face to wipe away his grin.

While she stood there petting me in front of you like an angel. Right after she thanked me for the ride. Which she coerced me into giving her, thanks to you telling her about friendship contracts.

The girl still had her fire. Kale looked over at Vera and caught her watching him. He ran a hand through his hair and nodded a greeting.

Hurry up, munch tote. Before I link her in and let her see how pathetic you really are.

I will castrate you and feed you your own male bits if you do, Kale warned, but he stepped toward the rest of the group anyway.

Ferrox laughed with glee. He'd finally found a threat that worked on Kale. And he'd use it to drive Kale mad. Kale didn't get to say hello before yet another visitor made their appearance. He smelled gingerbread and farmland just moments before the weaver strolled into the meadow carrying a covered dome in one hand.

"Hope you all don't mind. I seemed to have misplaced my invitation," greeted Marianna.

By the time everyone had settled back around the table, an extra stool pulled from a closet, Kale still hadn't managed to say one word to Vera. The girls cooed over the baby crows Marianna had brought in the covered cage. For the Crone, she'd said. Soon, they were discussing how to take care of baby birds, which turned to news of Eggbert. The chick had apparently found a taste for eggs. With Gage gone, he'd needed a new home. So Marianna had taken him in and told Vera to visit any time. Not a good idea at all, Kale wanted to point out.

"By the way, how's the magic sitting, dear?" asked Marianna. *And that's why.*

"Good. Sometimes it flexes, but I push it back down where no one can accidentally snag it and go-go-siphon-master or anything."

"That's good. Wouldn't want your own siphon to take notice of it either, of course" Marianna said.

"What do you mean?" asked Vera.

"Your siphon abilities are awake now. And they aren't likely to go back to sleep with that mess of magic curled up inside you. Best to keep it well out of reach."

"I can siphon magic already inside me?"

"Untrained the way you are now, yes. The world thread or your own magic from whatever else you are. If your siphon gets stronger than that other part of you, you could be in trouble."

"How do I make sure that doesn't happen?" asked Vera.

"The more you cultivate your other abilities, the better handle you'll have on keeping the siphon in check," answered Marianne, seemingly unconcerned.

"So, I need to what? Go to unicorn school before I siphon myself into a world-destroying psycho?"

"Something like that," said Marianne with a laugh.

"What happens if Vera siphons the world-thread?" Kale asked

"It's gone. Which is fine, so long as no one decides to go after the High Witches any time soon. But there's already one corrupt Siphon Master running amok on Earth. We don't need to add another."

"I've been looking for the Siphon Master, but he's gone off the radar," Addamas said.

"He's either learning to deal with magic withdrawal, or he's hunting down any humans with dormant magical talents like yours and draining them, drop by drop," said Marianne.

"That's why you've had Ferrox watching me," Vera said to Kale. The first time she'd looked at him that night.

Kale blinked, letting her make her own conclusions. He'd had Ferrox watching her for several reasons, not the least of which was the Siphon Master.

"All right. How do I begin training?" asked Vera.

"Kale could teach you how to defend yourself, so you don't have to add any more locks to your door," Mimi suggested.

Vera shot Mimi a look then cleared her throat, running a finger back and forth on the edge of her plate, and said quietly, "If you wouldn't mind. That might help ease my mind so I can worry about the siphon inside me instead."

"Sure," Kale said.

"Good." Weaver delivered the refilled cups to Kale for him to pass out. "The rest will be like working a muscle. You just need practice. For now, how about a toast?"

Kale slid a cup to Mimi and Addamas. Vera's fingers brushed Kale's when she took hers from his hand. She pulled back quickly, looking studiously at the inside of her cup.

Weaver raised her glass. "To bringing the world back together." Marianne took a deep swig.

With a few murmurs, Kale's friends followed suit. Kale took a mouth full and nearly spit it out when Vera began to glow. Everyone stared at the girl until she noticed. Her eyes grew panicked.

"Did I grow a horn?" Vera rubbed at the empty spot in the center of her forehead.

Kale leaned across the table and looped a finger through her hair, which glowed like Ferrox's eyes in waves of black and red. Vera's breath caught. Her eyes locked with his. Kale glanced at her lips for only a moment before pulling the lock forward to show her.

"I told you she was a redhead," crowed Addamas.

Mimi smacked him.

"I didn't know unicorns could do that," Vera whispered, eyes locked with Kale's.

"Neither did I," he said.

"What does it mean?" she wondered aloud.

"It means you're impossible to figure out," Kale answered ruefully. "It also means your training starts immediately. Before your luck gets you into any more trouble. Plus, you're running every day with Mimi because your endurance is terrible."

"You know you're a bossy jerk, right, Scotchie?" She bit the inside of her lip to keep from smiling.

Kale let her hair fall from his fingers and sat back in his chair with a smirk. "And you're a pain in the butt, Sprinkles."

Vera's heart lifted with the familiar banter. She'd finally made it back home.

KEEP READING for a sneak peak of
Tempest Song (Unraveled World- book 2)

AVAILABLE HERE FOR purchase or pre-order. Releases December 28, 2018

ALSO BY ALICIA

Want more Kale and Vera? Check out the next books in the Unraveled World Series. Available soon or now on pre-order.

Newsletter Sign Up
Get author updates, sneak peaks, special offers, and more!
www.AliciaFabel.com

ACKNOWLEDGMENTS

Holy cow! I'm writing acknowledgements, which means I really did this insane thing I set out to do. There are so many people who helped me get to this point. First off, my husband, who has been my biggest supporter from the start. And our kids, who put up with a distracted space-head for a mom. Thank you guys for not caring about having to eat on paper plates every day—we really should've bought stock in those, mac & cheese, and pizza rolls. Seriously though, this would not be possible without you guys.

Vicki, my friend, I would not have found the courage to finally pursue this path without your encouragement and advice as well. You are a rockstar for answering my billion-and-one questions. Sorry for all the ones that came to me at unholy hours of the night. And to all the other authors I've met along the way, who've made me feel a little more normal, thank you. You're the reasons I have any clue about what I'm doing right now.

When I set out to find people to help me get my stories ready for readers, I never expected to find people I would count as friends. I truly got lucky finding you guys. Lara

(Wynter Designs), you are incredibly talented. Chris (The Editing Hall), you not only made my stories sparkle, you gave me the tools and confidence to be a better writer. And Erin, for reading my stories in their earliest incarnations, you are a hero.

To everyone else who has cheered for me, offered support, and given feedback, thank you. To anyone taking the time to read these acknowledgements, you are part of the reason why this story is possible. And this is only the beginning. I cannot wait to share the other worlds churning in my head with you.

Here's to all the paper plate days to come!

ABOUT THE AUTHOR

Alicia Fabel got her degree in Resource Management from Iowa State University. Then, because she dreamed of a life with books but was too chicken to come out of the writer's closet, she pursued a teaching certificate for middle school language arts. She never finished that certification, though. Instead, she finally came to her senses and started writing for real. Now here she is, talking in third person and feeling like a weirdo. But hey, she did it!

Alicia is a socially awkward misfit, who loves all things fantasy, sugar-coated, and cozy. She lives on the high plains of the USA with her husband, their four children, and a spaztastic cat. If she can achieve her dreams, anyone can, with a little hard work and persistence. So go make those dreams happen! <3

TEMPEST SONG

UNRAVELED WORLD - BOOK 2

Chapter One

"You like him," Mimi singsonged across the dorm room Vera shared with her.

"You're crazy." Vera pulled a gray stocking cap over her messy bun and checked the mirror to be sure all of her hair was tucked underneath. She scowled at her flaming cheeks.

"Only as crazy as that man is adorable." Mimi threw herself across her unmade bed with an exaggerated sigh.

"Who's adorable?" Addamas asked, stepping out of a path from his room on the men's floor.

"No one," Vera answered at the same time as Mimi said, "The new librarian intern on campus."

"That's why you've been spending so much time at the library." Addamas plopped down beside Mimi. "You've got the hots for a nerd, girly?"

"No." Vera winced at the spike of pain through her temples. Her truth-telling superpower had raised the stakes since Summartir last year. What she wouldn't give to have her plain-old bells back. The world-thread curled up in Vera's gut shifted. She held it down until it settled.

"Hold up. I have a picture of him." Mimi leaped from the bed to retrieve her tablet.

"You took a picture of him?" Vera spun around to gape at her friend, but Mimi ignored her. "Do we need to discuss how humans feel about stalkers?"

Addamas whistled appreciatively when Mimi turned the screen toward him. "Good work, Vera."

"I've never even met him," Vera protested. "Neither has Miss Paparazzi over there."

"Oh, but that'll change tonight," Mimi assured. "Noah's scheduled to work when our psych group's meeting. And I have a plan."

"How do you know his name?" Vera asked with increasing alarm. "And how do you know his schedule?"

Mimi shrugged with an impish gleam in her eyes. "I may have taken a peek at some files while you were hunting down another book on mythical creatures yesterday."

"You told me you had to pee."

"I pee fast."

Vera smacked a hand to her face, covering one eye. "We're going to end up with a restraining order, aren't we?"

"Pshh." Addamas waved a dismissive hand. "One minute with you and Noah's the one who'll need restraining."

Dear Lady, help me. Addamas and Mimi were teaming up against her. The only time those two were ever on the same page was when they were trying to hook Vera up with a guy. With their meddling powers combined, they were unstoppable.

"Can we just go already?" Vera asked—begged. "I'm hungry."

"For something other than book-boy?" teased Addamas,

making no move to open a path to the meadow for their mid-week check-in. A.K.A. family dinner. A.K.A. a condition of Vera being allowed to attend college while a Siphon Master still roamed Earth.

"We're supposed to be there in two minutes," Vera pointed out. "Think Kale's on his way yet?"

Last time they were late, Kale had stormed the campus. They'd had to hide the Guardian in the closet while security went door to door looking for a madman with a sword. Later that night, Kale had insisted Mimi and Addamas join Vera's training session. He wanted to be sure they could protect his charge if some baddie *had* found her. The only reason he'd even agreed to let Vera enroll full-time last semester was because Addamas and Mimi had volunteered to enroll with her. How could the Guardian say no when she had a satyr bounty hunter and a morph queen for bodyguards? Truthfully, Addamas and Mimi were thrilled to be living a human-college-kid life. To make sure Kale didn't pull the plug on their fun, they followed his rules to the T when it came to Vera's protection. Even if that meant sparring with the thousand-plus-years-old Guardian to prove they were capable. They'd passed that night, but none of them walked straight for days. They were never late again.

Addamas stood and grumbled, "Gotta suck the fun out of everything, don't you?"

"Oh, yes. Because this has been so much fun," Vera said with more irritation than she'd intended.

"You okay?" Mimi frowned. "You seem like something's bothering you."

"I'm fine," Vera apologized. "It's just been a long day."

"I'm sorry for giving you a hard time about Noah." Mimi's shoulders slumped.

Dang it. Now I've made Mimi feel bad. Vera had been

determined to get through the day without making anyone else miserable. *Way to fail.*

"It's not you. I'm just tired. Spring break needs to hurry up and get here." Vera did her best impression of a smile.

Mimi nodded in understanding but still seemed deflated.

"You really think Noah will like me?" Vera asked.

That perked the girl up. "I'm totally sure."

"If not, you're taking me out for frozen custard after the library," Vera said.

"Hun, I'm taking you for frozen custard either way, but you'll be glowing not moping."

Addamas winked at Vera when Mimi wasn't looking. A path appeared in the middle of the room, looking like a portal into the woods. The boundary forest to be exact, where the gates to all the realms of the world were tethered. All those gates circled the meadow where Kale lived, and unlike Earth, the meadow was saturated with magic. Addamas gestured for the girls to proceed.

Vera wrapped her fingers around the two charms hanging from her neck. The small white disk with an acorn etched in it was a piece of Summartir eggshell. A symbol of good luck, she'd been told. While she didn't believe in good-luck charms, she wore it to remind herself of the sacrifices made to protect the world from humans. And that's where the black teardrop-shaped charm came in. It was a cloaking charm, which hid her powers and muzzled her siphon. With it, Vera couldn't accidentally suck up the magic around her and become a magic-addicted, world-destroying monster like humanity's ancestors. That's what got them all banished to Earth in the first place. Heading into the meadow was like heading into a crack den for her siphon. A scary prospect even with her cloak.

"You'll be fine," Mimi said, obviously sensing Vera's reluctance. "We'll make sure of it."

"Sometimes I wish I could just go back to being human."

"I know." Mimi squeezed Vera's hand.

"That's pretty selfish, huh? When the magic inside me keeps everyone here safe." The world-thread stitched Earth to the rest of the world. Without it, the seams would unravel, and Earth would fall away. In a spectacular display of fiery-death and destruction for all her kind.

"Not selfish." Mimi shook her head. "That thread also keeps the siphon inside you awake and hungry. It's never selfish to wish for peace inside your own skin."

"Since none of us wants you to destroy Earth to get that peace, let's get to the meadow and work on waking up the good power inside you," piped Addamas. "Those siphon urges won't stand a chance against your unicorn, girly."

"At this point, I wouldn't even complain about a horn sprouting from my forehead if I could just get a leash on my monster," said Vera.

Mimi raised a doubtful brow at that. "Mm-hmm."

"Fine, I'd complain," Vera admitted. "Just like you'd complain if your paws turned to hooves like Addamas's."

"Gods." Mimi shivered dramatically. "Don't say stuff like that."

"Woman," Addamas said to Mimi. "You only wish you could morph into a sexy-ass satyr instead of a flea-bitten cat."

The corners of Vera's mouth tipped up. Their bickering was soothing in its normalcy. It was just a normal day. "All right. Let's do this," she said.

***

KALE PICKED AT HIS THUMBNAIL. He'd barely been able to eat the lasagna he'd summoned for dinner—Vera's favorite. Vera hadn't eaten more than a couple of bites either, which worried him. He wondered if he should let his plan go. Maybe she did just want to forget.

Goddess save me from your incessant worrying. Were you like this before we were bound together? asked Ferrox.

What if she cries or something? Kale scrutinized Vera. She smiled at Mimi, but it was shaky.

Balls, she looks like she's two seconds from a breakdown already, Ferrox observed through Kale's eyes. *Best of luck with that, old man. I'm headed out.*

And you call me a coward.

If she loses it, the last thing you want is for her siphon to latch onto the demon in the meadow. That would be bad news for all of you.

She's wearing a cloak, Kale reminded.

Yeah, and magicked items have never been known to fail. Ferrox moved into the borderlands.

So, you're leaving for our protection? That's the story you're sticking with?

Just like you're sticking with the story that you're only worried about the girl's feelings right now.

What else would I be worried about? asked Kale.

Oh, I don't know. Why don't you man-up and give her your gift? See if you figure it out yourself.

You're a bastard.

Like all my brothers. Ferrox slipped through a gate and their link severed. Kale caught the scent of sandalwood and smoke in the air. The demon horse had decided to spend the night prowling around his home realm.

"Anyone want dessert?" Kale headed for the cupboard before he could talk himself out of it.

"Uh, you've got to ask?" Addamas asked around a mouthful of food and pushed his plate aside. "Bring it on."

"Nice." Mimi glowered at Addamas.

Addamas blew a kiss and her nose flared.

As always, the cupboard conjured precisely what Kale wanted. Right down to the twenty flickering candles. Vera's eyes weren't the only ones to widen when he set the cake on the table in front of her.

"Happy birthday, Vera," he said. *Stars blast me if this goes badly.*

Vera froze. "How'd you know?"

"You mentioned it once." Kale lifted one shoulder slightly. "The cake is only your first gift."

"Wait." Mimi finally found her tongue. "Today's Vera's birthday? And you didn't tell me?"

"That was your second gift," Kale told Vera.

There were definitely tears in her eyes, but Vera blew out her candles before saying, "It's exactly what I wanted."

"What?" Mimi's voice rose. "How could you not want me to know it's your birthday?"

"I don't love my birthday." Vera's sad smile made Kale's chest heavy. "Suzie died three days before I turned eighteen. She went to pick out a birthday gift for me and never made it home."

Mimi let out a breath. "Oh, honey."

A single tear spilled down Vera's cheek. She swiped it away quickly. "You know, I didn't think I'd ever want another birthday gift after that. Then, last year you gave me the best gift I could've asked for," Vera said to Mimi with a dry laugh. "You shoved me out of that tree and knocked me uncon-scious. I got to sleep through my birthday." She turned to

Kale. "And this year, I get to spend it with you guys. Which is actually kind of all right."

Kale tipped his head. "I have one more gift, but maybe you won't like it so well."

"I'm sure I'll love it."

"It's outside."

Vera stilled. "If it's my own demon horse, I take it back. I don't want it."

"It's not a demon or a horse," Kale assured. "Or a lizard or snake or spider either."

"You know me so well."

"I hope so."

Kale led them all out the front door, down the porch steps, and around the cabin. Beneath Vera's window, he'd planted lilac bushes. He'd been babying them for weeks so they didn't die.

"Suzie's favorite." Vera knelt to take in the spicy scent of the tiny lavender blooms just beginning to open.

"Those aren't just her favorite," Kale said. "Those are her bushes. I transplanted them from your old apartment building."

"You dug them out of the planters?" Shock colored Vera's words.

That's exactly what he'd done.

Vera stroked one of the blooms. "Each time she planted lilacs, the landlord ripped them out because he didn't want water wasted on 'useless weeds.' And every time he did, Suzie planted new ones. She said those planters were meant to hold beauty, and they should get to fulfill their purpose. Eventually, the landlord gave up and let her keep them."

"I thought Suzie would want you to have them," Kale said simply. "I put roses in their place. If he wants to take those out, he'll have to get bloodied for his efforts."

Vera choked and covered her mouth with a hand. *Infernals take me. I shouldn't have told her that.* Jumping up, Vera swung around and threw her arms around his ribs. She buried her face in his chest and squeezed.

"Thank you, Kale."

Kale swallowed hard. She hadn't touched him, other than for training, in almost a year. As quickly as she'd wrapped her arms around him, she pulled away.

With a brave smile, she said, "Can we eat cake now?"

Kale didn't miss how she wouldn't meet his gaze. And he didn't miss the lock of hair trailing down the back of her neck, glowing red. Glowing hair wasn't a unicorn trait. It wasn't something Vera siphoned either. No creature in the world had that ability for her to siphon. He figured it had to be a quirk of her mixed-magical heritage, but the phenomena seemed to upset her. She'd started wearing stocking caps during her visits, even though the meadow was perpetually warm. So far, the meadow was the only common factor in the sporadic glowing. It had happened a handful of times when they sparred, a few times when she sat eating dinner, and once last fall during finals week, when she'd fallen asleep on the couch after dinner. Sometimes it wouldn't glow for weeks. As Vera wiped tears from her cheeks and walked arm-in-arm with Mimi back inside, Kale had a new hypothesis. Next time they trained, he was going to test it out. Vera was not going to like it.

***

VERA TOOK another bite of cherry cake. She never would've

guessed that Kale had remembered her tale of birthday woes from their escape through the Velvet Woods.

"Any special plans for spring break?" Kale asked the group.

"I'm headed home to make sure my brothers aren't terrorizing anyone," Mimi answered. "Thank the gods it's only one week. Summer break will be murder."

"Three words," said Addamas. "Florida, girls, and booze."

"Pig," Mimi mumbled.

"You're welcome to join," Addamas informed her. "The less you wear, the better."

"How have I never seen a video of a satyr crashing spring break?" Vera asked. "I'd think with that many people, you'd be all over the news."

"Because I'm a complete gentleman. Strictly look, don't touch." Addamas stretched both tattooed arms up to rest behind his head. "And I keep my pants on."

Vera gave him a look. "I find that hard to believe."

"Oh, I believe it," said Mimi. "Humans start passing around pictures of a moron satyr, and Kale will hunt Addamas down and kick his fluffy tail. While I cheer him on."

"My tail is not fluffy," Addamas objected.

"Oh. That makes sense," Vera said to Mimi.

"My tail is not fluffy!" Addamas stood when no one acknowledged his proclamation and put his hands on the button of his pants. "Want me to show you?"

"Oh, good gods, no!" Mimi said with horror.

"Enough, Dam," Kale said. "Keep your pants on. I don't know how Vera puts up with you two every day."

"Aww, she loves us." Addamas fell back into his seat with a grin.

"When should I plan on you?" Kale asked Vera.

"Plan on me for what?" Vera didn't follow.

"You're coming to stay here while Mimi and Addamas are gone," Kale said as if it was already decided.

"I didn't know that was the plan," Vera said carefully.

Mimi suddenly became interested in cleaning all the pink frosting from her plate.

"I thought you'd know." Kale picked at his thumbnail. "I can't leave you there without anyone to watch over you."

"Uh, yeah, you can," Vera said. "Because I can take care of myself. And I'm just going to be in my room reading all week anyway. So unless books start stealing souls, I'll be fine."

"Couldn't you read here?" Kale asked. "If you need help carrying all your books—"

"I don't need help carrying my books," Vera snapped then pressed her lips together.

Kale watched her like she was a keg about to blow.

Calmly, she said, "It's only a week. You can even send Ferrox to spy on me and collect me for my usual training."

"I'll be more comfortable with you here," Kale persisted.

"But I wouldn't be more comfortable here," Vera argued.

Kale's expression became unreadable. He tipped his head to meet Vera's gaze. Since her truth-telling was not public knowledge, that had become Kale's silent way of asking her to listen for the truth. In this instance, his own. "I promise I'm never a danger to you."

"Huh?" Vera frowned at the man. *What's he talking about?* Then it sank in. Vera's eyes widened. "It's not you that I'm worried about," she rushed to explain. "It's me. I can't stay here for a week around all this magic."

Everyone around the table seemed to exhale. *Why would they think I'm worried about Kale?*

"Maybe it would be a good opportunity to stretch your unicorn powers," Kale suggested.

"I can't stretch what I can't find. Not on purpose anyway. Give me a shot of poison and, sure, I'm grand. But that's all I can do."

"I can help you," Kale said.

"No, you can't," Vera said as gently as possible. "Don't get me wrong, I appreciate all of you trying, but no one here knows how to help me. None of you are unicorns."

"Maybe I could talk to Kuwari," Addamas began.

"He already said no," Kale pointed out.

"But maybe we don't need him to come here," Addamas said.

"You think they'll welcome a siphon half-breed, who needs help mastering kargadan magic, into Nibiru?"

"Whoa. You two are talking Greek, you know that, right?" Vera asked. "Wanna try all that in English?"

"Actually, Addamas is the only one speaking Greek," Mimi corrected. "Kale's speaking some dead language he won't tell us the name of, and I'm speaking Canaan. You're the only one speaking English, hun." Mimi cocked her head in a very cat-like way. "You really don't hear the difference, do you?"

"No," Vera admitted. "Add it to my list of weird. I forget that you all use magic to understand each other. Until you start throwing out words which don't translate. Kargadan is a unicorn, but what are coo-war-ree, and nee-beer-rue?"

"Kuwari is a kargadan Addamas knows," Kale explained. "He's from a realm called Nibiru."

"And Kuwari could teach me to be a unicorn?" Vera asked Addamas.

The satyr shot Kale a sideways look and didn't answer.

Vera narrowed her eyes at Kale. "I'll take that as a yes. Let me guess. You didn't tell me because it's not safe?"

Addamas coughed and covered his mouth with a hand while Kale and Vera stared off.

"I didn't tell you because Kuwari cannot help you." As soon as the words left Kale's mouth, he ran a hand through his hair. The lie reverberated through Vera's skull. "Let me explain," he said.

"This should be good." Vera folded her arms while Mimi looked back and forth between them with a weird expression.

"Kargadan no longer leave their realm, not since Kuwari's last escort disappeared a few years ago. He was on a trip, looking for answers to their depleting numbers, and his bodyguard vanished. The herd realized they could've lost Kuwari instead. Since they cannot afford to lose their healer, he's not permitted to leave Nibiru. That's why he cannot come teach you." Kale finished, still picking at his thumb. There was a red stain where it had been bleeding at some point. Vera wondered if he even knew. The meadow must have healed it, but if he didn't cool it, he was going to start bleeding again.

"I can go to him," Vera said.

"You cannot..." Kale paused. "It is not safe for you to go to Nibiru."

"It wasn't safe for me to go to Summartir either. But we did all right."

"That was different," Kale said. "I could go to Summartir with you."

Now Vera was getting the picture. "You don't want me to go because I'd have to go alone? Couldn't Addamas come with?"

"Ah, yeah, we've all been banned not just Kale,"

Addamas said. "Although, I do sneak by and see Kuwari occasionally. I'm pretty sure Kuwari informs the marduk—the king—when I do, but so long as I stay invisible and don't cause trouble, he allows it."

"What did you all do?"

"Killed the kargadan prince who was supposed to be the next marduk," Addamas said cheerfully. "Actually, Kale let me kill him. Then he took the blame so I wouldn't be executed for it."

"You went to a different realm and killed someone? But that's against the world's laws. Kale should've killed you himself," Vera said.

"Eh, it's a gray area," Addamas replied.

"How?"

"Technically, Nibiru is my home realm," Addamas answered. "That's where I grew up."

"Kuwari is Addamas's adopted dad," added Mimi.

"The prince I killed was married to my sister. When she miscarried again, he murdered her. Kargadan don't divorce, so it was the only way for the prince to get himself a new wife. A kargadan woman is only valuable if she can produce spawn."

"They went to confront the prince and found out that he was trafficking young girls from off-realm," Mimi expanded. "When he was done with one, he killed them and ordered another one from the Tablilu Clan—nasty people with tails like scorpions."

"Sounds like a lovely place." Vera made a face. "But I'm still going."

"No," Kale said.

"Try to stop me, buddy."

"First of all, I don't have to stop you because you'd never

be able to find the gate. Second of all, it's not safe for you there. You're a woman."

"Glad you're aware of that." Vera poked at her right boob. "I was afraid these weren't obvious enough."

Mimi giggled and high-fived her.

"While the prince's actions don't reflect the ideals of the kargadan people, all kargadan men are over-protective when it comes to women," Kale said.

"You should all start a club," Vera suggested.

Addamas quirked a smile at that. "The girl has a point."

"Addamas," Kale said darkly.

"All right, all right," Addamas conceded. "Vera, gods love you, girly. You are much too feisty to survive Nibiru, even with the progressive Kuwari as your guardian and mentor. Kargadan expect their women to be demure and obedient."

"I can be obedient for a week."

Kale barked a laugh. "Until someone pisses you off. Like when you see a man bossing around his woman."

"Okay, yeah, that would be hard."

"What happens if you get in trouble?" asked Kale. "What happens if you upset the wrong guy, and they decide you need to be punished for your own good?"

"They'd learn that's a bad idea," answered Vera.

"Exactly." Kale looked very satisfied with himself. "And that's why you're never going to Nibiru."

"You don't think I can take care of myself for one week around a bunch of misogynistic unicorns?"

"Fine, you want one more birthday present?" asked Kale. "As soon as you can knock me off my feet in a sparring match, I'll summon the gate for you."

"Deal. Let's go." Vera stood, tipping over her stool.

"I didn't mean now." Kale's jaw jumped. "You're not

ready yet. And I planned to give you tonight off for your birthday."

"No. I wanna go now." Vera headed for the door. "It's my party, and I'll knock you on your ass if I want to."

AVAILABLE HERE TO PURCHASE OR **pre-order!**
   Releases December 28, 2018

Printed in Great Britain
by Amazon